A HUNGER ARTIST
AND OTHER STORIES

JOYCE CRICK taught German at University College London for many years. She has written on Kafka's first English translators Willa and Edwin Muir, and edited Coleridge's translation of Schiller's *Wallenstein* for Princeton University Press's Collected Coleridge. For Oxford World's Classics she has translated Kafka's *The Metamorphosis and Other Stories*, a selection of Grimms' *Tales*, and Freud's *Interpretation of Dreams* (1st edition), which was awarded the Schlegel–Tieck Prize in 2000.

RITCHIE ROBERTSON is Taylor Professor of German at Oxford and a Fellow of the Queen's College. He is the author of *Kafka: A Very Short Introduction* (2004) and has written the introductions and notes to *The Trial* (trans. Mike Mitchell), *The Metamorphosis and Other Stories* (trans. Joyce Crick), and *The Castle* (trans. Anthea Bell) for Oxford World's Classics. He has also translated Hoffmann's *The Golden Pot and Other Stories* for the series, and introduced editions of Freud and Schnitzler. He is the editor of *The Cambridge Companion to Thomas Mann* (2002), and his most recent work is *Mock-Epic Poetry from Pope to Heine* (2009).

T0054935

OXFORD WORLD'S CLASSICS

*For over 100 years Oxford World's Classics have brought
readers closer to the world's great literature. Now with over 700
titles—from the 4,000-year-old myths of Mesopotamia to the
twentieth century's greatest novels—the series makes available
lesser-known as well as celebrated writing.*

*The pocket-sized hardbacks of the early years contained
introductions by Virginia Woolf, T. S. Eliot, Graham Greene,
and other literary figures which enriched the experience of reading.
Today the series is recognized for its fine scholarship and
reliability in texts that span world literature, drama and poetry,
religion, philosophy, and politics. Each edition includes perceptive
commentary and essential background information to meet the
changing needs of readers.*

OXFORD WORLD'S CLASSICS

FRANZ KAFKA

A Hunger Artist
and Other Stories

Translated by
JOYCE CRICK

With an Introduction and Notes by
RITCHIE ROBERTSON

OXFORD
UNIVERSITY PRESS

OXFORD

UNIVERSITY PRESS

Great Clarendon Street, Oxford OX2 6DP

Oxford University Press is a department of the University of Oxford.
It furthers the University's objective of excellence in research, scholarship,
and education by publishing worldwide in

Oxford New York

Auckland Cape Town Dar es Salaam Hong Kong Karachi
Kuala Lumpur Madrid Melbourne Mexico City Nairobi
New Delhi Shanghai Taipei Toronto

With offices in

Argentina Austria Brazil Chile Czech Republic France Greece
Guatemala Hungary Italy Japan Poland Portugal Singapore
South Korea Switzerland Thailand Turkey Ukraine Vietnam

Oxford is a registered trade mark of Oxford University Press
in the UK and in certain other countries

Published in the United States
by Oxford University Press Inc., New York

Translation © Joyce Crick 2012
Editorial material © Ritchie Robertson 2012

The moral rights of the author have been asserted
Database right Oxford University Press (maker)

First published as an Oxford World's Classics paperback 2012

All rights reserved. No part of this publication may be reproduced,
stored in a retrieval system, or transmitted, in any form or by any means,
without the prior permission in writing of Oxford University Press,
or as expressly permitted by law, or under terms agreed with the appropriate
reprographics rights organization. Enquiries concerning reproduction
outside the scope of the above should be sent to the Rights Department,
Oxford University Press, at the address above

You must not circulate this book in any other binding or cover
and you must impose this same condition on any acquirer

British Library Cataloguing in Publication Data

Data available

Library of Congress Cataloging in Publication Data

Data available

Typeset by Cenveo, Bangalore, India
Printed in Great Britain
on acid-free paper by
Clays Ltd, Elcograf S.p.A.

ISBN 978-0-19-960092-2

13

CONTENTS

BIOGRAPHICAL PREFACE

FRANZ KAFKA is one of the iconic figures of modern world literature. His biography is still obscured by myth and misinformation,
yet the plain facts of his life are very ordinary. He was born on 3 July
1883 in Prague, where his parents, Hermann and Julie Kafka, kept a
small shop selling fancy goods, umbrellas, and the like. He was the
eldest of six children, including two brothers who died in infancy
and three sisters who all outlived him. He studied law at university,
and after a year of practice started work, first for his local branch of
an insurance firm based in Trieste, then after a year for the state-run
Workers' Accident Insurance Institute, where his job was not only to
handle claims for injury at work but to forestall such accidents by
visiting factories and examining their equipment and their safety precautions. In his spare time he was writing prose sketches and stories,
which were published in magazines and as small books, beginning
with *Meditation* in 1912.

In August 1912 Kafka met Felice Bauer, four years his junior, who
was visiting from Berlin, where she worked in a firm making office
equipment. Their relationship, including two engagements, was
carried on largely by letter (they met only on seventeen occasions, far
the longest being a ten-day stay in a hotel in July 1916), and finally
ended when in August 1917 Kafka had a haemorrhage which proved
tubercular; he had to convalesce in the country, uncertain how much
longer he could expect to live. Thereafter brief returns to work alter-
nated with stays in sanatoria until he took early retirement in 1922.
In 1919 he was briefly engaged to Julie Wohryzek, a twenty-eight-
year-old clerk, but that relationship dissolved after Kafka met the
married Milena Polak (née Jesenská), a spirited journalist, unhappy
with her neglectful husband. Milena translated some of Kafka's work
into Czech. As she lived in Vienna, their meetings were few, and the
relationship ended early in 1921. Two years later Kafka at last left
Prague and settled in Berlin with Dora Diamant, a young woman
who had broken away from her ultra-orthodox Jewish family in
Poland (and who later became a noted actress and communist activist).
However, the winter of 1923–4, when hyperinflation was at its height,
was a bad time to be in Berlin. Kafka's health declined so sharply that,

after moving through several clinics and sanatoria around Vienna, he died on 3 June 1924.

The emotional hinterland of these events finds expression in Kafka's letters and diaries, and also—though less directly than is sometimes thought—in his literary work. His difficult relationship with his domineering father has a bearing especially on his early fiction, as well as on the *Letter to his Father*, which should be seen as a literary document rather than a factual record. He suffered also from his mother's emotional remoteness and from the excessive hopes which his parents invested in their only surviving son. His innumerable letters to the highly intelligent, well-read, and capable Felice Bauer bespeak emotional neediness, and a wish to prove himself by marrying, rather than any strong attraction to her as an individual, and he was acutely aware of the conflict between the demands of marriage and the solitude which he required for writing. He records also much self-doubt, feelings of guilt, morbid fantasies of punishment, and concern about his own health. But it is clear from his friends' testimony that he was a charming and witty companion, a sportsman keen on hiking and rowing, and a thoroughly competent and valued colleague at work. He also had a keen social conscience and advanced social views: during the First World War he worked to help refugees and shell-shocked soldiers, and he advocated progressive educational methods which would save children from the stifling influence of their parents.

Kafka's family were Jews with little more than a conventional attachment to Jewish belief and practice. A turning-point in Kafka's life was his encounter with Yiddish-speaking actors from Galicia, from whom he learned about the traditional Jewish culture of Eastern Europe. Gradually he drew closer to the Zionist movement: not to its politics, however, but to its vision of a new social and cultural life for Jews in Palestine. He learnt Hebrew and acquired practical skills such as gardening and carpentry which might be useful if, as they planned, he and Dora Diamant should emigrate to Palestine.

A concern with religious questions runs through Kafka's life and work, but his thought does not correspond closely to any established faith. He had an extensive knowledge of both Judaism and Christianity, and knew also the philosophies of Nietzsche and Schopenhauer. Late in life, especially after the diagnosis of his illness, he read eclectically and often critically in religious classics: the Old and New Testaments, Kierkegaard, St Augustine, Pascal, the late diaries of the convert Tolstoy, works by Martin Buber, and also extracts from the Talmud. His religious thought, which finds expression in concise and profound aphorisms, is highly individual, and the religious allusions which haunt his fiction tend to make it more rather than less enigmatic.

During his lifetime Kafka published seven small books, but he left three unfinished novels and a huge mass of notebooks and diaries, which we only possess because his friend Max Brod ignored Kafka's instructions to burn them. They are all written in German, his native language; his Czech was fluent but not flawless. It used to be claimed that Kafka wrote in a version of German called 'Prague German', but in fact, although he uses some expressions characteristic of the South German language area, his style is modelled on that of such classic German writers as Goethe, Kleist, and Stifter.

Though limpid, Kafka's style is also puzzling. He was sharply conscious of the problems of perception, and of the new forms of attention made possible by media such as the photograph and cinema. When he engages in fantasy, his descriptions are often designed to perplex the reader: thus it is difficult to make out what the insect in *The Metamorphosis* actually looks like. He was also fascinated by ambiguity, and often includes in his fiction long arguments in which various interpretations of some puzzling phenomenon are canvassed, or in which the speaker, by faulty logic, contrives to stand an argument on its head. In such passages he favours elaborate sentences, often in indirect speech. Yet Kafka's German, though often complex, is never clumsy. In his fiction, his letters, and his diaries he writes with unfailing grace and economy.

In his lifetime Kafka was not yet a famous author, but neither was he obscure. His books received many complimentary reviews. Prominent writers, such as Robert Musil and Rainer Maria Rilke, admired his work and sought him out. He was also part of a group of Prague writers, including Max Brod, an extremely prolific novelist and essayist, and Franz Werfel, who first attained fame as avant-garde poet and later became an international celebrity through his best-selling novels. During the Third Reich his work was known mainly in the English-speaking world through translations, and, as little was then known about his life or social context, he was seen as the author of universal parables.

Kafka's novels about individuals confronting a powerful but opaque organization—the court or the castle—seemed in the West to be fables of existential uncertainty. In the Eastern bloc, when they became accessible, they seemed to be prescient explorations of the fate of the individual within a bureaucratic tyranny. Neither approach can be set aside. Both were responding to elements in Kafka's fiction. Kafka worries at universal moral problems of guilt, responsibility, and freedom; and he also examines the mechanisms of power by which authorities can subtly coerce and subjugate the individual, as well as the individual's scope for resisting authority.

Placing Kafka in his historical context brings limited returns. The appeal of his work rests on its universal, parable-like character, and also on its presentation of puzzles without solutions. A narrative presence is generally kept to a minimum. We largely experience what Kafka's protagonist does, without a narrator to guide us. When there is a distinct narrative voice, as sometimes in the later stories, the narrator is himself puzzled by the phenomena he recounts. Kafka's fiction is thus characteristic of modernism in demanding an active reading. The reader is not invited to consume the text passively, but to join actively in the task of puzzling it out, in resisting simple interpretations, and in working, not towards a solution, but towards a fuller experience of the text on each reading.

INTRODUCTION

THE short fiction that makes up this volume consists of two complete collections published by Kafka, and a number of important uncollected works, most of them published only posthumously. They show the aspect of Kafka's writing that Heinz Politzer, in one of the best and best-known studies of his oeuvre, summed up as parable and paradox. Politzer described their enigmatic quality as follows: 'There is not one self-explanatory word in a typical Kafka narrative. His mature prose shows nothing but a surface spread over happenings that remain profoundly impenetrable.'[1] Kafka's texts may be impenetrable, however, but they are not unintelligible. They are not riddles to be solved, but subtle literary artefacts to be explored by each individual reader. The purpose of this introduction is to present some contextual information, to suggest useful avenues of inquiry, and to elucidate some of the hints that Kafka does occasionally seem to have inserted into his fiction.[2]

The present volume contains two of the seven books that Kafka allowed to be published during his lifetime: *A Country Doctor: Little Tales* and *A Hunger Artist: Four Stories*, together with a large number of miscellaneous texts. Two of them, 'The Aeroplanes at Brescia' and 'The Rider on the Coal-Scuttle', were published by Kafka in periodicals. The former is a report that Kafka wrote on an aeronautical display that he attended when on holiday with friends in northern

---

[1] Heinz Politzer, *Franz Kafka: Parable and Paradox* (Ithaca, NY: Cornell University Press, 1962), 17.

[2] In writing this introduction I have drawn heavily on the *Kafka-Handbuch: Leben—Werk—Wirkung*, ed. Manfred Engel and Bernd Auerochs (Stuttgart: Metzler, 2010), an invaluable encyclopaedic compendium. I am also much indebted to the tireless researches of Hartmut Binder, notably to his edited *Kafka-Handbuch*, 2 vols. (Stuttgart: Kröner, 1979), especially the first, biographical volume, written entirely by Binder; his *Mit Kafka in den Süden: Eine historische Bilderreise in die Schweiz und zu den oberitalienischen Seen* (Prague: Vitalis, 2007); and *Kafkas Welt: Eine Lebenschronik in Bildern* (Reinbek bei Hamburg: Rowohlt, 2008). I thank Theresa Holz for her generosity in giving me the last-mentioned book as a present. For Kafka's biography, I have relied especially on Peter-Andre Alt, *Franz Kafka: Der ewige Sohn. Eine Biographie* (Munich: Beck, 2005); Reiner Stach, *Kafka: Die Jahre der Entscheidungen* (Frankfurt a.M.: Fischer, 2002) and *Kafka: Die Jahre der Erkenntnis* (Frankfurt a.M.: Fischer, 2008). Stach's first volume is now available in English; his second volume and Alt's biography are being translated but to the best of my knowledge have not yet appeared.

Italy in 1909; the latter is a gentle fantasy inspired by the fuel short-age that afflicted Central Europe in the later stages of the First World War. In addition, we have a selection of texts of varying length from Kafka's manuscripts that were published only after his death, usually with titles supplied by his friend and editor Max Brod. Our criteria for choosing them are various. Some of the texts have become part of the Kafka canon, and their absence would have disappointed many readers. That applies to the substantial narratives 'Investigations of a Dog' and 'The Burrow', explorations of frustration and para-noia respectively, and also to such concise pieces as 'On Parables' or the little dialogue 'Give it up!' which Politzer used, in the intro-ductory pages of his study of Kafka, as a model of how Kafka's texts both invite and resist interpretation.[3] The fragments com-posing 'The Huntsman Gracchus', and the more self-contained 'At the Building of the Great Wall of China', belong in this category. Others, such as 'The Knock on the Courtyard Gate', are particularly fine illustrations of recurrent situations in Kafka's fiction, or, like 'The Spinning-Top', fictional distillations of Kafka's philosophical reflections.

Kafka the thinker, in contrast to Kafka the artist, has often been underestimated. His own modest claim that he thought only in images has been taken too much at face value.[4] He was, after all, a trained lawyer, schooled in legal argument, and he was able to give Brod some astute comments on the latter's arguments about aesthetics.[5] But one need not follow Brod to the other extreme and attribute to Kafka a coherent philosophical doctrine.[6] The mode in which Kafka preferred to formulate his reflections was the aphorism, a concise formulation in which a difficult thought is often condensed into a poetic image. In the winter of 1917–18, when Kafka, recently diagnosed with tubercu-losis, was staying for the sake of his health on his sister's farm at Zürau (now Siřem) in the northern Bohemian countryside, he wrote many such aphorisms in his notebooks. His diaries for 1920 also con-tain a sequence of aphorisms, published by Brod under the title 'He'

---

[3] Politzer, *Franz Kafka*, 1–22.

[4] e.g. by Hartmut Binder, 'Jugendliche Verkennung. Kafka und die Philosophie', *Wirkendes Wort*, 34 (1984), 411–21.

[5] Published by Max Brod in *Der Prager Kreis* (Stuttgart: Kohlhammer, 1966), 94–5.

[6] Max Brod, *Franz Kafkas Glauben und Lehre* (Winterthur: Mondial-Verlag, 1948), repr. in Brod, *Über Franz Kafka* (Frankfurt a.M.: Fischer, 1974), 221–99.

(because so many of them begin with the third-person pronoun). Both these sequences are presented here.

Another facet of Kafka's writing that receives too little credit is his humour. The popular myth of Kafka, or of the 'Kafkaesque', sees him as the creator of nightmarish fantasies in which a helpless protagonist is subjected to psychological torture by incomprehensible authorities and threatened also with the physical torture that is imagined in such gruesome detail in *In the Penal Colony*. That description applies, at least partially, to *The Trial*, especially to the scene with the Thrasher (written at about the same time as *In the Penal Colony*), but even in *The Trial* there is plenty of light relief, as in the skilfully drawn character of the agitated uncle whom Josef K. calls 'the ghost from the country', and much more in the other two novels, *The Man who Disappeared* and *The Castle*. It is in the later short fiction, however, that Kafka's brand of gentle, sad humour is most fully developed, and while this collection contains many specimens, perhaps the most obviously appealing is the incomplete and relatively little-known story presented here as 'Blumfeld, an Elderly Bachelor'.

The Aeroplanes at Brescia

Kafka was fascinated by the latest technology. The first chapter of his novel *The Man who Disappeared*, which he began working on early in 1911, was, he assured his publisher, set in 'the most ultra-modern New York'.[7] Skyscrapers, seemingly endless road traffic, telephones and telegrams, a hotel with thirty lifts, and a desk with a hundred drawers that can be rearranged by turning a handle all feature in the novel, along with the dark side of technology as a means of extracting yet more work from wage-slaves. Kafka's own work, in an insurance office dealing with industrial accidents, also showed him the dangers of misapplied technology, and his inspection reports on safety standards in factories are full of drawings of industrial machinery.[8]

By comparison, 'The Aeroplanes at Brescia' is a light-hearted text, showing the liberating potential of technology. The aeronautic display

---

[7] Letter to Kurt Wolff, 25 May 1913, in Franz Kafka, *Briefe 1913–März 1914*, ed. Hans-Gerd Koch (Frankfurt a.M.: Fischer, 1999), 196.

[8] See Franz Kafka, *The Office Writings*, ed. Stanley Corngold, Jack Greenberg, and Benno Wagner, tr. Eric Patton with Ruth Hein (Princeton and Oxford: Princeton University Press, 2009).

held at Brescia from 8 to 20 September 1909 aroused international interest and was attended by Italy's notables from King Vittorio Emmanuele III downwards, including the writer Gabriele d'Annunzio and the composer Giacomo Puccini (both mentioned in Kafka's account). Kafka happened to be on holiday nearby in Riva, on Lake Garda (a locality that was to reappear in 'The Huntsman Gracchus'), with Max Brod and the latter's brother Otto. When they read in the newspaper about the air show Kafka urged the others to take the opportunity of seeing aeroplanes for the first time in their lives, so they spent Saturday 11 September at the display.[9] To encourage Kafka in his writing, Max Brod suggested that they should both compose accounts of the event and then compare them. An abridged version of Kafka's text appeared in the German-language Prague newspaper *Bohemia* on 29 September; the full text, which is translated here, was first published by Brod in his biography of Kafka in 1937.

Kafka conveys the excitement surrounding aviation, which was at its peak at this very time. It was less than six years since the Wright brothers had made their first flight in a petrol-powered aeroplane. That summer, Louis Blériot and Hubert Latham had been in competition to achieve the first flight across the English Channel. Latham's attempt on 19 July had been frustrated by engine failure. Six days later, Blériot's engineer Alessandro Anzani insisted that he should take advantage of the first clear day, and Blériot, though still in pain from a burned foot, successfully flew the Channel in thirty-seven minutes at an altitude of about 76 metres. Hence the excitement surrounding Blériot in Kafka's report.

No description by Kafka is ever just a description. Here, as always in his prose, the circumstantial detail allows metaphorical overtones to emerge faintly into view. The long and rather grumpy accounts of laborious travel which begin the narrative fall into place when we read them as contrasting the mundane struggles of everyday life with the liberation made possible by air flight. In watching an aviator, Kafka notices how one imaginatively adopts the pilot's perspective: thus, when the American aviator Glenn Curtiss flies towards the distant forests, they 'seem only now to be rising into view', as though the

---

[9] See Peter Demetz, *The Air Show at Brescia, 1909* (New York: Farrar, Straus, & Giroux, 2002). Binder, *Mit Kafka in den Süden*, 51–84, reconstructs Kafka's experience in unsurpassable detail and with many contemporary illustrations.

earth-bound spectators could see them through Curtiss's eyes. It is tempting to read this not only as a report on a new experience—that of watching an aviator—but also as a metaphor for the adoption of a narrator's perspective when one reads a novel. Later, Henri Rougier is described as 'sitting at his controls like a gentleman at a desk'; the implicit association with a writing-desk briefly equates the pilot with a writer and aeronautics with the imaginative flights undertaken by an author. The end of the text emphasizes the contrast between sky and earth: Rougier is visible so high up that he seems to be among the stars, but down on the ground Kafka and his companions are embarking on their difficult journey back to their hotel.

A Country Doctor: Little Tales, 'At the Building of the Great Wall of China', 'Blumfeld, An Elderly Bachelor', and 'The Rider on the Coal-Scuttle'

The very diverse stories collected here were written in the winter of 1916–17. Since the beginning of 1915, when he abandoned work on *The Trial*, Kafka had not written much, though 'Blumfeld', a story about a bachelor who resembles an older and surlier Josef K., dates from early 1915. Many of Kafka's colleagues at work had been called up, and he himself volunteered, but he was deemed indispensable. His increased work-load, the anxiety of the war, the shortages of food and other commodities, the reports from friends and relatives such as his brothers-in-law about terrible conditions at the front, all hindered literary creation, as did the noise in Kafka's lodgings. In November 1916, however, his sister Ottla rented a house at Zlatá ulička 22 (the 'Alchimistengäßchen' or Alchemists' Alley) on the Hradčany hill, near the castle and the cathedral. Kafka used this tiny house, which tourists nowadays can visit, as a working space in the evenings. Fourteen of the stories written there, some of which had previously been published in periodicals, were assembled in the volume *A Country Doctor: Little Tales*, with the dedication 'To my Father', in the spring of 1920 (though with the official date 1919) by the Kurt Wolff Verlag, where Kafka's earlier fiction had appeared. 'The Rider on the Coal-Scuttle' was originally intended to form part of this collection, but Kafka withdrew it and published it separately in 1921.

These stories suggest certain ways of reading Kafka, and suggest also other ways which are better avoided. When reading a story by

Kafka, we should not, for example, ask anxiously 'What does it mean?' as though the meaning were a secret message which Kafka had planted in the text and laboriously disguised. Rather, we should follow the narrative and allow further implications, metaphorical or metaphysical, to arise in the course of our reading. We should not be put out by the physical impossibilities which the stories require us to accept. A war-horse becomes a lawyer; an ape transforms himself (by his own account) into a human being; gigantic horses crawl out of a pigsty and transport the country doctor to his destination almost instantaneously. Like the metamorphosis of Gregor Samsa into an insect, these events do not need to be explained, only to be accepted, and the reader is invited to explore the imaginative implications at which Kafka hints with characteristic ambiguity.

The tone of the collection is set by the two stories which frame it, 'The New Advocate' and 'A Report to an Academy', and by the title story, 'A Country Doctor'. All three convey a sense of cultural pessimism. From a better state of affairs, now recorded only in myths, life has declined until the present, which at the end of 'A Country Doctor' is described with startling explicitness as 'this most calamitous age'. The ape who reports to an academy on how he has found a niche in human society tells his hearers: 'I come from the Gold Coast.' This evokes not only the West African territory now known as Ghana but also the myth of the Golden Age and the account, given most influentially by Rousseau, of modern civilization as a decline from primeval standards of happiness and virtue. In his 'Discourse on the Arts and Science', itself submitted to an academy, that of Dijon, in 1750, Rousseau argued that the simple honesty of primitive society had been corrupted by the progress of civilization into vice, dissimulation, and artifice. As the civilized arts acquired by the ape in the course of his humanization include spitting, smoking, and drinking brandy, Kafka offers a similar satire on so-called progress.

Moreover, modern society is spiritually adrift. In 'The New Advocate', the India to which Alexander the Great led his army figures less as a literal place than as a spiritual goal to which nobody can now lead the way. Whereas Alexander could indicate a direction by pointing his sword, the many people who have swords nowadays—in an age of increased democracy and widely diffused authority—can only wave them about futilely.

Another theme which emerges from all three stories is the question of what it means to be human, and where the dividing-line runs—if there is one—between humans and animals. This theme was already addressed in *The Metamorphosis*, where Kafka makes great play with the discrepancy between Gregor's human consciousness and his animal body and appetites. At a key moment there, Gregor's loss of physical appetite, and his new appreciation of music as a potential source of spiritual nourishment, make him wonder: 'Was he a beast, that music should move him like this? He felt as if the way to the unknown nourishment he longed for was being revealed.'[10] In 'The New Advocate', the transformation of Alexander's war-horse Bucephalus into a present-day lawyer is just as unexplained as Gregor's metamorphosis. Both events enable Kafka to play games with the reader. What we learn about Gregor's insect body does not correspond to any actual creature, and Kafka insisted that the insect should not be illustrated. Bucephalus is equally impossible to visualize. Does he look like a man or a horse? Climbing stairs, he lifts his legs high, like a horse, and the 'ringing' of his feet on the marble suggests that he is wearing horseshoes, yet, despite what seem obvious clues, it takes a habitué of the racetrack, presumably an expert on horses, to suspect anything equine about him.

The boundary between humanity and animality, however, is not only a source of Kafka's discreet humour. In the wake of Darwin, it was an urgent philosophical question. Darwin's *Origin of Species* (1859), which appeared the following year in German translation, dethroned humankind from its special status and placed it firmly within the animal kingdom. Theories of evolution were relatively easy to accept in the German-speaking world, because they fitted the assumption of a gradual and purposive development running through all organic life which was already a commonplace of the German Romantic philosophy of science.[11] Nietzsche, especially in his later writings, repeatedly asks what kind of animal man is, and argues that man is distinguished from other animals by being '*the* sick animal'.[12] While other animals are adapted to their environment, man is

[10] Franz Kafka, *The Metamorphosis and Other Stories*, tr. Joyce Crick, Oxford World's Classics (Oxford: Oxford University Press, 2009), 66.

[11] See Gregory Moore, *Nietzsche, Biology and Metaphor* (Cambridge: Cambridge University Press, 2002), 26.

[12] Friedrich Nietzsche, *On the Genealogy of Morals*, tr. Douglas Smith, Oxford World's Classics (Oxford: Oxford University Press, 1996), 100 (Third Essay, §13).

uncomfortable and at odds with his. But this maladaptation gives humankind the potential to develop in intriguing and unforeseeable ways, for we are 'the most unsuccessful animal, the sickliest, the one most dangerously strayed from its instincts—with all that, to be sure, the most *interesting*!'[13]

While the story of Rotpeter, the ape who has become human, can be read as a Rousseauesque narrative of decline from primitive health to civilized corruption, it can also be read as a humorously Darwinian narrative in which Rotpeter actively accelerates the process of evolution in his own person. In doing so he is driven by the need to avoid being confined in a cage—an imperative just as urgent as the struggle for survival that underpins evolution. The desperation with which he learns human behaviour is emphasized by the image of the whip: 'Oh, you learn when you have to; you learn if you want a way out; you learn mercilessly. You oversee yourself with the whip; you flay yourself at the slightest resistance.' This in turn recalls Nietzsche's interpretation of evolutionary theory. One of Nietzsche's criticisms of Darwin was that the latter placed too much stress on the effect of the environment in promoting evolution, whereas Nietzsche's wide reading in biology encouraged him to attribute more importance to an internal force of development which he identified with his favourite concept of the will to power. Rotpeter's evolution into a human is driven by his powerful will. His image of the whip is reminiscent of Nietzsche's speculations in *The Genealogy of Morals* about how humanity, in its remote prehistory, was forcibly made into an animal that can keep promises. This must have been done, Nietzsche thinks, by a prolonged exercise in cruelty. In a passage which seems also to have left its mark on *In the Penal Colony*, he surmises that the beginnings of memory and hence morality must have been inculcated, not by reason or persuasion, but by violence: 'Things never proceeded without blood, torture, and victims, when man thought it necessary to forge a memory for himself.'[14]

But have his prodigious efforts actually made Rotpeter into a

---

[13] *The Antichrist*, §14, in Nietzsche, *Twilight of the Idols and The Antichrist*, tr. R. J. Hollingdale (Harmondsworth: Penguin, 1968), 124.

[14] Friedrich Nietzsche, *On the Genealogy of Morals*, 42 (Second Essay, §3). The relevance of this passage was first pointed out by Malcolm Pasley, 'Introduction', in Franz Kafka, *Der Heizer, In der Strafkolonie, Der Bau* (Cambridge: Cambridge University Press, 1966), 1–33 (p. 18).

human being? The point of the story is surely that they haven't. Rotpeter is an unreliable narrator who boasts of his achievements while constantly undercutting his own claims. He has been admitted into human society, not as a human being, but as an entertainer who makes his living in the music-hall by showing how well he has learnt to imitate human behaviour. So the story suggests the sad conclusion—and Rotpeter, by the tone of resignation with which he ends his report, seems to acknowledge it—that his unremitting five-year struggle has not really accomplished very much. Moreover, he undermines his claims by uneasy references to his own lingering animality. He is very indignant at a journalist's claim, which he nevertheless does not deny, that he is in the habit of taking his trousers down in public to show his wound, and his companion is 'a little half-trained chimpanzee' with whom he enjoys himself at night 'in the apish fashion'. But one can go still further and suggest that Rotpeter involuntarily undermines, not only his claim to have become human, but the very existence of a barrier between humans and animals in the first place. If 'apedom' is as remote from his hearers as from him, it is also equally close, in that his academic listeners are also products of evolution. The journalists who attack him are 'news-hounds' ('Windhunde' in the original), humorously implying that they too are basically animals, and illustrating Kafka's fondness—especially in *The Metamorphosis* and 'Josefine, the Singer'—for everyday expressions that undercut the distinction between animals and humans.

The critique of civilization in these stories is further developed by the repeated suggestion that to be civilized is to be physically damaged, and in particular damaged in one's sexuality. Rotpeter was captured on the Gold Coast by members of an animal-collecting expedition, who shot him first on the cheek and then 'below the hip'. To represent the transition from nature to culture as a wound which permanently destroys an original physical vitality or a harmonious unity of human faculties is a familiar trope. A famous example occurs in Schiller's *Letters on the Aesthetic Education of Mankind* (1795–6), where Schiller deplores the over-specialization that is inseparable from cultural development: 'It was civilization itself which inflicted this wound upon modern man.'[15] The location of Rotpeter's wound

---

[15] Friedrich Schiller, *On the Aesthetic Education of Man in a Series of Letters*, tr. Elizabeth M. Wilkinson and L. A. Willoughby (Oxford: Clarendon Press, 1967), 33.

'below the hip', or in the genital area, evokes overtones of castration, and links it with the war-wound whose scar is displayed by the father in *The Judgement* and with the mysterious wound 'in the region of the hips' that afflicts the boy in 'A Country Doctor'. Gerhard Neumann, one of Kafka's most astute interpreters, has called Rotpeter's experience 'the primal scene of culture', noting that what pushes him across the threshold 'from the naked body to the social law' is pain.[16]

The country doctor himself, though not wounded, is clearly someone of low sexual vitality. Hence the symbolic importance of the disused pigsty and the beings who emerge from it. The two enormous horses, 'mighty beasts with powerful flanks', and the brutish groom who addresses them as 'brother' and 'sister', embody raw physical energy, alarmingly manifested also in the groom's assault on the servant-girl Rose. On the other hand, it is remarkable that the groom refers to his victim by her name, whereas until then the doctor has only referred to her as 'my servant-girl' or 'the girl'. The groom at least has something of a personal relation to her, whereas the doctor describes her, too late, as 'that lovely girl, who has for years been living in my house while I have scarcely noticed her'.

The doctor represents a type of character central to several of Kafka's major works: a professional man, used to an unvarying routine, morose and desiccated, whose life is changed by the intervention of a new and incomprehensible force. He has counterparts in the bank manager Josef K. in *The Trial*, in the commercial traveller Gregor Samsa, and in the elderly bachelor Blumfeld whose story is included in the present collection. Just as Josef K. unwittingly invited the Court's guards into his bedroom by ringing the bell for his breakfast, the country doctor absent-mindedly kicks the door of the disused pigsty. He thereby summons up the vital forces which have been locked away in a place associated with dirt, rather like the lumber-room in Josef K.'s bank where a scene of horrific violence is enacted in the 'Thrasher' chapter of *The Trial*. Rose's innocent remark, 'You never know what you'll find in your own house', applies not only to the doctor's living-space but to his psychic economy. It strikingly resembles Freud's contemporaneous statement that 'the ego . . . is not

---

[16] Gerhard Neumann, 'Kafka als Ethnologe', in Hansjörg Bay and Christof Hamann (eds.), *Odradeks Lachen: Fremdheit bei Kafka* (Freiburg i.Br.: Rombach, 2006), 325–45 (p. 336).

even master in its own house'.[17] The psychic drives that the doctor has repressed for so many years emerge with uncontrollable strength.

The emotional centre of the story is the doctor's discovery of his patient's wound. Although at first he could see nothing wrong with the boy, the neighing of the horses—a hint at their supernatural function—alerts the doctor to an impossibly huge wound, populated by equally impossible many-legged worms. Commentators talk of a 'metaphysical' wound, referring to the boy's later description of the wound as the only 'portion' bestowed on him at his birth. But, if we think again of Nietzsche, we could see the boy as representing man, the animal who is by definition sick. Moreover, the wound is surrounded by intense and bewildering emotional associations. Horrifying and disgusting, it is also beautiful, and is compared to a flower. It evokes the horror that is felt when internal organs become visible, and in particular it evokes male fear of the female body and the anxiety that focuses on the vagina. The boy's sister meanwhile is waving a blood-soaked handkerchief, with a suggestion of menstrual blood, and the wound itself, in being compared to a mineshaft, resembles a huge gash torn in the body of Mother Earth. Above all, the wound is associated with the servant-girl Rose. The sentence describing it begins with the word 'Rose-red' (in the original 'Rosa', meaning pink), which thus acquires a capital letter and a clear link to the servant's name. The doctor's sexual anxieties acquire a homosexual tinge when he is placed in the bed beside the boy.

Finally, the doctor differs from the other professional men depicted by Kafka hitherto in being offered, and refusing, a more than personal responsibility. At one time Kafka intended to entitle the entire collection *Responsibility*.[18] One reason for discarding this title, however, may have been that the doctor so conspicuously fails in his mission. His patients, as he complains, expect him to replace the priest, in whose ministrations nobody, even the priest himself, believes any longer: 'That's what the people in my region are like. Always demanding the impossible of their doctor. They have lost their old faith; the

---

[17] *Introductory Lectures on Psycho-Analysis*, in *The Standard Edition of the Complete Psychological Works of Sigmund Freud*, ed. James Strachey, 24 vols. (London: Hogarth Press, 1953–74), xvi. 285.

[18] Letter to Martin Buber, 22 Apr. 1917, in Franz Kafka, *Briefe 1914–1917*, ed. Hans-Gerd Koch (Frankfurt a.M.: Fischer, 2005), 297. See Malcolm Pasley, 'Kafka and the Theme of "Berufung"', *Oxford German Studies*, 9 (1978), 139–49.

priest sits at home and picks his cassocks into shreds, one by one; but the physician is supposed to do everything with his delicate surgical hand' (p. 16). Even a country village is part of a modern, increasingly secular society that respects science instead of religion. The doctor, however, cannot play the role of a secular saviour. Unable to save the wounded boy, he escapes through the window, only to meet his nemesis. The supernatural horses that brought him to the patient instantaneously now seem unable to take him home: they creep slowly through the snow, with the inevitable result that he will freeze to death. The other protagonists, Bucephalus and Rotpeter, who admittedly face no such challenge, do not seek to engage with society; they opt for quiet lives, the one immersed in legal tomes, the other, having renounced any hope of freedom, moderately content with the 'way out' provided by his ambiguous status in human society.

The theme of responsibility runs through much of the collection. In 'An Ancient Manuscript' a city with a Chinese atmosphere has been invaded by terrifying nomads who devour raw flesh and seem to undermine the distinction between nature and culture, humanity and animality. The Emperor has retreated into the interior of his palace, and the small shopkeepers on the city's main square find that the impossible task of driving away the nomads has descended on their shoulders. The Chinese setting reappears in 'A Message from the Emperor', itself extracted from the longer, unpublished narrative 'At the Building of the Great Wall of China'. Here some unexplained obstacle, ingrained in the nature of reality, means that the messenger entrusted with a message by the dying Emperor can never take it to its destination, and can never even force his way through the crowds occupying the innumerable corridors and forecourts of the imperial palace. Time and space are again represented as dangerously fluid in 'The Next Village', while in 'On the Gallery' two views of the situation are juxtaposed. One is hypothetical: if a circus artiste were really suffering, the young man in the audience would dash down and command the show to stop; the other, in which the artiste loves her act and is loved by the audience, is presented as real, yet it reduces the young man to tears. Which view corresponds to the truth, and why does the saccharine happiness of 'reality' make the spectator weep? How is responsible intervention possible if the world is so ambiguous?

Some of the stories also imply an ironic comment on the possibility of actual intervention in the real world. The opening sentence of 'An

Ancient Manuscript', written in March 1917, 'It is as if the defence of our country has been much neglected', was distinctly pertinent after two-and-a-half years of warfare. The privations of warfare are evident in 'The Rider on the Coal-Scuttle', whose protagonist, a victim of the fuel shortage, ends up heading into an icy waste, like the country doctor. Kafka, on the other hand, showed public spirit by composing an eloquent petition calling for the establishment of a clinic to treat soldiers suffering from what would now be called post-traumatic stress disorder, though he refused to serve on the organizing committee.

Several of Kafka's friends, especially Brod, were enthusiastic members of the Zionist movement, which had one of its most active centres in Prague. Kafka regarded Zionism with some scepticism. The story 'Jackals and Arabs', apparently set in Palestine, can be read as a satire on the impractical messianic fantasies of some extreme Zionists. At the same time it satirically exaggerates the negative Zionist view of Diaspora Jewry: the smell from the jackals' mouths recalls the anti-Semitic charge of 'Jewish smell' or *foetor judaicus*; their 'wailing tone' was conventionally attributed to Jews; and the absurd scissors the jackals produce reminds us that tailoring was a traditional Jewish profession.[19] The story was published in *Der Jude* (*The Jew*), a monthly founded by Martin Buber in 1916 to promote the serious discussion of Jewish political and cultural issues, along with 'A Report for an Academy', under the collective title 'Two Animal Stories'.

Since Buber chose these two stories, out of a dozen that Kafka offered him, one wonders what Jewish theme Buber can have found in 'A Report'. The answer is given by Max Brod's description of the story as the most brilliant satire ever written on Jewish assimilation.[20] The ape's uneasy position, inside but also outside human society, corresponds to the grudging and incomplete acceptance which—in the view of many Jews, not only Zionists—was the best that Jews could hope for in an increasingly intolerant Gentile environment.[21] To this extent the satirical view of the ape, an unreliable narrator who does

[19] See Sander L. Gilman, *Franz Kafka, the Jewish Patient* (London: Routledge, 1995), 150; Iris Bruce, *Kafka and Cultural Zionism: Dates in Palestine* (Madison, Wisc.: University of Wisconsin Press, 2007), 154–7.
[20] Quoted in Hartmut Binder, *Kafka Kommentar zu sämtlichen Erzählungen* (Munich: Winkler, 1975), 226.
[21] For a fuller interpretation along these lines, see Ritchie Robertson, *Kafka: Judaism, Politics and Literature* (Oxford: Clarendon Press, 1985), 164–71.

not fully comprehend his own situation, anticipates the increasing commitment to practical (as opposed to political) Zionism that Kafka would make in his later years. A hint of Zionism may be found in 'Blumfeld', where the celluloid balls that plague the reclusive bachelor are blue and white, the Zionist colours. And as they prevent Blumfeld from drinking brandy and smoking, make him perform an unaccustomed athletic feat, and send him out the next day feeling refreshed, they may embody a message that Zionism is good for you. It was a familiar Zionist theme that simple nourishment and hard manual labour in Palestine could transform the unhealthy, cerebral, town-bred Western Jew into a strong and healthy character in both mind and body. The antithesis between Eastern and Western Jews is also hinted at in 'At the Building of the Great Wall of China', another text composed in Kafka's productive phase in the winter of 1916–17. The building of the wall is said to unite 'two great armies of labourers, the eastern and western armies', and to generate a spirit of national solidarity otherwise hard to achieve among a population spread over such a huge territory: 'Unity! Unity! Shoulder to shoulder, a round-dance of the people, blood, no longer imprisoned in the narrow confines of the body's veins, but circulating sweetly and still returning through the infinite expanse of China.' Kafka was deeply interested in the Jews from Eastern Europe who came to Prague as refugees from advancing Russian armies and Cossack atrocities in the first winter of the war. In 1916 he pressured his fiancée Felice Bauer to teach in a school for Jewish refugee children in Berlin. Jewish nationalism envisaged Palestine as a place where secular Jews from Western Europe and religious Jews from Russia and Eastern Europe might overcome their differences in a national endeavour. However, Kafka's narrator, seeking an explanation for the obvious impracticality of the wall-building project—the system of piecemeal building, which was bound to leave gaps, and the uselessness of the wall for the population remote from China's northern borders—increasingly questions the meaning of all such nationalistic undertakings and approaches the conclusion that the wall was really built, not to keep the nomads out, but to unify the population and to counterbalance the obscurity surrounding the office of Emperor. The surmise that the wall might serve as the foundation for a second Tower of Babel may be read as an additional reminder of the dangers of nationalism.

Two stories are particularly enigmatic. The story of Odradek, an animated contrivance who declares in a dry little voice that he has no fixed abode, has invited many attempts at decoding, of which the most plausible may be Wilhelm Emrich's association with the Czech *odra-diti*, 'to dissuade', so that Odradek's name would mean 'Little Dissuader'.[22] But perhaps the narrator's philological meditations are a deliberate red herring. We might see the point of the story rather in the contrast between the nomadic Odradek and the stationary house-holder, uneasily aware of Odradek as representing an alternative way of living, a possibility that haunts him throughout his life and will continue to exist after his death. 'A Brother's Murder' again poses the question of responsibility. Pallas, the onlooker at an apparent crime of passion which is also a re-enactment of the original fratricide, invites the question: 'Am I my brother's keeper?'[23] On the other hand, it may be that, rather than trying to interpret the story, we should read it as an exercise in transferring cinematic techniques to literature. The accelerated narrative, with many verbless sentences; the highly con-spicuous gestures, as when Schmar sharpens his knife or Frau Wese falls on her husband's corpse; the harsh contrasts of darkness and moonlight; the focus on passion and violence—all these recall the silent film of which Kafka was a devotee.[24]

We have in addition two fragments written earlier, 'Before the Law', which also forms part of *The Trial* but is here presented as a self-contained narrative, and 'A Dream', in which the novel's pro-tagonist, Josef K., dreams about his own death and burial. Besides these, there are two stories which form an exception within Kafka's oeuvre in that they do seem to require a kind of decoding. These are 'Eleven Sons' and 'A Visit to the Mine'. About the former, Kafka told Brod that the sons were simply eleven stories on which he was cur-rently working.[25] Following this hint, Malcolm Pasley succeeded in identifying the sons with ten of the stories composing *A Country Doctor*, plus 'The Rider on the Coal-Scuttle'. He then turned to

[22] Wilhelm Emrich, *Franz Kafka* (Wiesbaden: Athenaion, 1975), 92–3. For further surmises, see Binder, *Kafka Kommentar*, 232.

[23] See Breon Mitchell, 'Ghosts from the Dungeons of the World Within: Kafka's "Ein Brudermord"', *Monatshefte*, 73 (1981), 51–62 (p. 53).

[24] See Hanns Zischler, *Kafka Goes to the Movies*, tr. Susan H. Gillespie (Chicago and London: University of Chicago Press, 2003), and for a detailed study of the story's filmic aspects, Peter-André Alt, *Kafka und der Film: Über kinematographisches Erzählen* (Munich: Beck, 2009), 128–44.

[25] Brod, *Über Franz Kafka*, 122.

'A Visit to the Mine' and argued that Kafka was inspired to write it by receiving an anthology of recent literature, *Der neue Roman* ('The New Novel') issued by his own publisher, Kurt Wolff, which contained exactly ten contributions. Each of the engineers corresponds to one of the authors in the anthology, and Kafka figures by implication as a lowly miner to whom the grandees of contemporary literature are paying a visit.[26]

These allusions, or as Pasley calls them, Kafka's 'semi-private games', may be considered irritating or trivial, but there is no doubt that Kafka did include in his texts glancing allusions to his own writing and his position as a writer which only he could be expected to understand. Thus the mysterious Odradek may, among other things, represent an incomplete work by Kafka, the fragments entitled 'The Huntsman Gracchus', with its many loose ends; if Odradek's voice sounds like 'the rustling of dry leaves', that may also allude to the pages (the German *Blatt* means both 'leaf' and 'page') of Kafka's text. On the other hand, the pursuit of such possible allusions may produce decreasing returns, especially if it excludes attention to the publicly accessible meanings of Kafka's work which can be disclosed by the familiar techniques of literary analysis.

One cannot avoid pursuing private allusions, however, in the text 'The Huntsman Gracchus' itself. The fragments assembled under this title are preserved in various places, some in notebooks, some in Kafka's diary. Max Brod tried to weld the fragments into a coherent story, incorporating an adjacent but unconnected passage. Rather than repeat such editorial interventions, we have decided to present the fragments as they stand. The basic narrative pattern that emerges—sometimes through third-person narrative, sometimes through dialogue between Gracchus and an unidentified speaker—links a modern setting with a mythical story. The setting is Riva on Lake Garda, where Kafka had stayed with Max and Otto Brod in September 1909 and which he again visited in September and October 1913, when his relationship with Felice Bauer was in crisis. The myth turns on a figure who many centuries before died yet remained alive because the ship bearing him to the land of the dead

---

[26] See Malcolm Pasley, 'Drei literarische Mystifikationen Kafkas', in Jürgen Born *et al.*, *Kafka-Symposion* (Berlin: Wagenbach, 1965), 21–37; 'Franz Kafka: "Ein Besuch ins Bergwerk"', *German Life and Letters*, 18 (1964–5), 40–6; 'Kafka's Semi-Private Games', *Oxford German Studies*, 6 (1971–2), 112–31.

took the wrong course. We have a suggestion here of Charon's boat in which he ferried the dead to the underworld imagined by the Greeks, and also of Wagner's Flying Dutchman, who sails the seas of the world and cannot die until a woman's selfless love redeems him—though Gracchus does not even have that possibility.

The fragments also have a more personal resonance. Kafka knew that Gracchus, the name of a famous family in ancient Rome, meant 'jackdaw', as his own surname did in Czech. The choice of name implies a degree of identification with his undead protagonist. When in Riva in 1913, Kafka developed a close relationship with an eighteen-year-old Swiss woman who has never been identified. The relationship, though brief, meant a great deal to him, and he promised to keep it secret, but did confess it to Felice Bauer.[27] This may lie behind Gracchus' otherwise unexplained guilt. But the occasion of Gracchus' fall, his pursuit of a mountain goat, also has a coarser sexual innuendo, for the original word is 'Gemse' (chamois), which in Kafka's day was a slang term for a prostitute.[28] So the story can be understood in part as a deeply veiled admission of sexual guilt.

A Hunger Artist

The last book that Kafka authorized for publication appeared in late August 1924, almost three months after his death on 3 June. He corrected proofs on his deathbed. Two of the stories, 'First Sorrow' and 'A Hunger Artist', were written in 1922; 'A Little Woman' probably dates from the end of 1923; 'Josefine, the Singer' was written early in 1924, when his health was rapidly declining. An atmosphere of finality, of approaching death, hangs over the whole collection.

Three of the stories are obviously about artists; less obviously, so is 'A Little Woman'. Instead of writers like Kafka, or painters like Titorelli in *The Trial*, the artists here are public performers of various kinds. The hunger artist belongs to a type that still existed in Kafka's time. So-called starvation artists would display themselves to the public under the supervision of guards who ensured that they did not nibble on the sly, and the duration of their fast would be

---

[27] Letter to Felice Bauer, 29 Dec. 1913–2 Jan. 1914, in *Briefe 1913–März 1914*, 311.

[28] See Frank Möbus, *Sünden-Fälle: Die Geschlechtlichkeit in Erzählungen Franz Kafkas* (Göttingen: Wallstein, 1994), 18–19.

carefully recorded.[29] In 1880 visitors to New York's Clarendon Hall paid twenty cents each to see Henry Tanner becoming increasingly emaciated over a forty-day period. A little later, Giovanni Succi toured all Europe's major cities, like Kafka's hunger artist, thrilling callous visitors by the sight of his famished body. A Viennese society lady told Arthur Schnitzler that she would go to see Succi after he had been starving for twenty-nine days and would look really terrible.[30] When the fashion for hunger artists declines, perhaps because many Europeans experienced real starvation in the later years of the First World War, Kafka's artist retreats to a circus, which is also the venue where the trapeze artist of 'First Sorrow' not only works but lives. Josefine is a singer, appearing before the other mice in performances whose value and meaning are persistently questioned by the narrator. And the woman in 'A Little Woman' can be interpreted as a Muse who, rather than inspiring the male protagonist, constantly nags and berates him in order to remind him of his duty.

Kafka's choice of performing artists reflects both his own enthusiasm for the circus and his increasing interest in the relations between the artist and the public. An artist dedicated to perfecting his art resents having to compromise with the demands of a commercial society. Thus the hunger artist can never starve for as long as he feels capable of doing, because his manager, alert to public preferences, insists on bringing his performances to an end after forty days. Not only the perfectionism but also the integrity of the hunger artist is highlighted. To show his guards that he does not eat surreptitiously, he sings, but the world refuses to believe in his honesty. Near the end of his life, neglected both by the public and by the employees of the circus where he has taken refuge, he is able to starve indefinitely because nobody thinks of feeding him, but his feats of starvation are not recorded. He himself comes to doubt his own integrity, insisting to the indifferent keeper that his fasting does not deserve admiration because he did it only because there was no food he liked. Is this a

[29] See Walter Vandereycken and Ron van Deth, *From Fasting Saints to Anorexic Girls: The History of Self-Starvation* (London: Athlone, 1994), ch. 5: 'Hunger Artists and Living Skeletons'; Breon Mitchell, 'Kafka and the Hunger Artists', in Alan Udoff (ed.), *Kafka and the Contemporary Critical Performance: Centenary Readings* (Bloomington, Ind.: Indiana University Press, 1987), 236–55.

[30] Arthur Schnitzler, *Tagebuch 1893–1902* (Vienna: Verlag der Österreichischen Akademie der Wissenschaften, 1989), 183 (13 Apr. 1896).

profession of modesty or a neurotic self-criticism? By implication, it dismantles the Romantic conception of the artist's special gifts by reinterpreting these gifts as a deficiency which disqualifies the artist from leading the 'normal' life he longs for. In one of Kafka's favourite stories, Thomas Mann's *Tonio Kröger*, the protagonist declares: 'Literature isn't a profession at all, I'll have you know—it's a curse.'[31]

While the hunger artist may be a tragic figure, other Kafka artists invite a different response through the childishness which makes them out of place in the adult world. As the trapeze artist in 'First Sorrow' lives on his trapeze, we may attribute this choice not just to devotion to his art, but also to an unwillingness to compromise with the human world. This awkwardness makes it difficult for his obviously caring manager to take him on tour, since the acrobat insists on travelling in the luggage-rack of his train. However, this solitary and self-centred existence proves unsatisfying. His lament—'Only this one bar in my hand—how can I live?'—suggests further semi-private meanings: the isolation required by a literary calling which requires one constantly to hold a pen, and the sexual solitude that finds relief in masturbation. At the end of the story, the trapeze artist's 'smooth and child-like brow' is furrowed by the cares that will make his sheltered existence ultimately unsustainable.

Josefine, the singing mouse, is also an immature person, treated with humorous detachment by the anonymous narrator. If her audience is slow to assemble, she stamps and swears, and she thinks so highly of the value of her art that she demands to be exempted from work. Her nation, the mouse people, treat her tantrums with indulgence, looking after her as a father looks after a child. But the question the narrator ponders is why they take so much trouble on Josefine's behalf. After all, what does her art consist in? She 'pipes', but then so do all the mice. Kafka's word, 'pfeifen', usually translated as 'pipe' or 'whistle', is not the normal word for the squeaking of a mouse, but Kafka does use it elsewhere in this sense.[32] So the point of the story seems to be that Josefine's performance simply enacts before an audience the everyday sound made by the mice. The value of her

[31] Thomas Mann, *Death in Venice and Other Stories*, tr. David Luke (London: Vintage, 1998), 159.

[32] Letter to Felix Weltsch, 15 Nov. 1917, in Kafka, *Briefe 1914–1917*, 365.

art cannot therefore consist in what she does, but in something else, and that something appears to lie in the performance as such, which brings the mice together in a warm unity and creates a feeling of national solidarity among them.

It gradually emerges that this national unity is the central value of the story. Kafka not only uses the emotionally charged word 'Volk' for the nation of the mice, but also describes individual members of the nation as 'Volksgenossen' (translated here as 'our fellows' and in the singular 'one of its own'), a term which was soon to be monopolized by the political right and is now unusable. The story was written at a time when Central European nationalism had been boosted by the Treaty of Versailles which encouraged the establishment of independent states by many of the peoples of the now defunct Austrian Empire, including, of course, the First Czechoslovak Republic of which Kafka was now a citizen. Moreover, although Kafka was more interested in practical than in political Zionism, he was by this time contemplating emigration to Palestine from an increasingly intolerant post-war Europe. The question whether the story alludes specifically to the Jewish people has often been asked, but never conclusively answered. While the precarious existence of the mice certainly suggests that of the Jews in the Diaspora, the story may be read first and foremost as a meditation on nationalism and on the sources of national unity.

Kafka had addressed this question already in 'At the Building of the Great Wall of China'. Both there and in 'Josefine' we find a note of cautious scepticism. In the earlier text, the building of the wall was gradually revealed as an impractical and even dangerous project whose undisclosed purpose was to promote a sense of unity among the Chinese. Here, Josefine's performances turn out to have no intrinsic artistic value, and even to be dangerous inasmuch as assembling together in one place exposes the mice to an attack from their enemy (presumably the cat), but to serve a purpose quite different from their declared aim. Josefine represents a central figure in modern nationalism, the bard or singer who gives voice to the national soul by using the national language (in this case, squeaking). But unlike nationalist thinkers, Kafka exposes the bard as deluded and her performances as an unwitting instrument of nation-building.

The story has another and sadder dimension as the last text Kafka wrote. After his diagnosis of tuberculosis in September 1917, prolonged periods of recuperation in the countryside and at sanatoria had only postponed his death. From September 1923 to March 1924 he lived in Berlin with his lover Dora Diamant, in considerable hardship owing to hyperinflation, and supported by food parcels sent by his family in Prague. Early in 1924 his health declined rapidly. The cause was diagnosed as tubercular lesions of the larynx, which made it increasingly difficult for him to speak or swallow. Hunger and thirst accelerated his death. Near the end he communicated with those around him by writing on slips of paper, some of which were preserved; Brod records (whether spoken or written is unclear) a poignantly paradoxical statement, typical of Kafka in constructing a double-bind—'If you don't kill me, you're a murderer'.[33] Against this background, the contortions of Josefine's 'fragile throat' suggest not only the exertions of the singer but also her creator's increasing difficulty in speaking. Her final disappearance anticipates Kafka's own. And the narrator's assurance that the life of the mouse community will go on much the same without her is Kafka's final profession of modesty and his last rebuke to the vanity of the artist.

Miscellaneous and Shorter Pieces

The text 'Investigations of a Dog', written probably in September and October 1922, and seemingly unfinished, has important features in common with the earlier 'At the Building of the Great Wall of China' and the later 'Josefine'. All three texts are not so much stories as meditations. The narrator, or the speaking voice, stands somewhat apart from his community and reflects on the foundations of its solidarity and on the practices that hold the community together. In this instance, the speaker has devoted much of his life to experimentally testing the beliefs on which the life of the canine community is based. For example, the dogs are convinced that they obtain their food from the earth, by watering it and by dancing, singing, and uttering spells. They are not troubled by the constantly observed fact that the food reaches them not directly from the earth but from above, and they snap up most of it before it even reaches the ground. It is only the speaker who is troubled by this contradiction. He undertakes a series of experiments to see whether food appears when he refrains from

[33] Brod, *Über Franz Kafka*, 185.

dancing, or what happens when the food arrives but he fails to pick it up (in which case the food follows him through the air), or what happens if he does not look for food at all but starves himself.

All these experiments, however, are condemned in advance to futility by the limitations of the dogs' perceptual apparatus. The story's premise is that the dogs are unaware of the existence of human beings. They sometimes wonder why it is that despite their natural desire to live in a warm huddle they actually live so far apart, and can only occasionally 'bond together' 'in moments of euphoria', but they never realize that it is because they have human owners. Their belief that by urinating, jumping about, and barking they actually produce the food which their owners throw to them so flatters their vanity that none of them, apart from the speaker, ever investigates its contradictions. And this sheds an ironic light on metaphysical inquiries conducted not only by dogs but also by us. Suppose our minds are so constituted that we can never know the truth about the world, never answer the basic questions of existence? When Heinrich von Kleist, one of Kafka's favourite authors, read Kant and learnt that the real nature of things, the 'Ding an sich', is forever inaccessible, he fell into a mood of despair in which he wrote, in a famous letter to his fiancée:

If all mankind had green spectacles instead of eyes, they would be obliged to conclude that the objects they saw through them *were* green—and they would never be able to decide whether their eyes showed them things as they are, or whether something was being added that was part of the eye rather than of the things. That is how the intellect works. We cannot decide whether what we call truth is truly truth, or whether it only seems so to us.[34]

Kafka's dog seems to be in a similar predicament without knowing it.

A different slant on the story is possible, however, if we emphasize the words 'science' and 'investigations'. Kafka's word 'Wissenschaft' does not mean 'natural science', but systematic knowledge in general. In the text such an approach to knowledge is contrasted with that offered by art. Admittedly, art, or rather the artist, is presented satirically through the 'aerial dogs', who are presumably lapdogs sitting on

---

[34] Letter to Wilhelmine von Zenge, 22 March 1801, in Heinrich von Kleist, *Sämtliche Werke und Briefe*, ed. Ilse-Maria Barth *et al.*, 4 vols. (Frankfurt a.M.: Deutsche Klassiker Verlag, 1989), iv. 205.

the knees of their invisible owners, and who typify a rarefied form of art, remote from the firm ground of ordinary existence. But a quite different version is represented by music. Already in *The Metamorphosis*, written ten years earlier, music implied a higher reality to which Gregor gained access only a little before his death, and which seemed to signify a loftier alternative to the earthly food he could no longer eat. Here the music encountered by the narrator-dog is an overwhelming experience, communicated by an 'awe-inspiring voice'. And although the dog, when he hears it, is in an advanced state of starvation, it drives him back into life, 'in the most marvellous leaps and bounds'. If art, represented here by music, is a separate realm, it is not a self-enclosed or self-sufficient one; contact with it is invigorating and forces one willy-nilly to carry on living with renewed energy. In contrast to the ascetic art of the hunger artist, this is a full-blooded, Dionysian conception of art. Like the Greek tragic theatre, in which the Nietzsche of *The Birth of Tragedy* saw a conjunction of Dionysus and Apollo, music and poetry, it sustains life not through its appeal to reason, but through its sheer vital power.

'The Burrow', written between November 1923 and January 1924, dates from a few months before Kafka's death, and it is tempting to explain the unspecified burrowing animal's resistance against a perhaps imaginary enemy as expressing Kafka's awareness of a growing enemy in his body that would soon kill him. In this perspective, the mysterious 'piping noise' that the creature hears would represent the wheezing that Kafka could hear in his failing lungs.[35] More generally, however, the story asks to be read as a description of paranoia by an unreliable narrator who reports faithfully on his situation but does not see that his ever-increasing precautions, the elaboration of his burrow to forestall the intrusion of an unknown enemy, render him vulnerable by making the burrow ever harder to defend. The narrator would then be like the narrator-dog in 'Investigations of a Dog', committed to a task whose futility is apparent to the reader but not to him.

With the remaining short texts, an attempt at detailed interpretation would spoil them. It may suffice to indicate ways of approach and some correspondences to other places in Kafka's oeuvre. 'The Knock

---

[35] For this and other possible autobiographical references, see Malcolm Pasley, 'Introduction', Kafka, *Der Heizer, In der Strafkolonie, Der Bau*, esp. p. 27.

on the Courtyard Gate' again illustrates the situation in which a slight, casual, even involuntary action brings about disaster. As the country doctor says: 'Once you have been led astray by the sound of the night-bell, it can never be put right.' Once the narrator's sister has knocked—or perhaps merely threatened to knock—on the gate, an apparatus of pursuit, arrest, trial, and punishment springs into action, as it does for Josef K. in *The Trial*.

'The Bridge' reads like a startling erotic fantasy. The narrating voice has been variously understood as female or male, but in either event, the human bridge suffers a violent assault 'right in the middle of my body', plunges down, and is 'torn apart and pierced' by sharp stones. Other scenes of eroticized violence in Kafka come to mind, notably the scene with the Thrasher in *The Trial*; but there are strong overtones of homosexual violence and masochistic pleasure in *The Metamorphosis* and *In the Penal Colony*. Mark Anderson has compared 'The Bridge' to the episode in *The Metamorphosis* where Gregor, like the bridge, lies face down and is pelted with apples by his father.[36] The sexual violence in 'The Bridge' is made more shocking, as Anderson also notes, by its idyllic Romantic setting—a summer evening on a trout-stream among the mountains. The attack is also an assault on nature, and to the bridge a previous delightful natural setting turns violent, colluding with the assailant to impale the victim on the sharp points of the stones.

In 'The Truth about Sancho Panza' Kafka takes one of literature's classic odd couples, Cervantes's knight Don Quixote who believes he is living in a world of chivalric adventures and his down-to-earth squire Sancho Panza, and uses them to represent the duality of the artist's existence. Such a duality can already be found in *The Judgement*, where Georg Bendemann's professional and erotic success is gained by repressing an alternative self, the friend who is wasting away in Russia. Here, Don Quixote, who lives in an imaginary world, may be taken to represent the authorial self, while Sancho Panza embodies the everyday self. His authorial persona is not a higher existence, but a devil that would destroy him if not diverted with chivalrous romances. Having found this method, Sancho Panza is able to lead a peaceful and even entertaining life. But isn't this really

---

[36] Mark Anderson, 'Kafka, Homosexuality and the Aesthetics of "Male Culture"', *Austrian Studies*, 7 (1996), 79–99 (p. 91).

the picture of a Philistine who has artistic potential but neutralizes it with vulgar mockery?

Some other short pieces encapsulate what may be called philosophical problems. The text to which Brod gave the title 'Little Fable', here called 'Cat and Mouse', varies the situation of 'Before the Law': a whole life dedicated to a single purpose turns out, when it is too late, to have been misguided. 'The Spinning-Top' can be linked with 'Investigations of a Dog' as illustrating how not to understand the world. The world, like the top, is constantly in motion. It refuses to stand still while the philosopher examines it. When the philosopher picks up the top, its essential quality—its motion—has vanished, leaving nothing for him to study. The children who enjoyed the motion of the top without trying to analyse it were wiser than he was. 'On Parables' is a puzzling piece about the relation between figurative and literal speech, and imagined and real existence; by a logical sleight-of-hand, it ends by devaluing reality in favour of the parable, and making a success in reality seem worthless by comparison with a loss on the figurative level. 'Give it up!' again offers us a vision of the world in which the slightest everyday action becomes impossible once one starts to reflect on it, rather as in 'The Next Village' a short journey could become a perilous enterprise lasting a lifetime. This side of Kafka's attitude to the everyday world is conveyed in a letter about him that his one-time lover Milena Jesenská wrote to Max Brod: 'For him life is something quite different than for anyone else. Above all, money, the stock market, the currency exchange, a typewriter are entirely mystical things (which indeed they are, but not for the rest of us), for him they are the strangest enigmas, to which his attitude is quite different from ours.'[37] Kafka's awestruck amazement before the complications of day-to-day life must often have been irritating; but to a sympathetic soul like Milena it revealed a different and deeper attitude to reality, a touch of mysticism, which helped to mark Kafka out as an exceptional person.

The Aphorisms

Kafka's shorter writings include two groups of aphorisms—concise reflective statements, in which a difficult thought is often expressed

---

[37] Franz Kafka, *Briefe an Milena*, revised and enlarged edn., ed. Jürgen Born and Michael Müller (Frankfurt a.M.: Fischer, 1983), 363.

through images. The first group, often known as the 'Zürau Aphorisms', was written in the winter of 1917–18. That was a critical period for Kafka. On the morning of 13 August 1917 he had woken up to find himself spitting blood. This haemorrhage was diagnosed as resulting from pulmonary tuberculosis. Kafka took extended sick-leave and went to recuperate in the country at Zürau/Siřem, where his sister Ottla was running a farm.[38] Zürau was a village with 400–500 inhabitants, where Kafka was able to live quietly, become accepted in the community, help a little on the farm, read, and think. His reading included an eclectic choice of religious writers, including works by Søren Kierkegaard and the late, heavily Christian diaries of Leo Tolstoy. The discovery of his almost certainly terminal illness, and the final dissolution of his five-year on–off engagement to Felice Bauer, required him, he felt, to rethink his own life and, more gener-ally, to ponder ultimate questions. On a brief visit to Prague in December 1917 he told Brod: 'What I have to do, I can do only by myself. Become clear about the last things.'[39] His thoughts found expression in a large number of aphorisms and brief narratives writ-ten in his notebooks. Later he selected over a hundred of his aphor-isms, numbered them, and copied them out in a sequence to which Brod subsequently gave the title 'Reflections on Sin, Suffering, Hope, and the True Way'.

In a broad sense, the Zürau aphorisms articulate the perennial questions of religion—about the purpose of life, about one's place in the universe, about how to conduct oneself towards one's fellow-beings. But to say any more about their religious framework is diffi-cult. They do not seem to presuppose belief in a personal god. Crucial to understanding the collection is no. 50:

Man cannot live without an enduring trust in something indestructible in himself, though both the indestructible as well as the trust may remain for ever hidden from him. Remaining hidden has one possible expression in the belief in a personal god.

The belief in a personal god is evidently an illusion which conceals from us the 'indestructible' basis of life. Similarly, in no. 13 the hope of being rescued by 'the Lord' is a remnant of faith which impedes

---

[38] For a detailed account of Zürau with many evocative photographs, including even the view Kafka could see from his window, see Binder, *Kafkas Welt*, 527–43.

[39] Brod, *Über Franz Kafka*, 147.

true insight into the nature of the world. The concept of the 'inde-structible' comes from Arthur Schopenhauer. In Volume II of *The World as Will and Representation*, which consists of essays supplementing the reflections in Volume I, Schopenhauer has a long essay entitled 'On Death and its Relation to the Indestructibility of our Essential Being'. Here he argues that death should not be feared, because our existence as distinct individuals—what Schopenhauer calls the *principium individuationis*—is itself illusory.[40] Our true being is as a species. In the Will, which for Schopenhauer is the ultimate force propelling all life, there is no distinction between the individual and the species; death is simply the transition from one temporary individual embodiment to another, whence the widespread belief in metempsychosis or reincarnation—another source of imagery in Kafka's aphorisms. Kafka does not necessarily take on board Schopenhauer's theory of the Will, but he does seem to accept a belief in the essential unity of humankind. The question is how to live in accordance with this insight. In an aphorism from his Zürau notebooks which he did not include in his final selection, Kafka wrote: 'Faith means: liberating the indestructible in oneself, or rather: liberating oneself, or rather: being indestructible, or rather: being.'[41]

Within this context, the aphorisms turn on human duality. We are inhabitants both of a material and of a spiritual world. Only the spiritual world is real. Life is a perilous journey towards the spiritual world. On this journey there are many temptations: from vanity, from despair, from sexuality. The erotic attraction which the world exerts even on the would-be ascetic is drastically represented by the image of a faithful dog, already dying, which insists on licking its helpless owner with its already putrefying tongue. But the image of a journey, with its implication of a passage through time, is also exposed as illusory. For since there is only a spiritual world, time is illusory, and hope, directed towards the future, becomes pointless. Another recurring image is that of expulsion from and return to paradise. But since time is illusory, this image is again misleading, so it is possible that we are still in paradise, only without knowing it. Our task is therefore one

---

[40] See Dale Jacquette, *The Philosophy of Schopenhauer* (Chesham: Acumen, 2005), 108–44 (ch. 4: 'Suffering, Salvation, Death, and the Renunciation of the Will to Life').

[41] Franz Kafka, *Nachgelassene Schriften und Fragmente II*, ed. Jost Schillemeit (Frankfurt a.M.: Fischer, 1992), 55.

of accurate knowledge ('Erkenntnis', implying an active, dynamic form of insight).

However, knowledge is not enough. The quest for knowledge can be an excuse for not engaging in action (see the end of no. 86). Kafka distinguishes between knowing and being. If you know the truth, you are yourself separate from the truth as an object of knowledge; you are therefore not yourself part of the truth, hence you are a lie (no. 80). The point is to transform oneself. And for this, mere effort is not enough (no. 45). Someone who was astonished at his rapid progress on the path to eternity failed to realize that he was actually moving backwards (no. 38). Kafka calls instead for a humble concentration on oneself, even on the negative task of destroying oneself, and for a dialectic between humble prayer and active effort (no. 106). If one is really making spiritual progress, one may well not realize it, just as a wooden stair hollowed out by people's feet is, from its own point of view, a mere worthless piece of wood, yet is also the means by which people rise (no. 59). This progress means an increase in suffering. But thereby it also means an increase in solidarity, through suffering, with other people (nos. 102, 103). It is through shared suffering that one may ultimately overcome the world—certainly not through assailing it head-on. The unnumbered aphorism that Kafka placed last in the series advocates utter stillness as the way to bring the world to one's feet. Here Kafka seems momentarily to join hands with the world's great mystics.

The second group of aphorisms, which Brod was to publish under the heading 'He', dates from early in 1920. Kafka wrote them at what he felt to be a critical stage in his life, soon after he had severed his engagement to Julie Wohryzek. They occur together in Kafka's diary, but nothing suggests that he revised or arranged them; some are incomplete. At least one, the anecdote about the two children, reads like an account of an actual event, though it is almost certainly fictionalized to suggest metaphysical overtones, and another is a first-person recollection of how the speaker—surely Kafka himself—once pondered his vocation. These are not so much general statements about the world as formulations of one person's existential position.

Their leading themes include the sense of captivity. The speaker feels that he is imprisoned, whether as 'a captive on the earth' or in his own cage. Yet the captivity seems voluntary: he is in a cage whose bars are so far apart that he could easily step out; or he is thirsty yet separated from a spring only by a few bushes. The double meaning of captivity is summed up in the equation: 'My prison cell—my stronghold.' A related theme is the extreme difficulty of everyday life. Yet again this difficulty seems to be self-induced, or to result from the speaker's character: he himself blocks his own path just by living; or, in a more drastic physical image, he is always beating against his own forehead.

While these notes continually emphasize the speaker's isolation, they also suggest that the isolation is temporary or even illusory. He feels as though he had originally been part of a group monument, but the other figures have been dispersed, so that in his solitude he still feels the imprint of the absent community. Or his sense of being part of a larger entity is expressed through the feeling that somebody somewhere is worried about him. He has a feeling of responsibility, but he is not sure to whom: it feels as though he were living under the pressure of an unknown family who impose on him a responsibility from which he cannot be discharged.

The theme of responsibility links these diary entries with the *Country Doctor* volume and warns us, finally, against a frequent misapprehension about Kafka. Despite the way he often stylizes himself in his diaries, he was not a recluse or a hermit. Rather, he inhabited what he himself calls, in a note of 29 October 1921, a 'borderland between solitude and community'.[42] His fictions and his reflections are the product of solitude, but they also reveal his awareness of forming part of a community and having a responsibility towards it.

[42] Franz Kafka, *Tagebücher*, ed. Hans-Gerd Koch, Michael Müller, and Malcolm Pasley (Frankfurt a.M.: Fischer, 1990), 871.

NOTE ON THE TEXT

A Country Doctor: Little Tales and *A Hunger Artist: Four Stories* were published, or authorized for publication, during Kafka's lifetime, as were 'The Aeroplanes at Brescia' and 'The Rider on the Coal-Scuttle'. The texts here translated are those of the first published editions as reproduced in the volume of the Critical Edition of Kafka's works entitled *Drucke zu Lebzeiten*, edited by Wolf Kittler, Hans-Gerd Koch, and Gerhard Neumann (Frankfurt a.M.: Fischer, 1996). The critical apparatus, published as a separate volume, includes the—not extensive—variants in Kafka's surviving manuscripts. 'The Aeroplanes in Brescia' appeared in an abridged form in the Prague newspaper *Bohemia* on 29 September 1909; the full text was published after Kafka's death by Max Brod and is supplied here from the text and apparatus volumes of *Drucke zu Lebzeiten*. The remaining texts are taken from volumes of the Critical Edition containing Kafka's diaries and notebooks: *Tagebücher*, edited by Hans-Gerd Koch, Michael Müller, and Malcolm Pasley (Frankfurt a.M.: Fischer, 1990); *Nachgelassene Schriften und Fragmente I*, edited by Malcolm Pasley (Frankfurt a.M.: Fischer, 1993); and *Nachgelassene Schriften und Fragmente II*, edited by Jost Schillemeit (Frankfurt a.M.: Fischer, 1992), 143–217.

NOTE ON THE TRANSLATION

IN translating a second selection of Kafka's shorter pieces, I found, not surprisingly, not only a continuation of those problems I had met in the first, but a further range as well, which is only a different way of saying that he extended his stylistic scope considerably in his two later published collections, and was still doing so in many of the pieces he left unfinished. Some are longer, the prose looser, allowing the translator greater freedom. Others continue the density of the prose poem; 'In the Gallery', for example, where the more various forms of the German conditional are put to more ambiguous use than the narrower range available in English can do. 'First Sorrow', on the other hand, has its strongest poetic resource not so much in its grammar as in the expressive rhythms of its sentences—indeed, apart from the implied metaphor in the central figure these are its single poetic resource, and so ask for close imitation. The characteristic ambiguities and indeterminacies persist, forcing the translator into 'either/or' choices when 'both/and' or 'both-but-not-at-the-same-time' would be preferable. I found myself quite often reverting to a more or less literal version, particularly of the Aphorisms, simply because this would at least preserve a certain openness.

A number of the pieces here, such as 'A Hunger Artist' and the unfinished 'Blumfeld, an Elderly Bachelor', are, like the novels and the definitive stories of the first selection, narrated in that insecure mode of 'style indirecte libre' or 'erlebte Rede'. This is not simple interior monologue, for there is no 'I', and the past tense of the storyteller still, just about, holds sway, for in Kafka's stories it is often the 'only just' past; rather, the reader is brought close to the limited perspectives of the protagonist's thinking and immediate reacting, with a narrator functioning more as a hidden stage-manager of the action than as an open, knowledgeable voice. A translator needs to be alert to tenses here, and to ways of rendering the German subjunctive of indirect speech. The usual, rather heavy-handed trick is to insert an unobtrusive 'he thought', 'she said'. However, in the present selection an important group, the longer animal stories—'A Report to an Academy', 'Josefine, the Singer or the Mouse-People', the unpublished 'Investigations of a Dog', and 'The Burrow' (unfinished)—but

others too, such as 'At the Building of the Great Wall of China' and
'A Little Woman', are actually monologues, told by an 'I' with a char-
acterized voice, sometimes strongly, like Rotpeter's, sometimes more
elusively as in the 'Great Wall of China'. The translator's aim here
was to re-create a distinct voice, a dramatized persona, in English.
But the peculiar problem of Kafka's prose in this respect is that
although these sentences are certainly spoken and speakable (actors
have frequently performed 'A Report'), they are not, strictly speaking,
colloquial, but still literary, still constructed, and they will frequently
rise to the syntactical complexity characteristic of so much that is
familiar from *The Judgement* and the novels—for example, towards
the end of 'A Little Woman', where the speaker ties himself up in self-
defensive self-deceptions very similar to Georg Bendemann's, wryly
comic this time. On other occasions the complexity appears to be a
rhetoric of crisis, as when the Dog encounters the musical dogs; or
when the complex syntax becomes the immediate expression of the
theme, as when the scrabbling maker of the burrow describes his labyrinth in labyrinthine sentences, or when the historian of the Wall
imagines the incommunicable distance between the centre of authority and the waiting recipient in a seeming endless sequence of short,
effortful actions. But through all these complexities, it is important to
maintain the distinctive voice, and also—though this is much more
difficult—a certain lightness where these figures, who take themselves
so seriously, are in their different ways comic, delicately, sadly,
absurdly, grotesquely, ambivalently. I have had a great deal of pleasure in simply attempting it. But attempting it is one thing . . .

But the stories in Kafka's two collections are very various, and not
all are obviously characteristic. 'A Brother's Murder' seems to be an
exception in its precision and concision as much as in its violence
and impersonality, rather like an Expressionist woodcut—I was
unable to make anything as brief and exact in English as the mapping
of the streets where Schmar will murder Wese, or as the minute
reporting of their every movement along them. But this apparent
lucidity obscures great unknowns: who is whose brother? Is Pallas
more than a voyeur? What is Frau Wese really feeling? And so on.

The markers of indeterminacy and uncertainty, 'quite', 'almost',
'nearly', the reactive 'positively', 'perhaps', and the rest, are as ubi-
quitous in these pieces as in the earlier ones, particularly—or does it
merely seem so?—'as if', that curious figure which introduces a

metaphor, follows it with a speculative subjunctive, not with a confident indicative, and so at the same time signals its own imprecision and inadequacy. The effect is indeed one of imprecision, insecurity, even of doubting that language itself is adequate to naming. The problem in translating here lies in German's employment of the subjunctive, which is falling out of use in English, and is often confused with the conditional, so that if one reverts to older forms ('as if it were . . .') there is a risk of gratuitous heaviness just where it should be light.

There is a further, extraneous, element of uncertainty at some points in the pieces that Kafka did not publish or did not finish. How far is what may be (or what this translator thinks may be) a possible ambiguity or uncertainty attributable simply to lack of revision? For example, where as a rule Kafka's sentences, however elaborately they may zigzag and gyrate, always manage to land beautifully on their feet, some of the more complex sentences in 'The Burrow', his last, unfinished (unfinishable?) piece, seemed to get out of hand. And in 'Investigations of a Dog', the occasional slide from 'Hundeschaft' (mainly rendered as 'pack') to 'Volk' (mainly rendered as 'people') made me wonder how far this slippage was purposeful or how far merely intrusive. In the ambivalent fable of the diva Josefine (Kafka at his most many-layered, and most charming), 'people' is in the title and essential to the theme; in the dog's story, the analogy with human society, though it is certainly present, is less dominant. 'Hundeschaft' would have served consistency; 'Volk' seems to be pushing the analogy harder than literary tact requires. I may be just inventing difficulties. After all, 'Volk' is what Kafka wrote.

'Volk', together with its combinations, is itself problematic, or rather it has become so historically. Its association in Kafka's lifetime and after with an increasingly tainted nationalism, racial ideology, ethnicity, or collective governance, disparate ideas all collapsible into a single word, make it almost impossible to find an innocent equivalent now. I have mainly used the all-purpose 'people', which is suitable enough for the range required for 'Josefine', though varying it on occasion to 'nation' was useful insofar as it accommodates readings that take into account the nationalisms, Zionist and Czech, which most preoccupied Kafka and his circle. Cognates, such as 'völkisch' (here: 'national'), and combinations such as 'Volksgenosse' (here: 'fellow'), which both, notoriously, entered Nazi discourse, were more intractable, and my renderings consequently weaker.

The Aphorisms I found the most intractable of all to translate, largely, I suspect, because of this translator's stubborn (and scarcely successful) attempt to understand first what it was she was translating, but partly too because of a tension between the authoritative lapidary form, and the exploratory content of so many of them. Shortest of all, the cage in search of a bird sounds very like a metaphor in search of a correlative. Translation, perhaps?

My debts in translating this selection have been once again to my editors Judith Luna and Ritchie Robertson, but even more so this later time round: to Judith for taking the gamble of inviting me to take it on in the first place and holding me to it so tactfully; to Ritchie for throwing light on my frequent bafflement, for correcting my errors and suggesting improvements, and in general for continuous support throughout. Remaining errors and remaining bafflement are my own.

J. C.

SELECT BIBLIOGRAPHY
(CONFINED TO WORKS IN ENGLISH)

Translations of Kafka's Non-Fictional Works

The Collected Aphorisms, tr. Malcolm Pasley (London: Penguin, 1994).

The Diaries, tr. Joseph Kresh (Harmondsworth: Penguin, 1972).

Letters to Friends, Family and Editors, tr. Richard and Clara Winston (New York: Schocken, 1988).

Letters to Felice, tr. James Stern and Elizabeth Duckworth (London: Vintage, 1992).

Letters to Milena, expanded edn., tr. Philip Boehm (New York: Schocken, 1990).

Letters to Ottla and the Family, tr. Richard and Clara Winston (New York: Schocken, 1988).

Biographies

Adler, Jeremy, *Franz Kafka* (London: Penguin, 2001).

Brod, Max, *Franz Kafka: A Biography*, tr. G. Humphreys Roberts and Richard Winston (New York: Schocken, 1960).

Diamant, Kathi, *Kafka's Last Love: The Mystery of Dora Diamant* (London: Secker & Warburg, 2003).

Hayman, Ronald, *K: A Biography of Kafka* (London: Weidenfeld & Nicolson, 1981).

Hockaday, Mary, *Kafka, Love and Courage: The Life of Milena Jesenská* (London: Deutsch, 1995).

Murray, Nicholas, *Kafka* (London: Little, Brown, 2004).

Northey, Anthony, *Kafka's Relatives: Their Lives and His Writing* (New Haven and London: Yale University Press, 1991).

Stach, Reiner, *Kafka: The Decisive Years*, tr. Shelley Frisch (San Diego and London: Harcourt, 2005).

Storr, Anthony, 'Kafka's Sense of Identity', in his *Churchill's Black Dog and Other Phenomena of the Human Mind* (London: Collins, 1989), 52–82.

Unseld, Joachim, *Franz Kafka: A Writer's Life*, tr. Paul F. Dvorak (Riverside, Calif.: Ariadne Press, 1997).

Introductions

Gray, Richard T., Ruth V. Gross, Rolf J. Goebel, and Clayton Koelb, *A Franz Kafka Encyclopedia* (Westport, Conn.: Greenwood Press, 2005).

Preece, Julian (ed.), *The Cambridge Companion to Kafka* (Cambridge: Cambridge University Press, 2002).

Robertson, Ritchie, *Kafka: A Very Short Introduction* (Oxford: Oxford University Press, 2004).

Rolleston, James (ed.), *A Companion to the Works of Franz Kafka* (Rochester, NY: Camden House, 2002).

Speirs, Ronald, and Beatrice Sandberg, *Franz Kafka*, Macmillan Modern Novelists (London: Macmillan, 1997).

Critical Studies

Alter, Robert, *Necessary Angels: Tradition and Modernity in Kafka, Benjamin and Scholem* (Cambridge, Mass.: Harvard University Press, 1991).

Anderson, Mark, *Kafka's Clothes: Ornament and Aestheticism in the Habsburg Fin de Siècle* (Oxford: Clarendon Press, 1992).

——'Kafka, Homosexuality and the Aesthetics of "Male Culture"', *Austrian Studies*, 7 (1996), 79–99

Boa, Elizabeth, *Kafka: Gender, Class and Race in the Letters and Fictions* (Oxford: Clarendon Press, 1996).

Corngold, Stanley, *Lambent Traces: Franz Kafka* (Princeton: Princeton University Press, 2004).

Dodd, W. J., *Kafka and Dostoyevsky: The Shaping of Influence* (London: Macmillan, 1992).

Duttlinger, Carolin, *Kafka and Photography* (Oxford: Oxford University Press, 2007).

Eilittä, Leena, *Approaches to Personal Identity in Kafka's Short Fiction: Freud, Darwin, Kierkegaard* (Helsinki: Academia Scientiarum Fennica, 1999).

Flores, Angel (ed.), *The Kafka Debate* (New York: Gordian Press, 1977).

Gilman, Sander L., *Franz Kafka, the Jewish Patient* (London and New York: Routledge, 1995).

Goebel, Rolf J., *Constructing China: Kafka's Orientalist Discourse* (Columbia, SC: Camden House, 1997).

Heidsieck, Arnold, *The Intellectual Contexts of Kafka's Fiction: Philosophy, Law, Religion* (Columbia, SC: Camden House, 1994).

Koelb, Clayton, *Kafka's Rhetoric: The Passion of Reading* (Ithaca and London: Cornell University Press, 1989).

Pascal, Roy, *Kafka's Narrators: A Study of His Stories and Sketches* (Cambridge: Cambridge University Press, 1982).

Politzer, Heinz, *Franz Kafka: Parable and Paradox* (Ithaca, NY: Cornell University Press, 1962).

Robertson, Ritchie, *Kafka: Judaism, Politics and Literature* (Oxford: Clarendon Press, 1985).

Sokel, Walter H., *The Myth of Power and the Self: Essays on Franz Kafka* (Detroit: Wayne State University Press, 2002).

Spilka, Mark, *Dickens and Kafka: A Mutual Interpretation* (Bloomington, Ind.: Indiana University Press, 1963).

White, J. J., 'Endings and Non-Endings in Kafka's Fiction', in Franz Kuna (ed.), *Franz Kafka: Semi-Centenary Perspectives* (London: Elek, 1976), 146–66.

Zilcosky, John, *Kafka's Travels: Exoticism, Colonialism, and the Traffic of Writing* (Basingstoke and New York: Palgrave Macmillan, 2003).

Zischler, Hanns, *Kafka Goes to the Movies*, tr. Susan H. Gillespie (Chicago and London: University of Chicago Press, 2003).

Historical Context

Anderson, Mark (ed.), *Reading Kafka: Prague, Politics, and the Fin de Siècle* (New York: Schocken, 1989).

Beck, Evelyn Torton, *Kafka and the Yiddish Theater* (Madison, Wisc.: University of Wisconsin Press, 1971).

Bruce, Iris, *Kafka and Cultural Zionism: Dates in Palestine* (Madison, Wisc.: University of Wisconsin Press, 2007).

Gelber, Mark H. (ed.), *Kafka, Zionism, and Beyond* (Tübingen: Niemeyer, 2004).

Kieval, Hillel J., *The Making of Czech Jewry: National Conflict and Jewish Society in Bohemia, 1870–1918* (New York: Oxford University Press, 1988).

Robertson, Ritchie, *The 'Jewish Question' in German Literature, 1749–1939* (Oxford: Oxford University Press, 1999).

Spector, Scott, *Prague Territories: National Conflict and Cultural Innovation in Franz Kafka's Fin de Siècle* (Berkeley, Los Angeles, and London: University of California Press, 2000).

'The Aeroplanes at Brescia'

Demetz, Peter, *The Air Show at Brescia* (New York: Farrar, Straus, & Giroux, 2002).

A Country Doctor: Little Tales

Boa, Elizabeth, 'Kafka's "Auf der Galerie": A Resistant Reading', *Deutsche Vierteljahrsschrift*, 65 (1991), 486–501.

Campbell, Karen J., 'Dreams of Interpretation: On the Sources of Kafka's "Landarzt"', *German Quarterly*, 60 (1987), 420–31.

Cohn, Dorrit, 'Kafka's Eternal Present: Narrative Tense in "Ein Landarzt" and Other First-Person Stories', *PMLA* 83 (1968), 144–50.

Martens, Lorna, 'Art, Freedom and Deception in Kafka's "Ein Bericht für eine Akademie"', *Deutsche Vierteljahrsschrift*, 61 (1987), 720–32.

Mitchell, Breon, 'Ghosts from the Dungeons of the World Within: Kafka's "Ein Brudermord"', *Monatshefte*, 73 (1981), 51–62.

Pasley, Malcolm, 'Franz Kafka: "Ein Besuch ins Bergwerk"', *German Life and Letters*, 18 (1964–5), 40–6.

Timms, Edward, 'Kafka's Expanded Metaphors: A Freudian Approach to "Ein Landarzt"', in J. P. Stern and J. J. White (eds.), *Paths and Labyrinths: Nine Papers from a Kafka Symposium* (London: Institute of Germanic Studies, 1985), 66–79.

Triffitt, Gregory B., *Kafka's 'Landarzt' Collection: Rhetoric and Interpretation* (New York: Peter Lang, 1985).

A Hunger Artist: Four Stories

Gross, Ruth V., 'Of Mice and Women: Reflections on a Discourse in Kafka's *Josefine, die Sängerin oder Das Volk der Mäuse*', *Germanic Review*, 60 (1985), 59–68.

Minden, Michael, 'Kafka's *Josefine, die Sängerin oder Das Volk der Mäuse*', *German Life and Letters*, 62 (2009), 297–310.

Mitchell, Breon, 'Kafka and the Hunger Artists', in Alan Udoff (ed.), *Kafka and the Contemporary Critical Performance: Centenary Readings* (Bloomington, Ind.: Indiana University Press, 1987), 236–55.

Norris, Margot, 'Sadism and Masochism in Two Kafka Stories: "In der Strafkolonie" and "Ein Hungerkünstler"', *Modern Language Notes*, 93 (1978), 430–47.

Sheppard, Richard W., 'Kafka's "Ein Hungerkünstler": A Reconsideration', *German Quarterly*, 46 (1973), 219–33.

Stern, J. P., 'Franz Kafka on Mice and Men', in J. P. Stern and J. J. White (eds.), *Paths and Labyrinths: Nine Papers from a Kafka Symposium* (London: Institute of Germanic Studies, 1985), 141–55.

'Investigations of a Dog'

Fickert, Kurt J., 'Kafka's Search for Truth in *Forschungen eines Hundes*', *Monatshefte*, 85 (1993), 189–97.

Kohlenbach, Margrete, 'Religious Dogs in Nietzsche and Kafka', *Oxford German Studies*, 39 (2010), 213–27.

Leadbeater, Lewis W., 'The Sophistic Nature of Kafka's *Forschungen eines Hundes*', *German Life and Letters*, 46 (1993), 51–8.

Winkelman, John, 'Kafka's *Forschungen eines Hundes*', *Monatshefte*, 59 (1967), 115–31, 204–16.

'The Burrow'

Boulby, Mark, 'Kafka's End: A Reassessment of *The Burrow*', *German Quarterly*, 55 (1982), 175–85.

Coetzee, J. M., 'Time, Tense and Aspect in Kafka's *The Burrow*', *Modern Language Notes*, 96 (1981), 556–79.

Heinemann, Richard, 'Kafka's Oath of Service: *Der Bau* and the Dialectic of the Bureaucratic Mind', *PMLA* 111 (1996), 256–70.

The Aphorisms

Gray, Richard T., *Constructive Destruction. Kafka's Aphorisms: Literary Tradition and Literary Transformation* (Tübingen: Niemeyer, 1987).
Milfull, Helen, 'The Theological Position of Franz Kafka's Aphorisms', *Seminar*, 18 (1982), 169–83.
Robertson, Ritchie, 'Kafka's Zürau Aphorisms', *Oxford German Studies*, 14 (1983), 73–91.
Sandbank, Shimon, 'Surprise Technique in Kafka's Aphorisms', *Orbis Litterarum*, 25 (1970), 261–74.

Further Reading in Oxford World's Classics

Kafka, Franz, *The Castle*, tr. Anthea Bell, ed. Ritchie Robertson.
—— *The Man who Disappeared*, tr. and ed. Ritchie Robertson.
—— *The Metamorphosis and Other Stories*, tr. Joyce Crick, ed. Ritchie Robertson.
—— *The Trial*, tr. Mike Mitchell, ed. Ritchie Robertson.

A CHRONOLOGY OF FRANZ KAFKA

1883 3 July: Franz Kafka born in Prague, son of Hermann Kafka (1852–1931) and his wife Julie, née Löwy (1856–1934).

1885 Birth of FK's brother Georg, who died at the age of fifteen months.

1887 Birth of FK's brother Heinrich, who died at the age of six months.

1889 Birth of FK's sister Gabriele ('Elli') (d. 1941).

1890 Birth of FK's sister Valerie ('Valli') (d. 1942).

1892 Birth of FK's sister Ottilie ('Ottla') (d. 1943).

1901 FK begins studying law in the German-language section of the Charles University, Prague.

1906 Gains his doctorate in law and begins a year of professional experience in the Prague courts.

1907 Begins working for the Prague branch of the insurance company Assicurazioni Generali, based in Trieste.

1908 Moves to the state-run Workers' Accident Insurance Company for the Kingdom of Bohemia. First publication: eight prose pieces (later included in the volume *Meditation*) appear in the Munich journal *Hyperion*.

1909 Holiday with Max and Otto Brod at Riva on Lake Garda; they attend a display of aircraft, about which FK writes 'The Aeroplanes at Brescia'.

1910 Holiday with Max and Otto Brod in Paris.

1911 Holiday with Max Brod in Northern Italy, Switzerland, and Paris. Attends many performances by Yiddish actors visiting Prague, and becomes friendly with the actor Isaak Löwy (Jitskhok Levi).

1912 Holiday with Max Brod in Weimar, after which FK spends three weeks in the nudist sanatorium 'Jungborn' in the Harz Mountains. Works on *The Man who Disappeared*. 13 August: first meeting with Felice Bauer (1887–1960) from Berlin. 22–3 September: writes *The Judgement* in a single night. November–December: works on *The Metamorphosis*. December: *Meditation*, a collection of short prose pieces, published by Kurt Wolff in Leipzig.

1913 Visits Felice Bauer three times in Berlin. September: attends a conference on accident prevention in Vienna, where he also looks in on the Eleventh Zionist Congress. Stays in a sanatorium in Riva. Publishes *The Stoker* (= the first chapter of *The Man who Disappeared*) in Wolff's series of avant-garde prose texts 'The Last Judgement'.

1914 1 June: officially engaged to Felice Bauer in Berlin. 12 July: engage-
ment dissolved. Holiday with the Prague novelist Ernst Weiss in the
Danish resort of Marielyst. August–December: writes most of *The
Trial*; October: *In the Penal Colony*.

1915 The dramatist Carl Sternheim, awarded the Fontane Prize for
literature, transfers the prize money to Kafka. *The Metamorphosis*
published by Wolff.

1916 Reconciliation with Felice Bauer; they spend ten days together in the
Bohemian resort of Marienbad (Mariánské Lázně). *The Judgement*
published by Wolff. FK works on the stories later collected in
A Country Doctor.

1917 July: FK and Felice visit the latter's sister in Budapest, and become
engaged again. 9–10 August: FK suffers a haemorrhage which is
diagnosed as tubercular. To convalesce, he stays with his sister
Ottla on a farm at Zürau (Siřem) in the Bohemian countryside.
December: visit from Felice Bauer; engagement dissolved.

1918 March: FK resumes work. November: given health leave, stays till
March 1919 in a hotel in Schelesen (Želená).

1919 Back in Prague, briefly engaged to Julie Wohryzek (1891–1944).
In the Penal Colony published by Wolff.

1920 Intense relationship with his Czech translator Milena Polak, née
Jesenská (1896–1944). July: ends relationship with Julie Wohryzek.
Publication of *A Country Doctor: Little Stories*. December: again
granted health leave, FK stays in a sanatorium in Matliary, in the
Tatra Mountains, till August 1921.

1921 September: returns to work, but his worsening health requires him
to take three months' further leave from October.

1922 January: has his leave extended till April; stays in mountain hotel in
Spindlermühle (Špindlerův Mlýn). January–August: writes most of
The Castle. 1 July: retires from the Insurance Company on a pension.

1923 July: visits Müritz on the Baltic and meets Dora Diamant (1898–1952).
September: moves to Berlin and lives with Dora.

1924 March: his declining health obliges FK to return to Prague and in
April to enter a sanatorium outside Vienna. Writes and publishes
'Josefine, the Singer or The Mouse-People'. 3 June: dies. August:
A Hunger Artist: Four Stories published by Die Schmiede.

1925 *The Trial*, edited by Max Brod, published by Die Schmiede.

1926 *The Castle*, edited by Max Brod, published by Wolff.

1927 *Amerika* (now known by Kafka's title, *The Man who Disappeared*),
edited by Max Brod, published by Wolff.

1930   *The Castle*, translated by Willa and Edwin Muir, published by Martin Secker (London), the first English translation of Kafka.

1939   Max Brod leaves Prague just before the German invasion, taking Kafka's manuscripts in a suitcase, and reaches Palestine.

1956   Brod transfers the manuscripts (except that of *The Trial*) to Switzerland for safe keeping.

1961   The Oxford scholar Malcolm Pasley, with the permission of Kafka's heirs, transports the manuscripts to the Bodleian Library.

A HUNGER ARTIST
AND OTHER STORIES

The Aeroplanes at Brescia

WITH delight *La Sentinella Bresciana* announces: We have unprece-
dented crowds of people in Brescia, not seen even in the days of the
great automobile races; distinguished foreign visitors from Venetia,
Liguria, Piedmont, Tuscany, Rome, even from as far as Naples, great
lords and ladies from France, England, America throng our squares,
our hotels, every corner of our private houses: prices are all rising
splendidly; transportation will not be enough to carry the crowds to
the circuito aereo; the restaurants at the airfield are able to serve meals
of excellent quality to two thousand people, but confronted with the
many thousands arriving, they are bound to fall short—they could do
with the army to protect the bars; fifty thousand people fill the cheap
standing-room every day.

When my two friends and I read this news, we are at the same time
both emboldened and alarmed. Emboldened because where there are
such terrible crowds, things usually follow the ways of the dear old
plebs and where there isn't any room at all, you don't have to go looking for it: alarmed at the thought of the Italian organization of such
occasions, alarmed at the committees who are going to look after us,
alarmed at the railways, as the *Sentinella* pays tribute to their famous
four-hour delays. All our expectations are false; all our memories of
Italy get somehow mixed up the moment we are back at home, get
muddied, unreliable.

Even while our train is still entering the black hole of the railway
station at Brescia, with people shouting as if the ground beneath their
feet were on fire, we warn one another earnestly that whatever happens we should stay together. Aren't we already arriving with a kind
of hostility?

We alight; a carriage, not quite steady on its wheels, picks us up;
the driver is in a very good mood; we drive through near-empty streets
to the palace where the committees are lodged—where they pass over
our inner ill-will as if it didn't exist; we find out everything we need.
At first sight the inn where they send us seems to be the dirtiest we
have ever seen, but very soon that is no longer an exaggeration. A dirt
once simply there, a dirt that no longer gets remarked on, that no
longer changes, which has become endemic and has made human life
to some extent more solid and rooted, a dirt out of which our host

hurries, proud on his own behalf, humble on ours, constantly touching his elbows, and with his hands (every finger a salutation) casting fresh shadows across his face, bowing his body all the time in a way we all recognize—at the airfield, for instance, in Gabriele d'Annunzio*— who, you have to ask, would resent such dirt as this?

The airfield is located in Montechiari; it can be reached in a mere hour by the local train to Mantua. This local train runs on a track reserved for it on the main highway, allowing it to travel modestly along, no higher, no lower than the rest of the traffic, between cyclists riding into the dust with half-shut eyes, between the utterly unusable carts and carriages of the entire province which pick up passengers, as many as you like, and go so fast into the bargain, you'd scarcely believe—and between automobiles, often of monstrous size, which practically fall over themselves the moment they are let loose, as the speed turns their multitudinous hooting into one mindless din.

From time to time you lose all hope of reaching the circuito in this miserable train. But all around people are laughing, from right and left they laugh into the train. I stand on the outside platform, squashed up against a giant of a man, who stands with legs stretching across the buffers of two carriages, in a shower of soot and dust coming down from the shaking carriage roofs. Twice the train stops to wait for one coming in the other direction, as long and patiently as if it were just waiting for a casual encounter. A few villages pass slowly by, here and there excited posters for the last gathering of automobiles appear of the walls; all the roadside plants are unrecognizable beneath the colour of olive-leaves left by the white dust.

Because it cannot go any further, the train finally stops. A group of motor-cars brake at the same time; through the flying dust we can see lots of little flags waving not far away; we are still held up by a herd of cattle running wild and stumbling on the hilly ground, who practically charge into the motor-cars.

We have arrived. In front of the aerodrome there is another large open space with dubious wooden sheds which we might have expected to have frontages announcing something very different from 'Garage', 'International Cuisine', and so on. Enormous beggars, grown fat in their little carts, stretch out their arms in our way; in our haste we are tempted to jump over them. We overtake several people, and several of them overtake us. We look up into the sky, which after all is what it is all about here. No one is flying yet, thank heavens! We don't give way, but in spite of that we are not run over. Between and behind and towards the thousand vehicles skips the Italian cavalry. Order and road accidents appear to be equally impossible.

Once we had arrived in Brescia, late in the evening, we wanted to get quickly to a particular street we thought was quite distant. A driver asks for three lire; we offer two. The driver refuses the trip, and only out of the goodness of his heart he describes to us how positively fearsome the distance to this street is. We begin to be ashamed of our offer. Fine, three lire. The carriage makes three turns round some very short alleys and we are at the place we wanted to get to. Otto,* more energetic than the other two of us, declares that he wouldn't dream of paying three lire for a journey that has taken one minute, not at all. One lira is more than enough. Here's one lira. Night has already come on. The alley is empty. The driver is powerful. He promptly gets into a passion, as if the dispute had already gone on for an hour: What?—That's a swindle.—What are you thinking of?—Three lire was agreed, three lire must be paid. Come up with the three lire or you'll get a shock. Otto: 'The list of fares or the town guard!' 'List of fares? There isn't one. Where are you going to find a list of fares for this trip?'—It was a contract for a night-time tour, but if we pay him two lire, he'll leave us be. Otto, enough to frighten him: 'The list of fares or the town guard!' After some shouting and hunting around, a list of fares is produced on which nothing can be seen but dirt. So we settle on one lira fifty, and the coachman drives further down the narrow alley, where he is unable to turn round, not only angry, but melancholy too, it seems to me. For I am sorry to say our manners were not as they should have been; in Italy it is not done to behave like that; it may be all right elsewhere, but not here. Oh well, who stops to think about that when they are in a hurry! It's nothing to cry over; one can't turn into an Italian in one little week of flying.

But remorse mustn't spoil our pleasure on the airfield, that would only produce fresh remorse, and we leap into the aerodrome rather than walk, in this sudden rush of excitement coming over us, one after the other, in every joint, here, under this sun.

We go past the hangars, each of them standing there with its curtains drawn, looking like the stage of a troupe of wandering players before the show has opened. Their gable-ends carry the names of the aviators whose machines they are concealing, above them the flags of their countries. We read the names of Cobianchi,* Cagno,* Calderara,*

Rougier,* Curtiss,* Moncher* (who comes from Trentino, and wears the Italian colours—he has more confidence in them than in ours), Anzani,* Roman Aviation Club. And Blériot?* we ask. Blériot, the one we have been thinking about all the time. Where is Blériot?

Inside the fenced-off space in front of his hangar Rougier is walking to and fro in his shirt-sleeves, a small man with a remarkable nose. He is in a state of total activity difficult to make out, swinging his arms, hands vigorously on the go, patting himself all over as he paces; he sends his workmen behind the hangar curtain, calls them back, goes within himself, driving everyone off, while to one side his wife looks out into the empty heat; she is wearing a close-cut white dress, a little black hat pushed deep in her hair, her legs in a short skirt, delicately parted, a business-woman with all the cares of the business in her little head.

In front of the neighbouring hangar Curtiss is sitting quite alone. His machine can be seen where the curtains part slightly; he is taller than they say. As we are going past, he holds up a copy of the *New York Herald* high in front of him and reads a line at the top of one page; after half an hour we come back again; he is still pausing in the middle of the same page; after another half-hour he has finished the page and is starting on a new one. Obviously he is not going to fly today.

We turn and see the open field. It is so vast that everything on it looks forsaken: the boundary post nearby, the signalling-mast far in the distance, the starting-catapult somewhere to the right, an official automobile carrying one of the little yellow flags, taut in the wind, describes a curve across the field, comes to a halt in its own dust, and starts off again.

An artificial desert has been created here in an almost tropical countryside, and the nobility of Italy, dazzling ladies from Paris, and thousands of others are all together here, to gaze with narrowed eyes for several hours into this sunny desert. There is nothing in this space to bring variety as there is on other sports fields, none of the dainty hurdles for the horse-races, none of the white markings for tennis, none of the fresh grass for football, only the stony up and down of the tracks for auto- and cycle-racing, only a procession of colourful riders trotting across the plain two or three times. The horses' feet are invisible in the dust; the monotonous sunlight does not change until almost five hours after noon. And so that nothing should get in the way of viewing this plain, there is no music either, only the whistling of the masses in the cheap seats endeavours to satisfy the needs of ear and impatience. From the better seats behind us, though, that crowd of people could just as well, with no distinction, merge into one with the empty plain.

At one point by the wooden fence there are several people standing together. 'How small!' cries a French group, as it were with a sigh. What's going on? We push our way through. And there, standing on the airfield, quite near us, is a small aeroplane, painted in a real, yellowish colour, and being made ready for flight. Now we can also see Blériot's hangar and next to it the hangar belonging to his pupil Leblanc;* they have been built on the airfield itself. Leaning against one of the two wings and promptly recognized, Blériot, his head set firmly on his shoulders, is keeping a close eye on his mechanics as they work on the engine.

He's intending to go up in the air on this scrap of a thing? Folk who sail on water have it easier. They can practise first in puddles, then in ponds, then in rivers, and only much later they can venture on the ocean—but for this fellow here, there is only the ocean.

Blériot is already sitting in his seat, holding his hand on some lever or other, but he lets the mechanics carry on still, as though they were over-active children. He takes a long look at us, then looks away from us and somewhere else again, but keeps his gaze always to himself. Now he is going to fly—nothing is more natural for him. This attitude comes from his feeling that it is natural, together with the general feeling, which he can't prevent, that it is extraordinary.

A workman takes hold of one blade of the propeller to start it spinning; he pulls hard on it; it gives a jerk; we hear something like a powerful man's sudden intake of breath as he sleeps; but the propeller doesn't move any further. They try once again, they try ten times; sometimes the propeller stops straight away; sometimes it offers a couple of turns. The problem is the engine. New work on it begins. The spectators tire more quickly than those closely involved. The engine is oiled from all sides; hidden screws are loosened and tied; a man runs into the hangar to get a spare part; that doesn't fit either; he hurries back and, crouching on the hangar floor with it between his knees, belabours it with a hammer. Blériot changes places with a mechanic, the mechanic changes places with Leblanc. First one of them pulls at the propeller, then the other, but the motor is unyielding, like a schoolboy who is always getting help; the entire class tells him the answers, no, he just can't, again and again he gets stuck, again and again he gets stuck at the same place, a hopeless failure. For a little while Blériot sits unmoving in his seat; his six colleagues stand around him without stirring; they all seem to be dreaming.

The spectators can now breathe again, and look around themselves. Young Madame Blériot with her maternal face comes past, trailing two children. When her husband is unable to fly, she's not happy about it, and when he does fly, she's anxious; and on top of that, her beautiful dress is rather too heavy for this weather.

Again they turn the propeller, perhaps better than before, perhaps not; the engine starts up with a great noise, as if it were a different motor; four men steady the back of the machine, and in the midst of the calm air round about the draught from the rotating propeller-blades blows in gusts through their working-clothes. Not a word can be heard; only the noise of the propeller seems to be in command; eight hands let go of the machine, which takes its time as it moves over the bumpy ground, like a clumsy walker on a parquet floor.

They make many such attempts, which all end to no purpose. Each of them makes the public rise into the air, standing on the basket chairs, where you can stretch out your arms, keeping your balance and at the same time demonstrating your hope, fear, and pleasure. In the intervals, however, the party from the Italian nobility parades along the stands. They greet one another, bow, salute one another again, there are embraces, they move up and down the steps to the stands. They point out Principessa Laetitia Savoia Bonaparte to one another, and the Principessa Borghese, an elderly lady whose face has the colour of dark yellow grapes, and the Contessa Morosini. Marcello Borghese attends all the ladies and none; from a distance he seems to have a sensible face, but nearby his cheeks close over the corners of his mouth in a very curious way. Gabriele d'Annunzio, small and frail, dances timidly, it seems, before Conte Oldofredi, one of the most important gentlemen of the Committee. Looking over the railings we can see the strong face of Puccini, with a nose that you could call a drinker's nose.

But you only notice these personages if you are looking for them; otherwise everywhere it is the tall ladies of today's fashion that you see, who put everyone else in the shade. They prefer to walk, rather than sit; their clothes are not made for sitting. Their faces, veiled in the Eastern mode, are all worn in faint shadow. Seen from the back, the dress, loose over shoulders and bosom, makes the figure as a whole appear rather timid; it makes a mixed, uneasy impression when such ladies appear timid. The bodice is low, almost too low to hold; the waist appears less slim than usual, because everything is so slender; these women want to be embraced more closely.

Up until now it is only Leblanc's machine that has been on display. But now comes the machine in which Blériot flew over the Channel; no one has told us; everybody just knows. A long pause, and Blériot is in the air; we can see his head and shoulders upright above the wings, his legs deep inside as part of the machinery. The sun has begun to set, and through the canopy over the stands it lights up the soaring wings. Enraptured, everyone looks up at him; there is no room for another in any heart. He flies a short lap, and then reappears above us, almost at a vertical. And craning their necks, everyone can see how the monoplane hesitates, how Blériot gets a grip on it, and it even rises higher. What is going on? Up there, twenty metres above the earth, is a man trapped in a wooden frame, defending himself against a freely undertaken, invisible peril. We on the other hand are standing down below, thrust entirely into the background, insubstantial, gazing at this man.

It all ends well. At the same time the mast signals that the wind has become more favourable, and that Curtiss is going to fly in an attempt to win Brescia's Grand Prize. So he will fly after all? The public has hardly agreed on it before Curtiss's engine is roaring; we have hardly glanced in his direction before he has flown away from us, flying over the plain as it opens out before him, to the forests in the distance, which seem only now to be rising into view. His flight over those forests is long and slow; he disappears; we look at the forests, not him. From beyond houses, God knows where, he emerges at the same height as before, and flies towards us; when he rises you can see the surfaces underneath the biplane darkening, when he sinks, the upper surfaces shine in the sun. He flies round the signalling-mast and turns, indifferent to the noise of the welcome, straight to where he has come from, only so that he can become small and solitary again. He flies five laps of this kind, covering fifty kilometres in forty-nine minutes and twenty-nine seconds, and with this feat he wins Brescia's Grand Prize, thirty thousand lire. It is a flawless performance, but flawless performances cannot be properly appreciated, ultimately everyone thinks he is capable of a flawless performance, a flawless performance doesn't seem to require courage. And while Curtiss labours alone, there above the forests, and while his wife, well known to everyone, worries about him, the crowd has almost forgotten him. Everywhere all they do is complain that Calderara is not going to fly (his machine is damaged), that Rougier has been messing around for two days on his Voisin-designed plane without leaving it alone, that Zodiac, the Italian dirigible, has still not arrived. So many rumours are doing the rounds about Calderara's bad luck, all to his honour, that you would think the nation's affection would raise him higher into the air than his Wright-designed plane.

Curtiss has not yet finished his flight before the engines in three hangars are already beginning to start up as though inspired. Wind and dust together descend upon the crowd from opposite directions. Two eyes are not enough. People spin on their chairs, stagger, cling on to somebody, apologize, somebody staggers, brings someone down with them, gets thanked. Evening begins to fall, early as always in the Italian autumn; on the airfield nothing can be seen distinctly any more.

Just as Curtiss walks past after his winning flight, smiling slightly and taking off his cap without looking towards us, Blériot starts flying in a small circuit, which everyone already knew he was capable of doing. They don't know whether they are applauding Curtiss or Blériot, or Rougier in advance, as his great heavy machine now hurls itself into the air. Rougier is sitting at his controls like a gentleman at a desk you can reach from behind his back by a little ladder. He climbs in tight circles, flies above Blériot, turning him into a spectator, and goes on climbing higher and higher.

If we are still to get a cab, it is high time we left; a lot of people are already pushing past us. For of course they know this flight is only a trial run; as the time is already approaching seven o'clock, it will no longer be registered officially. In the forecourt of the aerodrome the chauffeurs and servants are standing on their seats, pointing up at Rougier; the drivers are standing on the many cabs scattered about, pointing up at Rougier; three trains, full to the last buffer, are not moving on account of Rougier. Fortunately we get a cab; the driver crouches in front of us (there isn't a box), and, turning at last into autonomous beings once again, we drive off. Max makes the very just observation that they could and should organize something like this in Prague too. It doesn't have to be aeroplane racing, in his view, though even that would be worth it, but surely it would be easy to invite an aviator, and no one who took part would regret it. It would be so simple; Wright* is flying in Berlin right now; Blériot will be flying in Vienna shortly, Latham* in Berlin. They would only have to persuade the people there to make a small detour. The other two of us say nothing in reply, first because we are tired, and secondly because in any case we would have no objections. The road bends, and Rougier appears so high up that you would think his position could only be identified from the stars, on the verge of becoming visible in the darkening sky. We keep turning round; Rougier is just about still climbing, but as for us, our way takes us in the end deeper into the Campagna.

A COUNTRY DOCTOR

LITTLE TALES

To my father

The New Advocate

WE have a new advocate, Doctor Bucephalus.* There is little in his outward appearance to recall the time when he was Alexander of Macedon's battle-charger. True, there are a few things that someone acquainted with the circumstances will notice. Though recently I saw a lowly court-usher gazing in wonderment, with the expert eye of the regular small race-goer, as our advocate lifted his haunches and mounted the outside stairs, step by ringing marble step.

On the whole the bar approves of Bucephalus' admission. With astonishing insight they say to themselves that under the present social order Bucephalus is in a difficult situation, so for that reason as well as for his significance in world history, at the very least he deserves some concessions to be made. Today—it cannot be denied—an Alexander the Great does not exist. True, there are plenty who know how to murder; and there is no lack of skill in using a lance to strike a friend across the banqueting-table; and for many Macedonia is too restricted, making them curse Philip, the father—but no one, no one can lead an army toward India. Even in those days the gates of India* were inaccessible, but the royal sword pointed towards where they lay. Nowadays the gates have shifted in a very different direction, further and higher; no one points the way; there are many bearing swords, but only to wave them about; and the gaze ready to follow them is bewildered.

So perhaps the best thing really is to do what Bucephalus has done—to immerse oneself in the statute books. Free, flanks unconfined by the rider's thighs, in the quiet of the lamplight, far from the tumult of Alexander's battle, he reads and turns the pages of our ancient tomes.

A Country Doctor

I WAS in sore straits; I had an urgent journey ahead of me; a patient, gravely ill, was waiting for me in a village ten miles away; driving snow covered the distance between him and myself; I had a trap, light with high wheels, just the kind suitable for our country roads; packed into my fur greatcoat, my instrument-bag in my hand, I was standing in the yard all ready to travel, but there was no horse, no horse. My own horse had perished the night before, overstrained in this icy winter; my servant-girl was running around the village now to borrow one; but it was hopeless, I knew, and getting more and more covered with snow, more and more unable to move, I stood pointlessly there. The girl appeared at the gate, alone, swinging her lantern; of course, who's going to lend their horse out now, for a journey like mine? I crossed the yard once again; I couldn't think of a possible way; distracted, anguished, I kicked at the crumbling door of the pigsty, unused for years. It fell open, banging to and fro on its hinges. Warmth and the smell of horses came out from it. Inside, a dim stable lantern swung on a rope. A man, crouching in the low shack, revealed his open, blue-eyed face. 'Shall I harness up?' he asked, crawling out on all fours. I didn't know what to say, and only stooped to see what else was still in the sty. The maid was standing next to me. 'You never know what you'll find in your own house,' she said, and we both laughed. 'Hey, brother! Hey, sister!' the groom called, and two horses, mighty beasts with powerful flanks, tucking their legs close to their bodies and lowering their finely formed heads like camels, pushed their way just by the strength of their haunches through the doorway one after the other, filling it completely. But straight away they stood up, tall-legged, their bodies steaming in dense clouds. 'Help him,' I said, and the willing girl was quick to pass him the harness for the carriage. But scarcely has she reached the groom when he grabs her in his arms and thrusts his face against hers. She screams and seeks refuge with me; two rows of teeth are impressed red on the girl's cheek. 'You brute,' I shout in rage, 'are you asking for the whip?', but straight away I reflect that he is a stranger here, that I don't know where he comes from, and that he is helping me of his own free will where all the others have refused. As if he knows what I am thinking, he doesn't take offence at my threat, but, still busied with the horses, he turns towards me just once. 'Get in,' he says then, and everything is in fact ready. I've never driven with such a fine pair of horses,* and I cheerfully climb in. 'But I'll take the reins—you don't know the way,' I say. 'I'm certainly not coming with you. I'm staying with Rose.' 'No,' Rose screams, and rightly anticipating her inevitable fate, she runs into the house. I can hear the chain on the door rattling as she fastens it; I can hear the lock engaging; I can see how she is putting out the light in the hall, and running on through the rooms putting out all the other lights too, to make it impossible to find her. 'You're coming with me,' I say to the groom, 'or I'll abandon the journey, urgent though it is. I wouldn't dream of handing the girl over to you as your price.' 'Look lively,' he says, clapping his hands; the trap is swept away like trees in a torrent; I can still hear the sound as the door to my house bursts open and splinters under the groom's onslaught; then a roaring fills my eyes and ears, assailing all my senses with equal intensity. But even that is only for a moment, for there, as if opening right in front of the gate to my own yard, is the yard of my patient, and I am already there; the horses are standing quietly; the snow has stopped; moonlight all around; the parents of the sick boy come hurrying out of the house, his sister after them; they almost lift me out of the trap; I can't make anything of their confused words; in the sickroom the air is scarcely breathable; the stove, neglected, is smoking; I'll push the window open; but first I want to see the patient. Thin, without fever, neither cold nor warm, empty-eyed, shirtless, the boy pulls himself up beneath the coverlet, throws his arms about my neck, and whispers in my ear, 'Doctor, let me die.' I look around; no one has heard; the parents are standing, bent forward, waiting for my judgement; the sister has fetched a chair for my bag. I open it, and rummage among my instruments; all the time the boy keeps stretching his hand towards me to remind me of his entreaty; I pick up a pair of tweezers, look at them closely in the candlelight, and put them down again. 'Oh yes,' I think blasphemously, 'the gods come to your help in cases like this; they send you the missing horse; they add a second one for speed, and if that weren't too much already, they even make a gift of the groom.' It is only now that Rose comes into my head again. What can I do, how can I save her, how can I drag her out from under this groom, ten miles away from her, with unruly horses in front of my trap? These horses, who now seem to have loosened their straps in some way, are pushing the windows open from outside—how, I can't tell—each thrusting a head through a window and, unperturbed by the family's cries, observing the sick boy. 'I'll drive back right now,' I think, as if the horses were challenging me to make the journey, but I allow the sister, who believes I have been overcome by the heat, to take off my fur greatcoat. A glass of rum is placed before me, the old man claps me on the shoulder; giving up his treasure justifies this familiarity. I shake my head; to the old man's limited thinking I might be feeling queasy; that is my only reason for refusing to drink it. The mother is standing by the bed, beckoning to me. I follow her, and while one horse whinnies loudly at the ceiling, I lay my head on the boy's chest and he shudders beneath my damp beard. This confirms what I know: the boy is healthy; circulation rather poor, soaked in coffee by his doting mother, but healthy, and the best thing would be to turn him out of his bed with a good shove. I am no world reformer, and I let him lie. I am appointed by the district authorities, and I do my duty to the limit, to the point where it becomes almost too much. Badly paid, but all the same I am generous and ready to help the poor. I still have Rose to look after—and then, well, the boy could well be in the right, and I shall want to die too. What am I doing here in this endless winter! My horse is dead, and there is no one in the village who will lend me his. I have to drag my pair from the pigsty; if they didn't chance to be horses, I'd have to be pulled by swine. That's the way it is. And I nod to the family. They know nothing about it, and if they did, they wouldn't believe it. Writing out prescriptions is easy; on the other hand, relating to people is hard. Well, at this point my visit might be over; once again people have put me to unnecessary trouble; I'm used to that; with the help of my night-bell the entire district torments me. But that this time I have to surrender Rose as well, that lovely girl, who has been living in my house for years while I have scarcely noticed her—that sacrifice is too great, and inside my head I have to improvise some specious account of it to myself just so that I don't vent my feelings on this family, who cannot, with the best will in the world, give Rose back to me. But when I shut my bag and gesture for my coat, the family closes up, father sniffing at the rum glass in his hand, mother, it seems, disappointed—what on earth do these people expect?—tearful, and biting her lips, with the sister waving a badly blood-soaked handkerchief, and I am somehow ready to concede, given the circumstances, that perhaps the boy is sick after all. I go towards him; he smiles as I come, as if I were bringing him a bowl of the heartiest soup—oh, now both horses are whinnying! The noise is ordained by higher authority* to make the examination easier, I suppose—and now I discover that indeed the boy is sick. In his right side, in the region of the hips, a wound as large as the palm of my hand has opened. Rose-red, in many shades, dark in the depths, growing light towards the margins, delicately crusted, the blood welling intermittently, wide as an open-cast mine. That is how it looked from a distance. Close up, it shows further worsening. Who can look at it without whistling softly? Worms, as thick and long as my little finger, coloured rose from their own blood, but also bespattered, caught fast in the heart of the wound, with little white heads and many little legs, writhe towards the light. Poor boy, there is nothing to be done for you. I have discovered your great wound; you will be destroyed by this bloom in your side. The family is happy; they can see me at work; the sister tells the mother, the mother tells the father; the father tells some guests, who come tiptoeing in through the moonlight from the open door, balancing with outstretched arms. 'Will you save me?' whispers the boy through his sobs, quite dazzled by the life in his wound. That's what the people in my region are like. Always demanding the impossible of their doctor. They have lost their old faith; the priest sits at home and picks his cassocks into shreds, one by one; but the physician is supposed to do everything with his delicate surgical hand. Well, if that's how they want it. I didn't volunteer, but if you're using me for your religious ends, I'll even let you do that with me; what better could I wish for, an old country doctor, robbed of my maid! And they come, the family and the village elders, and they strip me of my clothes; a school choir, led by their teacher, is standing outside the house and singing an utterly simple melody to the text:

> Strip him of his clothes, and then he'll heal you,
> And if he doesn't heal you, kill him!
> He's just a doctor, just a doctor.

And then I am unclothed, and, fingering my beard, with my head bowed I gaze calmly at the people. I am thoroughly composed and above them all, and I remain so, even though it doesn't help me in the least, for now they are picking me up by my head and feet and carrying me to the bed.* They lay me down on it next to the wall, on the side of the wound. Then they leave the room; the door is closed; the song falls silent; clouds cover the moon; the bedclothes are warm around me; the horses' heads sway in the window like shadows. 'You know,' I hear a voice in my ear, 'I don't have much confidence in you; and you've been dropped off any old where, haven't you? You didn't come here of your own accord. Instead of helping, you're just crowding me on my deathbed. More than anything I'd like to scratch out your eyes.' 'That's right,' I said, 'it's a shame. But I'm a physician. What am I to do? Believe me, it's not easy for me, either.' 'And I'm expected to be satisfied by this excuse? Oh, I suppose I have to be. I always have to be satisfied. I came into the world with a beautiful wound; it was my only portion.' 'My young friend,' I say, 'your mistake is you don't have an overall view of things. I tell you—and I have been in every sickroom far and near—your wound is not all that bad. Made in a spot where you can't see with two blows of an axe. There are many who offer their side and can scarcely hear the axe in the forest, let alone that it is coming closer to them.' 'Is that really so, or are you deceiving me in my fever?' 'It really is so—take the word of honour of a district physician with you on your way.' And he took it, and grew still. But now it was time to think of saving myself. The horses were still standing faithfully in their places. Clothes, greatcoat, and bag were quickly snatched up; I didn't want to delay by getting dressed; if the horses raced as fast as they had on the way here, I would jump, you might say, straight from this bed into my own. Obediently, one horse withdrew from the window; I threw the bundle into the carriage; my greatcoat flew too far, but it caught on a hook by just one sleeve. Good enough. I leapt onto the horse. The straps dragging loose, one horse scarcely harnessed to the other, the trap swaying to-and-fro, the fur coat trailing last in the snow. 'Look lively!' I said, but lively the ride was not; as slowly as old men we moved through the wastes of snow; for a long time the sound of the children's song—a new one, but quite mistaken—followed us:

> 'Rejoice, rejoice, ye patients,
> The doctor's put in bed with you.'

I'll never get home like this; my flourishing practice is lost; a successor is stealing from me, but to no avail, for he can't replace me; that foul groom is running wild in my house; Rose is his victim; I can't bear to think of it further. Naked, exposed to the frost of this most calamitous age, with an earthly carriage, unearthly horses, I wander up and down, an old man. My fur greatcoat is hanging behind the trap, but I cannot reach it, and not one of that agile gang of patients moves a finger. Deceived! Deceived! Once you have been led astray by the sound of the night-bell, it can never be put right.

In the Gallery

IF some frail, consumptive circus rider were being driven in a circle around the ring for months without cease, on a faltering horse, before an unflagging audience, by a remorseless, whip-wielding ringmaster, pirouetting on her horse, throwing kisses, swaying from the waist, and if this performance continued amid the incessant roaring of orchestra and ventilators into the ever-widening grey future, accompanied by the falling and fresh-rising clapping of applauding hands that are really steam-hammers—perhaps then a young gallery-goer would rush down the long set of steps through all the rows, dash into the ring, and cry 'Stop!' through the fanfares of the ever accommodating orchestra.

But as that is not the way it is, a lovely lady, white and red, flies in between curtains opened before her by proud retainers in their livery; the ringmaster breathes towards her in devotion, cowering like an animal; lifts her up with care onto her dapple-grey horse, as if she were his best-beloved granddaughter setting off on a perilous journey; hesitates to give the signal with his whip; finally brings himself to crack it; runs along next to the horse, open-mouthed; follows the rider keen-eyed as she leaps; can scarcely comprehend her skill; tries to warn her with cries in English; furiously exhorts the grooms holding the hoops to be most particularly attentive; just before her death-defying leap raises his hands, beseeching the orchestra to fall silent; finally lifts the little creature from her trembling horse, kisses her on both cheeks, and deems no homage from the audience sufficient; while she herself, supported by him, on the very tips of her toes, in a cloud of dust, with arms outstretched and head thrown back, wants to share her joy with the entire circus—as this is the way it is, the gallery-goer lays his head on the railing, and sinking into the final march as in a deep dream, he weeps, without being aware of it.

An Ancient Manuscript

IT is as if the defence of our country has been much neglected. We have not been worried about it until now, and have just got on with our work; however, recent events have given us cause for concern.

I have a shoemaker's workshop in the square in front of the Imperial Palace.* No sooner do I open my shop at dawn than I see the entries to all the lanes that enter the square occupied by armed men. They are not our soldiers though, but obviously nomads from the north. In some way I cannot comprehend they have penetrated as far as the capital, which is a very long way from the border, after all. Anyhow, there they are; it seems that every morning there are more of them.

As is their nature, they camp under the open sky, for they abhor dwelling-houses. They keep themselves busy with sharpening their swords, honing their arrows, exercising on horseback. They have turned this quiet square, which has always been kept meticulously clean, into a sty. It's true, we do attempt sometimes to dart out from our shops and clear away at least the worst of the filth, but that happens less and less frequently, for the effort is pointless, and besides it puts us in danger of falling beneath the wild horses or being hurt by the whips.

It is impossible to talk with the nomads. They do not know our language; indeed, they scarcely have one of their own. Among themselves they communicate rather like jackdaws.* One hears this jackdaw's cry constantly. Their incomprehension of our way of life, our institutions, is on a par with their indifference to them. Consequently they respond to any kind of sign language by rejecting it. You can dislocate your jaw and wrench your hands from your wrists, but they still won't have understood you and they never will understand you. They will often contort their features; then they turn up their eyeballs till the white shows, and foam at the mouth, but it doesn't mean they want to say anything, or even to frighten you; they do it because it's just their way. What they need, they take. You can't say that they use force. When they grab something, you step aside and let them have the lot.

They've taken a fair amount of my goods too. But I can't complain about it when I see how things are for the butcher opposite, for example. He hardly gets in his stock before it is all seized from him and devoured by the nomads. Their horses are meat-eaters too; a rider will often lie down next to his horse, and the two of them will eat from the same piece of meat, one from each end. The butcher is afraid, and doesn't dare stop the meat-supplies. But we understand this, pool our money, and support him. If the nomads didn't get their meat, who knows what they might think of doing—though who knows what they will think of, even when they do get their daily meat.

Recently, the butcher thought he might at least spare himself the trouble of slaughtering, and in the morning he brought them a living ox. He must never do that again. I lay on the ground for a good hour right at the back of my workshop with all my clothes, blankets, and cushions heaped over me, just so as not to hear the bellowing of the ox, which the nomads leapt on from all sides so as to tear pieces from its warm flesh with their teeth. It was quiet for a long time before I dared go out; like drinkers around a barrel of wine they lay drowsily around the remains of the ox.

That was just at the time when I thought I saw the Emperor himself at a window in the palace; he never enters these outer chambers at other times; he always lives only in the innermost garden; but this time he was standing—at least, that's how it seemed to me—at one of the windows, gazing with head bowed at the goings-on in front of his palace.

'How will it all end?' we all ask ourselves. 'How long will we endure this burden, this torment? The Imperial Palace has attracted the nomads here, but doesn't know how to drive them away again. The gate is kept locked; the guards, who in the old days always marched ceremonially in and out, stay behind barred windows. The salvation of our country has been entrusted to us, craftsmen and traders; but we are not up to such a task; and we have never boasted that we were capable of it, either. It is a misunderstanding; and it will be our ruin.'

Before the Law

BEFORE the law stands a doorkeeper. A man from the country comes up to this doorkeeper and begs for entry into the law.* But the door-keeper says he cannot grant him entry now. The man considers, and then asks whether this means that he might be allowed entry later.

'It is possible', says the doorkeeper, 'but not now.' As the gateway to the law is open as always, and the doorkeeper moves to one side, the man stoops so as to see inside the gate. When the doorkeeper notices this, he laughs, saying: 'If it tempts you so much, go on, try, even though I forbade you. But take note: I am powerful. And I am only the lowliest of the doorkeepers. From hall to hall there are doorkeepers, each mightier than the last. The mere sight of the third is something even I cannot bear.' Difficulties like this were something the man from the country did not expect; surely the law should be accessible to all, always, he thinks, but when he looks more closely at the doorkeeper in his great fur coat, with his sharp nose and long, thin Tartar's beard,* he decides after all rather to wait until he receives permission to enter. The doorkeeper gives him a stool, and lets him sit down to one side of the door. There he sits for days and years. He makes many efforts to be let in, and wearies the doorkeeper with his pleading. The doorkeeper will often arrange a little interrogation with him, questioning him about his homeland and a great deal besides, but his questions show no interest; they are put as great lords might put them, and in the end he tells him again and again that he cannot let him in yet. The man, who has equipped himself well for his journey, uses everything, however valuable, to bribe the doorkeeper. The latter, indeed, accepts everything, saying as he does so: 'I am taking it only so that you do not think that you have left anything out.' In the course of the many years the man watches the doorkeeper almost constantly. He forgets the other doorkeepers, and this first one seems to him to be his only obstacle to entering the law. He curses this unfortunate accident, loudly and recklessly in the early years, but later, as he grows old, he only grumbles to himself, and, as his years of studying the doorkeeper have allowed him to perceive even the fleas in his thick fur collar, he even begs the fleas to help him change the doorkeeper's mind. In the end his sight begins to fail, and he cannot tell whether it is really growing darker around him, or whether his eyes are just deceiving him. But he does indeed perceive a radiance in the dark, breaking forth inextinguishably from the door. Now he has not much longer to live. On the brink of death, everything he has experienced in all his time there concentrates in his mind into one question which he has not yet put to the doorkeeper. He beckons him over, for he can no longer raise his stiffening body upright. The doorkeeper has to bend low to him, for the difference in their heights has changed, very much to the man's disadvantage. 'What more do you want to know now?' asks the doorkeeper, 'You're insatiable.' 'Surely everyone aspires towards the law?' said the man. 'How is it that in all these many years no one except me has demanded entry?' The doorkeeper perceives that the man is already near his end, so to reach him as his hearing fails, he bellows at him: 'Nobody else could be granted entry, for this entrance was meant only for you. I shall go now and close it.'

Jackals and Arabs

WE were camping in the oasis. My travelling companions were asleep. One Arab, tall and dressed in white, came past me; he had been attending to the camels and was going to his sleeping-quarters.

I flung myself on my back in the grass; I tried to sleep; it was impossible; the howl of lament from a jackal in the distance; I sat up again. And what had been so far away was suddenly near. A horde of jackals around me, dark golden eyes gleaming, vanishing; slender bodies, their movements drilled and nimble as if driven by a whip.

One came from behind, pushing under my arm as if it needed my warmth, then stepped in front of me and spoke, almost eye to eye with me:

'I am the oldest jackal far and near. I am glad to be able to greet you here still. I had almost given up hope, for we have been waiting for you for an eternity; my mother waited for you, and her mother, and before her all their mothers, down to the mother of all jackals. Believe what I say!'

'I'm astonished,' I said, and forgot to light the pile of wood lying ready to repel the jackals with its smoke, 'I am most astonished to hear that. It is only by chance that I have come to this place from the far north, and I am midway through a short journey. What is it you want, jackals?'

And as if encouraged by my perhaps over-friendly words they drew their circle more closely around me, all of them panting and snarling.

'We know', began the eldest, 'that you come from the north; that is exactly what we are building our hopes on. In those parts there is the good sense that is not to be found here among the Arabs. From their cold arrogance, you know, there is not one spark of good sense to be struck. They kill animals to eat them, and they despise carrion.'

'Don't talk so loud,' I said, 'there are Arabs sleeping nearby.'

'You really are a stranger here', said the jackal, 'otherwise you would know that never in the history of the world has a jackal been afraid of an Arab. You think we're afraid of them? Isn't it misfortune enough that we've been cast out among such people?'

'May be, may be', I said, 'I wouldn't be so bold as to judge things that are so remote from me; it seems to be a very ancient quarrel; so it might well be in the blood; and so perhaps it will only end in blood.'

'You are very clever,' said the old jackal, and their breath came thicker and faster, with lungs panting, although they were still all standing motionless; a sour smell, tolerable for a brief while only if one grits one's teeth, came pouring from their open mouths, 'you are very clever; what you say accords with our ancient wisdom. So we will relieve them of their blood, and the quarrel is at an end.'

'Oh!' I exclaimed, more fiercely than I intended, 'they'll defend themselves; they will shoot you down with their rifles, pack by pack.'

'You misunderstand us', he said, 'after the human fashion, which, it seems, still persists, even in the far north. Of course we still won't kill them. All the waters of the Nile would not be enough to wash us clean. In any case, we run away at the mere sight of their living flesh, away into purer air, into the desert; that is why it is our home.'

And all the jackals round about, who had meanwhile been joined by many more from far away, laid their heads between their front legs and cleaned them with their paws; it was as if they were trying to hide a loathing so terrible that I wanted most of all to take a great bound and escape from their circle.

'So what do you intend to do?' I asked, and made to get up; but I couldn't; two young jackals had bitten fast into the back of my jacket and shirt, and I had to stay sitting down. 'They are holding your train,' explained the old jackal solemnly, 'a mark of honour.' 'Tell them to let me go,' I cried, turning first to the old jackal, then to the young ones. 'They will, of course,' said the old jackal, 'if you want them to. But it will take a little while, for according to our custom they have bitten very deep, and they will have to unclench their jaws only very slowly. Meanwhile, hear our petition.' 'Your behaviour hasn't made me very receptive,' I said. 'Don't make us pay for our ill grace,' he said, and now for the first time he resorted to the wailing tone that was his natural voice, 'we are poor creatures; all we have is our teeth;

for everything we want to do, good and bad, we have only our teeth.'
'What do you want, then?' I asked, only slightly pacified.

'Sir,' he cried, and all the jackals raised a howl; in the farthest distance it sounded to me like a melody. 'Sir, you must end this quarrel
which splits the world in two. Even as you are, so have our forebears
described him who shall do so. We must have peace from the Arabs;
breathe pure air; the view all round the horizon cleansed of them; no
cries of lamentation from the sheep under the Arab's knife; every
beast shall die serenely; it shall be drunk by us in peace to the last
drop and cleansed down to the bone. Purity, nothing but purity,* is
what we desire,' and now they all wept and sobbed—'how can you
endure it in this world, oh noble heart and tender bowels? Filth is
their white; filth is their black; their beard is a horror; one cannot help
spitting at the sight of the corner of their eye, and if they lift their
arm, all hell is revealed in their armpit. Therefore, O master, therefore, dear, dear master, with the aid of your all-skilful hands, with the
aid of your all-skilful hands, cut their throats with these scissors!' And
at a jerk of his head a jackal came forward, carrying by his eye-tooth
a small, age-rusted, pair of sewing-scissors.

'The scissors at last then, and that's enough!' called the Arab leader
of our caravan, who had crept up on us against the wind, and was now
raising his giant whip.

They all scattered in haste, but they still remained at a distance,
cowering close together, the many beasts so close and motionless that
they seemed to be standing in a narrow pen, surrounded by flying will
o' the wisps.

'So you too, sir, have seen and heard this performance,' said the
Arab, laughing as cheerfully as the reserved habit of his tribe allowed.
'So you know what the beasts are after?' I asked. 'Of course, sir,' he
said, 'everyone knows that; as long as there are Arabs, these scissors
will wander through the desert and will go on wandering with us till
the end of time. The offer is made to every European to do the great
deed; every European is the very one they think seems to be called to
it. It's a crazy hope these beasts have; they are fools, real fools. We
love them for it; they are our dogs; more beautiful than yours. Just
look, a camel died in the night and I've had it brought here.'

Four bearers came and threw the heavy cadaver down before us.
It scarcely lay there before the jackals raised their voices. Each one
drawn irresistibly as if by a rope, they came forward, hesitantly, bodies

brushing the ground. They had forgotten the Arabs, forgotten their hatred; obliterating everything else, the presence of the steaming corpse cast a spell on them. One was already clinging to the neck, and with its first bite found the artery. Like a little pump frantically trying to put out a mighty blaze, single-mindedly and hopelessly, every muscle of the jackal's body tugged and twitched in its place. And all of them working away at the same task, they were already lying on the corpse, piled mountain-high

Then the Arab leader struck powerfully out at them on all sides with his keen whip; they raised their heads, half intoxicated, half fainting; saw the Arabs standing in front of them; felt the whip on their muzzles; leapt back, running backwards for a stretch. But pools of the camel's blood already lay there, smoking; its body was torn open in several places. They couldn't resist; once again they were there; once again the leader raised his whip; I seized his arm.

'You are right, sir,' he said, 'we'll leave them to their calling; and it is time to start on our way. You've seen them. Wonderful animals, aren't they? And how they hate us!'

A Visit to the Mine

TODAY the top engineers* came to visit us down below. The management has issued orders of some kind to open up new galleries, so the engineers have come to make the first of the surveys. How young these people are, but all of them so different too! They have all developed freely, and the sharply defined nature of each already displays itself without constraint even now in their early years.

One of them, black-haired, lively, lets his eyes roam all around.

A second, with a notepad, makes sketches as he walks, looks around him, compares, makes notes.

A third, hands in pockets so that everything on him is strained taut, walks upright; preserves his dignity; biting his lips all the time is the only sign of impatient, irrepressible youth.

A fourth is giving explanations to the third, who hasn't asked for them; smaller than the third, running along at his side like a tempter, index finger constantly in the air, he appears to be reciting a litany to him about everything to be seen here.

A fifth, perhaps the highest in rank, prefers to walk unaccompanied;

at one moment he is in front, at another in the rear; the group takes its route from him; he is pale and frail; responsibility has made hollows of his eyes; often as he ponders he presses his hand against his brow.

The sixth and seventh walk slightly bowed, head close to head, arm in arm, in intimate conversation; if this site were not obviously our coalmine and our place of work in the deepest gallery you might believe that these bony, beardless, knob-nosed gentlemen were young clerics. The one is laughing to himself, mostly with a feline purr; the other, also smiling, is doing the talking, with his free hand keeping some sort of time. How sure these two gentlemen must be of their position, indeed what service they must already have rendered our mine despite their youth, that here, on such an important inspection, under their superior's very eyes, they are permitted to be so nonchalantly absorbed only in their own concerns, or at least concerns that had nothing to do with their present task. Or might it possibly be that despite all their laughter and inattention they are noticing the essentials perfectly well? One hardly risks a definite judgement about gentlemen like that.

On the other hand, there can be no doubt that the eighth, for example, is incomparably more on top of the job than they are, indeed than all the other gentlemen. He has to lay his hands on everything, and tap it with the little hammer he is constantly taking out of his pocket and constantly putting back for safe keeping. Sometimes, regardless of his elegant clothes, he will kneel down in the dirt and tap the ground; then again just as he is going along, he will tap the walls or the roof above his head. Once he lay down for a long time, lying there quite still; we thought some accident had occurred, but then he leapt up with a little shake of his slender body. So he'd only been investigating again. We think we know our mine and its stones, but what this engineer is constantly investigating in this way is beyond our comprehension.

A ninth pushes a kind of perambulator in front of him, which contains the measuring instruments. Extremely valuable instruments, packed deep in the finest padding. Actually the attendant ought to be pushing this trolley, but it is not entrusted to him; an engineer had to be called, and he does it gladly, as we can see. He is probably the youngest; perhaps he doesn't understand all the instruments yet, but he keeps his eye on them all the time and that sometimes makes him run the risk of bumping the trolley into a wall.

But there is another engineer who walks along next to the trolley and prevents this. He obviously understands the equipment thoroughly and seems to be its true custodian. From time to time he takes some component of the equipment out of the trolley, looks it over, tightens or loosens a screw, shakes it and taps it, puts it to his ear and listens; and finally, mainly when the trolley-driver is standing still, carefully replaces the little object, scarcely visible from a distance, back into the trolley. This engineer is rather domineering, but only on behalf of the equipment. Already at ten paces ahead of the trolley, at a wordless gesture from his finger, we are supposed to step aside, even where there is no space to give way.

Behind these two gentlemen the attendant walks along, unoccupied. The gentlemen have long ago cast off any arrogance—given their great knowledge that goes without saying—but the attendant by contrast appears to have concentrated it all into himself. With one hand in the small of his back, the other in front guarding his gilt buttons or stroking the fine cloth of his liveried coat, he nods frequently to right and to left as if we had greeted him and he were responding, or as if he assumed we had greeted, but could not, from his lofty position, be sure of it. Of course we don't greet him, but the sight of him might almost make you believe it was a colossal thing to be Chancery Attendant to the Management of Mines. It's true, we laugh behind his back, but since even a thunderclap wouldn't make him turn round, he still remains in our reflections as something beyond our comprehension.

Today not much more work will get done; the interruption was too extensive; a visit like that dismisses all thought of work. It is far too tempting to gaze after the gentlemen into the darkness of the trial gallery into which they have all disappeared. Our shift will also come to an end soon; we shall no longer join those who will be watching the gentlemen's return.

The Next Village

MY grandfather used to say: 'Life is astonishingly short. Now when I remember, it is all so compressed together that I can scarcely grasp, for example, how a young man can decide to ride to the next village without being afraid that—quite apart from unhappy accidents—even the time-span of an ordinary life as it passes happily by is not nearly enough for such a ride.'

A Message from the Emperor

THE Emperor—so it is said—has sent to you, the solitary, the miserable subject, the infinitesimal shadow who fled the imperial sun to far and furthest parts, to you and none other, the Emperor has from his deathbed sent a message. He had the messenger kneel at his bedside and whispered the message in his ear; so important to him was it that he had it repeated in the messenger's ear once more. With a nod he confirmed that what had been said was correct. And in the presence of the entire audience for his death—all the walls that might be in their way are demolished, and the grandees of the empire are standing in a circle on the wide, high sweep of the outer flight of steps—in the presence of all those assembled he sent the messenger on his way. The messenger has set off at once; a sturdy man, unwearying; stretching forward first one arm, then the other, he pushes his way through the crowd; if he meets with resistance, he points to his chest, which bears the sign of the sun; and he moves forward with an ease no one can match. But the crowd is so vast, their dwellings never come to an end. If open country stretched out before him, how he would fly, and soon, no doubt, you would hear the commanding sound of his fists beating upon your door. But instead, how uselessly he labours; he is still forcing his way through the chambers of the innermost palace; he will never get through them; and if he managed that, there would be nothing gained; he would have to fight his way down the stairs; and if he managed that, there would be nothing gained; the courtyards would have to be crossed; and after the courtyards, the second, outer palace; and again more stairs and more courtyards; and again a palace; and so on through the millennia; and if at last he emerged, stumbling, through the outermost gates—but that can never, never happen—the imperial city still lies before him, the centre of the world, piled high with its own refuse. No one will get through here—and certainly not with a message from the dead.—You, though, will sit at your window and conjure it up for yourself in your dreams, as evening falls.

Odradek, or Cares of a Householder

SOME say the word Odradek is Slavonic in origin, and they try on this basis to demonstrate the word's construction. Others are of the opinion that its origin is German, and that it is only influenced by Slavonic. But the uncertainty of both interpretations probably allows us to conclude that neither applies, especially as neither of them offers any help in discovering the meaning of the word.

Of course, no one would be concerned with such studies if there were not really a being with the name of Odradek. It looks at first like a flat, star-shaped spool for thread, and it does in fact appear to be wound round with thread, though it seems as if these are only old, torn scraps of yarn of various kinds and colours knotted into string, but also matted together. But it is not only a spool: a little rod sticks out crosswise from the middle of the star, and another one is fitted into this rod at a right angle. With the aid of this little rod on one side and one of the rays of the star on the other the whole thing can stand upright as if on two legs.

One might be tempted to believe that this construction once had a form fit for some purpose and is only broken now. That doesn't seem to be the case; at least there is no indication of it to be found; nowhere are there damaged places or worn surfaces to be seen which might suggest as much. In any case, there is little to be said by way of further detail, as Odradek is extraordinarily nimble and elusive.

He will change his dwelling-place from the attic to the stairwell, to the corridors or the hall. Sometimes he is not to be seen for months; that is when he has probably moved to other buildings; but then he will inevitably return to ours. Sometimes, if you come out through a door and he happens to be leaning against the bannisters, you would like to speak to him. Of course, you don't ask him any difficult questions, but you treat him—it's his tiny size that tempts you to do it—like a child. 'What's your name, then?' you ask him. 'Odradek,' he says. 'And where do you live?' 'No fixed abode,' he says, and laughs; but it is only the kind of laughter that can be produced without lungs. It sounds rather like the rustling of fallen leaves. And that is usually the end of the conversation. In any case, you can't always get even these answers; he is often silent, like the wood that he seems to be made of.

In vain I ask myself what will become of him. Is it possible for him to die? Everything that dies has had some sort of prior purpose, some sort of occupation, and has worn itself to nothing doing it; that does not apply to Odradek. So will he one day tumble down the stairs, perhaps under the feet of my children or grandchildren, trailing his threads after him? He obviously does no harm to anyone; but the idea that he should still outlive me, does almost give me pain.

Eleven Sons

I HAVE eleven sons.*

The first is very unattractive in appearance, but serious and clever; nevertheless, although I love him as my son, as I do all the others, I do not have a very high opinion of him. His way of thinking seems to me too simple. He looks neither to right nor left, nor far ahead; he is constantly running in circles round his narrow range of thought, or rather, he rotates.

The second is beautiful, slender, well-built; it is delightful to see him in a fencing pose. He is clever too, but he has some experience of the world as well; he has seen a lot, and so it seems that even nature itself in his own home country will converse with him more intimately than with the stay-at-homes. Nevertheless, this special quality is not due only or not even essentially to his travels; rather it belongs to the inimitable characteristics of this child, which are acknowledged for example by everyone who tries to emulate his acrobatic dive into the water, say, as he somersaults over and over while still under downright ferocious control. Their courage and pleasure last them as far as the end of the diving-board, but instead of diving, the imitator will sit down all of a sudden and raise his arms in apology.—And despite all this (after all, I really ought to be happy to have such a child) my relations with him are not unclouded. His left eye is slightly smaller than the right and winks a lot; only a little flaw, certainly, making his face even more cheeky than it would have been otherwise, and considering how inimitably self-contained he is by nature no one would notice that smaller eye with the wink and find fault with it. I, his father, do. Of course, it is not this physical flaw alone that grieves me, but also a kind of counterpart to it, a slight irregularity of mind, some toxin astray in his blood, some inability to fulfil the disposition of his life, apparent only to me. On the other hand, though, this is exactly what makes him my own true son, for this flaw of his is at the same time the flaw of our entire family; it is only more distinct in him.

My third son is also beautiful, but it is not a beauty that gives me pleasure. It is the beauty of the singer; the curving lip; the dreamy eye; the head that needs some rich drapery behind it to make an effect; the extravagant swelling breast; the hands quick to rise and much too quick to drop; the legs that strike an attitude because they cannot carry weight. And more: the tone of his voice is not full; deceives only for a moment; makes the connoisseur sit up and listen; but runs out of breath soon afterwards. Even though, in general, everything tempts me to show this son off, I still prefer to keep him under wraps; he himself doesn't push himself forward, but not because he knows his faults, rather from naivety. Also, he feels a stranger in our time; as though he belonged to my family but beyond that to another as well, lost to him for ever, so he is often listless, and nothing can cheer him up.

My fourth son is perhaps the most sociable of all. A true child of his time, he can be understood by everybody; he stands on ground common to everybody, and everybody wants to greet him. Perhaps this general recognition gives his nature a quality of ease, his movements a certain freedom, his judgements a certain light-heartedness. People are often fond of repeating some of his sayings, but only some, for taken all in all, he still suffers from being far too lightweight. He is like someone who makes an amazing leap, cleaves the air like a swallow, but then still ends miserably in the dusty wasteland, a nothing. Such thoughts sour the sight of this child for me.

My fifth son is kind and good; promised far less than he fulfils; used to be so insignificant that in his presence you felt virtually alone; but he has still come a long way and acquired some standing after all. If you were to ask me how this has come about, I can scarcely give an answer. Perhaps naivety is what makes its way most easily through the tumultuous elements of this world, and naive he surely is. Perhaps far too naive. Friendly with everyone. Perhaps far too friendly. I confess, I become uneasy when he is praised to my face. After all, it means making praise too easy for yourself if you praise a person as obviously praiseworthy as my son is.

My sixth son seems, at least at first glance, the deepest thinker of all. Hangs his head in misery, but still chatters. That is why you can't get close to him. If he is the loser, he is overcome with grief; if he gains the ascendancy, he will keep it by chattering away. But I don't deny he possesses a certain passion, when he is lost to the world; in broad daylight he often fights his way through his thoughts as though in a dream. Without being ill—on the contrary, he has very good health—he will sometimes stagger, particularly in poor light, but he doesn't need any help, he doesn't fall down. Perhaps this phenomenon is due to his physical development: perhaps he is too tall for his age. Taken all in all, that makes him look unlovely, in spite of strikingly beautiful single features, for example his hands and feet. His brow is unlovely too, by the way; shrunken in skin as well as in bone-structure.

My seventh son is perhaps more my own than all the others. The world does not know how to appreciate him; they do not understand his particular kind of wit. I do not overestimate him; I know he is insignificant enough; if there was nothing wrong with the world besides its failure to appreciate him, it would still be flawless. But within the family, I wouldn't be without this son. He brings disturbance as well as respect for tradition, and he combines both, at least as I see it, into an unassailable whole. But he himself is the last to know what to do with this whole; he is not the one to set this wheel of the future rolling; but this disposition of his is so cheering, so hopeful; I would want him to have children, and these to have children in turn. Unfortunately there seems to be little sign that this wish will be fulfilled. With a self-satisfaction which I can understand, it's true, but by the same token do not welcome, and which in any case is vastly contrary to the opinions held round about him, he drifts about alone, has no interest in girls, and in spite of all this, he will never lose his good temper.

My eighth son is the child of my sorrow, and I really cannot tell why. He looks at me like a stranger, and yet as his father I feel a close bond with him. Time has healed a great deal; I used to be overcome sometimes with trembling if I merely thought about him; he goes his own way; he has broken off all connections with me; and with his hard skull and athletic little body—only as a boy his legs were pretty weak, though meanwhile that may well have righted itself—he will make his way wherever he chooses. I have often felt the urge to call him back, and ask him how he is really faring, why he has cut himself off from his father in this way, and what, deep down, are his intentions, but now he is so far away and so much time has gone by, let it all stay the way it is. I have heard that he is the only one of my sons to wear a beard; of course, that doesn't look particularly fine on such a short man.

My ninth son is very elegant, with an attractive eye for women—so attractive that on occasion he can even seduce me, even though I know that a damp sponge is literally enough to wipe away all this unearthly glory. But the curious thing about this boy is that he is not at all intent upon seduction; he would be satisfied with spending his entire life lying on the sofa and wasting his eyesight on the ceiling or even more with letting it rest beneath his eyelids. If he is in this favourite position of his, he will talk readily and well; tersely and vividly; but only within narrow limits; if he oversteps them, which is unavoidable, as they are so narrow, what he has to say becomes quite vacuous. You might signal him to stop, if you had any hope that this sleepy gaze was capable of noticing it.

My tenth son is regarded as a dishonest character. I won't entirely dispute this failing, nor entirely confirm it. What is certain is that anyone who sees him coming, with a pomposity far beyond his years, his morning coat always buttoned up tight, wearing his old, but carefully polished, black hat, with his rather prominent chin, his heavy-lidded eyes, two fingers sometimes on his lips—anyone who sees him like that, will think: there goes an unbounded hypocrite. But just listen to him speaking! Sensibly; prudently; crisply; cross-questioning with lively malice; in astonishing, taken-for-granted and joyful accord with the universe, an accord which is bound to stiffen the sinews and raise the head high. Some, who consider themselves very wise and for that reason, so they thought, felt put off by his appearance, have been greatly drawn by his words. But then again there are people who have nothing against his appearance but find his words hypocritical. As his father, I don't want to decide between them here, but I must admit that in any case the latter judges are more worthy of respect than the first.

My eleventh son is delicate, probably the weakest amongst my sons; but his weakness is deceptive; at times he can be strong and decisive, but even then this is still somehow founded on his weakness. But it is not a weakness to be ashamed of, rather it is something that only on this our earth seems to be weakness. For example, isn't a readiness for flight also a weakness, being still hesitation and uncertainty and dithering? Something of that sort can be seen in my son. Of course such characteristics do not make a father happy; they obviously end in destroying the family. Sometimes he looks at me as if he wanted to say: 'I'll take you with me, father.' Then I think: 'You would be the last I would trust.' And then his eyes seem to say in reply: 'At least let me be the last then.'

These are my eleven sons.

A Brother's Murder

IT has been proved that the murder occurred in the following way:

Towards nine o'clock in the evening on a moonlit night, Schmar, the murderer, took up a position at the street corner which Wese, the victim, was bound to turn as he came out of the street where his office was located in order to enter the street where he lived.

Cold night air, chilling everyone through and through. But Schmar had only put on thin blue clothing; and besides, his jacket was unbuttoned. He didn't feel any cold; he was also constantly on the move. His murder-weapon, half bayonet, half kitchen knife, he held tight in his grasp, unsheathed. Looked closely at his knife reflecting the moonlight; the blade flashed; not enough for Schmar; he struck it against the bricks of the pavement so that it gave out sparks; regretted it perhaps; and to make good the damage he stroked it like a violin bow across the sole of his boot; standing on one leg, crouching forward, he listened to the sound of the knife on his boot and at the same time out into the fateful side street.

Why did Pallas, the rentier who was observing everything from his window on the second floor nearby, allow it all to happen? Sound the depths of human nature! Collar turned up high, dressing-gown belted round his large waist, shaking his head, he looked down.

And five houses further on, diagonally opposite him, Frau Wese, fox-fur coat over her nightdress, was looking out for her husband, who was taking an unusually long time.

At last the bell on the door outside Wese's office rings out—too loud for such a bell—over the town and up to the skies—and Wese, ever the conscientious night-worker, walks out of the building there, in this street still out of sight, only announced by the signal of the bell; at once the pavement counts his steady steps.

Pallas leans far forward; he mustn't miss a thing. Frau Wese, reassured by the bell, shuts the window with a clatter. But Schmar kneels down; since for the moment no other part of him is exposed, he presses only his face and hands against the stones; where everything is frozen, Schmar is glowing.

Just at the edge where the streets separate, Wese pauses; supported only by his walking-stick he enters the street beyond. A whim. The night sky has lured him, the dark blue and the gold. All unawares he gazes at it, all unawares he smoothes his hair beneath his lifted hat; there is no movement up there to warn him of the immediate future; everything remains in its meaningless, unfathomable place. In itself, it is perfectly sensible that Wese should continue walking on his way; but he walks right into Schmar's knife.

'Wese!' Schmar shouts, standing on tiptoe, his arm stretching up, the knife descending sharply. 'Wese! Julia will wait in vain!' And to right of the throat and to left of the throat and the third time deep into the belly Schmar stabs. Ships' rats, slit open, utter a sound like Wese's.

'Done!' says Schmar, and hurls the knife, the blood-stained excess ballast, against the nearest house-front. 'Oh, bliss of murder! Ecstasy from the flow of another's blood!' Wese, my old night-shadow, friend, drinking-companion, you are trickling away in the dark street depths. Why aren't you simply a blister filled with blood, so that I could sit on you and you'd disappear entirely. Not everything is fulfilled, not all the dreams of our youth bear fruit;* your remains are lying here in all their weight, already inaccessible to any step. What can the meaning of your silent question be?'

Pallas, retching on all the poisons churning in his body, the double-doors of his house springing open, stands in the doorway, 'Schmar! Schmar! I noticed it all! Missed nothing!' Pallas and Schmar eye each other. Pallas is satisfied. For Schmar there is no end. Frau Wese, with a crowd from the people on either side, rushes up, her face quite aged with horror. Her fur coat flies open; she falls upon Wese; her body in its nightdress belongs to him; the fur coat closing over the married couple like grass on a grave belongs to the crowd.

Schmar, stifling the final bout of nausea, his mouth pressed against the shoulder of the policeman who leads him away with tripping step.

A Dream

JOSEF K. was dreaming:

It was a beautiful day and K. intended to go for a stroll. But he had scarcely taken two steps before he was already in the graveyard. The paths there were quite artificial, winding to little purpose; still, he glided above one of them as he might over raging waters, securely, serenely, hovering. Even from a distance he noticed the mound of a freshly dug grave, and proposed to stop there. This mound attracted, almost enticed, him, and as he saw it, he couldn't reach it nearly quickly enough. But sometimes he could hardly see the mound; it was hidden from him by flags, which waved and flapped against one another with great force; the flag-bearers were not to be seen, great rejoicing seemed to prevail.

Even as he had still been gazing into the distance, suddenly he saw the same mound next to him at the wayside, indeed he almost went past it. He jumped quickly onto the grass. As the path went on racing beneath his feet while they were making the leap, he stumbled and fell on his knees just in front of the mound. Two men were standing behind the grave, and between them they were holding up a gravestone in the air; K. had scarcely appeared before they drove the stone into the earth, where it stood as if cemented in. At once a third man emerged from the bushes; K. recognized him straight away as an artist. He was dressed only in trousers and an ill-buttoned shirt; he had a velvet beret on his head; in his hand he held an ordinary pencil, which he was already using to describe figures in the air as he drew near.

With this pencil he now began working on the stone from the top downwards; the stone was very tall; he didn't need to crouch at all, but he did have to bend forward, for the mound, which he didn't want to tread on, cut him off from the stone. So he stood on the tips of his toes and supported himself with his left hand on the stone's surface. By some particularly cunning skill, he managed with this ordinary pencil to produce gold lettering; he wrote: 'Here rests —'. Each letter appeared clear and beautiful, deeply incised and in perfect, pure gold. When he had written the two words, he looked back at K.; K., who was very eager to see how the inscription would continue, was scarcely concerned with the man, but gazed only at the stone. The man actually started work again on writing further, but he couldn't; there was some obstacle; he lowered his pencil and turned round to K. again. Now K. looked at the artist too, and noticed that he was much distressed, but couldn't say what the cause was. All his previous energy had disappeared. This made K. distressed too; they exchanged helpless glances; there was a hateful misunderstanding present, which neither of them could resolve. On top of that, at just the wrong time, a small bell began tolling from the chapel by the grave, but the artist gave an abrupt wave with his raised hand, and it stopped. After a little while it started again, this time very quietly and, without being specifically ordered, breaking off straight away; it was as if it only wanted to test out its sound. K. was inconsolable at the artist's predicament; with his hands to his face he began a long weeping and sobbing. The artist waited until K. had calmed down, and then decided, as he could find no other way out, to continue writing anyway. The first little stroke he made was for K. a deliverance, though it was obvious that the artist got it done only with the utmost reluctance; the script was no longer so beautiful, either; above all, there seemed to be no gold; pale and uncertain, the stroke trailed off, but the letter became very big. It was a J; it was almost finished when the artist stamped angrily into the mound with one foot, so that the earth flew up round about. At last K. understood him; there was no more time to beg his pardon; he dug with all his fingers in the earth, which offered hardly any resistance; everything seemed prepared; a thin crust of earth had been raised just for show; right behind it a great hole with sloping sides opened up, and into this, turned on his back by a gentle current, K. sank. But while down below, his head still raised, he was already being received by the impenetrable depths, up above his name drove with mighty flourishes across the stone.

Delighted at the sight, he awoke.

A Report to an Academy

WORTHY Gentlemen of the Academy,

You have done me the honour of inviting me to present a report on my previous life as an ape.

In terms of your request, I am unfortunately unable to comply with your invitation. Almost five years separate me from the estate of apedom, a short time perhaps measured by the calendar, but infinitely long to gallop through as I have done, for stretches accompanied by excellent human beings, advice, applause, and orchestral music, but fundamentally alone, for accompanying of all kinds will stop short—to maintain the metaphor—a long way before the barrier. This achievement would have been impossible if I had wanted to cling on wilfully to my origins, to my memories of my youth. For to give up a full will of my own was above all the supreme commandment I had imposed upon myself; I, as a free ape, submitted to this yoke. This caused my memories for their part to close themselves off more and more from me. Although at first I was free to return—if the humans had let me—I could have returned at first through the vast gateway the heavens form over the earth, but it grew smaller and narrower, even as my development was being driven forwards with cruel speed; I felt more comfortable and included in the human world; the storm that blew me out of my past has eased; today it is merely a breeze that keeps my heels cool; and that gap in the distance through which it comes, and through which I once came, has become so small that, even if I had sufficient will and energy to run there, I would have to skin the hide off my back to get through it. To speak frankly, however much I like choosing my metaphors for these things, to speak frankly: your apedom, gentlemen—insofar as you have something of the sort behind you—cannot be further away from you than mine is from me. But there is an itch in the heels of everyone who walks here upon earth, little chimpanzee and great Achilles* alike.

However, in a limited sense I am perhaps able to answer your questions, and indeed I do so with great pleasure. The first thing I learned was to shake hands; shaking hands testifies to frankness; I trust that today, when I am at the height of my career, the first handshake may also be followed by frank words. They will not make an essentially new contribution to the Academy and will fall far short of what has been asked of me, and of what I am with the best will in the world unable to say—nevertheless they should point the general direction along which a quondam ape entered the human world and settled there. But certainly I would not say even the trivialities that follow if I were not completely sure of myself, and if my position on all the great music-hall stages of the civilized world were not firmly established, indeed unshakeable:

I come from the Gold Coast. For the story of how I was captured I am dependent on others' accounts. A hunting expedition from the firm of Hagenbeck*—I have since enjoyed many a good bottle of wine with its leader, by the way—was camped in a hide among the bushes on the river bank when I ran down in the midst of a group of my fellows at evening to drink. They shot; I was the only one to be hit; I received two gunshots.

One in the cheek, a slight one; but it left a large red bare patch which put me down with a name I hate, utterly inappropriate and literally invented by an ape: Redpeter—as if I were trying to distinguish myself from Peter,* the performing ape who had recently kicked the bucket, merely by the red patch on my cheek. This by way of digression.

The second shot struck me below the hip. It is due to this that I still have a slight limp. I read an article lately by one of the ten thousand news-hounds* who hold forth about me in the press: my essential inner ape is not yet entirely suppressed; as proof he claimed that when I have visitors I prefer to take off my trousers to show where the shot entered. That fellow should have every finger of his writing hand shot away one by one. As for me, I can take off my trousers in front of anyone I wish; they will find nothing there but a well-kept hide and the scar left by a—in this context let us choose a specific word for a specific purpose, which nevertheless I would not wish you to misunderstand—the scar left by a wicked, criminal shot. Everything is open to the light of day; nothing is to be hidden; if it is a matter of truth, all those of noble mind will cast aside even the most refined of good manners. On the other hand, if that hack were to take off his trousers when visitors came, it would certainly look very different, and I am ready to accept it as a sign of reason that he doesn't. In that case, he and his delicate feelings can get off my back!

After those shots I woke up—and this is the beginning of my own memories—in a cage between decks on the Hagenbeck steamer. It wasn't a four-sided cage with bars, rather there were only three sides fastened to a crate, so the crate formed the fourth side. The whole thing was too low for me to stand upright and too narrow for me to sit down. So I squatted with my knees bent and trembling all the time, and, because it seems that at first I didn't want to see anybody and wanted to remain in the dark, I turned to face the crate, while the bars at my back cut into my flesh. Keeping wild animals like this initially is regarded as beneficial, and today I cannot deny that in my experience this is, in human terms, in fact the case.

But that wasn't what I was thinking about then. For the first time in my life I had no way out; at least there wasn't a direct one. Directly in front of me was the crate, plank fixed firmly to plank. True, there was a gap running between the planks, which I welcomed, when I first discovered it, with howls of idiot delight, but this gap was not nearly wide enough even to stick my tail through, and impossible to make any wider, not with all the strength of an ape.

I am supposed to have made unusually little noise, they told me later, from which they concluded either that I was bound to perish soon or, if I managed to survive the first critical period, that I would be very suitable for training. I survived this period. Sobbing quietly, searching painfully for fleas, listlessly licking a coconut, butting the side of the crate with my skull, sticking out my tongue if anyone came near me—these were my first activities in my new life. In all of it, though, still the one feeling: no way out. Naturally, what I felt then as an ape I can only retrace today in human words; consequently I misrepresent it, but even though I can no longer attain my old truth as an ape, at least my description points in its direction. There is no doubt of that.

I had had so many ways out until then, and now not one. I was stuck fast. If they had nailed me down, it would not have made my need for freedom of movement any the less. Why should that be? Scratch the flesh between your toes raw, and you won't find the reason. Press your back against the bar until it nearly cuts you in two, and you won't find the reason. I had no way out, but I had to make one for myself, for without it I could not live. Always against the wall of this crate—I would indubitably have snuffed it. But under Hagenbeck, apes belong tied to the wall of a crate—well then, I would stop being an ape. A lucid, beautiful train of thought which I must have hatched out of my belly somehow—for apes think with their bellies.

I am afraid that you will not understand exactly what I mean by a way out. I use the word in its fullest and most customary sense. I deliberately do not say freedom. I do not mean this great feeling of freedom on all sides. Perhaps as an ape I may have known it, and I have been acquainted with humans who yearn for it. But for my own part I had no desire for freedom, neither then nor today. By the by: all too often humans deceive themselves with freedom. And just as freedom belongs among the noblest of feelings, the corresponding delusion is also among the noblest. Often in the music hall, just before my entrance, I have seen a pair of artistes performing their tricks on the trapeze high in the ceiling. They swayed, they swung, they flew into each other's arms, one held the other in his teeth by the hair. 'That too is human freedom,' I thought, 'self-mastery in movement.' What a mockery of sacred nature! No building could withstand the laughter of apedom at this sight.

No, it was not freedom I wanted. Only a way out; to right, to left, in any direction; it was my sole demand; even if a way out too was only a delusion; my demand was small, the delusion would not be any greater. Move on further, further! Anything but stand still with arms raised, pressed against the wall of a crate.

Today I can see it clearly; without the greatest inward calm I would never have been able to escape. And in fact, perhaps I owe everything I have become to the calmness that came over me after the first days there on the ship. But on the other hand, I probably owed that calm to the ship's crew.

They are good people, in spite of everything. Even today I am glad to remember the sound of their heavy steps, which re-echoed in my half-sleep at the time. It was their habit to set about everything extremely slowly. If one of them wanted to rub his eyes, he would lift his hand like a drop-weight. Their joking was coarse but friendly. Their laughter always had coughing mixed in with it, which sounded dangerous but meant nothing. They always had something in their mouth to spit out, and they didn't care where they spat it. They always complained that my fleas jumped over onto them; all the same, they never seriously meant me ill on that account; they just knew that fleas flourish in my coat and that fleas will jump; they were content with that. In their free time, some of them would sometimes sit around me in a half-circle; they hardly spoke, just grunted to one another; smoked a pipe, stretched out on the crates; slapped themselves on the knee as soon as I made the slightest movement, and now and again one of them would take a stick and tickle me where I like to be tickled. Today, if I were invited to take part in a voyage on these ships, I would certainly refuse the invitation, but it is just as certain that I haven't only unpleasant memories to recall from my days down there between decks.

Above all, the calmness I acquired in the company of these people held me back from any attempt at flight. From my present perspective it seems to me that I had at least an inkling that I would have to find a way out if I wanted to live, but that this way out was not to be reached by flight. I can't remember whether flight was possible, but I believe it was; for an ape flight should always be possible. With the present state of my teeth, I have to be careful even cracking nuts, but with time I should have been able to bite through the lock on the door. I did not. And what would have been gained by it? I would scarcely have put my head round the door before they would have captured me again and locked me up in an even worse cage; or I could have fled unobserved to one of the other animals opposite me, maybe to the giant snakes, and breathed my last in their embraces; or I might have succeeded in stealing up on deck and jumping overboard, when I would have been tossed on the ocean for a while and would have drowned. Acts of desperation. I did not calculate in these human terms, but under the influence of my environment I behaved as if I had been calculating.

I did not calculate, but calmly and quietly I was certainly observing. I watched these humans walking up and down, always the same faces, always the same movements—it often seemed to me as if there was only one of them. So this human, or these humans, went their ways without interference. A great purpose dawned upon me. No one promised me that if I became like them, they would open the cage door. Such promises, apparently impossible to fulfil, are not made. But if you do bring about the fulfilment, the promises will also appear retrospectively in just the place where you had once sought them in vain. Now there was essentially nothing about these humans that particularly attracted me. If I had been a devotee of that freedom I mentioned, I would certainly have chosen the way out offered by the ocean, as the melancholy eyes of those humans had shown. But in any case I had already been observing them for a long time before I thought of such things, indeed it was my accumulated observations that first urged me to take this particular direction.

It was so easy to mimic these people. I learned to spit in the very first days. Then we spat into each other's face; the only difference was that afterwards I licked my face clean, they didn't lick theirs. I was soon puffing at a pipe like an old smoker; then if I pressed my thumb into the bowl as well, the whole crew cheered; only for a long time I didn't grasp the difference between a pipe that was empty and one that was full of tobacco.

I had most trouble with the brandy bottle. The smell was a torment; I forced myself with all the strength I had, but it took weeks before I could get the better of myself. Remarkably, people took these inner struggles of mine more seriously than anything else about me. I don't distinguish between those people even in my memories, but there was one who came again and again, alone or with his mates, at all hours of the day and night; he would take up his position in front of me with a bottle, and instruct me. I mystified him; he wanted to solve the enigma of my being. He would uncork the bottle slowly, and then look at me to see if I had understood; I confess, I always watched him with a fierce, intense attention; there is not a human teacher on the whole round earth who will have such a student of humanity as I to teach. After the bottle was uncorked, he would lift it to his mouth; I follow him all the way with my eyes, right into his gullet; he nods, satisfied with me, and puts the bottle to his lips; I, delighted with my dawning knowledge, squeal as I scratch myself up and down and across wherever it happens to itch; he is pleased, raises the bottle, and takes a drink; I, impatient and desperate to emulate him, foul myself in the cage, which again gratifies him hugely; and now, stretching the bottle well away from himself and swinging it up again and leaning back with pedagogic exaggeration, he drinks it right down in one draught until the bottle is empty.

Now the practical exercises begin. Am I not all too exhausted already by the theory? Certainly, all too exhausted. That is part of my destiny. In spite of this, I grab as best I can after the bottle held out to me; tremble as I uncork it; with my success fresh energies gradually appear; scarcely distinguishable from the original, I raise the bottle, put it to my lips and—throw it in disgust, in disgust, although it is empty and filled only by the smell, throw it in disgust to the ground. To my mentor's sorrow and to my own even greater sorrow; it is no consolation either for him or for myself that I have not forgotten, even after throwing away the bottle, how to pat my stomach beautifully, grinning as I do so.

Only too often this is how the lessons went. And all honour to my mentor: he didn't get angry with me. True, he sometimes took his lighted pipe to my fur until it began to burn in a place I couldn't reach; but then he would put it out himself with his huge, kind hand; he wasn't angry with me; he perceived that we were fighting on the same side against the apish nature, and that I had the more difficult part.

All the same, what a victory it was for him, and for me, when one evening, in front of a big circle of spectators—perhaps there was some celebration, a gramophone was playing, an officer was taking his ease among the crew—when that evening, unnoticed for the moment, I seized a bottle of brandy left by accident outside my cage, and amid increasing attention from the company present, uncorked it just as I had been taught, put it to my mouth, and without hesitating, without wincing, like an expert drinker, with eyes rolling and throat spilling, I really and truly drank it right down until the bottle was empty; threw the bottle away no longer in desperation, but as an artist; true, I forgot to pat my stomach; but I made up for that, because I couldn't help it, because I had an urge to, because my senses were intoxicated, in short, when I called out 'Halloo!', breaking into human sounds, and with this call made the leap into the human community. And its echo: 'Listen, he's talking!' felt like a kiss over all my sweating body.

I repeat: there was no attraction for me in mimicking humans; I mimicked them because I was looking for a way out, for no other reason. In any case, that victory still did not achieve very much. I promptly lost my voice again; it only returned after months; my aversion to the brandy-bottle was even stronger. But anyhow, my direction once and for all was there for me to take.

When I was handed over to my first trainer in Hamburg, I soon had the measure of the two possibilities open to me: the Zoological Gardens or the music hall. I said to myself: make every effort to get into the music hall; that is the way out; the zoo will only be a new cage with bars; if they put you in that, you are lost.

And I learned, gentlemen. Oh, you learn when you have to; you learn if you want a way out; you learn mercilessly. You oversee yourself with the whip; you flay yourself at the slightest resistance. The nature of the ape in me rampaged, tumbling over itself, out of me and away, so that my first mentor almost went ape himself; he soon gave up instructing me, and had to be put into a mental home. Fortunately, he soon came out again.

But I used up several teachers, indeed several of them at the same time. Once I had become more assured of my capacities, more certain that the public was following my progress step by step, and that my future was dawning bright, I took on teachers myself, sat them down in five adjoining rooms, and studied with them all at the same time, leaping successively from one room to another.

Oh, this step-by-step progress! Oh, this penetration of the awakening brain from all sides by the radiance of knowledge! I won't deny it filled me with joy. But I will also admit that even then I did not overestimate it, much less now. By an effort which to this day has not been repeated the whole world over, I have attained the average educational level of a European. That would in itself perhaps be nothing at all, but it is still something insofar as it did help me out of the cage, and made this particular way out available to me, this human way out. There is a phrase that puts it very neatly: taking to the hills; that is what I have done: I've taken to them there hills. I had no other way, always assuming that freedom was not an option.

If I review my development and its purpose up to this point, I am not complaining, nor am I satisfied. With my hands in my trouser-pockets, a bottle of wine on the table, I half-sit, half-recline in my rocking-chair, looking out of the window. If I have visitors, I receive them with all propriety. My impresario sits in the anteroom; if I ring, he will come and listen to what I have to say. In the evening I almost always have a performance, and my success, I might say, could scarcely rise any higher. When I come home late at night from a banquet, or from some scientific society, or a friendly get-together, a little half-trained chimpanzee is waiting up for me, and I take my pleasure with her after the apish fashion. I have no wish to see her by day; you see, she has the crazy, confused look of the trained animal in her eyes; I am the only one to recognize it, and I cannot endure it.

In any case, I have on the whole achieved what I wanted to achieve. Do not say it was not worth the trouble. Besides, I am not asking for a judgement from any human, my only wish is to make these insights more widely known; I am simply reporting; to you too, honoured gentlemen of the Academy, I have been simply making a report.

The Rider on the Coal-Scuttle

ALL the coal used up; the scuttle empty; the shovel useless; the stove breathing cold; the room filled with frosty air; the trees outside the window stiff with rime; the heavens a silver shield against anyone looking to them for help. I must have coal; I can't freeze to death; behind me the pitiless stove, before me the just as pitiless heavens, so consequently I have to ride the hair's breadth between them and go in search of help from the coal-dealer. But by now he is hardened to my usual pleas; I must prove to him exactly that I haven't a single little speck of coal left, so that for me he signifies the very sun in the firmament. I must go to him like the beggar dying of hunger and about to utter his last gasp on the doorstep, so that the master's cook might bring herself to pour the last dregs of coffee into his mouth; and likewise the coal-dealer, even as he fumes, is bound, in the light of the commandment 'Thou shalt not kill', to toss a shovelful into my scuttle.

From the start, the way I drive up must be what decides him; so I shall ride there on the scuttle. As the Rider on the Coal-Scuttle, my hand upon the handle on top, simplest of bridles, I make my way with some difficulty down the winding stairs; but once at the bottom my scuttle rises up magnificently, magnificently; camels lying low to the ground and rousing themselves beneath their driver's stick do not arise more beautifully. Through the frozen street we ride with a regular trot; I am often lifted up to first-floor height; I never sink down as low as the house doors. And at an extraordinary height I hover before the vault of the coal-dealer's cellar, where he crouches in the depths, writing at his little table; to let out the extreme heat he has opened the door.

'Coal-dealer!' I call, in a voice burnt hollow with cold, wrapped in smoking clouds from my breath, 'please, coal-dealer, give me a little coal. My scuttle is so empty I can ride on it. Be so kind. As soon as I can, I'll pay you.' The dealer raises his hand to his ear. 'Am I hearing right?' he asks his wife over his shoulder. She is on the bench by the stove, knitting. 'Am I hearing right? A customer.'

'I can hear nothing,' says his wife, breathing peacefully in and out over her knitting-needles, her back cosy and warm.

'Oh yes,' I call, 'it is I; an old customer; your humble servant; only with no money at the moment.'

'Wife,' says the dealer, 'it is—it is someone; I'm not deceiving myself that much; it has to be an old customer, a very old one, to be able to speak to my heart in this way.'

'What's the matter with you, man?' said his wife, and, pausing in her work for a moment, she clutches her knitting to her breast, 'it's no one. The street is empty; all our customers are well supplied; we can shut the shop for days and take a rest.'

'But I'm still sitting here on the coal-scuttle,' I cry, and numb tears of cold veil my eyes, 'please, please look up; you'll find me straight away; I'm begging you for one shovelful; and if you give me two, you will make me more than happy. All your other customers are already supplied, after all. Oh, I just heard a rattling inside the scuttle!'

'I'm coming,' the coalman says, about to climb the cellar steps on his short legs, but his wife is already at his side; she grasps him firmly by the arm, and says: 'You're staying here; if you don't stop being so pig-headed, I'll go up myself. Remember how badly you were coughing last night. But to do a bit of business, even if it is only imaginary, you forget your wife and child and sacrifice your lungs. I'll go.' 'Then tell him all the sorts of coal we keep in stock; I'll call the prices out after you.' 'Right,' says his wife, and she climbs up to the street. Of course, she sees me at once. 'Mrs Coal-dealer,' I call, 'humble regards; just one shovel of coal; straight here into the scuttle; I'll transport it home myself; a shovelful of the poorest sort. I'll pay the full price of course, but not right now, not right now.' What a bell tolling resounds in those three words, 'not right now', and how confused one's mind becomes as they blend with the evening bells one can hear from the church tower nearby!

'What is it he wants, then?' the dealer shouts. 'Nothing,' his wife shouts back, 'there's really nothing; I see nothing; I hear nothing; only the bells ringing for six o'clock, so we'll shut the shop. The cold is monstrous. Likely we'll have a lot of work tomorrow.'

She sees nothing and hears nothing; but she undoes her apron-strings all the same, and attempts to wave me away with her apron. Unfortunately, she is successful. My scuttle has all the virtues of a good riding-horse; but he has no power of resistance; he is too light; a woman's apron can chase his legs off the ground.

'You wicked woman,' I go on calling back to her as she shakes her hand about in the air, half in scorn, half in satisfaction, 'you wicked woman! I begged you for a shovelful of the poorest sort, and you didn't give it to me.' And with these words I rise up into the regions of the Ice Mountains and I am lost, never to return.

A HUNGER ARTIST

FOUR STORIES

First Sorrow

A TRAPEZE artist—this art, practised high in the music-hall domes, is acknowledged to be one of the most difficult of any attainable by mankind—had so arranged his life, first out of his striving for perfection and later out of habit turned tyranny, that as long as he worked in the same firm he would remain night and day high up on his trapeze. All his needs—very slight, by the way—were met by servants, who took over from one another, staying on the lookout below and pulling up and down everything required above, in specially constructed containers. This way of life did not present any particular difficulties for the world around; only during the other acts on the programme it was slightly disturbing that he remained up there, unhidden, and that, although at such times he mainly stayed quite still, now and again a glance from the audience would wander off towards him. But the management forgave him for this, because he was such an extraordinary, irreplaceable artist. They also perceived of course that he did not live thus out of wilfulness, and really only thus could he keep himself in constant practice, only thus maintain his art in all its perfection.

In any case, it was in all other respects perfectly healthy up above; in the warmer season, when all the side windows round the roof were opened, and with the fresh air the sun entered the shadowy space in all its glory, it was even beautiful there. True, his human contact was limited, but sometimes a fellow acrobat would clamber up to him on the rope ladder; then they would both sit on the trapeze, lean to right and to left on the support-ropes, and chat; or builders might be repairing the roof, and would exchange a few words with him through an open window, or a fireman inspecting the emergency lighting in the topmost gallery would shout a few respectful but not very comprehensible words to him. Otherwise everything about him was still; once in a while some employee, wandering into the empty theatre of an afternoon for instance, would look thoughtfully up into the heights, so far away they almost escaped from view, where the trapeze artist, with no means of knowing that someone was watching him, would be practising his skills, or resting.

The trapeze artist could have gone on living undisturbed in this way if it had not been for the unavoidable travelling from place to place, which was extremely distressing for him. True, the impresario saw to it that the trapeze artist was spared anything that prolonged his suffering; for driving him in the cities they used racing automobiles which would charge through the empty streets, whenever possible at night or early in the morning, at the fastest speed they could, but still too slowly to satisfy the trapeze artist's wishes; on the railway, they would reserve an entire compartment, where the trapeze artist would spend the journey in a miserable substitute for his usual way of life—at least an attempt at one—up in the luggage-rack; in the next place where they were due to give a guest performance, long before the trapeze artist had arrived, his trapeze was already in place in the theatre, all the doors leading into the auditorium were opened wide, all the aisles kept free—but still, it was always the best moment of the impresario's life when the trapeze artist set his foot on the rope ladder and in an instant was suspended once more from his trapeze on high.

However many journeys the impresario had managed with success, he still found every new one upsetting, for quite apart from everything else, in any case these tours had a ruinous effect on the trapeze artist's nerves.

On one occasion they were travelling together again in the same way: the trapeze artist lay in the luggage-rack dreaming, the impresario leaning back in the window corner opposite him, reading a book, when the trapeze artist addressed him softly. The impresario was at his service at once. Biting his lip, the trapeze artist said that instead of the one trapeze he had used for his exercises up to now, he must have two, two trapezes, opposite each other. The impresario assented at once. But, as if he wanted to indicate that in this respect the impresario's agreement was as immaterial as his opposition, the trapeze artist said that from now on he would never, not under any circumstances, perform on only one trapeze. He seemed to shudder at the very idea that this might still happen one day. Hesitantly, watchfully, the impresario yet again declared his complete assent: two trapezes were better than one, and besides, this new arrangement also had the advantage of giving greater variety to the performance. Then suddenly the trapeze artist began to weep. Profoundly startled, the impresario leapt to his feet asking what had happened, and when he received no reply, he jumped up on the bench, stroked him, pressed his face against his own, so that the trapeze artist's tears overflowed that as well. But only after lots of questions and words of flattery, the trapeze artist said with a sob: 'Only this one bar in my hand—how can I live?' It was already easier now for the impresario to console the trapeze artist; he promised to telegraph from the very next station to the next place where they were due to perform about the second trapeze; reproached himself that for so long he had allowed the trapeze artist to work on one trapeze; thanked him and was loud in his praises that at last he had drawn the impresario's attention to this great error. In this way he managed to calm the trapeze artist down gradually and was able to return to his corner. But he himself had not calmed down; secretly and with a heavy heart he observed the trapeze artist over the top of his book. If such thoughts once began to torment him, would they ever completely stop? Could they not but grow in intensity? Were they not a threat to life and livelihood? And the impresario really believed he could see how, at this moment, in the seemingly peaceful sleep in which the weeping had ended, the first furrows began to inscribe themselves on the trapeze artist's smooth and child-like brow.

A Little Woman

SHE is a little woman; quite slim naturally, but still heavily corseted; I always see her in the same dress, made of yellowish-grey material, rather like the colour of wood, with a few bobbles or things like buttons of the same shade dangling from it; she is always without a hat; her dull-blond hair is smooth, and not untidy, but worn very loose. Although she wears a corset, she is quick and agile, but she does, I admit, overdo the agility; she is fond of putting her hands on her hips and turning from the waist all in one movement with surprising speed. I can only render the impression she makes on me by saying that I have never seen a hand where the fingers are as sharply separated as they are on hers; and yet her hand has no anatomical peculiarity about it whatever; it is a perfectly normal hand.

Now this little woman is most dissatisfied with me; she is always finding fault with me about something, I always offend her, I vex her at every turn; if you could divide life up into the smallest of small parts, and judge *ex parte* each separate little part separately, every particle of my life would assuredly be a vexation to her. I have often thought about why I vex her so much; it may be that everything about me is incompatible with her feeling for beauty, her sense of justice, her habits, her traditions, her hopes. There are incompatible natures of this kind, but why does she suffer so much from mine? There is absolutely no relationship between us at all that would compel her to suffer on my account. She would only have to make up her mind to look on me as a complete stranger, which after all I am, and I wouldn't defend myself against such a decision, but welcome it; she has only to make up her mind to forget my existence, which after all I have never forced upon her, nor would I ever do so—and all her suffering would clearly be over. I am not thinking of myself here, nor that her behaviour is of course distressing to me too; I disregard it because I can see perfectly well that all this distress is nothing in comparison with her suffering. All the same, I am fully aware that there is no love in her suffering; she does not care in the least about really reforming me, especially as everything she finds fault with in me is not of the kind that would hinder how I myself am getting on. But how I get on is not what really bothers her either; all she is concerned about is her own personal interest, and that is to take her revenge for the torment I cause her, and prevent the torment I cause from threatening her in the future. I once tried to point out to her how best to put an end to this constant vexation, but simply by doing so I put her into such an outburst of passion that I shan't attempt to repeat it again.

Also I do bear, if you like, a certain responsibility, for even though the little woman is almost entirely a stranger to me, the only relationship between us is almost entirely the vexation I cause her, or rather the vexation she uses me to cause for herself, it cannot after all be a matter of indifference to me to see how she also suffers physically from this vexation. From time to time news reaches me, increasingly of late, that in the mornings she is once again pale, bleary-eyed, racked by headaches, and almost incapable of working; her relatives are worried by this; they cast around at a loss for the cause of the state she is in, and up to now they have not yet found it. I am the only one who knows: it is the old, ever-new vexation. Now it's true, I do not share her relatives' worries; she is strong and tough; anyone who can get quite so vexed is probably quite able to get over the consequences of their vexation; I even suspect that she is—at least partly—only pretending to suffer, to divert the world's suspicion in this way on to me. She is too proud to state openly how much I torment her by merely existing; she would feel she was demeaning herself to bring her appeal before others in her case against me. It is only revulsion, never-ending revulsion perpetually driving her on that makes her so obsessed with me; and on top of that, discussing this grubby matter in public would be too much for her sense of shame. But on the other hand it is also too much for her to remain completely silent about the matter that constantly oppresses her. And so with her woman's wiles she tries a middle way; by remaining silent, only by the outward signs of her secret suffering, she is minded to bring the matter before the open court of the world at large. Perhaps she even hopes that if society once takes a hard look at me, there will arise a universal public vexation with me, which, with the great powers it has at its disposal, will judge me all the way to the ultimate court of appeal faster and more forcibly than her private vexation—relatively weak in any case—is able to do; but then she can withdraw, heave a sigh of relief, and turn her back on me. Well, if that's what she is really hoping for, she is deceiving herself. Society will not take over her role. Society will not find so much never-ending fault with me, even if it puts me under its most powerful lens. I am not such a useless person as she thinks; I don't want to boast, particularly not in the present context; but even if I am not distinguished by my specific usefulness, I certainly won't be conspicuous for the opposite either; only to her, in the almost white-hot light of her eyes, am I like that; she will never be able to convince anyone else of it. So in this respect I could be quite reassured? No, not really, for if it becomes widely known that I make her downright ill by my behaviour, and a few spies, the most zealous of the tell-tales, are already close to seeing through it, or at least to pretending they do, and the world comes and asks me why I torment the poor little woman by being so utterly incorrigible and do I intend to drive her to her death, and when will I finally have the good sense and the simple human sympathy to stop—if the world asks me this, it will be difficult to answer. Am I supposed to admit to them that I have no great belief in these symptoms of illness, and give the disagreeable impression that just to free myself of guilt I lay the blame on others, and with such ill manners, too? And could I go so far as to say openly that even if I did believe she was ill really, I haven't the least sympathy for her, as the woman is a total stranger to me, and the relationship that exists between us has been contrived by her alone, and exists only from her side? I don't mean to say that they won't believe me, rather that they will neither believe nor disbelieve me; they certainly wouldn't go as far as discussing it; they would simply register the answer I have given regarding a weak, sick woman, and that would hardly do me any good. In this answer as in any other, I would be thwarted by the world's stubborn inability in a case like this to deny that it suspects a love affair, even though it is glaringly obvious that such a relationship does not exist, and that even if it did, I would sooner be the one to start it, for in fact I might find it in me to admire the little woman anyway for her hard-hitting judgement and her relentless logic, as long as I wasn't constantly being chastised by these very virtues. But in any case, on her side there is not a trace of a well-disposed relationship to me; in this she is honest and true; my last hope rests upon that; she would not once, though it might suit her battle-plan to make such a relationship seem plausible, forget herself so far as to do anything of the kind. But in this respect the wider world is utterly insensitive; it will stick to her judgement and always decide against me.

So the only thing that would be left for me is the prospect of changing, in good time, before the world interferes, to the extent not of getting rid of the little woman's vexation, which is unthinkable, but still of moderating it a little. And I have in fact often asked myself whether I am so satisfied with my present state that I don't want to change it at all, and whether it mightn't be possible to make certain changes in myself, even if I didn't do it out of any conviction that it was necessary, but only to mollify the woman. And I have honestly tried, painstakingly and conscientiously—it was even congenial, it almost amused me; single changes arose of their own accord, and were visible far off, I didn't have to draw her attention to them, she notices anything like that sooner than I do, she actually notices how my mere demeanour already expresses my intentions; but success was not granted me. And how would it be possible, anyway? Her displeasure with me is, indeed, I can see now, a matter of principle. Nothing will remove it, not even removing myself. Her outbursts of fury at the news of my suicide, for instance, would have no bounds. Now I cannot imagine that this sharp-witted woman doesn't see this as well as I do, I mean the hopelessness of her labours as much as my innocence, my inability even with the best will in the world to live up to her demands, but being a born fighter she forgets it in the passion of the fight; and my unfortunate nature is so made—and I cannot choose another, for that is how it was given me—that to anyone who has lost all control I am inclined to murmur words of gentle rebuke. Of course we will never get on well like this. Day after day, for instance, I will leave the house enjoying the early morning, and I will see this face, bad-tempered because of me, the ill-humoured curl of the lip, the scrutinizing eye that already knows the result of the scrutiny, that looks me over briefly and that nothing, however fleeting, can escape, the bitter smile painfully hollowing her prim little face, the plaintive heavenward gaze, the hands planted on her hips to steady herself, the growing pallor, the palpitations.

Recently, for the very first time, as I admitted to myself with astonishment as I did so, I gave a good friend some hint of the situation, just in passing, lightly, in a few words; I reduced the importance of the whole thing, slight though it is to me fundamentally with regard to the outside world, to just a little less than the truth. Strange that nevertheless my friend did not disregard it, indeed, he gave it greater importance of his own accord, would not be put off, and persisted in his opinion. All the same, even stranger that on one crucial point, in spite of everything he still underestimated the matter, for he advised me in all seriousness to go travelling for a while. No advice could be more incomprehensible. It's true, things are quite simple; on closer inspection anyone can see through them, but still, they are not so simple that everything, or at least the most important things, could be sorted out tidily if I were to go away. On the contrary, I should rather be wary of going away; if I am to follow any kind of plan at all, then at least let it be one that will keep the thing within its previous narrow limits, which have not so far dragged in the outside world, that is, to stay quietly where I am and refuse to admit any conspicuous changes this affair might have caused, which also involves not talking to anyone about it, but all of this not because it might be some kind of dangerous secret, rather because it is a small, purely personal matter, and as such easy to bear anyway and because it has to remain like that always. In this respect my friend's remarks were not unhelpful; they didn't tell me anything new, but they strengthened me in my fundamental opinion.

Considered more closely, it becomes clear that the changes the situation seems to have undergone in the course of time are not changes in the affair itself, but only developments in the way I have come to view it, insofar as this view has partly become steadier, more masculine, closer to the heart of the matter, though it is also partly that under the influence of the constant emotional upsets—which are impossible to get over, however slight—there is a certain increase in nervous strain.

I become calmer facing the matter when I think I realize that, however large it sometimes seems to loom ahead of me, it will probably not yet come to a crucial decision after all; one is easily inclined, especially as a young man, to overestimate greatly the pace at which decisions happen; the moment my little judge, worn out at the sight of me, sank sideways into a chair, one hand clutching the back of the seat, the other nestling round her stays, tears of rage and despair rolling down her cheeks, I would always think: now is the critical moment, and I am about to be called on to justify myself. But not a word about decision, not a word about justification; women readily feel ill; the world hasn't enough time to keep its eye on every case. And what has actually happened in all these years? Only that instances like this were repeated, now stronger, now weaker, so now their sum total is the greater, and people hang around near at hand and would love to interfere if they could find an opportunity, but they can't, so they rely on their nose for trouble, and a nose for trouble, it's true, is sufficient to give its possessors plenty to keep them busy, but is no use for anything else. But that is how it has been all the time; all the time there have been these idlers hanging around and sniffing the air who will find any more-than-cunning excuse for happening to be nearby, the best one being that they are relatives; all the time they have been on the watch, all the time their noses have had their fill of sniffing and sensing, but the end-result of it all is simply that they are still around. The only difference is that I have gradually come to recognize them, distinguish their faces; I used to believe that they would gather together from all sorts of places; that the scale of it all would increase and of itself force a decision; today I think I know that the whole thing has always been there, from long, long ago, and had nothing, or very little, to do with the looming decision. And the crucial decision itself? Why am I giving it such a grandiose name? If it once came to the point— certainly not tomorrow, nor the day after, and probably never—that the wider world would be concerned with the affair after all—where, as I shall keep repeating, it has no jurisdiction—I shall not, I admit, emerge from the proceedings undamaged, but it will surely be taken into consideration that I am not unknown in the wider world, have lived fully in its light for years, trusting and trustworthy, and that consequently this unhappy little woman, who arrived late in my life, and whom, by the way, perhaps anyone but myself would long ago have recognized as a clinging vine and would have trampled beneath his boot silently and out of the world's hearing, that this woman could at worst only add an ugly little flourish to the diploma with which the world at large had long ago declared me to be its estimable member. That is how things stand at present, a situation hardly liable to upset me.

With the passage of time I have become rather less calm, though, but that has nothing at all to do with the real significance of the whole affair; it simply can't be borne to go on vexing someone all the time, even when you know perfectly well that the vexation is groundless; you become upset; you begin, partly just physically, to be watching out for decisions, even though rationally you don't much believe they will happen. But it is also partly just a sign of age; youth makes everything look appealing; unlovely individual features are lost in the ceaseless fountain of youthful energy; if someone had a rather wary eye as a boy, no one thinks badly of him for it, it is simply not noticed, not even by the boy himself, but what is left when he is older are remnants; each one is necessary, not one is renewed, each one is under observation, and the wary eye of an ageing man is just that, quite clearly a wary eye, and not hard to detect. But even in this context it is still not really a change for the worse in the actual situation.

So from whatever angle I look at it, it becomes clearer every time—and I shall stick to this—that if I keep my hand covering this little affair over even quite lightly, I shall be able to go on with my life as before for a very long time, calmly, undisturbed by the world, despite all that little woman's raging.

A Hunger Artist

IN recent decades, interest in hunger artists has greatly diminished. Where it once paid to organize major performances of the kind, under the personal direction of the performer himself, nowadays it is completely impossible. They were different times. In those days the hunger artist engaged the attention of the entire town; from hunger-day to hunger-day interest increased; everyone wanted to see the hunger artist at least once each day; during the later days there were subscription-holders who would sit all day long before the bars of the little cage; at night too tours were arranged to view him—lit by torches, to heighten the effect; on fine days the cage was brought into the open, and then it was especially for the children that the hunger artist was put on show; while he was often just an amusement for the adults, who only attended because it was the fashion, the children would gaze in astonishment, open-mouthed, holding each other's hands for safety, at how he would sit, pale, in his black singlet, with sharply jutting ribs, on a floor of scattered straw, scorning even a chair, and at how, with a single courteous nod, he would make an effort to answer questions, and stretch out an arm through the bars for his audience to feel how thin he was, but then would sink into himself, paying attention to no one, not even to the clock, the only furniture in the cage, as it struck the hour so important to him, but would merely gaze ahead with eyes almost closed, and sip now and again from a tiny glass of water, to moisten his lips.

Apart from the changing spectators, there were also permanent watchmen elected by the public—curiously, they were usually butchers—always three at a time, who had the job of observing the hunger artist night and day, to see that even so he did not in one way or another take some secret nourishment. But it was simply a formality, introduced to appease the masses, for the initiated knew perfectly well that during the period of fasting the hunger artist would never, not under any circumstances, even if coerced, have eaten even the tiniest morsel; the honour of his art forbade it. Of course, not every watchman could understand that; sometimes there were groups of night-watchers who carried out their duties very sloppily, deliberately sitting huddled together in a corner far from him, absorbed in a card-game, with the obvious intention of granting the hunger artist the opportunity of a little refreshment, which, so they thought, he was able to produce from some secret supplies. Nothing was more of a torment to the hunger artist than these watchers; they made him melancholy; they made his hungering terribly difficult; sometimes he would conquer his frailty and sing during their watch, just so as to

hold out long enough to show these people how unjustly they suspected him. But it didn't help very much; they only marvelled at his
skill at eating and singing at the same time. He much preferred the
watchmen who sat close to the bars, who were not satisfied with the
dim lighting in the hall at night, but shone a light on him with the
electric pocket-torches the impresario put at their disposal. The harsh
light didn't disturb him in the least, sleep was impossible for him in
any case, and he was always able to doze a little in any kind of lighting
and at any hour, even in the noisy, overcrowded hall. With these
watchmen he was gladly prepared to pass the night entirely without
sleep; he was ready to joke with them, tell them stories about his travels, and listen to their tales in turn—and all just to keep them awake,
to be able to show them all the time that there was nothing to eat in
his cage, and that he hungered in a way none of them possibly could.
But he was happiest of all when morning came and they were
served—at his expense—with a sumptuous breakfast which they
hurled themselves upon with the appetite of healthy men after a hard
night on the watch. There were even people who suspected this breakfast of improperly influencing the watchmen, but that was going too
far, and when they were asked if they would take on the night watch
themselves just for the sake of proving their point, and without the
breakfast, they withdrew—but they still kept their suspicions.

This particular suspicion was simply one among the many that
were in any case inextricably part and parcel of the hungering. Nobody
of course was in a position to spend all their days and nights continuously with the hunger artist, so nobody could know from seeing for
himself whether his hungering had been really continuous and without fault; only the hunger artist himself could know that, so only he
could be at the same time the fully satisfied spectator of his own hungering. But then again there was another reason why he was never
satisfied; perhaps it was not hungering at all that had made him grow
to be so very emaciated that many, to their regret, had to stay away
from the performances because they could not bear to look at him,
but he had only become so emaciated out of his own dissatisfaction
with himself. For he alone knew what no other initiate knew: how easy
hungering was. It was the easiest thing in the world. He didn't hide it,
either, but nobody believed him, at best they thought him modest,
but mostly they thought he was after publicity or was even a swindler
who found hungering easy anyway because he knew how to make it

easy for himself, and then even had the nerve to half-confess it. He had to take all that; in the course of the years he had even got used to it, but inwardly this state of dissatisfaction gnawed at him, and he had never, not after any period of hungering—they had to testify to that—ever left the cage voluntarily. The uttermost length of time for hungering had been set by the impresario at forty days; he never allowed hungering to go beyond that, not even in the great cities, and with good reason. For forty days or so he knew from experience that by gradually intensifying the advertising he could whip up the interest of a town higher and higher; but then the public would take no more; bookings, it was clear to see, became substantially thinner; in this respect of course there were slight differences between the towns and the provinces, but as a rule forty days was the uttermost time. Then, on the fortieth day, the door of the cage, all garlanded with flowers, would be opened; an ecstatic crowd of spectators filled the amphitheatre; a military band would play; two physicians would enter the cage to carry out the necessary measurements on the hunger artist; the results would be announced to the hall by megaphone, and finally two young ladies would arrive, delighted that they were the very ones selected by lot, and they would attempt to lead the hunger artist out of the cage down a few steps, where on a little table a carefully chosen light meal was waiting for him. And at this moment the hunger artist always resisted. True, he still placed his skeletal arms freely into the hands the young ladies stretched out to help him as they bent towards him, but he would not stand up. Why stop just now, after forty days? He would have held out for a long time, a time without limit, even yet; why stop just now, when he was still at the height of hungering, indeed, not yet at the height? Why did they want to rob him of the fame of hungering still further, of becoming not only the greatest hunger artist of all times, which, indeed, he probably was already, but also to outperform himself far beyond all comprehension, for he felt there were no bounds to his capacity for hungering. Why did this mob, who claimed to admire him so much, have so little patience with him; if he could endure hungering still further, why wouldn't they endure it? He was weary too; he was sitting comfortably in the straw, and now he was supposed to stand up tall and straight and go and eat, the mere thought of which made him feel sick, though out of regard for the ladies he refrained with some effort from demonstrating it. And he looked up into the eyes of these ladies, apparently so kind, in reality so cruel, and shook his too-heavy head on its frail neck. But then there happened what always happened. The impresario arrived, lifted his arms silently—the music made speaking impossible—above the hunger artist as if he were inviting heaven to behold its work here for once, on the straw, this pitiful martyr, which the hunger artist was anyway, but in a quite different sense. He clasped the hunger artist round his shrunken waist with exaggerated care to make them believe what a fragile thing it was he had to do with here; and he handed the hunger artist over—not without secretly giving him a little shake so that he swayed to and fro, his legs and upper body out of control—to the young ladies, who had meanwhile turned deathly pale. The hunger artist now put up with everything; his head drooped on his chest, it was as though it had rolled away and inexplicably remained where it was; his body was hollowed out; his legs, in some instinct of self-preservation, were tightly pressed together, but they still scraped along the ground as if it were not the real ground and they were just searching after the real ground, while the entire weight of his body, though very light, lay on one of the ladies. The lady, seeking for help and with panting breath—this was not how she had imagined her office of honour—first craned her neck as far as possible to keep at least her face from touching the hunger artist, and then—as this did not work and her more fortunate companion did not come to her aid, but tremulously contented herself with holding the hunger artist's hand, this little bundle of bones, at a distance—she burst into tears, to the delighted laughter of the hall, and had to be relieved by a servant long stationed in readiness to do so. Then came the meal, which the impresario slipped down the hunger artist's throat, just a little, as he half-fainted, half-slept, while he himself chattered merrily to draw attention from the hunger artist's condition; then a toast was raised to the public, which the impresario claimed had been whispered in his ear by the hunger artist; the orchestra reinforced it all with a great flourish; the audience broke up, and nobody had any right to be dissatisfied with what had happened, nobody, only the hunger artist, always and only the hunger artist.

For many years, with short breaks for rest, he lived like this, in apparent glory, honoured by the world, but for all that mostly in a dark temper of mind, which became all the darker because no one had the discernment to take it seriously. How were they supposed to console him anyway? What more could he wish for? And if some good-natured person turned up who was sorry for him and tried to explain to him that his sadness probably came from the hungering, it could happen, especially at an advanced stage of the hungering-period, that the hunger artist would reply with an outburst of rage and to everyone's horror begin to shake at the bars of his cage like an animal. But for situations of this kind the impresario had a punishment he was fond of using. He would make excuses for the hunger artist before the assembled public, admitting that only the irritability provoked by the hungering, not readily comprehensible to the well-fed, could excuse the hunger artist's behaviour; and then in this connection he would go on to speak of the hunger artist's assertion, which also needed some explanation, that he could go on hungering for much longer than he did—he would praise the noble aspiration, the good-will, the great self-denial that were assuredly also contained in this assertion, but then he would proceed to contradict the assertion simply enough by displaying photographs, which were sold at the same time, for in the pictures the public saw the hunger artist in the fortieth day of hungering, lying in bed, enfeebled and almost fading away. This distortion of the truth, certainly nothing new to the hunger artist but every time grating on his nerves afresh, was too much for him. The consequence of ending his hungering prematurely was being represented here as its cause! To struggle against this stupidity, this world of stupidity, was impossible! Again and again he had gone on listening avidly and in good faith to the impresario as he clung to the bars, but every time the photographs appeared he would let go of the bars, sink sighing back into the straw, and the public, much appeased, was able to approach once more and view him.

If the witnesses to such scenes thought back on them a few years later, they often couldn't understand their own attitude. For meanwhile the drastic change already referred to had set in. It happened almost suddenly; there may have been deeper reasons for it, but who cared to discover them; in any case, one day the pampered hunger artist found himself deserted by the pleasure-seeking masses, who preferred to go in their droves to gaze at other spectacles. Once again the impresario chased through half Europe with him to see if the old interest might not be rediscovered here or there; all in vain; as if by some secret understanding, an outright revulsion against hungering for show had developed everywhere. Of course, in reality it could not have arrived like that all of a sudden, and now in retrospect they recalled a number of portents which they had in the headiness of success not heeded well enough at the time, nor dealt with well enough, but it was too late to do anything to counteract it now. True, one day the time for hungering would certainly return again, but for the living that was no consolation. What was the hunger artist supposed to do now? The performer who had been surrounded by the cheering of thousands could not make a display of himself in the booths of village fairs, and the hunger artist was not only too old to take up another calling, but was above all too fanatically devoted to hungering. So he dismissed the impresario, companion of a career without compare, and accepted an engagement with a big circus; to spare his delicate sensibility, he did not cast a single glance at the conditions in his contract.

A big circus, with its countless human beings and animals and apparatus, can find a use for anyone at any time, including a hunger artist with his, of course appropriately modest, demands, and besides, in this particular case it wasn't just the hunger artist himself who was being engaged, but also his name, famous from old times. Indeed, given the peculiar nature of his art, which did not diminish with increasing age, one could not even say that an old trouper past his prime was taking refuge in a quiet circus job; on the contrary, the hunger artist declared, entirely credibly, that his hungering was just as good as it used to be, indeed, he even declared that if they would let him have his way—and this they promised him without more ado—he would actually, now for the first time, give the world cause for justified astonishment, an assertion, however, which, given the temper of the times, brought only a smile from the professionals.

Deep down, though, even the hunger artist did not lose his sense of the real state of affairs, and he took it for granted that they did not exactly set him up as the star number with his cage in the middle of the ring, but outside, in a position—one otherwise perfectly accessible—near the stables. Big coloured signs framed the cage, announcing what was to be seen there. During the intervals in the shows, when the public surged to the stables to view the animals, it was almost impossible for them to avoid passing by the hunger artist and pausing there for a moment; they might have stayed longer with him if the crowds coming after them, not understanding this pause on the way to the eagerly awaited stables, had not made longer, peaceful contemplation impossible. This was also the reason why, when these visiting times came round, which naturally as his life's purpose he longed for, the hunger artist would tremble nevertheless. In the early days he could hardly wait for the intervals; he had looked with delight towards the masses as they thronged forward, until only too soon—even the most stubborn, almost conscious self-deception could not withstand what he experienced so often—he became convinced that they were, most of them intentionally, over and over again, without exception, nothing more than visitors to the stables. And this view of them from a distance still remained the best one. For when they came right up to his cage, the shouts and curses of the constantly shifting factions instantly stormed around him, the ones—the hunger artist soon found these more embarrassing than the rest—who wanted to look at him at their ease, not out of sympathy, but on a whim and just to be stubborn, and the second group, who most of all just wanted to get to the animals. Once the main crowd was over, then came the stragglers, but although these were no longer being prevented from stopping for as long as they liked, they went hurrying past, taking long strides, almost without a side glance, so as to reach the animals in good time. And it was a none-too-frequent happy chance when the father of a family came along with his children, and would point with his finger at the hunger artist, explaining in detail what it was all about, telling of earlier years when he had attended similar, but incomparably more impressive, performances, and then the children, lacking the satisfactory grounding from school or from life, would still, it is true, remain uncomprehending—what did hungering mean to them?—but in spite of that would still reveal in the brightness of their inquiring eyes something of new, more merciful times to come. Perhaps, the hunger artist would sometimes tell himself then, everything would get slightly better if his position were not quite so near the stables. That made the choice too easy for people, to say nothing of how much the smell from the stables, the restlessness of the animals at night, the raw meat carried past him for the beasts of prey, the howling at feeding-time, offended and constantly depressed him. But to make representations to the management was too much for him to dare; in any case he was beholden to the beasts for the mass of visitors, among whom there might be someone meant for him; and who knew where they might hide him if he were to remind them of his existence, which would also remind them that he was, strictly speaking, only an obstacle on the way to the stables.

A small obstacle, it is true, an obstacle which was becoming smaller and smaller. People became used to how strange it was in the present day to expect attention to be paid to a hunger artist, and with this familiarity the verdict on him was pronounced. Well might he hunger as much as he would and could—and he did—but nothing could save him further; they passed him by. Just try to explain to someone the art of hungering! Anyone who doesn't feel it, can't be brought to understand it.* The beautiful signs became dirty and illegible. People tore them down, no one thought to replace them; the little board registering the number of hunger-days completed, which in the beginning had been renewed daily with care, had long remained unchanged, for after the first weeks the attendants had had enough of even this small chore; and so, it is true, the hunger artist went on hungering as he had once dreamed of doing, and he succeeded effortlessly, just as he had foretold at the time, but no one counted the days, no one, not even the hunger artist himself, knew the scale of his achievement so far, and his heart grew heavy. And if once in a while some idle stroller stopped and made fun of the old figures and spoke of fraud, it was in this sense the most stupid lie it was possible for indifference and inborn malice to invent, for it was not the hunger artist who cheated—he laboured honestly—but the world cheated him of his reward.

But many more days passed, and that too came to an end. One day a supervisor happened to notice the cage, and asked the servants why this perfectly good cage with its rotten straw, which they could put to good use, had been left empty; no one knew, until someone, helped by the board and its figures, remembered the hunger artist. They poked at the straw with poles and found the hunger artist. 'What, you're still hungering?' asked the supervisor. 'When are you going to stop?' 'Forgive me everyone,' whispered the hunger artist; only the supervisor, who had his ear to the cage, could understand his words. 'Of course,' said the supervisor, pointing his finger at his forehead, as a sign to the attendants of the hunger artist's state of mind, 'we forgive you.' 'I always wanted you to admire my hungering,' said the hunger artist. 'And we do admire it,' said the supervisor, obligingly. 'But you shouldn't admire it,' said the hunger artist. 'Well, then we won't admire it,' said the supervisor. 'Why shouldn't we admire it?' 'Because I have to hunger; I cannot do otherwise,' said the hunger artist. 'Well, now,' said the supervisor, 'why can't you do otherwise?' 'Because,' said the hunger artist, lifting his frail head slightly and speaking with lips puckered as if for kissing, right into the supervisor's ear so that not a word was lost, 'because I could not find the food that was to my taste. If I had found it, believe me, I would not have caused a stir, and would have eaten my fill, like you and everybody else.' These were his last words, but his exhausted eyes still held the firm, though no longer proud, conviction that he was still continuing to hunger.

'Now clear up, let's have some order!' said the supervisor, and they buried the hunger artist along with the straw. But into the cage they put a young panther. It was a recovery that even the bluntest of senses could feel, to see this wild beast leaping around in the cage that had been desolate for so long. It lacked for nothing. The keepers did not have to reflect for long about bringing it the sustenance that was to its taste; it didn't even seem to miss its freedom; this noble body, equipped nearly to bursting with all the necessaries, seemed to carry its freedom around with it too; it seemed to have it hidden somewhere in its teeth; and its joy of life came with such fiery breath from its jaws that it wasn't easy for the spectators to resist it. But they held out, surged around the cage, and wouldn't stir from the spot.

Josefine, the Singer or The Mouse-People

OUR singer is called Josefine. If you haven't heard her, you do not know the power of song. There is no one who is not carried away by her singing—something that counts so much the more, as on the whole our kind has no love of music. To us the sweetest music is the stillness of peace. Our life is hard; even when we have tried to cast off all our daily cares for once, we can no longer rise to things that are as remote from the rest of our life as music is. But we do not greatly complain about it, we don't even get that far; a certain practical guile, which, it's true, we have a pressing need for as well, is in our view our greatest asset, and the smile of this cunning is our usual comforting way of getting through everything, even if we were for once—not that it happens—to feel that yearning for happiness which, it may be, flows from music. But Josefine is the exception; she loves music, and she knows how to share it too; she is the only one; with her departure music will—who knows for how long?—disappear from our life.

I've often thought about what there really is to this music. After all, we are completely unmusical; how is it that we understand Josefine's singing, or at least—for Josefine denies that we do understand it—believe we understand it. The simplest answer would be that the beauty of her singing is so great that even the dullest cannot resist it. But this isn't a satisfactory answer. If that were really so, listening to her song, one could not help having the sense—in the beginning and for ever after—that out of this throat something extraordinary is sounding which we have never heard before, and which we are not capable of hearing either, something that only this one-and-only Josefine and no one else enables us to hear. But that, in my opinion, is exactly what is not the case. I don't feel it, and I haven't seen anything of the kind in others either. Among ourselves we admit quite openly that as singing goes, Josefine's singing does not represent anything extraordinary.

Is it in fact singing at all? In spite of our unmusicality, we do have certain traditions of song; in the past ages of our people there was song; our legends tell of it, and some songs have even been preserved, though it's true, no one can sing them any more. So we have a faint idea of what song is, and Josefine's art does not really fit this idea. Is it in fact song at all? Is it perhaps only piping? And of course we are all familiar with piping; it is our people's one real skill, or rather, it is not a skill at all, but a characteristic expression of our life. We all of us pipe, but truly, nobody thinks of claiming it as an art, we pipe without paying any attention to it, indeed, without noticing, and there are even many among us who have no idea at all that piping is among our distinctive characteristics. So if it were true that Josefine doesn't sing, but only pipes, and perhaps doesn't even—at least so it seems to me—go beyond the limits of the usual piping—indeed, perhaps her strength isn't even up to the usual piping, which a common toiler in the earth can do with ease while he is working—if all that were so, it would certainly refute Josefine's claim for her alleged art, but then the riddle of the great effect she has would more than ever demand a solution.

Anyway, it is not just piping that she produces. If you stand some distance away from her and listen, or better still, if you test yourself as you listen, and maybe Josefine is singing among other voices, and you set yourself to recognize her voice, then there is no doubt that you will make out nothing but ordinary piping, noticeable—slightly—at best by the delicacy, or thinness, of its quality. On the other hand, if you are standing right in front of her, it is not merely piping. To understand her art you need not just to hear her, but also to see her. Even if it were only our everyday piping, you are still starting from the curious situation that here is someone ceremoniously presenting herself—in order to do nothing different from the usual thing. Cracking a nut is truly not an art, which is why no one would dare summon an audience before them and, to entertain it, crack nuts. But if someone does so all the same, and it works, then it just can't be a matter of simply cracking nuts. Alternatively, it *is* a matter of cracking nuts, but it turns out that we have ignored this art because we master it so effortlessly, and that this new nut-cracker simply reveals to us the true nature of the art; indeed, it could even be useful for the effect if the performer is a little less competent at cracking nuts than most of us.

Perhaps Josefine's singing is a similar case; we admire in her what we do not admire at all in ourselves; on this point, by the way, she agrees with us completely. I was once present when someone drew her attention, as often happens of course, to the piping common to our people, quite modestly indeed, but for Josefine that was already too much. I have never seen such an insolent, arrogant smile as the one she assumed then; she is, I say, to outward appearance the perfection of delicacy, strikingly delicate even for our kind, which is so rich in women of this type, but at that moment she appeared just plain crude. She may, with her great sensitivity, have felt this at once, and pulled herself together. Anyway, that is how she repudiated any connection between her artistry and our piping. For those who hold the contrary opinion she has only contempt and, it would seem, unacknowledged hatred. This is not ordinary vanity, for the opposition, to which I too half-belong, certainly admires her no less than the crowd does, but Josefine doesn't want to be merely admired, but admired in the particular way she demands; admiration alone means nothing to her. And if you are sitting in front of her, you understand her; being in opposition is only possible at a distance; if you are sitting in front of her, you know: what she is piping here is not piping.

As piping is one of our unthinking habits, you might perhaps expect her audience would pipe up with their own response to her singing; her artistry makes us feel good, and when we're feeling good, we pipe away; but her audience does not pipe up; they are as quiet as mice; we are as silent as if we were sharing in the peace we so long for, and which at least our own piping keeps us from hearing. Is it her

singing that transports us, or rather perhaps the solemn silence surrounding that thin little voice? It once happened that some silly little
thing began to pipe up in all innocence while Josefine was singing.
Well, it was exactly the same as we were hearing from Josefine; up
there in front of us the piping, still hesitant, despite the practised
routine, and down here in the audience the childish peeping, quite
lost to the world; it would be impossible to identify the difference. All
the same we hissed and piped the interrupter into silence, though it
wasn't in the least necessary, for she would surely have crept away in
fear and shame without it, while Josefine struck up her triumphant
piping, quite beside herself, with her arms outspread and a neck that
could not possibly be stretched any higher.

That is how she always is; she will take the slightest incident, any
accident, any awkward moment, creaking in the stalls, teeth grind-
ing, a lighting failure, as an opportunity to heighten the effect of her
singing; indeed, in her opinion she is singing to cloth ears; there is
plenty of enthusiasm and applause, but she has long ago learnt to do
without real understanding, as she sees it. So any kind of disturbance
suits her book; anything from outside that opposes the purity of her
song, that is easily fought and conquered, indeed without her fighting
it, simply by confrontation, can contribute to rousing the crowd and
to teaching it if not understanding, then a dim, though respectful
awareness.

But if the slightest thing can serve her in this way, how much more
so the greatest! Our life is full of disturbances; each day brings something to take us by surprise, alarms, hopes, and terrors, so that one
individual could not possibly endure them all if he did not always,
night and day, have the support of his fellows; but even then it is often
very hard; sometimes even a thousand shoulders tremble beneath the
burden that was only meant for one. That is when Josefine considers
her time has come. She is ready and waiting, the delicate creature,
trembling alarmingly, especially below her breast. It is as if she had
concentrated all her energy in her singing; as if everything in her that
did not directly serve her singing had been drained of all her energies,
almost of every possibility of life; as if she were exposed, abandoned,
given over only to the protection of kindly spirits; as if, while she is
dwelling enraptured in her song, a cold breath brushing past might
kill her. But it is the very sight of her at such a moment that makes us
so-called opponents say to ourselves: 'She can't even pipe; she has to

make such a terrible effort to force—not song, we're not talking about song, but just our usual piping—out of her.' That is how it looks to us, but, as I have already said, this is an impression, unavoidable, it's true, but a fleeting one that quickly passes. We too immerse ourselves in the feelings of the crowd, fervently listening, bodies packed close, hardly daring to breathe.

And in order to gather round her these crowds of our people, who are always on the move, darting to and fro to uncertain purpose, Josefine has to do no more than assume the pose—head flung back, mouth half-open, eyes raised aloft—that indicates that she intends to sing She can do this whenever she wants—it doesn't have to be a space that is visible far and wide—any hidden cranny, chosen on a chance whim of the moment, will do just as well. News that she is about to sing spreads at once, and soon they are thronging there, processions of them. Well, sometimes in spite of everything, obstacles do occur. It is in times of disturbance that Josefine prefers to sing. Trouble and distress of various kinds force us then to take a number of different routes. With the best will in the world it is not easy for us to gather together as quickly as Josefine would wish, and on these occasions she might be posing in her grand attitude for quite some time without a large-enough audience—then of course she will get furious, then she will stamp her feet, curse in a way most unbecoming in a young girl, indeed, she will even bite. But even behaviour like this does not damage her reputation; instead of trying to curtail her excessive demands, the people make the effort to live up to them; messengers are sent out to bring in the audience; they keep it from her that this is happening; that is when you see stewards posted at the waysides round about beckoning to the members of the audience as they draw near, urging them to hurry; all this for as long as it takes until a tolerable number has been gathered together.

What drives the people to go to such lengths for Josefine? A question no easier to answer than the related one that queries Josefine's singing. You could remove it and subsume it entirely into the second question, if it could be said more or less that the people have surrendered absolutely to Josefine's singing. But that is simply not so; absolute surrender is something scarcely known to us; our people, who are above all fond of guile—harmless, of course—childish whispers, chatter, gossip mouthed in silence—innocent, of course—a people of this kind simply cannot surrender itself absolutely anyway.

Very probably Josefine feels this too—it is what she fights against with every effort of her fragile throat.

One shouldn't go too far, though, in making such general judgements; our people are devoted to Josefine nevertheless—only not absolutely. For example, they wouldn't be capable of laughing at Josefine. It may be admitted privately that there's a great deal about Josefine simply asking to be laughed at; and we are by nature never far from laughter; despite all the tribulations of our life, a quiet laugh is always, you might say, at home among us. But we do not laugh at Josefine. I sometimes have the impression that our people think of their relationship to Josefine as one in which this frail, vulnerable creature who is somehow marked out—in her opinion, marked out by her singing—has been given to them in trust, and they would be bound to look after her; no one is clear about why this should be so, only the fact of the matter seems quite certain. But there is no laughing at what has been given to one in trust; laughing would be a breach of duty; ultimately, the most malicious remark that the most malicious among us can make about Josefine is when they sometimes say: 'the sight of Josefine is no laughing matter.'

So the people care for Josefine as a father does, accepting a child who stretches out her little hand towards him—uncertain whether as a plea or a demand. You would think that our people are not fit to fulfil such fatherly duties, but in reality they do perform them, in this case at least, in model fashion. No individual could do what in this respect the people as a whole is capable of doing. Of course, the difference in strength between the people and the individual is so enormous that the people only have to draw their ward into the closeness of their warmth, and she is protected enough. Not that anyone dares to talk to Josefine about such things, though. 'I don't give a hoot for your protection,' she will say then. 'Hoot?' we think, 'You mean squeak.' And besides, this is not refuted, truly, when she rebels, for that is rather just the way children behave and show their gratitude, and it is the way of fathers not to mind.

However, some other factor is also in play that is not so easy to explain by this relationship between the people and Josefine. For Josefine holds quite the contrary opinion. She believes that she is the one who protects the people. It is her song, she claims, that delivers us from a terrible political or economic situation; it brings about nothing less than that; and though it does not banish misfortune, at least it gives us the strength to bear it. She doesn't put it like that, and she doesn't put it differently, she actually says very little anyway, she is silent among all the chatterboxes, but her eyes will flash, it can be understood from the way she will shut her mouth—there are only a few among us who can keep their mouths shut. Whenever the news is bad—and there are many days when such reports come thick and fast, the false and the half-true among them—she will arise at once; though she is usually drawn wearily to the ground, she will arise and crane her neck and attempt to survey her flock like a shepherd before the storm. Certainly, children too make similar claims in their wild, untamed fashion, but in Josefine's case, her claims are not as groundless as theirs. Of course, she doesn't deliver us; she doesn't give us strength; it is easy to build yourself up as the saviour of this people, inured as it is to suffering, unsparing of itself, quick in its decisions, acquainted with death, only seemingly timid in the reckless atmosphere it lives in all the time, and as fecund withal as it is courageous—it is easy, I say, to build yourself up as saviour of this people, which has always somehow managed to save itself, even at the cost of sacrifices that make the historians—in general we neglect historical enquiry entirely—freeze with terror. And yet it is true that above all in times of trouble we are more attentive to Josefine's singing. The threats hanging over us make us quieter, humbler, more submissive to Josefine's bossiness; we are glad to gather together; we are glad to huddle close, especially as the occasion for it is far away from the main thing that is distressing us; it is as if we were hastily drinking—yes, haste is necessary, Josefine forgets that far too often—one last cup of peace together before the battle. It is not so much a song recital as a people's assembly, an assembly which, apart from the thin little piping out in front, is completely still; the hour is far too solemn for us to have any inclination to chatter it away.

A relationship of this kind could certainly not satisfy Josefine, of course. Despite all the nervous unease her ambiguous position causes her, there is still a great deal she doesn't see, blinded as she is by her own sense of herself, and it doesn't take much effort to persuade her to overlook even more; in this respect—one useful to us all, in fact—a swarm of flatterers is busy all the time. But to perform merely from the sidelines, unnoticed, in a corner of an Assembly of the People, she would certainly not sacrifice her song, great though the sacrifice would be, for that.

Nor does she have to, for her artistry does not go unnoticed. Although fundamentally we are still concerned with totally different things, and the silence certainly does not reign only on account of her song, and many do not look up at all, but nestle their faces into their neighbours' fur, so that Josefine seems to labour up there in vain, still, there's no denying, something of her piping does indisputably break through to us. This piping, which rises when silence is enjoined upon everyone else, reaches the individual almost like a message from the people. Josefine's thin pipe in the midst of hard decisions is almost like the miserable existence of our people in the midst of the tumult of a hostile world. Josefine asserts herself; this nothing of a voice, this nothing in achievement of any kind asserts itself and makes its own way to us—it is good to think on that. A really great singing artist, if such a one were to be found among us one day, would be unendurable to us at such a time, and we would unanimously reject the pointlessness of such a performance. Let Josefine be spared seeing that the simple fact that we are listening to her is evidence against her song. She probably has some obscure awareness of this, otherwise why would she refuse so passionately to believe that we listen to her, but she will keep on singing, piping her way over and past this awareness.

But there might be yet another consolation for her: to some extent we do listen to her after all, probably in much the same way as we listen to a great singer; she achieves effects that a great singer would aim for in vain among us, and which are granted only to her inadequate voice. This is likely to be connected mainly to our way of life.

Among our people, youth is something we do not know, scarcely even a brief childhood. It is true, demands are regularly made to grant children a particular freedom, a particular consideration, their right to be carefree for a while, to romp about a little to no purpose, to play a little; we are asked to acknowledge this right and help to fulfil it; such requirements make their appearance and almost everyone approves of them; there is nothing we could approve of more, but there is nothing in the reality of our lives that is less possible to grant; we approve the demands; we try out experiments along those lines; but things quickly revert to old ways. For our life is such that, as soon as a child can take a few steps and begin to make out the world around him, he has to look after himself just like an adult; the regions where, for economic reasons, we have to live scattered are too vast, our enemies are too numerous, the dangers ready for us too incalculable—we cannot keep our children far away from the struggle for existence; if we did, it would be their premature end. These sad reasons are supplemented by one that is uplifting: the fertility of our kind. One generation—and every one is numerous—presses hard upon the other; the children do not have time to be children. The children of other peoples may well be nurtured with care, schools for the little ones may well be set up there, the children there, the people's future, may well come pouring out of these schools, they are still the same children emerging, day in, day out, over a long period. We have no schools, but from our people huge swarms of our children pour out in the shortest of time-spans, merrily cheeping and peeping until they are able to pipe, scrambling or rolling under their own weight until they are able to trot, clumsily carrying all before them by their sheer mass until they are able to see. Our children! And not, as in those other schools, the same children, no, again and again new ones, without end, without interruption. A child has scarcely appeared before it is no longer a child, but behind it new children's faces are already pressing, indistinguishable in their numbers and haste, rosy with joy. Of course, however beautiful this may be, and however much others might justly envy us for it, we are simply unable to give our children a real childhood. And that has its consequences. A certain surviving, ineradicable childishness pervades our people; in direct contradiction to our best characteristic, our infallible common sense, we sometimes act foolishly, in the way children act foolishly, that is, pointlessly, extravagantly, generously, frivolously, and all of it often just for a little joke. And even if naturally our pleasure no longer has the full strength of a child's pleasure, something of theirs is still alive in ours, certainly. And among those who have long profited from this childishness is Josefine.

But our people are not only childish, they are also to some extent prematurely old; childhood and age develop differently among us than among others. We have no youth, straight away we are adults, and then we are adults for too long. A certain weariness and hopelessness arise from this, which pervade the nature of our people and leave their mark, though on the whole we are so tough and strong in hope. Our unmusicality is probably connected to this; we are probably too old for music; the excitement, the lift to the heart it produces is not fitting to our gravity; wearily we wave it away; we have withdrawn into piping; a little piping now and again, that's the right thing for us.

Who knows whether there aren't musical talents among us, but if there are, the character of our fellows is bound to stifle them before they have developed. On the other hand, Josefine can pipe or sing or whatever she wants to call it as she pleases; that suits us; we can live with that very well; if that happens to contain something of music, then it is reduced to the slightest of nullities; a certain musical tradition gets preserved, but without our being in the least encumbered by it.

But Josefine has more to give a people of this temper. At her concerts, particularly in grave times, it is only the very young who are still interested in the singer as singer, only they gaze with astonishment at the way she puckers her lips, exhales the air between her dainty front teeth, swoons in admiration at the sounds she herself is producing, and uses her dying fall to spur herself on to new feats, further and further beyond her own understanding; but the real multitude, it is clear to see, has withdrawn into itself. Here, in the brief pauses between battles, the people dream; it is as if the limbs of each individual relaxed, as if the restless might for once stretch out at his pleasure in the great warm bed of the people. And now and again, Josefine's piping chimes into these dreams; she calls it trilling; we call it puffing-and-panting; but anyway it is in its rightful place here, as it is nowhere else, in the way music hardly ever finds the right moment waiting for it. Something of our poor, brief childhood is in it, something of happiness lost, never to be found again, but something of our busy present life is also in it, something of its small, incomprehensible cheerfulness, which abides and cannot be destroyed. And truly, this is not said in grand tones, but lightly, in a whisper, intimately, sometimes rather hoarsely. Of course it is piping. What else? Piping is the language of our people. Only there are some who pipe all their lives and don't know it. But here, piping is freed of the fetters of daily life, and it also sets us free, for a short while. It is certain: we would not want to miss these performances.

But from this to Josefine's assertion that at such times she gives us new strength and so on and so on, it is still a long way. For ordinary people perhaps, not for Josefine's flatterers. 'How else,' they say quite blatantly, 'how else could you explain the huge crowds she draws, especially in a time of urgent present danger, when this has sometimes even got in the way of making an adequate, timely defence against that very danger.' Now, this is unfortunately true; but it is hardly among Josefine's claims to glory, particularly when you add that when such assemblies were unexpectedly broken up by the enemy and many of our people unavoidably lost their lives, Josefine, who was responsible for it all, who indeed had probably attracted the enemy with her piping, was always in possession of the safest spot, and protected by her hangers-on was the first, very quietly and very hurriedly, to disappear. But deep down everybody knows this too, and in spite of that they will scurry along again on the next occasion, somewhere, at some time, that Josefine chooses to rouse herself to sing. You might conclude from this that Josefine is almost beyond the law, and can do whatever she wants, even if it endangers the group as a whole, and still be forgiven. If this were so, then it would also be possible to understand Josefine's claims, indeed to some extent you might see this freedom the people give her, this extraordinary gift granted to no one else, which is actually counter to the law, as an admission that the people do not understand her, just as she declares they don't, that they are helplessly in awe of her art, feel unworthy of it, and are endeavouring by this almost desperate act to compensate for the suffering they cause her. And, just as her art is beyond their understanding, they have also placed her person and her wishes beyond their authority. That is not at all the right way to put it though. Perhaps as individuals the people do capitulate too quickly to Josefine, but just as the people capitulates unconditionally to no one, it does not capitulate to her either.

For a long time now, perhaps since the beginning of her artistic career, Josefine has been fighting to be free of any kind of work, for the sake of her singing; we ought to relieve her of worrying about her daily bread and of everything else bound up in our struggle for existence, and—in all likelihood—shift the burden on to the people as a whole. A ready enthusiast—and there were some—might conclude, simply from the unusualness of this demand and from the attitude of mind that was capable of thinking up such a thing, that it was inherently justified. But our people draw different conclusions, and calmly reject her demand. They don't take a great deal of trouble over refuting her reasons for making the request either. Josefine points out, for example, that the strain of work damages her voice, that the strain of work is admittedly slight in comparison with the strain of singing, but it deprives her of the opportunity to rest sufficiently after singing and recover her strength for new song, that she would inevitably be utterly

exhausted when she sang, and even if she did, under these circumstances she would never attain her peak of performance. The people
listen to her and ignore it. This people, so easily moved, is sometimes
not to be moved at all. Their dismissal is sometimes so hard that even
Josefine is astonished. She appears to acquiesce, works her stint, sings
as well as she can, but all just for a while, then she takes up the fight
again with new strength—and her strength seems to have no limits.

Now it is clear of course that Josefine is not really aiming at what in
so many words she is demanding. She is reasonable, she is not afraid
of work, indeed being afraid of work is something quite unknown to
us; even if her demand were granted, she would certainly be living no
differently from before, work would not be in the way of her song at
all, and her singing would certainly not become more beautiful
either—so what she is aiming at is simply the public and unambigu-
ous recognition, outliving the ages, transcending all that has been
known before, of her art. Perhaps right from the start she should have
steered her attack in a different direction, perhaps now she can see the
error for herself, but now she is no longer able to retreat, retreat would
mean she would be untrue to herself, now she has to stand or fall with
this demand.

If she really has enemies, as she says she does, she could watch this
struggle and enjoy it without having to stir a finger herself. But she
has no enemies, and even if there are a few who raise objections to her
now and again, no one enjoys this struggle, if only because here the
people appear in their cold, judgemental posture, which is seen in us
only very rarely. And though some individual might approve of this
posture in this particular case, the mere idea that one day the people
might behave like this towards him excludes any pleasure. What is at
issue in their refusal is very similar to what was at issue in her demand:
not the matter itself, but that a people is able to close ranks against
one of its own so impenetrably, all the more impenetrably when
otherwise it looks after that very one with a father's care, indeed, with
more than a father's care, with humility.

If just one man were standing here in place of the whole people,
you might think that he has been giving in to Josefine all along, wishing fervently all the time to put an end to this compliance; he has
given in to her wishes more than is humanly possible in the firm belief
that nevertheless his compliance would find its proper limit; indeed,
he has given in to more than was necessary only so as to bring the

matter to a head, only so as to indulge Josefine and drive her into making more and more demands until she really produced this ultimatum. At that point, though briefly, it is true, because it has been coming for a long time, he has resolved on the definitive refusal. Now, that is most certainly not how it is; the people don't need to use such tactics; their veneration for Josefine is true and tested, and in any case Josefine's demand is so great that any innocent child could tell her how it would end. All the same, it may be that suspicions of this kind played a part in Josefine's own thoughts on the matter, and added bitterness to the rejected singer's pain.

But even if she did have such suspicions, she did not let them frighten her away from the struggle. Recently, it has even intensified; up to now she has waged it only with words, but now she is beginning to use other weapons, which in her opinion are more effective, and in our view are more of a danger to herself.

Many believe Josefine has become so insistent because she senses that she is growing old, and that her voice is showing signs of weakness, and so it seems to her high time to fight the last battle for recognition. I don't believe it. Josefine wouldn't be Josefine it this were true. As she sees it, there is no ageing and no weakness in her voice. When she demands something, she is not driven by externalities, but by an inner logic. She is not reaching for the highest laurels because just at the moment the crown is hanging a little lower, but because they are the highest. If it were in her power, she would hang them even higher.

In any case, this contempt of hers for external difficulties doesn't prevent her from resorting to the most dishonourable means. In her eyes, her rightful claim is beyond all doubt; so what does it matter how she reaches it; particularly when in this world, as she imagines it, it is after all the honourable means above all that are bound to fail. Perhaps it is even the reason why she has transferred the battle for her rights from the field of song to another one, less precious to her. Her hangers-on have circulated remarks of hers declaring that she feels thoroughly capable of singing so that it would give real joy to the people, in all walks of life down to the most underground opposition, real joy, not as the people mean it, for of course they maintain they have always enjoyed Josefine's singing, but the joy that Josefine longs to produce. But, she adds, since she cannot debase the high nor flatter the low, things have to stay as they are. However, it is different when it comes to the struggle for relieving her from work; that too is a struggle on behalf of her singing, but in this case she is not fighting with the precious weapon of her song, so every means she employs is good enough.

So, for example the rumour is put about that if they don't give in to her, Josefine intends to shorten her coloratura passages. I don't know anything about coloratura. I have never detected anything like coloratura in her singing. But Josefine intends to make hers shorter; not, for the time being, remove them, just shorten them. They say she has already carried out her threat, but speaking for myself, I have not noticed any striking difference from her earlier performances. The people as a whole listened as it always does, without remarking on her coloratura, and its treatment of Josefine's demand has not changed either. By the way, at times there is something undeniably charming about her thinking—just as there is in her figure. For example, after that performance, as if her decision regarding her coloratura had been too harsh or too peremptory, she announced that next time she would sing the coloratura passages in full after all. But after the next concert she had second thoughts: now it was time to put an end once and for all to her long passages of grand coloratura, and until a decision in Josefine's favour was reached they would not be coming back. Well, the people pay little attention to all these declarations, decisions, and changes of mind, just as an adult deep in thought will pay little attention to a child's prattle, fundamentally benevolent, but remote.

Josefine, on the other hand, does not give in. Recently, for example, she maintained that she had injured her foot while at work, and this made it difficult for her to stand while singing; but as she could only sing while standing, she was now compelled even to shorten her performances. In spite of her limp and in spite of letting herself be supported by her hangers-on, no one believes she has been really injured. Even allowing for the particular sensitivity of her little body, we are still a working people and Josefine too is one of us; but if we were all to limp on account of every scratch, the entire people would never stop limping. All the same, even though she allows herself to be led along like a cripple, even though she makes her appearance in this pitiful state more often than usual, the people listen to her song with gratitude and delight, as before, but can't be bothered about the shortened performance.

As she can't go on limping for ever, she thinks up something else. She pleads tiredness, distress, fragility. So now as well as a concert we have high drama. Behind Josefine we can see her hangers-on begging her and pleading with her to sing. She would gladly sing, but she simply cannot. She is comforted, flattered, almost carried to the spot—already chosen—where she is supposed to sing. Finally, amid enigmatic tears, she gives in. But, just as she is, obviously with a final effort of will, about to begin, weary, her arms no longer outspread as they used to be, but hanging lifelessly from her body—which gives one the impression that perhaps they are a little too short—just as she is getting ready to sing, well, she can't do it after all, as a reluctant twitch of her head announces, and she sinks to the ground before our eyes. But then in spite of everything she rouses herself again and sings—it's my belief not very differently from usual; perhaps if you have an ear for the subtlest of nuances you can hear a slight, rare, agitation in her song, though that is only of benefit to her cause. And at the end, she is even less tired than before. Firm of step, if that's what you can call her scurrying pitter-patter, she sweeps out, refusing any help from her hangers-on and scrutinizing the crowd with a cold eye, as it reverently makes way for her.

That is how things stood recently, but the latest is that at a point in time when she was expected to sing, she had disappeared. Not only her hangers-on went searching for her, very many rallied to the search. In vain. Josefine has disappeared. She does not want to sing. She does not even want to be asked to sing. This time she has deserted us completely.

Strange, how badly she miscalculates, the clever creature, so badly that you might think she doesn't calculate at all, but is only driven onward by her destiny, which in our world can only be a very sad one. She herself is withdrawing from her song, she herself is destroying the power she has won over our hearts and minds. How was she ever able to win this power, when she has so little understanding of our hearts and minds? She goes into hiding, and refuses to sing. But the people, calmly and without any visible disappointment, masterfully, a unified mass, which literally, even if appearances are against it, can only give gifts, never receive them, not even from Josefine, this people continues on its way.

But with Josefine, things are bound to go downhill. Soon the time will come when her last peep will sound and fall silent. She is a small episode in the eternal story of our people, and we will get over her loss. It will not be easy for us; how will our assemblies be possible, held in total silence? Weren't they silent, though, even with Josefine? Was her real piping truly any louder and livelier than our memory of it will be? Even when she was still alive, was it anything more than a mere memory? Isn't that rather the very reason why our people in their wisdom have placed Josefine's song on such a high pedestal, because in this way it could never be lost?

So perhaps we won't be missing all that much. Josefine, on the other hand, delivered from the earthly torment which in her opinion is the lot of the elect, will lose herself happily in the numberless host of our people's heroes, and, since we don't go in for history, she will soon, redeemed and transfigured, be forgotten, like all her brethren.

Blumfeld, an Elderly Bachelor

ONE evening Blumfeld, an elderly bachelor, was going upstairs to his flat, a laborious climb, for he lived on the sixth floor. As he climbed he thought, as he often had of late, how wearisome was this utterly lonely life he led, how he was obliged to climb these six flights literally in secret now to get to his empty room up there, put on his dressing-gown, again literally in secret, light his pipe, read for a little in the French newspaper he had subscribed to regularly for years, while reading take a sip of the cherry brandy he had made himself, and after half an hour finally go to bed, not without first being obliged to rearrange the bedclothes completely because the cleaning-woman, deaf to any reproof, always flung them around as she pleased. To Blumfeld, any companion, any spectator for these activities would have been most welcome. He had already considered whether he shouldn't get himself a little dog. An animal like that is fun, and above all appreciative and faithful; a colleague of Blumfeld's has a dog like that; he is attached to no one but his master, and if he hasn't seen him for just a minute or two he will promptly greet him with a tremendous barking, by which he obviously wants to express his joy at having found his master, this extraordinary benefactor, once more. On the other hand there are disadvantages about a dog, too. Even if he is kept ever so clean, he will foul the room. There is no way at all to avoid that; you can't give him a hot bath every time you let him into the room, besides, his health wouldn't stand it. But for his part, Blumfeld can't stand having his room fouled; the cleanliness of his room is something indispensable to him; several times a week he has a quarrel with the unfortunately not very punctilious cleaning-woman about it. As she is hard of hearing, he usually drags her by the arm to the places where he has a complaint about cleanliness. By being as strict as this he has managed to have the tidiness of his room come close to what he wants, more or less. But by introducing a dog he would practically of his own free will be bringing in the dirt he had until now so carefully kept at bay. Fleas, a dog's constant companions, would move in. Once fleas were there, it would not be too long before he would abandon his cosy room to the dog and look for another room. But uncleanliness was only one disadvantage in a dog. Dogs also fall ill, and nobody really understands dogs' illnesses. Then the animal will crouch in a corner, or shuffle about, whine, cough, gag on some sharp little pain; you wrap him in a blanket, whistle him a little tune, put some milk in front of him, tend him in the hope that it is only a passing infirmity, which of course is also possible, though on the other hand it could be a seriously nasty, contagious disease. And even if the dog is still healthy, it will still grow old eventually; you won't have felt able to give the faithful creature away in time, and there will come a day when your own age gazes out at you from the rheumy eyes of the dog. Then you will have the worry of a half-blind, wheezing dog, almost immobile with fat, and pay a high price for the pleasure you had from it earlier. However much Blumfeld might want a dog now, he would after all rather climb the stairs for another thirty years alone, instead of being burdened later by an old dog like that, who would drag himself up the stairs at his side, gasping louder than Blumfeld himself.

So Blumfeld will remain alone like this after all. He has nothing like the desires of an old maid who wants to have a living creature of some sort subordinate to her that she can shelter, cosset, which will always be at her service, so that for this purpose a cat, a canary, or even a bowl of goldfish will be enough for her. And if that cannot be, then she will be content with flowers outside her window. Blumfeld, by contrast, wants only someone at his side, an animal he doesn't have to worry about too much, which is not harmed by the occasional kick, which if needs be can also spend the night in the street, but which, whenever Blumfeld wants it, is at his disposal right away, barking, jumping, licking his hand. Something of that kind is what Blumfeld wants, but because, as he sees, he can't have it, he does without; still, being ruminant by nature, from time to time—this evening for instance—he comes back again to the same thought.

At the top, as he is taking his key out of his pocket, he notices a noise coming from his room. A peculiar clattering noise, but very lively, very regular. Since Blumfeld has just been thinking about dogs, it reminds him of the sound of paws pattering one after another on the floor. But paws don't clatter; it's not paws. He opens the door swiftly and turns on the electric light. The sight catches him unprepared. But this is a conjuring trick! Two little celluloid balls, white with blue stripes, are jumping up and down next to each other on the parquet floor; when one hits the ground, the other is in the air, and they carry on their game* without tiring. Once, when he was at school, Blumfeld had seen little globes leaping like this in a well-known electricity experiment, but the present balls are big in comparison, they are leaping in the open room, and there is no electricity experiment set up. Blumfeld bends down to them to look at them more closely. There is no doubt, they are ordinary balls; they probably contain a few smaller balls inside them, and these are producing the clattering noise. Blumfeld grasps into the air, to make sure that they are not perhaps hanging from any threads; no, they are moving quite independently. A pity that Blumfeld is not a small child, two balls like these would be a pleasant surprise for him, while now the whole thing makes more of an unpleasant impression on him. It is after all not entirely without merit to live only in secret as an unnoticed bachelor; now someone, no matter who, has brought the secret out into the open and sent him these two peculiar balls.

He tries to grab one, but they back away from him and lure him after them into the room. 'It's too silly,' he thinks, 'running after the balls like this.' He stops, and follows them with his eyes, seeing how, now that he seems to have given up pursuing them, they too stay on the same spot. 'I'll try and catch them all the same,' he thinks again, and dashes up to them. At once they take flight, but with legs outspread Blumfeld drives them into a corner, and in front of the trunk standing there he manages to catch one. The ball is cool and small, and wriggles in his hand, obviously anxious to escape. And the other ball too, as if he sees his companion in trouble, bounces higher than before, making the bounces higher and higher until he touches Blumfeld's hand. He strikes at this hand, strikes again, leaps faster and faster, changes his point of attack and, as he cannot do anything about the hand holding the other ball, bounces even higher, trying, apparently, to reach Blumfeld's face. Blumfeld could catch this ball too, and lock both of them up somewhere, but at the moment it seems to him too demeaning to resort to such measures against two little balls. After all, it's fun to have two little balls, and they'll soon get sufficiently tired to roll underneath a cupboard and leave him in peace. But in spite of this thought, Blumfeld dashes the ball to the ground in a kind of rage; it is a miracle that the thin, almost transparent celluloid skin doesn't smash to bits. Without transition, the two balls resume their earlier low-level bouncing in tune and time with each other.

Blumfeld undresses calmly, arranges his clothes tidily in the wardrobe—it is his habit to check closely to see if the woman has left everything in order. Once or twice he looks over his shoulder for the balls, which, now that they are not being pursued, even appear to be pursuing him; they have followed him and they are now bouncing right behind him. Blumfeld puts on his dressing-gown and tries to go across to the opposite wall to fetch one of his pipes, which are hanging there on a pipe-stand. Instinctively he gives a kick behind him before he turns round, but the balls know how to avoid it, and his foot misses them. Now when he makes for his pipe, the balls promptly latch on to him, he drags his slippered feet, takes irregular steps; nevertheless every step he takes is accompanied almost without interval by a bounce of the balls, they are keeping in step with him. Blumfeld turns round unexpectedly to see how the balls manage to do that. But he has scarcely turned round before the balls describe a semicircle and already they are behind him once again; and whenever he turns round they repeat it. Like inferior companions, they try to avoid stopping in front of Blumfeld. Until now, so it seems, they only dared do so to introduce themselves, but now they have already begun acting like servants.

Up until now, in any exceptional situation which was beyond his powers to control, Blumfeld has always chosen the expedient of behaving as if he had noticed nothing. It has often helped and in most cases at least improved the situation. So that is how he behaves now too; standing in front of the pipe-stand, his lips pursed, he selects a pipe, fills it with particular care from the waiting tobacco-pouch, and nonchalantly lets the balls go on with their leaping behind him. But he is slow to go back to his table. It almost gives him pain to hear their bounces keeping time with his steps. So he stays standing there, filling his pipe for an unnecessarily long time and examining the distance that separates him from the table. In the end he overcomes his weakness, and covers the length of the floor with such a stamping of his feet that he cannot hear the balls at all. However, when he sits down they are jumping behind his chair again, audible, as before.

Above the table, within arm's reach, a shelf has been fixed to the wall with the bottle of cherry brandy on it, surrounded by little glasses. Lying next to it there is a pile of his French newspapers. But instead of getting down everything he needed, Blumfeld sits still, looking into the bowl of his unlit pipe. He is on the alert; suddenly, quite unexpectedly, he relaxes his rigid position and in one sudden movement he and his easy-chair turn round. But the balls too are just as watchful, or else they are mindlessly following the law that governs them; at exactly the same time as Blumfeld turns round, they change their position too and hide behind his back. So now Blumfeld sits with his back to the table, the cold pipe in his hand. The balls are now bouncing under the table, and, because there is a rug there, there is very little to hear. That is a great improvement; there are only quite faint, dull sounds; one has to attend very closely to catch the sound in one's ear. Blumfeld, though, is very attentive and can hear them perfectly well. Probably after a little while he won't hear them any longer. Their inability to draw much attention to themselves on carpets seems to Blumfeld to be a great weakness in the balls. All one has to do is lay one, or better, two rugs underneath them and they are almost powerless. Only for a while, though, and besides, their mere existence already means a certain power.

Now Blumfeld could really use a dog, a young untrained animal would make quick work of the balls; he imagines the dog catching them in his paws, driving them from their places, chasing them up and down the room and in the end getting them between his teeth. It is very possible that before long Blumfeld will get himself a dog.

But for the moment the balls have only Blumfeld to fear, and he has no desire to destroy them now; it may be that he also lacks the resolution for it. In the evenings he comes home tired from work, and now, when he needs his peace and quiet so badly, he is greeted by this surprise. It is only now that he feels how tired he actually is. He will certainly destroy the balls, and do it soon, but not for the moment and probably not until tomorrow. If one looks at the whole thing without prejudice, the balls are behaving discreetly enough. They could, for instance, jump out, reveal themselves, and then go back to their corner, or they could jump higher and bang on the table-top to make up for having their sounds muffled by the rug. But they don't do that; they don't want to irritate Blumfeld needlessly; they are obviously confining themselves to the necessary minimum.

All the same, this necessary minimum is enough to ruin Blumfeld's respite at his table. He sits there only for a few minutes, thinking about going to bed already. One of his reasons is also that he can't smoke here because he has put the matches on his bedside table. So he would have to fetch the matches, but once he is at his bedside table, it is probably better to stay there and lie down. At the back of his mind he also had another thought: he believes that in their blind obsession with staying behind him all the time, they will bounce onto the bed, and that when he lies down, he will squash them there willy-nilly. The objection that even what was left of the balls would still be able to bounce he rejects out of hand. Even the extraordinary must have its limits. Balls that are all in one piece bounce on other occasions too; fragments of balls, on the contrary, never do, and they won't bounce here either.

'Up!' he cries, made almost defiant by the thought, and he stamps to bed, again with the balls behind him. His hopes seem to be confirmed; just as he stands deliberately close to the bed, one ball promptly jumps up on to it. On the other hand, the unexpected happens, and the other ball betakes itself under the bed. The possibility that the balls could also jump under the bed had simply not occurred to Blumfeld. He is quite indignant at the one ball, in spite of feeling how unjust that is, for by jumping under the bed, perhaps the ball is doing its job much better than the ball on the bed. Now everything depends on which place the balls decide on, for Blumfeld doesn't believe that they can work for long apart. And in fact, the very next moment the other ball leaps up onto the bed too. 'Now I've got them,' thinks Blumfeld, flushed with pleasure, flinging his dressing-gown from his body to hurl himself into bed, but straight away the same ball jumps under the bed again. In an excess of disappointment, Blumfeld practically collapses. The ball had probably just looked around up there, and didn't like what he saw. And now the other one follows him too and of course stays down there, because it's better down there. 'Now I'll have these drummers here for the whole night,' thinks Blumfeld, biting his lips together and nodding his head.

He is sad, though he doesn't actually know what the balls had in their power to do to him that night. He is an excellent sleeper; he can easily cope with the slight noise they might make. To make quite sure, in view of what he had just learned he pushes two rugs under them. It is as if he had a little dog and wanted to make a cosy, soft bed for it. And as if the balls too were tired and sleepy, their leaping was also lower and slower than before. As Blumfeld kneels at his bed and shines his bedside lamp underneath, he thinks once or twice that the balls will remain lying on the rugs for ever, they fall so feebly, they roll a little way so slowly. It's true, though, afterwards they dutifully rise up again. But it is easily possible that in the morning, when Blumfeld looks under the bed, he will find two children's balls there lying harmless and still.

But they seem unable to keep up their leaping, not even until morning, for the moment Blumfeld is lying in bed, he can no longer hear them. He strains to hear them, leans out of bed to listen—not a sound. The rugs can't be that effective; the only explanation for why the balls are no longer leaping is that they can't get enough purchase on the soft rugs to take off and so they have temporarily given up; alternatively, though—which is more likely—they will never leap again. Blumfeld could get up and see what the situation actually is, but content with peace and quiet at last, he prefers to stay lying there; now that the balls have settled down, he doesn't want to touch them, not even with a glance. He doesn't even mind going without smoking for the night, and turning on his side, he goes to sleep straight away.

But he does not remain undisturbed. Now too, as usual, his sleep is dreamless, but very restless. Countless times in the night he starts up, roused by the illusion that someone is knocking at the door. He also knows quite definitely that no one is knocking; who should be knocking at night at his lonely bachelor door? But although he knows this quite definitely, he starts up again and again, looking for a moment towards the door, tense and expectant, open-mouthed, wide-eyed, with his hair flopping onto his damp brow. He makes an attempt to count how often he has been wakened, but stunned by the enormous numbers that result, he falls asleep once more. He believes he knows where the knocking is coming from; it doesn't come from the door, but somewhere quite different, though he is so overcome by sleep that he can't remember why he should suppose so. He only knows that it takes many tiny, nasty little taps before they produce this loud, strong knocking. But he would be prepared to put up with all the nastiness of the little taps if he could avoid the knocking, but for some reason it is too late, he can't intervene, the opportunity is lost, he hasn't even words, his mouth opens only for a silent yawn, and he thumps his face into the pillows in his fury. That is how the night passes.

Next morning he is woken by the knocking of the cleaning-woman; with a sigh of release he welcomes the gentle knocking, though he had always complained about how inaudible it was. He is about to call 'Come in,' when he also hears another, different knocking, quiet, but downright aggressive. It's the balls under the bed. Have they woken up? Unlike himself, have they gathered new strength overnight? 'Coming,' Blumfeld calls to the woman; he jumps out of bed, cautiously though, so that he keeps the balls behind him; he flings himself to the floor, still with his back turned to them; twisting his head he looks for the balls—and almost wants to curse. Like children who have thrown off their horrid blankets in the night, the balls have, most likely by making repeated little jerks all through the night, pushed the rugs so far under the bed and out the other side that they themselves have parquet flooring beneath them, and are able to make a racket. 'Back onto the rugs,' says Blumfeld, scowling. Only when the balls have been silenced again thanks to the rugs, does he call the woman in. While she puts his breakfast on the table, and goes through the few motions necessary, this fat, dull-witted, stiff, straight-backed female, Blumfeld stands motionless at the side of the bed in his dressing-gown so as to keep the balls confined down there. He follows the cleaning-woman with his eyes to see if she notices anything. Deaf as she is, that's most unlikely, and Blumfeld puts it down to his being overwrought from too little sleep when he thinks he sees the woman pause now and again, hold on to some item of furniture, and listen, raising her eyebrows. He would be glad if he could get the woman to hurry up with her work, but she is if anything slower than usual. Fussing over each one, she loads herself up with Blumfeld's clothes and boots, and trails out into the corridor with them; she stays away a long time; the blows with which she belabours the clothes outside seem monotonous, each one quite isolated, as they sound across to him. And all this time Blumfeld has to hold out on his bed, mustn't move unless he wants to take the balls along behind him, and, though he likes to drink his coffee as hot as possible, has to let it grow cold, able to do nothing but stare at the lowered curtain on the window while behind it day is gloomily dawning. At last the woman is finished. She wishes him a good morning and is about to go. But before she finally takes off, she lingers at the door, moves her lips a little, and gives Blumfeld a long look. Blumfeld is about to take her to task when in the end she goes. What Blumfeld wants most is to fling open the door and scream after her what a stupid old dull-witted female she is. But when he considers what he actually has to object to in her, he can only discover the logical contradiction that she has undoubtedly noticed nothing and yet she wanted to give the impression that she had noticed something. How confused his thoughts are! And only from a bad night's sleep! He finds a small explanation for his broken sleep: yesterday evening he had departed from his usual habits and had not smoked, nor drunk his brandy. 'Whenever I don't smoke, nor drink my brandy, I sleep badly.' That is the final outcome of his reflections.

From now on he will pay more attention to his well-being, and begins by taking some cotton-wool from his medicine-cupboard, which is hung above his bedside table, and stopping his ears with two little plugs of cotton-wool. Then he stands up and takes a step by way of experiment. The balls do follow him, but they are almost impossible to hear; another bit of cotton-wool will make them completely inaudible. Blumfeld takes another few steps and things go without any particular discomfort. Each is on his own, Blumfeld and the balls alike; it's true, they are bound to each other, but they do not bother each other. Only once, when Blumfeld turns round more quickly and one ball is not able to make the counter-movement quickly enough, Blumfeld bumps his knee against him. That is the only accident; for the rest, Blumfeld drinks his coffee tranquilly; he is hungry not as if he had slept badly that night, but as if he had come a long way; he washes in cold, uncommonly refreshing water, and gets dressed. Up till now he hasn't opened the curtains, preferring out of caution to remain in semi-darkness; he doesn't need a stranger's eyes to see the balls. But just when he is ready to go out, in case they should dare—not that he thinks they will—he must somehow see to it that they don't follow him out into the street. He has a good idea for dealing with this: he opens the large wardrobe and plants himself with his back towards it. As if the balls had an inkling of his intention, they avoid the inside of the wardrobe; they use the small space between his back and the wardrobe and bounce, if there's nothing else for it, into the wardrobe for a moment, but immediately fly out again to escape the dark; they can't be persuaded any further than the threshold of the wardrobe; they would rather offend against their duty and almost cling to Blumfeld's side. But their little tricks shan't do them any good, for now Blumfeld himself steps backwards into the wardrobe and they will have to follow after all. This seals their fate, for there were various smaller objects lying on its floor, such as boots, boxes, small suitcases, which are all—Blumfeld regrets it now—perfectly tidy, but on the other hand get in the balls' way. And now, as Blumfeld, who has meanwhile almost closed the door, takes a great leap of the kind he hasn't done for years out of the wardrobe, and shutting the door tight, turns the key, the balls are locked inside. 'I managed it,' thinks Blumfeld, wiping the sweat from his face. What a noise the balls make in the wardrobe! It gives the impression that they are desperate. Blumfeld on the other hand is content. He leaves his room, and even the dreary corridor has a kindly effect upon him. He frees his ears of the cotton-wool, and the many sounds of the building as it wakes fill him with delight. He sees only a few people, it is still very early.

Down in the hall, outside the low doorway leading to the basement flat where his cleaning-woman lives, stands her small ten-year-old boy. The image of his mother, not one of the old woman's hideous features have been forgotten in this childish face. Bandy-legged, his hands in his trouser pockets, he stands there puffing and panting because at his age he already has goitre, and can only breathe with difficulty. But whereas at other times when Blumfeld comes upon the boy, he starts to walk faster to spare himself the spectacle as far as possible, today he is almost inclined to linger with him. Even if the boy was brought into the world by this woman and bears all the signs of his origins, he is for the present only a child after all; inside this ill-shaped head are a child's thoughts after all; if one were to speak to him sensibly and ask him something, he would probably answer innocently and respectfully in a clear, high voice, and after a small struggle you might be able to pat even these cheeks. That is what Blumfeld is thinking, but he walks past all the same. Out in the street he notices that the weather is kinder than he had thought when he was in his room. The morning mists part and patches of blue sky appear, blown clean by strong wind. Blumfeld has the balls to thank that he has come out of his room earlier than usual; he has even left his newspaper behind, unread on the table; anyway it has given him much more time, so he can now walk along slowly. It is remarkable how little he worries about the balls. As long as they were chasing after him, one could regard them as something belonging to him, something that in judging him as a person had also to be taken into account; now, on the other hand, they were just a toy at home in his wardrobe. As he thinks about it, it occurs to Blumfeld that he could neutralize the balls by steering them towards their proper vocation. The boy is still standing in the hall. Blumfeld will make him a gift of the balls, not just lend them, but explicitly give them, which is surely as good as bidding him destroy them. And even if they remain in one piece, still, in the boy's hands they will mean even less than they do in the wardrobe; the entire building will see the boy playing with them, other children will join in, the general view that these are balls to play with, and not what you might call Blumfeld's life-companions, will become immovable and irresistible. Blumfeld runs back into the building. The boy has just gone down the cellar steps and is about to open the door down below. So Blumfeld has to call the boy, and utter his name, which, like everything related to this boy, is ridiculous. He does it. 'Alfred, Alfred,' he calls. The boy hesitates for a long time. 'Do come up,' Blumfeld calls, 'I've a present for you.' The caretaker's two little girls come out of the door opposite, and plant themselves inquisitively to Blumfeld's right and left. They catch on much more quickly than the boy, and can't understand why he doesn't come up right away. They beckon to him, not letting Blumfeld out of their sight as they do, but they can't make out what kind of present Alfred is expecting. Hopping from one foot to the other, they are racked by curiosity. They make Blumfeld laugh as much as the boy does, who seems to have sorted it all out at last, and stiffly, clumsily, climbs the stairs. He hasn't even managed to throw off his mother's way of walking; she, incidentally, makes an appearance at the cellar door down below. Blumfeld shouts, his voice overloud, so that the woman too can understand him, and, if necessary, can keep an eye on the performance of his errand. 'Upstairs,' says Blumfeld, 'I have two fine balls in my room. Would you like to have them?' The boy merely screws up his mouth; he doesn't know how to respond; he turns round and looks questioningly down at his mother. The girls on the other hand immediately begin to bounce around Blumfeld and beg him for the balls. 'You can play with them too,' Blumfeld says to them, but still waits for the boy to answer. Meanwhile, without a word being exchanged, the boy has asked his mother for her advice, and nods in assent when Blumfeld asks again. 'Now pay attention,' says Blumfeld, who gladly overlooks the fact that he is not going to get any thanks here for his present. 'Your mother has the key to my room; you must borrow it from her; this key that I'm giving you is the key to my wardrobe, and in this wardrobe are the balls. Be careful, and lock the wardrobe and the room after you. But you can do what you want with the balls, and you don't have to bring them back. Have you understood me?' But unfortunately the boy has not understood. Blumfeld wanted to make everything particularly clear to this boundlessly thick-witted creature, but consequently, he simply repeated everything too often, now keys, now room, now wardrobe, and as a result the boy stares at him as if he were not a benefactor but a seducer. The girls, though, have understood everything at once, pressing close to Blumfeld and stretching out their hands for the keys. 'Wait,' says Blumfeld, already annoyed at them all. And time is passing, he can't stop any longer. If only the woman would finally say that she has understood him and will attend to it all for the boy. Instead of that, she is still standing down there, with the false smile of someone ashamed of being deaf, thinking perhaps that Blumfeld has taken a sudden fancy to her boy and is testing him on his tables up there at the top of the house. Blumfeld for his part really cannot go down the cellar steps and shout in the woman's ear, begging her for God's sake to let her boy set him free of the balls. It was as far as he could go to force himself into entrusting this family with the key to his wardrobe for the day. It's not to spare himself that he is offering the boy the key down here instead of taking him upstairs himself and handing over the balls to him there. But he really can't first give the balls away and then, as he foresaw was bound to happen, immediately take them from the boy again because he was drawing them along behind him as his retinue. 'So you don't understand me?' says Blumfeld, almost melancholy, after he embarked on a fresh explanation, but then beneath the boy's vacant gaze broke off again at once. A vacant gaze like that robs one of one's defences. It could tempt one to say more than one wants, only in order to fill this vacancy with intelligence.

'We'll fetch him the balls,' the girls cry. They are crafty, they have perceived that they can only obtain the balls somehow by way of the boy, but they will still have to bring this about themselves. A clock strikes from the caretaker's house, reminding Blumfeld to hurry up. 'You take the key, then,' says Blumfeld, not so much handing over the key as having it snatched from his hand. The certainty with which he would have given the key to the boy would have been incomparably greater. 'Get the key to the room from the good woman down below,' Blumfeld adds, 'and when you come back with the balls, you must give both keys to her.' 'Yes, yes,' cry the girls, running down the steps. They know everything, absolutely everything, and as though Blumfeld had been infected by the boy's thick wits he can't understand himself how quickly they have caught on to everything.

Now they are already downstairs, tugging at the cleaning-woman's skirt, but, tempting as it might be, Blumfeld cannot stay and watch how they will carry out their errand, not just because it is already late, but also because he doesn't want to be present when the balls are set free. He even wants to be some streets away when the girls first open the doors to his room up there. He has no idea at all what he can still expect from the balls! And so for the second time this morning he goes out into the open. The last he saw was the woman literally defending herself against the girls, and the boy was stirring his bandy legs to come to his mother's help. Blumfeld cannot understand why people like the cleaning-woman flourish in this world and multiply.

In the course of his way to the underwear factory where Blumfeld holds a position, thoughts of work gradually prevail over everything else. He quickens his steps, and in spite of the delay caused by the boy he is the first in his office. This office is a small room closed in by glass; it contains a writing-desk for Blumfeld and two high desks for the trainees under him. Although these high desks are as small and narrow as if they were meant for children, space is still very restricted in the office, and the trainees cannot sit down because then there would be no room for Blumfeld's chair. So they stand all day pressed close to their desks. That is certainly very uncomfortable for them, and also makes it difficult for Blumfeld to keep an eye on them. They often press up to their desks not to do any work but to whisper together or even to nod off. Blumfeld has a lot of trouble with them. They do not give him nearly enough support for the gigantic amount of work he is given to do. This work requires him to deal with the entire exchange of goods and cash with the home-workers who are employed by the factory to make certain finer products. To be in a position to judge the scale of this work, one has to have a greater insight into the overall situation. Ever since Blumfeld's immediate superior died a few years ago, however, no one left has possessed this insight, so Blumfeld cannot concede that anyone is justified in passing a judgement on his work either. The owner of the factory, Herr Ottomar, for example, obviously undervalues Blumfeld's work; naturally he recognizes the merit that Blumfeld has earned in the factory in the course of twenty years, not only because he has to, but also because he respects Blumfeld as a loyal, trustworthy person; but he undervalues his work all the same; he believes it could be organized more simply and hence in every respect more efficiently than Blumfeld arranges things. They say, and it is not implausible, that Ottomar shows up in Blumfeld's department so rarely just to spare himself the annoyance that the sight of Blumfeld's working methods causes him. To be misjudged in this way is certainly sad for Blumfeld, for after all he cannot

force Ottomar to spend, say, a month on end in Blumfeld's department to study the various kinds of work that have to be dealt with
here, apply his own allegedly better methods, and only then, following the department's collapse, which would be the inevitable consequence of all this, allow himself to be convinced by Blumfeld. So that
is why Blumfeld carries on with his work as blandly as before, and is
slightly startled when after a long interval Ottomar puts in an appearance; then, with the sense of duty of the subordinate, Blumfeld does
make a slight attempt at explaining to Ottomar this or that particular
set-up, whereupon the latter moves on with a silent nod and lowered
eyes, while Blumfeld is otherwise troubled not so much by this mis-
judgement as by the thought that if once he had to step down from his
position the immediate consequence would be vast confusion impossible for anyone to disentangle, for he knows no one in the factory who
could replace him and take over his position in a way that throughout
the months would avoid no more than the worst hold-ups. When the
head of a firm undervalues someone, then the employees tend to go
one better than him whenever they can. Hence everybody undervalues Blumfeld's work, nobody sees working in Blumfeld's department as essential to his training, and when new employees are taken
on, nobody is allotted to Blumfeld of his own accord. Consequently
there are no young successors for Blumfeld's department. There were
weeks of bitter struggle when Blumfeld, who had until then taken
care of everything in the department entirely on his own solely with
the support of one old odd-job man, demanded the appointment of
one trainee. Almost every day he would appear in Ottomar's office
and explain calmly and in detail why it was necessary to have one
trainee in this department. A trainee isn't necessary, he would explain,
because of any wish to spare himself work, he does his more-than-full
stint and has no thought of stopping, but Herr Ottomar really must
consider how the business has developed in the course of time, all the
departments have expanded in line with this, Blumfeld's department
is the only one to be forgotten. And how much the work has increased,
there above all! When Blumfeld first took up his post—Herr Ottomar
certainly won't remember those times—they had about ten sewing-
women to deal with there, now their number hovers between fifty
and sixty. Work like that requires energy. Blumfeld can guarantee that
he is wearing himself out with this work completely, but from now
on he can no longer guarantee that he can cope with it completely.

Now Herr Ottomar certainly never refused Blumfeld's submissions directly, he couldn't do that to an old member of the firm, but the way he had hardly listened, talking to other people across Blumfeld and his requests, half-assented to them and then after a few days had forgotten them—this was quite insulting. Not actually to Blumfeld; Blumfeld is not a fantasist—however fine honour and recognition may be, Blumfeld can live without them; he will hold out in his position in spite of it all for as long as is in any way possible; in any case, he is in the right, and the right in the end, even if it sometimes takes a long time, must be recognized. And Blumfeld did in fact even get two trainees—but what trainees, though! You might think that Ottomar understood how he could show his contempt for Blumfeld's department more clearly by granting him trainees than by refusing them. It was even possible that Ottomar had kept Blumfeld waiting for so long only because he was looking for two such trainees, and—understandably—was for a long time unable to find them. And now Blumfeld could not make a complaint, for of course the answer was foreseeable: didn't he get two trainees, when he had only asked for one? Ottomar had set it all up so cleverly. But of course Blumfeld did complain, but only because his dire situation positively forced him into it, not because he had any hope of further staff. And he didn't complain explicitly either, but rather only in passing, if a suitable occasion arose. Nevertheless, the rumour soon spread among his ill-wishing colleagues that someone had asked Ottomar whether it was possible that Blumfeld, who had now been given such extraordinary assistance, was still complaining; and Ottomar, it went, had replied that this was correct, Blumfeld was still complaining—but rightly so. He, Ottomar, had understood at last, and bit by bit he intended to allot Blumfeld one trainee for every sewing-woman, that is, about sixty in total. But that if this was still not enough for him, he would send more, and would not stop until the madhouse which had been developing in Blumfeld's department for years was complete. Now it's true, this remark was a good imitation of Ottomar's manner of speaking, but he himself, Blumfeld had no doubt, was far from ever expressing himself in a way even resembling this about Blumfeld's department. The whole thing was an invention of those layabouts in the offices on the first floor. Blumfeld passed over it; if only he could have passed over the trainees so calmly. But there they were, no longer to be moved. Feeble, pale-faced infants. According to their papers they are supposed to be old enough to have left school, but in reality one doubted it. Indeed, one wouldn't even want to entrust them to a teacher, they still belonged so clearly in their mother's care. They couldn't even move sensibly yet; standing for a long time tired them out dreadfully, especially when they first began. If one didn't keep an eye on them, they were so frail their limbs would give way under them at once; they stood in a corner, bent and leaning aslant. Blumfeld tried to make them understand that they would cripple themselves for life if they always yielded to making things easy for themselves in this way. It was a risk to give the trainees some small errand to do; at one time one of them was supposed to carry something for only a few paces; dashing there too eagerly, he knocked his knee against a desk. The room was full of women sewing, the desks were covered in materials, but Blumfeld was obliged to neglect everything, take the tearful trainee into the office, and make him a little bandage. But even this eagerness in the trainees was only superficial; like real children they sometimes wanted to shine, but far more often, or rather almost all the time, they only wanted to fool the sharp eye of their superior, and deceive him. Once, at the height of the working season, Blumfeld was rushing past them, dripping with sweat, and noticed them hidden between two bales of merchandise, exchanging stamps. He wanted to beat them on the head with his fists, it was the only possible punishment for such behaviour, but they were children, and Blumfeld couldn't beat children to death, could he? And so he went on giving himself grief over them. Originally he had imagined that the trainees would assist him in handing out the materials directly during the distribution period, which demanded great vigilance and effort. He had thought he would supervise it all and attend to the entries into the books, while the trainees would follow his orders and run to and fro handing everything out. He had imagined that his supervision, keen though it was, would not be adequate to deal with such a throng and would be supplemented by the vigilance of the trainees, that these trainees would gradually acquire experience, not depend on his orders in every detail, and would finally learn for themselves to distinguish between one sewing-woman and another in the matters of their demand for materials and their reliability. To judge by these trainees, his hopes were utterly empty. Blumfeld soon perceived that he couldn't allow them to talk with the sewing-women at all. They had not gone near many of them from the beginning because they were afraid of them or didn't like their looks; on the other hand there were others, the ones they preferred, they would run to the door to meet. They took them whatever they wanted, thrust it into their hands with a kind of furtiveness, even when the sewing-women were within their rights to take it; they would collect various scraps in a drawer for these favourites, remnants of no value, but even so, useful trifles; they would wave them at the girls gleefully from a distance, and in return have sweeties popped into their mouths. Blumfeld soon put an end to this disgraceful behaviour, and packed them off to his cabin of an office whenever the sewing-women came. But for a long time after they took it as a great injustice, they were defiant, wilfully broke their pens, and sometimes, though without daring to lift their heads, knocked on the glass panes to draw the attention of the sewing-girls to how badly in their opinion Blumfeld was treating them.

But they have no idea of how unjustly they themselves behave. For example, they almost always arrive too late at the office. Blumfeld, their superior, who from earliest youth has regarded it as self-evident that one should turn up at least half an hour before office-hours begin—not ambition, not an exaggerated sense of duty, only a feeling for the right thing makes him do it—Blumfeld has to wait for his trainees mostly for longer than an hour. Munching his breakfast roll, he usually stands behind the desk in the hall going through the final calculations in the sewing-women's little pay-books. Very soon he is deep in the work and thinking about nothing else. Then he is startled so suddenly that the pen in his hand continues to tremble for a while. One of the trainees storms in as if he is about to fall over; with one hand he hangs on tight to something, with the other he clutches his panting breast—but the whole performance means nothing more than creating an excuse for his late arrival, which is so ridiculous that Blumfeld deliberately doesn't hear it, for if he didn't do so, he'd be forced to thrash the boy, who deserves it. But as it is, he just looks at him for a while, points with outstretched hand to the cabin, and turns back to his work. Now even so one might expect the trainee to see the kindness his superior has shown him and hurry to his station. No, he is not in a hurry, he skips, he goes on tiptoe, he places one foot before the other. Is he trying to make a fool of his superior? Not that either. Again, it is this mixture of being afraid and being pleased with himself, against which one is defenceless. What other explanation can there be that today, when Blumfeld himself has arrived at the office

unusually late, now, after waiting a long time—he has no inclination
to check the women's books today—through the clouds of dust raised
by the firm's stupid menial and his broom he catches sight of the
two trainees in the street strolling along serenely. With their arms
clasped fast round each other's waist they seem to be telling each
other important things which certainly have nothing to do with the
business, unless an improper one. The closer they come to the glass
door, the more they slow down their pace. Finally, one of them seizes
the latch, but doesn't push it down, they are still telling each other
tales, listening, and laughing. 'Open it for our young gentlemen,'
screams Blumfeld to the menial. But as the trainees enter, Blumfeld
no longer feels like having a row, does not answer their greeting, and
goes to his desk. He begins his calculations, but looks up sometimes
to see what the trainees are up to. One of them looks very tired, yawn-
ing and rubbing his eyes; as he hangs his overcoat on the nail he takes
the opportunity to lean against the wall; he was lively on the street,
but being close to work makes him tired. The other trainee by contrast enjoys work, but only some of it. It has been his wish from the
beginning to be allowed to brush the floor. But that is not the kind of
work appropriate to him; it is the proper place only of the old menial
to brush the floor; Blumfeld indeed had nothing essentially against
the trainee's brushing the floor, let him do it, he can't do worse than
the servant, but if he does want to brush the floor, then he will have to
come earlier, before the menial begins brushing, and should not spend
the time on it which he is duty-bound to give strictly to his office
work. But if the boy is already proof against all reasonable considerations, at least the servant, this half-blind ancient, whom Ottomar
would certainly not tolerate in any other department but Blumfeld's,
and who is only alive by the grace of God and Ottomar, could be just
a little accommodating, and hand over the broom for a moment to the
boy, who is clumsy anyway, and will lose his pleasure in using the
broom right away and will run after the menial with it, if only to move
him to brush the floor again. But the menial seems to feel particularly
responsible for brushing the floor more than anything; the boy has
scarcely approached him before one sees the ancient attempting with
trembling hands to hold the broom tighter; more than that he stands
still, and leaves off brushing solely to draw everyone's attention to his
possession of the broom. The trainee does not put his request into
words because he is, certainly, afraid of Blumfeld who is doing his

calculations, and ordinary words would be useless, because one can only get through to the old man by shouting at the top of one's voice. So at first the trainee just plucks him by the sleeve. Naturally, the servant knows what it is all about; he looks darkly at the trainee, shakes his head, and clutches the broom closer to his breast. Now the trainee puts his hands together and begs. Of course, he doesn't expect to get anywhere by begging; begging is just fun for him, and so he begs. The other trainee accompanies the performance with quiet laughter, and obviously—though incomprehensibly—believes that Blumfeld can't hear him. The begging makes not the least impression on the old man; he turns round, believing now that he can use his broom in safety. But the trainee has followed him, skipping on tiptoe and holding his hands together in supplication, begging him now from this side. The menial turns round and the trainee skips after him over and over again. In the end the servant finds himself cut off on all sides and notices—and if he had been a little less simple he would have noticed right from the start—that he would tire more quickly than the trainee. Consequently he seeks help elsewhere, threatens the trainee with his finger, and points at Blumfeld, because he'll go and complain to him if the trainee doesn't stop. The trainee realizes that if he is to get the broom at all, he will have to hurry. So he makes a cheeky grab after the broom. An involuntary shout from the other trainee indicates the coming crisis. The old man saves his broom this time, it's true, by taking a step backwards and dragging it after him. But the trainee is not going to give in now. With mouth open and eyes blazing, he jumps forward, the servant tries to escape, but his old legs totter instead of running; the trainee snatches at the broom, and though he doesn't actually take hold of it, he does make it fall to the ground, and with that the broom is lost to the menial. But to the trainee as well apparently, for as the broom falls, they freeze, all of them, the two trainees and the menial, for by now everything must become obvious to Blumfeld. In fact, Blumfeld looks up at his special little window as if it is only now that he notices anything; he looks each one of them sternly and probingly in the eye, even the broom on the ground does not escape him. Whether because the silence lasts too long, or because the guilty trainee is unable to suppress his desire to brush the floor, anyway he stoops, though very cautiously, as if he were trying to take hold of an animal, not the broom, picks it up and makes a sweep across the floor, but promptly throws it away in terror as Blumfeld leaps up and emerges from the cabin. 'Get back to your work, both of you, and no more messing around,' he shouts, and with hand out-stretched points the trainees the way to their desks. They follow at once, but not with their heads lowered in shame; instead they turn towards Blumfeld and look him fixedly in the eye, as if they were try-ing in this way to stop him from striking them. And yet experience should have told them sufficiently by now that Blumfeld, on prin-ciple, never strikes. But they are too afraid, and always try to defend their real or supposed rights regardless.*

At the Building of the Great Wall of China

THE Great Wall of China has been completed at its northernmost
point. The construction was extended from the south-east and the
south-west and brought together here. This system of building it in
sections was also followed on a small scale within the two great armies
of labourers, the eastern and western armies. This was done by forming groups of about twenty workers, who had the task of building a
section of wall of about five hundred metres in length; a neighbouring
group then built a wall of the same length to meet it. But then, after
the union had been accomplished, construction was not in fact continued at one end of the thousand metres; rather, the groups of
labourers were sent off to other regions entirely to build the wall.
Of course in this way great gaps arose which were only filled slowly,
bit by bit, many of them not until after it was proclaimed that the
building of the wall had already been completed. Indeed, there are
said to be gaps that have never been filled in at all; according to some
they are much longer than the parts that have been built, though this
may be an assertion belonging to one of the many legends that have
arisen around the wall and which cannot be confirmed by any one
individual, at least not with his own eyes, nor his own measurements,
because the wall extends so far. Now you would think from the start
that there would in every sense be greater advantage in building continuously, or at least with continuity within the two main sections.
After all, as was widely proclaimed and well known, the wall was
intended as a defence against the tribes from the north. But how can
a wall that is not continuous be a defence? Indeed, a wall like that is
not only unfit to be a defence—the structure itself is in constant danger. Those sections of the wall standing in desert places can of course
be destroyed over and over again by the nomads, especially as these
tribes, alarmed by the building of the wall, changed their dwelling-
places with the incomprehensible speed of locusts—which is perhaps
why they had a better overview of the wall's progress than even we,
the builders, had. In spite of this, the building probably could not
have been carried out in any other way than it was. To understand
that, one has to consider the following: the wall was meant to be a
defence for centuries, so the most careful construction, the use of
building-lore from all times and all peoples, the constant feeling of

personal responsibility on the part of the builders, formed the indispensable basis of their work. For unskilled work, it's true, ignorant day-labourers from the people, men, women, children, anyone who offered themselves for good money, could be used, but even to lead a group of four day-labourers, a skilled building-worker, an intelligent man was needed, one capable of sympathizing deep in his heart with what was at stake here. And the higher his position, of course the greater the demands on him. And there were in fact men of this calibre at our disposal, and even if there weren't as many as the construction could have used, still a very great number. We had not approached the work frivolously. Fifty years before building was begun, throughout the part of China that was to be surrounded by the wall, architecture and building skills, particularly masonry, had been declared the most important study, and everything else recognized only insofar as it had some bearing on it. I can still remember clearly how, when we were little children, hardly steady on our legs, we stood in our teacher's garden and had to build a kind of wall out of pebbles, how our teacher picked up his skirts, ran at the wall, knocked everything down of course, and scolded us so hard for the failings in our construction that we ran off in all directions, howling to our parents. A tiny incident, but indicative of the spirit of the times. When I was twenty, I had the good luck to pass the highest examination of the lowest grade of school when the building of the wall had just begun. I say luck, because before that many who had previously attained the highest level of the training available to them had no idea for years what to do with their knowledge; they hung around uselessly with grandiose building-plans in their heads, and simply went to the dogs, in their masses. But the ones who came to the wall as group-leaders, even of the lowest rank, were in fact worthy of it; they were men who had given it thought, and never ceased to give it thought; with the first stone they set in the ground, they felt they had grown to be part of the structure. Such men were driven not only by their desire to perform the work thoroughly, but also by their impatience to see the wall rise at last in all its perfection. The day-labourer was unacquainted with this impatience; what drove him was only his pay; the leaders of higher rank, indeed even those of the middling order, saw enough of the complex growth of the wall for them to be strengthened in spirit; but the leaders of lower rank, men intellectually far above the outwardly small task assigned them, had to be provided for differently.

For example, they could not be left in an uninhabited mountain region, hundreds of miles from their homelands, laying stone against stone for months or even years; the hopelessness of such diligent labour which even in a long life would not come to an end would have made them despair, and above all would have made them less useful for the work. That is why the system of building in sections was chosen. Five hundred metres of wall could be erected in about five years; by then, it's true, the group-leaders were worn out; they had lost all confidence in themselves, in the wall, in the world, but then, still full of the triumphant celebration of the union of a thousand metres of wall, they were sent far, far away; here and there on their journey they would see finished sections of the wall soaring up, would pass the quarters of the higher-ranking leaders, who decorated them with honours, hear the cheers of fresh armies of labourers pouring from the depths of the provinces, see forests laid low, destined to be scaffolding for the wall, see mountains broken into stones for the wall; at the holy places they would listen to the hymns of the pious pleading for its completion. All this soothed their impatience; the peaceful life of their homeland, where they spent a while, gave them strength; the respect in which all the builders were held, the humble faith with which their reports were heard, the confidence of the simple, peaceful citizen that one day the wall would be completed, all this gave them new heart; like children eternally full of hope they bade their homeland farewell; their desire to take up the people's work again became uncontrollable, they journeyed from their homes sooner than necessary, half the village accompanied them for long stretches; cheers, pennants, flags all along their way; never had they seen how vast and rich and beautiful and worthy of loving their country was, every fellow countryman was a brother for whom they were building a defensive wall, and who thanked them all his life long with everything he had and was. Unity! Unity! Shoulder to shoulder, a round-dance of the people, blood, no longer imprisoned in the narrow confines of the body's veins, but circulating sweetly and still returning through the infinite expanse of China.

So this does make the system of piecemeal building comprehensible, but it probably had other causes as well. Nor is it strange that I should linger on this question for so long; it is the question at the heart of the entire project, slight as it first seems. If I want to convey the thinking and the experiences of those times, and make them understood, this is the question I cannot pursue deeply enough.

First of all, it must be said that achievements were reached at that time which were scarcely inferior to the building of the Tower of Babel,* though as to being pleasing unto the Lord, they represent, at least according to human reckoning, the direct opposite of that edifice. I mention this because in the early days of building a scholar wrote a book in which he drew this comparison very precisely. In it he sought to prove that the building of the Tower of Babel failed in its purpose, not at all for the causes generally stated, or at least that it was not among these known causes that the most important of all were to be found. His evidence consisted not only of written records and reports; on the contrary, he claimed he had conducted investigations on the site itself, and in the course of doing so had discovered that it was on account of the weakness of its foundations that the building failed, and was bound to fail. In this respect, however, our time was superior to that time long past; almost every educated contemporary of mine was a mason by profession, and on the question of laying foundations infallible. But this was not the point the scholar wanted to make; he maintained rather that only the Great Wall would for the first time in human history create a secure foundation for the Tower of Babel. So, first the Wall and then the Tower. At the time the book was in everyone's hands, but I admit, to this day I still do not exactly understand how he imagined the building of this tower. How was the wall, which didn't even form a circle, but only a kind of quarter- or semi-circle, supposed to make the foundations of a tower? That could only be meant as an intellectual concept. But then, what was the point of building the wall, which after all was something real, produced by the labour and the lives of hundreds of thousands? And what was the point of the plans for the tower sketched in the work, rather hazy plans, it's true, and of the detailed proposals for marshalling the labour-force for the new work in prospect? There was—this book is only one example—much confusion of mind in those days, perhaps just because so many people were doing their best to come together for a single purpose. Human nature, fundamentally wayward, light as dust in the air, cannot bear to be tied down; if it ties itself down, it will soon begin to shake wildly at its ties, tearing apart wall, chain, and self, and scattering them to the four winds.

It is possible that these considerations too, even though they made a case against building the wall, were not left unconsidered by the authorities when they decided on building in sections. It was only as we spelt out the decrees of the highest authorities that we—and I am surely speaking for many here—learned to know ourselves, find ourselves, for without their leadership neither our book-learning nor our common sense would have been up to even the lowly posts we held within the greater whole. In the council chamber of the Wall Authority—where it was and who was seated there no one that I asked knows, and no one knew—in this chamber there probably circled every human thought and wish, and in a counter-circle every human aim and its fulfilment, but through the window the radiance of divine worlds cast their reflection upon the hands of the Authority as it drafted its plans.

Hence the incorruptible observer cannot fully grasp that the Wall Authority, if it had seriously wanted to, could not have overcome even those difficulties facing the continuous construction of the wall. So we are left only with the conclusion that the Authority actually intended to build in sections. But building in sections was only an expedient, and not fit for purpose. We are left with the conclusion that the Wall Authority wanted something unfit for purpose. A strange conclusion indeed. And yet from another angle, it has not a few justifications going for it. Today they can perhaps be spoken of without danger. In those days it was the secret principle of many, and even of the best: seek with all your might to comprehend the decrees of the Authority, but only up to a certain point; then cease your reflections. A very wise principle, which, by the way, was given further interpretation in a parable which was frequently repeated later: cease reflecting further, not because it might harm you, for it is not even certain that it will. It is irrelevant to speak of harm or of no harm in this context. What will happen to you will be like the river in spring. It rises, grows mightier, nourishes the land on its long banks more powerfully; gradually it becomes more and more the ocean's peer and welcome guest. Thus far reflect the Authority's decrees within you. But then the river overflows its banks, loses its outlines and its form, slows its downward surge, attempts, contrary to its nature, to form little inland lakes, spoils the meadows, and cannot stay so broad and wide for long but flows into its banks again, indeed in the hot season that follows it even shrinks pitifully dry. Do not reflect the Authority's decrees within you as far as that.

Now while the wall was being built, this parable may well have been extraordinarily close to the bone, but for my present report it has at the least only limited value. My inquiry is after all only historical in aim; sudden lightning no longer flashes from long-past storm-clouds, so I may look for an explanation for the piecemeal building that goes further than the one we found sufficient in those days. The limits set by my capacity to think are narrow enough anyway; the field to be covered here, on the other hand, is endless.

Against whom was the Great Wall supposed to protect us? Against the tribes of the north. I come from the south-east of China. No northern tribe can threaten us there. We read about them in the books of the Ancients, the cruelties they commit consistent with their nature make us sigh aloud in our peaceful garden-houses; in artists' true-to-life pictures of them we see faces of the damned, gaping mouths, jaws with pointed fangs, narrowed eyes seeming to be already squinting after their prey, mouths ready to crush and tear it to pieces. If our children are naughty, we only have to show them these pictures, and straight away they fly crying to our arms. But we know nothing more than that about these northerners; we have not seen them, and if we remain in our villages, we never will see them, even if they are riding their wild horses and driving straight towards us. The country is too vast, and will not let them reach us; they will lose their way in the empty air.

So why, if that is how things are, do we forsake our homelands, the river and bridges, our mothers and fathers, our weeping wives, our children who need instruction, and move far away for training in the distant town, with our thoughts even further away at the wall in the north? Why? Ask the authorities. They know us. For all the tremendous cares they shoulder, they know about us, they know the trades we ply for our meagre livelihood, they see us all as we sit together in our lowly workshop; the prayers our household heads say at evening in the circle of their own folk are pleasing or displeasing to them. And, if I may allow myself such a thought about the Authority, I have to say that in my opinion it was already in existence earlier; it did not come together as, say, the high mandarins do: on an impulse from a beautiful morning dream, these hastily summon a meeting, hastily resolve on their decree, and that same evening they are already drumming the population out of their beds to carry it out, even if it is just to set up a display of illuminations in honour of a god who had shown favour to their Lordships, only, the next morning, with the lanterns hardly extinguished, to beat up the people in some dark corner.

Rather, the Authority has been in existence since time immemorial, and the decree to build the wall likewise.

I have always been deeply interested, intermittently while the wall was being built, and afterwards to this day almost exclusively, in comparing the history of different nations—there are certain questions where this offers the only means of approaching to some extent the heart of the matter; and in the course of my studies I have discovered that we Chinese possess certain ethnic and governmental institutions that are uniquely lucid, and on the other hand some that are uniquely obscure. I have always been, and am still, tempted to trace the roots of the latter phenomenon in particular, and the construction of the wall too is involved in these questions.

Now, one of the most obscure of all our institutions is the office of Emperor. In Peking of course, and certainly in court society, there is some clarity about it, although even this is more apparent than real; the teachers of constitutional law and history at our universities also claim to be exactly informed about these things and able to pass on this knowledge to their students; and the further you descend to the lower schools the more the doubts about one's own knowledge—understandably—vanish; and semi-education surges mountain-high around a few dogmas rammed into heads for centuries, which, it's true, have lost nothing of their eternal truth, but in all this mist and fog have also remained eternally unrecognized.

But it is on this very question of the office of Emperor that in my opinion the people should be the first to look to for an answer, for they after all are its ultimate support. In this respect though, I can once again speak only of my own homeland. Apart from the gods of the fields and their changing and beautiful service throughout the year, all our thoughts were devoted solely to the Emperor. But not to the present Emperor, or rather, they would have been devoted to the present Emperor as well if we had known him or known anything definite about him. It's true, we were also—the only thing we were curious about—always trying our hardest to find out something of the kind. But—however strange it sounds—it was scarcely possible to find out anything, not from the pilgrim, who traverses many lands, not in villages near or far, not from the boatmen who travel not only our small streams but also the sacred rivers. One heard many things, but there wasn't much to be had from the many things. Our country is so vast no legend can do justice to its vastness, the heavens can scarcely span

it. And Peking is only a speck and the Imperial Palace only the smallest of specks. The Emperor as such, though, is on the contrary great
on all levels, from high to low, in all the world. The living emperor is
a human being like us, like us he lies on his couch of rest, which is of
a generous size, but still might possibly be only short and narrow.
Like us he sometimes stretches his limbs, and if he is very tired he
will yawn with his finely drawn mouth. How are we to find out about
this, a thousand miles in the south where we still almost border on the
Tibetan Plateau? But apart from that, any news, even if it were to
reach us, would arrive much too late, would be long out of date.
Around the Emperor the brilliant but shadowy throng of court and
state gathers, the counterweight to the Imperial office, always intent
on bringing down the Emperor from his scale of the balance with
their poisoned arrows. The office of Emperor is immortal, but the
single Emperor will fall and come to grief, even whole dynasties will
sink in the end and breathe their last in one single death-rattle. The
people will never learn of these struggles and sufferings; like late-
comers, like strangers to the city, they stand at the end of the crowded
side streets, calmly taking a bite out of the provisions they have
brought, while far ahead in the middle of the market-place their lord
is being executed.

There is a legend that expresses this situation very well. The
Emperor—so it is said—has sent to you, the solitary, the miserable
subject, the infinitesimal shadow who fled the imperial sun to far and
furthest parts, to you and none other, the Emperor has from his
deathbed sent a message. He had the messenger kneel at his bedside
and whispered the message in his ear; so important to him was it that
he had it repeated in the messenger's ear once more. With a nod he
confirmed that what had been said was correct. And in the presence
of the entire audience for his death—all the walls that might be in
their way are demolished, and the grandees of the empire are standing in a circle on the wide, high sweep of the outer flight of steps—in
the presence of all those assembled he sent the messenger on his
way. The messenger has set off at once; a sturdy man, unwearying, a
swimmer without equal; stretching forward first one arm, then the
other, he pushes his way through the crowd; if he meets with resistance he points to his chest, which bears the sign of the sun; and he
moves forward with an ease no one can match. But the crowd is so
vast, their dwellings never come to an end. If open country stretched

out before him, how he would fly, and soon, no doubt, you would hear the commanding sound of his fists beating upon your door. But instead, how uselessly he labours; he is still forcing his way through the chambers of the innermost palace; he will never get through them; and if he managed that, there would be nothing gained; he would have to fight his way down the stairs; and if he managed that, there would be nothing gained; the courtyards would have to be crossed, and after the courtyards, the second, outer palace; and again more stairs and more courtyards, and again a palace; and so on through the millennia; and if at last he emerged, stumbling, through the outer-most gates—but that can never, never happen—the imperial city still lies before him, the centre of the world, piled high with its own refuse. No one will get through here—and certainly not with a message from the dead.—You, though, will sit at your window and conjure it up for yourself in your dreams, as evening falls.

This is exactly how our people, just as hopelessly and hopefully, regard the Emperor. They have no idea which Emperor is ruling, and there are even doubts about the names of the dynasty. At school a great deal of that sort of thing is learned in sequence, but the general uncertainty in this respect is so great that even the best student comes to share it. In our villages, Emperors long dead are placed on the throne, and one who only survives in song recently issued a proclam-ation which was read out before the altar by the priesthood. Battles from our most ancient history are only now being fought, and with his face ablaze, your neighbour comes crashing through your door with the news. The imperial ladies, reclining bloated in their imperial cushions, estranged by wily courtiers from noble ways, swollen with power-lust, vehement in greed, outspread in wantonness, practise their wicked deeds anew over and over again; the more distant in time, the more frightening and garish all the colours appear, and with a loud cry of horror the village learns one day how thousands of years ago an Empress drank great draughts of her husband's blood.

That is how, then, the people treat figures from the past; persons from the present, on the other hand, they mix up with the dead. If, for once, once in a lifetime, an imperial official travelling in the province arrives by chance in our village, and makes certain demands in the name of the ruler, scrutinizes the list of taxpayers, sits in on school classes, questions the priest about all our doings, and then before he gets into his palanquin summarizes it all in long exhortations to the community rounded up there to hear him, a smile crosses everyone's face, they exchange hidden glances, they bend down to the children so that His Honour cannot observe them. He is talking about a dead ruler as if he were alive, but this Emperor died long ago, the dynasty is extinct, our great official is making fun of us, but we'll behave as if we don't notice, so as not to offend him. But we will be serious about obeying no one but our present lord, for anything else would be a sin. And behind the official's speedily departing palanquin, some figure arbitrarily elevated rises from an already crumbling urn and stamps his way towards the village to be its lord.

If you wanted to conclude from such occurrences that fundamentally we do not have an Emperor at all, you would not be far from the truth. Again and again I have to say: there is perhaps no people more faithful to the Emperor than ours in the south, but our fidelity doesn't do the Emperor any good. On the little pillar where the village ends, it's true, the sacred dragon stands and breathes its fiery breath in homage in the exact direction of Peking, but Peking itself is more strange to the folk in the village than the life beyond. Is there really supposed to be a village where house stands next to house, covering entire fields, and stretching further than the view from our hill; and between these houses are there human beings standing night and day, head next to head? It is less difficult than imagining such a city for us to believe that Peking and its Emperor are one, rather like a cloud wandering tranquilly beneath the sun in the course of the ages.

The result of such views is to some extent a free life without the constraints of government. By no means immoral; on my travels I have hardly ever encountered such purity of morals as in my home country. Nevertheless, it is a life governed by no laws of the present day, and it obeys only the decree and direction that come down to us from ancient times.*

I am wary of generalizations, and I do not maintain that this is the situation in all ten thousand villages of our province, certainly not in all five hundred provinces of China. But I may say on the basis of the many writings I have read on this subject as well as on the basis of my own observations—in particular at the wall while it was being built, the human material there gave the sensitive observer an opportunity to journey through the souls of almost all the provinces—on the basis of all this I may say with some justification that the dominant attitude shown towards the Emperor again and again and everywhere shares a certain fundamental characteristic in common with the attitude in my home country. Now I certainly do not want to argue that this attitude is a virtue, on the contrary. True, on the one hand it is largely the fault of the government, which in the oldest empire in the world has to this day not been in a position—or else it has neglected it in favour of other matters—to develop the institution of empire into something so radiant that its rule could be effective, direct, and constant right to the furthest limits of the Imperial lands. Nevertheless, it is on the other hand a weakness of imagination or faith on the part of the people that as subjects of the empire they have not got as far as bringing it out of the benighted depths of the Peking past to full life and presence and holding it to their submissive breasts, which after all desire nothing better than to feel its touch for once, and so die.

So this attitude is scarcely a virtue. It is all the more striking that this very weakness appears to be one of the most important means of uniting the people, indeed, if I may venture so far, it seems to be the very ground on which we live. To develop the causes for this flaw in detail would mean not so much to shake our consciences as our legs—which is much worse. That is why for the present I do not wish to pursue this question.

It was into this world that the news of building the wall made its way. That too was late by about thirty years after its announcement. It was on a summer's evening. I was standing, ten years old at the time, with my father on the riverbank. Appropriately for the significance of this often-mentioned hour, I remember it down to the smallest circumstance. He was holding me by the hand, something he was fond of doing right into old age, and with his other hand his fingers played the length of his pipe—it was quite long—as if it were a flute. His long, thin, stiff beard was pointing at the sky as he enjoyed his pipe and gazed over the river and up into the air. His pigtail, object of reverence to the children, sank all the deeper, rustling softly on the gold-embroidered silk of his holiday gown. A barque drew up before us; the boatman beckoned to my father to come down the embankment, and he himself climbed up to meet him. They met halfway; the boatman whispered something in my father's ear, embracing him so as to get very close. I couldn't understand what they were saying, I saw only how my father didn't seem to believe the news, how the boatman attempted to convince him of the truth, how my father still couldn't believe it, and how the boatman, with the passionate nature of his kind, almost tore the garment on his breast to tatters in the effort to prove the truth, how my father grew more silent, and the boatman leapt thundering into his barque and sailed off. Thoughtfully my father turned to me, knocked out his pipe and tucked it in his girdle, stroked my cheek, and drew my head towards him. That's what I liked best, it made me very happy, and so we arrived home. There rice was already steaming on the table, a few guests had gathered, and the wine was just being poured into the cups. Paying no attention to this, while still on the threshold my father began to report what he had heard. Of course, I have no exact memory of his words, but their meaning sank in deeply because the circumstances were so extraordinary, compelling even the child, so that I can nevertheless still trust myself to repeat the gist, more or less. I shall do so because it was very characteristic of the popular attitude. My father said something like

The Huntsman Gracchus

Two boys were sitting on the wall of the quay, playing at dice. A man was reading a newspaper on the steps of a monument in the shade of the sabre-swinging hero.* A girl was filling her wooden tub with water at the fountain. A fruit-seller was lying next to his wares, gazing out on the lake. In the depths of a bar one could see through the gaping doors and windows two men sitting over their wine. The landlord was sitting towards the front, dozing. A barque floated gently, as if borne above the water, into the little harbour. A man in a blue smock disembarked and pulled the painter through the rings; after the boatswain, two men in black jackets with silver buttons came carrying a bier, on which, beneath a large, flower-patterned fringed silk pall, there clearly lay a human being. No one on the quay bothered about the new arrival, no one approached, not even when they set down the bier to wait for the helmsman, who was still working on the ropes, no one approached them, no one asked them any questions, no one looked at them closely. The helmsman was held up for a moment longer by a woman with hair unloosed, who now came out on deck, a child at her breast. Then he arrived, and pointed at a yellowish, two-storeyed house that rose straight up to the left, near the water. The bearers took up their burden and carried it through the gateway, low, but framed by slender pillars. A small boy opened a window, just long enough to notice how the group disappeared in the house, and closed the window quickly again. The gate too was now shut; it was made of black oak, carefully crafted. A flock of doves, which had been flying around the church tower until now, came and settled in front of the house. As if their food were kept inside the house, they gathered outside the gateway. One of them flew up to the first storey and pecked at the window-pane. They were well-tended birds, lively and light in colour. With a great sweep of her arm the woman threw them seeds from the barque; they gathered them up and then flew over to the woman. An old man in a top hat with a mourning-band came down one of the very steep, narrow little alleys leading to the harbour. He looked round attentively, everything bothered him, the sight of refuse in a corner made him wrinkle his nose. Fruit-peel was lying on the steps of the monument; he pushed it aside with his stick as he went by. He knocked at the pillared door, at the same time taking his top hat in his black-gloved right hand. It was opened at once; all of fifty little boys formed a line in the long entrance-hall, and bowed. The helmsman came down the steps, greeted the gentleman, and led him up. On the first floor, while the boys crowded after them at a respectful distance, they skirted the courtyard, which was surrounded by delicate, lightly built loggias, and entered a large, cool room on the far side of the house, where there were no longer any houses to be seen opposite, but only a bare, grey-black rock-face. The bearers were busied with setting up and lighting a number of tall candles at the head of the bier, but these gave little light; rather, shadows that were earlier at rest were simply startled into flickering on the walls. The pall on the bier was thrown back. A man lay there, with wildly matted hair and beard and tanned skin, looking rather like a huntsman. He lay motionless, seemingly without breathing, his eyes closed; nevertheless, only the circumstances indicated that perhaps this was a dead man.

The gentleman walked up to the bier, laid a hand on the brow of the figure lying there, then kneeled down and prayed. The helmsman signalled to the bearers to leave the room. They went out, drove off the boys who had gathered outside, and closed the door. But the gentleman did not seem to be satisfied by this stillness either. He looked at the helmsman, who understood and went through a side door into the next room. At once the man on the bier opened his eyes, turned his face to the gentleman with a painful smile, and said: 'Who are you?' The gentleman rose from his knees without further astonishment and replied: 'The Mayor of Riva.' The man on the bier nodded, pointed with feebly outstretched arm to a chair, and said, after the Mayor had followed his invitation, 'Of course I knew, Mr Mayor, but in the first moment I always forget everything, everything is spinning, and it is better that I ask, even if I do know everything. You too probably know that I am Gracchus* the huntsman.' 'Certainly,' said the Mayor. 'Your arrival was announced to me in the night. We had been long asleep. Then towards midnight my wife called me. "Salvatore,"*—that is my name—"look at the dove in the window!" It really was a dove, but as big as a cockerel. It flew up to my ear and said: "Tomorrow the dead huntsman Gracchus will arrive. Receive him in the name of the town."' The huntsman nodded, and drew the tip of his tongue between his lips. 'Yes, the doves fly ahead of me. But do you think, Mr Mayor, that I should stay in Riva?' 'I can't say yet,' answered the Mayor. 'Are you dead?' 'Yes,' said the huntsman, 'as you see. Many years ago, indeed, it must be an uncommonly great many years, in the Black Forest—that's in Germany—I fell from a cliff as I went in chase of a mountain-goat. Since then I have been dead.' 'But you are alive too, nevertheless,' said the Mayor. 'To some extent,' said the huntsman, 'to some extent I am alive too. My ship bearing the dead took the wrong course, a false turn of the wheel, a moment of inattention on the part of the helmsman, a diversion through my wonderfully beautiful homeland, I don't know what it was, I only know that I remained on earth, and that since then my ship has sailed on earthly waters.* This is how I journey after my death through all the lands of the earth, I, who wanted to live only among my mountains.' 'And you have no part in the beyond?' asked the Mayor, wrinkling his brow. 'I am', answered the huntsman, 'always on the great stairway that leads upwards. On this infinitely broad flight of stairs now up, now down, now to the right, now to the left, always on the move.* But whenever I take the highest leap of all, and the great gate above is already shining on me, I wake on my old ship, adrift in some earthly waters. The fundamental error of my sometime dying grins at me from all sides in my cabin; Julia,* the helmsman's wife, knocks and as I lie here on my bier she brings me the morning drink of whatever land whose coast we happen to be travelling along.' 'A terrible fate,' said the Mayor, his hand raised as if to ward it off. 'And that is in no way your fault?' 'None,' said the huntsman, 'I was a huntsman, is that my fault? I was appointed to be a huntsman in the Black Forest, where in those days there were still wolves. I would lie in wait, shoot, hit the animal, skin it—is that my fault? My work was blessed. The great huntsman of the Black Forest they called me. Is that my fault?' 'I am not called to decide on this,' said the Mayor, 'but it does not seem to me either that there is any fault in that.' 'But who does bear the blame then? The boatswain,' said the hunter.

* * *

'And now you are thinking of remaining here with us in Riva?' asked the Mayor. 'I'm not thinking of it,' said the huntsman with a smile, and to make up for his mockery, he laid his hand on the Mayor's knee. 'I am here. I know no more than that. I can do no more than that. My boat has no tiller, it sails with the wind that blows in the deepest regions of death.'

* * *

I am the Huntsman Gracchus, my home is the Black Forest in Germany.

* * *

No one will read what I write here; no one will come to help me;* if to help me were set as a task, all the doors of all the houses would stay shut, all the windows closed, everyone would lie in their beds with the covers pulled over their heads, the whole earth a shelter in the night. There is good sense in that, for no one knows of me, and if he did know of me, he would not know my resting-place, and if he did know my resting-place, he would not know how to keep me there, and if he did know how to keep me there, he wouldn't know how to help me. The thought of helping me is a sickness, to be healed in bed.

This I know, so I am not writing to summon help, even at moments when, uncontrolled as I am—right now, for example—it is a compelling thought in my mind. But it is probably enough to drive out such thoughts whenever I look round me and remind myself of where I am and where I have dwelt—I can surely say—for centuries. I am lying on a wooden plank as I write this, I am wearing—there is no pleasure in looking at me—a filthy shroud, my hair and beard are matted together past disentangling, my legs are covered with a large silk, flower-patterned, long-fringed pall. A church candle stands at my head, giving me light. On the wall opposite me there is a small picture, evidently a bushman,* who is aiming for me with his spear and covering himself as much as he can behind an extravagantly painted shield. On board ship one often comes upon any number of stupid representations, but this is one of the stupidest. Otherwise my wooden cage is quite empty. The warm air of the southern night drifts in through a porthole on the side wall, and I can hear the water lapping at the old barque.

I have been lying here since the time when I was still alive, Huntsman Gracchus, at home in the Black Forest, when I chased after a mountain-goat, and fell. Everything went in the right order. I chased, I fell, I bled to death in a ravine, and this barque was meant to bear me to the beyond. I can still remember how joyfully I stretched out on the bier for the first time; the mountains had never heard such song from my lips as these four walls, which were still lit, in those days, by the dim light of dusk. I had lived gladly, and I died gladly, I was happy to throw off from me, before I stepped on board, the use-less burden of my gun and bag, and the hunting-jacket I had always worn with pride, and I slipped into my shroud like a girl into her wedding-dress. I lay here and waited.

Then there happened

* * *

6 April 17*

In the small harbour, where apart from the fishing-boats only the two passenger-steamers that provide the ferry service on the lake usually stop, today there lay a foreign barque. A heavy old boat, quite low and bulging wide, filthy, as though dirty water had been poured over it, it still apparently reached the yellowish outer wall, its masts incredibly high, the top third of the mainmast bent, its yellow-brown sails, rough and crumpled, drawn all over the place between the spars, botched work that wouldn't stand up to the wind.

I gazed at it in astonishment for a long time, waiting for somebody to show themselves on deck. Nobody came. A workman came and sat down next to me on the wall of the quay. 'Who does that ship belong to?' I asked. 'This is the first time I've seen it.' 'It comes every two or three years,' said the man. 'And it belongs to Gracchus, the huntsman.'

* * *

'Is it really true,* Huntsman Gracchus, that you've been travelling for centuries in this old boat?'

'It's been fifteen hundred years now.'

'And always in this ship?'

'Always in this barque. Barque is the right name for it. You're not familiar with ships and ships' ways?'

'No, it's only since today that I've been concerned with it, since I knew about you, since I set foot on your ship.'

'Don't apologize. I'm an inland man myself too. I wasn't a seafarer, never wanted to become one; mountain and forest were all my joys, and now—the oldest seafarer of all, Huntsman Gracchus, the sailors' guardian spirit, Huntsman Gracchus, who receives the prayers of the ship's boy as he wrings his hands in fear up on the top mast on stormy nights. Don't laugh.'

'Laugh? No, truly not. I stood outside the door of your cabin with heart pounding; I came in with heart pounding. Your kind manner calmed me slightly, but I shall never forget whose guest I am.'

'Of course. You're quite right. Be that as it may, Huntsman Gracchus I am. Will you take some wine? I don't know what kind it is, but it is sweet and powerful. My patron supplies me well.'

'Not now, please. I'm too restless. Perhaps later, if you can put up with me for so long. Who is your patron?'

'The owner of the barque. These patrons are excellent people. Only I don't understand them. I don't mean their language, though often I don't understand their language either. But that's only by the way. I've learned enough languages in the course of the centuries and I could be the interpreter between their forefathers and the children of the present day. But I don't understand the patron's line of thinking. Perhaps you can explain it to me.'

'I don't have much hope of that. How am I to explain anything to you when in comparison with you I am just a babbling child?'

'Not at all, once and for all not in the least. You will give me great pleasure if you present yourself in a rather more manly, rather more self-confident way. What can I do with a shadow as my guest? I'd blow him out of the porthole onto the lake. I need a number of different explanations. You knock about the world outside, so you can give me them. But if you flounder about at my table, deceiving yourself about the little you do know, then you can be off. I speak my mind outright.'

'There's some rightness in what you say. In fact I am ahead of you in some respects. So I'll try to force myself. Ask away.'

'That's better, much better. You're exaggerating in this direction, and imagining there are some things where you are superior. Only you must understand me correctly. I am a human being like you, but that much more impatient by the few centuries that I am older. Now then, let us talk about the patrons. Pay attention. And drink some wine to sharpen your wits. Don't be afraid. Take a good long drink. There's still a whole shipful there.'

'Gracchus, this is an excellent wine. To your patron's health!'

'A pity that he died today. He was a good man, and made a peaceful end. His older children, who turned out well, stood at his deathbed, at its foot his wife fainted, and fell, but his last thoughts were of me. A good man, came from Hamburg.'

'Good heavens, from Hamburg! And here in the south you already know that he died today!'

'What? I'm not supposed to know when my patron dies? You're very simple, you know.'

'Are you trying to insult me?'

'No, not at all, I do so reluctantly. But you shouldn't let so much astonish you, and you should drink more wine. But as to the patrons, their situation is like this: originally, the barque belonged to no one.'

'Gracchus, a request. First tell me briefly but coherently, what is your situation? To tell the truth, I simply do not know. You take these things for granted, of course, and you assume, as is your way, that the entire world is in possession of your knowledge. But in the brief span of a human life—for life is brief, Gracchus, try to understand that—people have all their hands full getting on, themselves and their families. And interesting as the Huntsman Gracchus is—I'm convinced of that, I'm not just flattering—they have no time to think of him, ask after him, or even worry about him. Perhaps on our death-bed, like your man from Hamburg, I don't know. That's the place perhaps where for the first time a busy man has the time to stretch out for a moment, and at his leisure the green Huntsman Gracchus will pass through his thoughts. But otherwise, as I said, I knew nothing of you; I came down to the harbour here on business, I saw the barque, the gangplank was ready, I crossed over—I would now very much like to hear something coherent from you.'

'Oh, coherent. The old, old story. All the books are full of it, in all the schools the teacher chalks it on the blackboard, the mother dreams of it as her child nurses at her breast—and you, fellow, ask me for coherence. You must have misspent your youth in a remarkably wild way.'

'Possibly, as everyone misspends his own youth in his own way. But it would, I think, be very useful for you, if you were to look around you in the world a little. It may seem odd to you, I'm wondering a bit about it myself, but it is so. You are *not* the talk of the town; however many things they talk about, you are not among them; the world goes the world's way, and you make your journey, but until today I have never noticed that your paths have crossed.'

'Those are your observations, my dear fellow; others have made other observations. Either you are holding back what you know about me, and have some purpose in doing so—in that case, I tell you quite frankly: you are on the wrong track; or, on the other hand, you actually don't believe you can remember me because you are confusing my story with another one. In this case, I can only tell you: I am.—No,

I can't; everybody knows my story, and I'm the one they expect to tell it to you! It is such a long time ago. Ask the historians! They sit in their studies and gaze open-mouthed at the happenings of long ago, and never stop describing them. Go to them, and then come back. It is such a long time ago. How can I keep it all in this overloaded brain?'

'Wait, Gracchus. I'll make it easier for you. I'll question you. Where do you come from?'

'From the Black Forest, everyone knows that.'

'Of course, from the Black Forest. And so you went hunting there in about the fourth century?'

'Good Lord, man, do you know the Black Forest?'

'No.'

'You really do know nothing. My helmsman's little child knows more than you, truly, much more. Who on earth sent you in here? It's my fate. Your diffidence at the beginning was only too well founded. You are a nothing, which I've been filling with wine. So you don't even know the Black Forest. I hunted there until I was twenty-five. If the mountain-goat hadn't tempted me—well, now you know—I would have had a fine long life of hunting, but the mountain-goat tempted me, I fell, and smashed myself to death on the rocks. Here I am, dead, dead, dead. Don't know why I am here. Was laid on the ship of death, as was proper, a miserable dead man; the three or four things to be done were done with me, as with everyone, why make an exception with the Huntsman Gracchus; everything was in order; I lay stretched out in the boat

Investigations of a Dog

How my life has changed, and yet how, deep down, it has not! When I think back now and recall the times when I still lived in the midst of the pack, shared all their troubles, a dog among dogs, still, looking at it more closely I discover even so that for ages something had not been right, some little fracture was there; in the middle of the pack's most venerable tribal occasions some little discomfort would overcome me, indeed sometimes in a circle of friends, no, not sometimes, very frequently, the mere sight of a fellow-dog dear to me, the mere sight, seen somehow through fresh eyes, would make me distressed, horrified, helpless, indeed desperate. I tried in some sort to calm down; I confessed it to friends, who helped me; quieter times returned, times when these surprise moments certainly were not absent, but were accepted more equably, more equably fitted into my life; perhaps they made me weary and sad, but besides that they allowed me to continue as a dog—admittedly a rather cold, reserved, timid, calculating dog, but still, taken all in all, a proper dog. Without these breaks for recovery, how could I have made my way through to the age I now rejoice in, how could I have struggled through to the calm with which I contemplate the terrors of my youth and endure the terrors of age, how could I have reached the stage of drawing my own conclusions from my admittedly unhappy, or to put it more cautiously not very happy disposition, and live my life almost entirely as my conclusions have indicated? I live my life withdrawn, solitary, occupied only with my hopeless, but to me indispensable investigations; even so I have still not lost sight of a wider view of my kindred from a distance; news frequently gets through to me, and in my turn I let them hear from me now and again. I am treated with respect; they can't understand my way of life, but they don't take it ill, and even the young dogs I see now and again running past in the distance, a new generation whose childhood I can hardly remember even vaguely, do not refuse me a respectful greeting. It shouldn't be forgotten that in spite of my eccentricities, which are there for all to see, I am far from being a total deviant from my own kind. Indeed, when I reflect on it—and for reflection I have time, inclination, and aptitude—there is something strange about us dogs as a race. There are creatures of many kinds around, poor, paltry, and silent, restricted to certain cries.

Many of us dogs study them; we have given them names, and try to help them, train them, improve them, and the like. I am indifferent to them, as long as they don't try to pester me; I cannot tell them apart, and ignore them. But one thing is too remarkable to have escaped me, and that is how little, compared with us dogs, they keep together, how coldly and silently and with a certain hostility they pass each other by, how neither a noble nor a low common interest can give them any unity, rather all such interests only keep them further apart than their usual condition of stasis does. But we dogs by contrast! It could well be said that we all live pretty well in one great heap, all of us, differentiated as we otherwise are by the countless and profound variations that have developed over time. All in one heap! Something urgent drives us together, and nothing can prevent us from satisfying its urging. All our laws and institutions, the few I still remember and the countless I have forgotten, go back to the greatest joy that we are capable of, the warmth of togetherness. But nowadays its opposite! There are to my knowledge no other creatures who live their lives as widely dispersed as we dogs lead ours, or have such an immense number of distinctions in class, labour, and occupation. Our kind, which wants to bond together—and again and again in moments of euphoria we do succeed in spite of everything—we more than any lead lives separated from one another, pursuing strange occupations which our fellow dogs often cannot understand, clinging to rules which are not the law of the pack, and indeed are meant rather to go against it. What difficult things these are, things one would prefer not to touch on— I can understand this point of view, I can understand it better than I do my own—and yet they are things that utterly possess me. Why don't I do as the others do and live harmoniously with my kind, silently accepting anything that disturbs the harmony, ignoring it as a small error in the great reckoning, and always turning towards what happily binds us together, and not towards what, irresistibly every time, wrenches us out of the closed circle of our kindred. I remember one occasion from my childhood—I was in one of those blissful, inexplicable states of excitement such as every child probably experiences—I was still a very young pup, everything gave me pleasure, everything related to me, I believed that great things were going on around me and I was leading them and I had to give voice to them, things that would have to lie miserably on the ground if I didn't run to fetch them, wag my whole body for them—children's fancies, which vanished with the years. But at the time they were very power-ful, I was wholly under their spell. And then something happened, extraordinary, it's true, something that seemed to confirm my wild expectations. In itself it was nothing extraordinary, I have seen such things, and even more remarkable ones, often enough later, but at that time it struck me with a strong, first, ineradicable impression that set the course for many others. It was my encounter with a small group of dogs, or rather, I didn't encounter them, they came up to me. I had run a long way through the dark, with a vague sense of great things to come—a sense which can easily deceive, for I had always had it—up and down, blind and deaf to everything, led by nothing but this indef-inite longing. I stopped short suddenly, with the feeling that this was the right place for me, I looked up, and it was bright day, just a bit misty. I greeted the morning with little noises of bewilderment when—as if I had conjured them up—there emerged from some sort of darkness, creating a terrifying clamour such as I had never heard before, seven dogs, out into the light. If I hadn't clearly seen that these were dogs and that the clamour was coming with them, although I couldn't tell how they produced it—I might have run off straight away, but as it was, I stayed. At the time I still knew almost nothing of the musicality granted solely to the tribe of dogs, for my powers of observation were only just developing and my attention had been drawn to it only by hint and suggestion; so it was all the more surprising, indeed positively dispiriting to me to hear those seven great virtuoso musicians. They didn't talk, they didn't sing, they were generally silent, almost doggedly so, yet by their magic they conjured up music out of empty space. All was music, the way they lifted and placed their feet, the way they turned their heads with a certain motion, their running and resting, the attitudes they took up towards each other, the patterned movements they made with one another, rather like a round-dance, as one of them propped his front paws on another's back, and they arranged themselves so that the first, stand-ing upright on his hind legs, took the weight of all the others, or the serpentine designs they formed as their bodies stole along low to the ground—and they never put a foot wrong, not even the last, who was still a bit insecure and didn't always join in with the others and was sometimes slow to pick up the melody, but even so was only uncertain in comparison with the bravura certainty of the others, and even if he had been much more, indeed totally, uncertain, nothing could have

spoiled it when the others, great maestros all, kept time so unshak-
ably. But you scarcely saw them. You scarcely saw any of them. They
had made their appearance; inwardly I had welcomed them as dogs,
very confused by the noise that had accompanied them, but after all
they were just dogs, dogs like you and me; you observed them in the
usual way, like dogs you meet as you go on your way; you tried to
approach them and exchange greetings; they were also quite close, a
lot older than I was, it's true, and not my long-haired woolly breed,
yet not so alien in size and shape, but rather very familiar; I knew a
number of their breed, or something similar. But while you were still
caught up in these reflections, the music suddenly gained the upper
hand, practically seized hold of you, drew you away from these real
little dogs, and, wholly against your will, hackles rising and struggling
with all your might, howling as if you were being hurt, you could give
your mind to nothing but the music coming from all sides, from the
heights, from the depths, from everywhere, music surrounding, overwhelming, crushing the listener to a point beyond destroying him,
music still so near that it was already far away, almost inaudibly sounding its fanfares still. And then you were released, because you were too
exhausted by now, too shattered, too weak to hear it any more, you
were released, and watched the seven little dogs as they formed their
processions, did their jumps; you wanted to call to them, however
unwelcoming they looked, to ask them to tell you what they were
doing here—I was a child and believed I could always ask questions
of anyone—but I had hardly started, I had hardly felt the warm,
familiar dog-solidarity with the seven before their music was there
again, robbing me of my senses, whirling me round, as if I were one
of the musicians myself, when on the contrary I was only their victim;
it flung me this way and that however much I begged for mercy, and
finally rescued me from the force of its own presence when it drove
me into a tangle of wood that rose all around in those parts, though
I hadn't noticed it before. It held me fast and kept my head down for
me, and gave me the opportunity, however much the music might
thunder out there in the open, to pause and catch my breath a little.
Truly, what amazed me more than the seven dogs' art—that wasn't
only beyond my comprehension, but also quite beyond my capacities,
with nothing I could relate to—was the courage they showed in putting themselves so fully and openly at the mercy of what they were
creating, and the strength they had to endure it calmly without letting

it break their back. It's true, though, as I watched them more closely from my hiding-place, that their way of working was marked not so much by calm as by extreme tension, and that at every step their legs, with their seemingly sure movements, constantly trembled and twitched in anxiety; each stared at the other as if in desperation, and no sooner had they got their tongues under control than they hung limply from their mouths again. It couldn't be fear of failure that agitated them so much; a dog who dared what they did, and achieved it, couldn't be afraid any more.—What were they afraid of, then? Who was forcing them to do what they were doing here? And I couldn't restrain myself, especially as they now seemed so incomprehensibly in need of help, and so I shouted out my questions, loud and challenging through all the din. But they behaved—I couldn't, couldn't understand it!—as if I weren't there, dogs who don't answer to another dog's call! That is an offence against good manners, unforgivable in even the smallest or biggest dog, under any circumstances. Perhaps they weren't dogs? But why shouldn't they be dogs, for as I listened more closely I could now even hear the soft calls they were making as they encouraged one another, drew attention to difficulties, warned against mistakes; and I could even see the last, smallest dog, who attracted the most calls, looking at me frequently out of the corner of his eye as if he would very much have liked to answer me, but was keeping himself under a tight leash, because it was not allowed. But why wasn't it allowed? Why, this time, wasn't it allowed, when it is always an absolute requirement of our laws? Something in me rose up at that, outraged. I almost forgot the music. These dogs were offending against the law. Great magicians they might be, but the law also applied to them; I was a child, but I already understood that precisely. And from that position I noticed still more. They really had cause to be silent, assuming that they were silent from a sense of guilt. For, carried away by sheer music, I had not until now noticed how they were behaving. They had truly cast aside all shame; the miserable creatures were doing what was both the most ludicrous and the most indecent of things: they were walking upright on their hind legs. Shame on them! They exposed themselves and showed off their nakedness for all to see: they were proud of themselves, and, when for a moment they listened to their better impulses and dropped their forelegs, they were positively shocked, as if it were a mistake, as if Nature were a mistake. They lifted their legs once more and their eyes seemed to beg for forgiveness that they had had to pause for an instant in their sinfulness. Was the world turned upside down? Where was I? What had happened? For the sake of my own survival I could hesitate no longer; I tore myself free from the wood that held me in its clutches, leapt out with one bound, and tried to reach the dogs; the little novice was compelled to be their teacher, had to make them understand what they were doing, had to stop them from sinning further. 'Old dogs like that! Old dogs like that!' I kept repeating to myself. But I was scarcely free, with only two or three bounds separating me from the dogs, before once again it was the clamour that overwhelmed me. Perhaps in my zeal I might have withstood even that, for I had already just met it, if there had not rung out through its full power—terrible as that was, it still might be resisted—a clear, austere, single note, approaching steadily from a great distance, perhaps the true melody in the midst of the clamour, and forcing me to my knees. Oh, what music was it these dogs made that could drive you mad! I couldn't go on. I no longer wanted to teach them, let them go on spreading their legs, committing their sins, and tempting others to the mute sin of the spectator—I was such a very small dog, who could demand such a difficult task of me? I made myself even smaller than I was, I whimpered, if the dogs had asked me at the time what my opinion was, perhaps I would have said they were in the right. In any case, it didn't last long and they disappeared with all the clamour and all the light into the darkness they had come from.

As I said, this entire occurrence held nothing extraordinary; in the course of a long life many things happen to you which, taken out of context and seen with a child's eyes, would be much more astonishing. Besides, you can of course 'edit the story', as they say, as you can everything, and then what emerges is that here, seven musicians had gathered together to make music in the quiet of the morning, that a little dog had come straying, a tiresome audience, and they had tried—unfortunately in vain—to scare him off with music of a particularly terrifying or sublime kind. He was interrupting them with his questions, and, interrupted quite enough by the mere presence of the outsider, were they supposed to respond to this nuisance and make it worse by answering? And even though it is required by the law to answer someone, is such a minuscule stray pup a Someone worth mentioning? And perhaps they simply didn't understand him—after all, he probably yelped his questions incomprehensibly.

Or perhaps they understood him perfectly well, and, restraining themselves, did answer him, but being a little dog unused to music, he couldn't distinguish their answer from the music. And as for their hind legs, perhaps they really did walk on them, but as an exception. All right, so it is a sin, but they were alone, seven friends among friends, in an intimate circle, you might say within their own four walls, you might say completely alone, for friends are not the public, and where there is no public, it can't be created by an inquisitive little dog off the streets. In this case, however, isn't it as if nothing had happened? Not entirely, but nearly, and parents should teach their young to run around less and rather keep silent instead, and respect their elders.

If you have reached that point, the case is settled. Of course, what is settled for the grown-ups is not yet settled for the children. I ran around, told my story and asked questions, I complained and queried and tried to drag everyone to the place where it all happened, and show everyone where I had been standing and where the seven had been and where and how they had danced and made music, and if anyone had come with me instead of shaking me off and laughing at me I would probably have sacrificed my innocence and tried to stand on my hind legs just to explain everything exactly. Well, people think the worst of a child in everything, but in the end they also forgive him everything. But I have kept this childlike nature, and in the meantime I have become an old dog. In those days I never stopped discussing the episode out loud—though I don't regard it as so important now—and analysing it into its elements, trying it out on those present without any respect for the society I happened to be in, engrossed only in this subject, which I found as burdensome as everyone else, but which—and this made the difference—was my very reason for wanting to solve it totally by my investigations, so that I could free my vision for ordinary, peaceful, happy daily life. That is exactly how I have worked subsequently, even if my methods are less childish—though the difference is not very great—and even today have not come any further.

But it was with that concert that it began. I am not complaining; my inborn nature is at work here, and it is certain that if the concert hadn't happened it would have found some other occasion to break through. Only that it all occurred so early sometimes made me sorry; it robbed me of a great part of my childhood. The blissful puppy life which many dogs are capable of prolonging for years lasted for me only a few brief months. So be it. There are more important things than childhood. And perhaps in my old age there beckons to me, as the reward earned by a hard life, more childlike happiness than a real child would have the strength to bear, but which by then I shall enjoy.

In those days I began my inquiries with the simplest things. There was plenty of material. Unfortunately it was the sheer quantity of it that in my dark hours made me despair. I began to inquire what it is that nourishes the tribe of dogs. Now of course, if you like, that is not a simple question; it has engaged us since ancient times; it is the main subject of our reflections; our observations, our experiments, and our opinions in this field are countless; it has become a science which in its enormous extent exceeds not only the grasp of the individual's understanding, but also that of the entire body of scholars, and it has to be borne by no one but the tribe of dogs as a whole, and even this can only bear it incompletely and with a sigh, as it crumbles away in ancient, long-held traditions and has to be augmented laboriously, to say nothing of the difficulties and over-demanding assumptions of fresh research. No one, I hope, will raise all this as an objection, for what I know of it all is only what any average dog does; it wouldn't occur to me to get involved in the true science; I have all due respect for it, but to increase it—I do not have the knowledge or the diligence or the composure or—most of all, particularly for some years now—the appetite. I gobble down food when I find it—but to me it is not worth a systematic study of animal husbandry one little bit. In this respect I am satisfied with the distillation of all knowledge, the little rule with which mothers dismiss their infants from their breasts: 'Wet everything as much as you can.' And doesn't that really contain almost everything? Has the research our ancestors began anything essential to add to it? Details, details. And how insecure it all is. But this rule will persist as long as we dogs exist. It concerns our chief nourishment; certainly, we have other resources, but both in time of need and when the years are not too bad we are able to live on this as our chief nourishment; we find our chief nourishment on the earth but the earth needs our water, is fed by it, and merely for this price she gives us our nourishment, though we should not forget either that its provenance can be hastened with certain ritual words, chants, and motions. But in my opinion that is all; from this aspect, there is nothing fundamental to be added. And in this I am at one with the great majority of the tribe of dogs, strictly turning my back on all heretical views on the subject. I am truly not concerned with being special, or claiming to know it all; I am happy if I can agree with my own kind, and in this case, that is so. My own investigations, however, move in a different direction. My observation tells me that the earth, watered and tended according to the rules of science, produces nourishment, and does it in the quantities, in the way, in the places, and at the hours required by the laws likewise laid down or partly laid down by science. That I accept. But my question is: 'Where does the earth get this nourishment from?'—a question that people generally pretend they don't understand and which they answer at best with: 'If you haven't enough to eat, we'll give you some of ours.' Note this answer. I know it is not one of the virtues of the tribe to offer to share food that we have once acquired; life is difficult, the earth unyielding, science rich in knowledge but poor enough in practical results; if you have food, you keep it. That is not self-interest; it is the opposite; it is the law of the dogs; it is the unanimous decision of the people, come into being by overcoming selfishness, for the possessors are of course always in the minority. And that is why the answer: 'If you haven't enough to eat, we'll give you some of ours,' is a permanent catchword, banter, a joke. I have not forgotten that. But it had all the more significance for me, in the days when I was wandering the world with my questions, that in my case they set the joking aside; true, they still gave me nothing to eat—where could they have got it from so quickly? And if they did by chance have any food just then, in their raging hunger they would forget all other considerations, but they meant the offer seriously, and now and then I really did get a morsel if I was quick enough to snatch it. How did it come about that they behaved towards me in this particular way, gave me an easier time, put me first? Because I was a scrawny weakling of a dog, ill-fed and not concerned enough about food? But there are plenty of ill-fed dogs running round, and the rest take even the most miserable fare out of their mouths if they can, often not from greed but mainly on principle. No, they put me first. I couldn't support this with details, but it's rather that I had a definite impression of it. So was it my questions that gave them pleasure, and which they thought were particularly clever? No, they took no pleasure in them and thought they were all stupid. And yet it could only have been the questions that drew their attention.

It was as if they would rather commit the outrage of stopping my mouth with food—they didn't do so, but they wanted to—as tolerate my question. But then they would have done better to drive me away and refuse my questions. No, that wasn't what they wanted; true, they didn't want to listen to my questions, but it was on account of these very questions of mine that they didn't want to drive me away. However much I was laughed at, and treated as a silly little creature, and pushed around, it was actually the time of my highest standing; nothing like it was ever repeated later; I had entry everywhere; nothing was forbidden me; under the pretence of rough treatment I was actually being flattered. So everything was on account of my questions after all, on account of my impatience, my investigative zeal. Were they trying to pacify me with this treatment, trying without force to divert me almost lovingly from taking the wrong path, but all the same not one that was so undoubtedly wrong that it would have allowed them to use force? Also, a certain respect and fear held them back from using force. I sensed something of the sort at the time; today I know exactly, much more exactly than those who did hold back in those days. It is true: they were trying to coax me away from my path. It didn't work. They brought about the opposite; it sharpened my attention. I even discovered that it was I who was trying to tempt the others, and in fact the temptation was to some extent successful. It was only with the help of the pack that I began to understand my own questions. For example, when I asked 'Where does the earth get this nourishment from?' was I concerned, as it might seem, about the earth, was I concerned perhaps about the burdens on the earth? Not in the least. That, as I quickly recognized, was far from my mind. It was dogs I was concerned about, nothing else. For what is there besides dogs? Who else is there to call upon in the whole wide, empty world? All knowledge, the totality of all questions and all answers, is held in dogs. If only one could bring this knowledge to life, make it useful, if one could only bring it into the light of day, if only they didn't know so much more than they admit, than they admit to themselves. The most talkative dog is far more unforthcoming than the locations of the best food tend to be. You prowl round your fellow dog, your mouth is foaming with desire, you are flogging yourself with your own tail, you ask, you beg, you howl, you bite, and you get—you get what you would get anyway without all this effort: loving attention, warm caresses, respectful sniffs, rapt embraces, my howls

and thine blending into one, everything is arranged to this end, finding forgetfulness in ecstasy, but the one thing you wanted above all to
get at: an admission of knowledge—that is still refused. Your plea,
silent or loud, even if you have tried to tempt them to the limit, is
answered at best only by blank faces, wry glances, veiled and clouded
eyes. It is not very different from the time when I was a child, when I
called on the dog-musicians and they were silent. Now you could say:
'You are complaining about your fellow dogs, at their silence over
things that are crucial; you are maintaining that they know more than
they are admitting, more than they want to accept as true in life, and
this reserve, whose source and mystery of course they also withhold,
poisons life, makes it unbearable to you, you must change it or leave
it; that may well be, but after all you are a dog yourself, you have a
dog's knowledge too, so state it outright, not just in the form of a
question, but as an answer. If you state it, who will contradict you?
The great chorus of the pack will join in as if it had been waiting for
it. Then you will have truth, clarity, open admission, as much as you
like. The lid on our humble life, which you speak of so badly, will be
lifted, and dogs together, shoulder to shoulder, we will all rise up to
the heights of freedom. And if this last should fail, if it should be
worse than before, if the whole truth were to be more unbearable than
half-truth, if it should prove that the ones who kept their silence, the
upholders of life, were in the right, if out of the slight hope we have
now there were to come total hopelessness, utterance is still worth the
attempt, for the life that is permitted you is one you do not want to
live. Well then, why do you upbraid the others for their silence when
you are silent yourself?' Easy answer: because I'm a dog. In essentials
just as resolutely unforthcoming as the others, resisting my own questions, rigid out of fear. So strictly speaking, have I been questioning
the tribe, at least since I have been a grown dog, in the hope of getting
an answer? Are my hopes so foolish? How can I look at the foundations of our lives, sense their depths, see the labourers burrowing,
hard at their work in the dark, and still expect that because of my
questions all this will be ended, destroyed, abandoned? No, I no longer expect that, truly. I am only hounding myself with these questions, trying to work myself up by the silence that is my only answer
from all around. How long, I ask myself, will you endure the insight,
which your investigations have made increasingly clear to you, that
the pack is silent and will always remain so? How long will you endure

it? Beyond all my separate questions that is the real question of my life: it is meant for me alone, and does not plague anyone else. Unfortunately I can answer it more easily than my separate questions: I expect I shall hold out until my natural end; the calm of age will resist my restless questions more and more. I shall probably die peacefully in silence, surrounded by silence, and I look forward to it with composure. We dogs were given the cradle gifts of an admirably strong heart and lungs resistant to premature wear and tear, as if out of malice; we hold out against all the questions, even our own—bulwarks of silence that we are.

Increasingly of late I have been thinking over my life, looking for the decisive error I may have made, which is to blame for everything, and I cannot find it. And yet I must have committed it, for if I hadn't, and if I hadn't in spite of that achieved what I wanted by the honest labour of a long life, then it would prove that what I wanted was impossible, and the consequence would be utter hopelessness. Behold your life's work! Look first at your inquiries into the question: 'Where does the earth get our nourishment from?' As a young dog, deep down naturally keen and eager for life, I went without every pleasure, gave all amusements a wide berth, buried my head between my legs against temptation, and set about my work. It was not the work of a scholar, not as far as scholarship, method, or purpose was concerned. These were probably errors, but they could not have been crucial ones. I have learned little, for I left my mother early, soon grew used to being independent, led a free life, and premature independence is bad for learning systematically. But I have seen and heard a great deal, and talked with many dogs of the most various breeds and callings, and I wasn't bad, I think, at taking it all in and making connections between isolated observations. That has been some substitute for scholarly learning; besides, although independence may be a disadvantage in learning systematically, it has a certain advantage for individual research. In my case this was all the more necessary as I was not able to follow real scientific method, I mean, making use of work done by my predecessors, and associating with contemporary researchers. I had to rely entirely on myself, and began at the very beginning, with the awareness—heartening for the young, but extremely depressing for the old—that the chance stop I would put to it would necessarily also be the final one. Was I really so alone in my researches, now and from the beginning? Yes and no. It is impossible that there haven't always been individual dogs here and there in my situation, today as well as in the past. My position can't be all that bad. I am not by a hair's breadth an outsider to our natural being as dogs. Like me, every dog has the urge to ask questions, and like every dog, I have the urge to be silent. Everyone has the urge to ask questions. How else but by my questions could I have produced even mild excitement in my fellow dogs, which it was often my privilege and delight to see—though the delight was overdone, I admit. And that I have the urge to be silent needs, unfortunately, no special proof. So essentially I am no different from any other dog, and that is why, in spite of differences of opinion, and dislike, everyone will acknowledge me, and I shall not behave otherwise towards all other dogs. Only the combination of the elements is different; for the individual this is a very important distinction, but it is insignificant for the race. Am I to believe that these always available elements never, in past or present, happened to form a combination similar to mine—and, if you want to call mine an unfortunate combination, what if that one had turned out to be even more so? That would go counter to every other experience. We dogs engage in the strangest occupations, which you wouldn't believe at all if you didn't have most reliable reports about them. My favourite example is the aerial dogs.* When I first heard of one of them, I simply laughed, and wouldn't be in the least convinced. What! There was supposed to be a dog of the very smallest breed, not much bigger than my head, not even in its old age, and this dog, fragile of course, to all appearances an artificial, immature creation, clipped and cosseted, incapable of making an honest jump, this dog, they said, was supposed to be able to move along mostly high in the air, yet without showing any visible signs of working at it, but floating at rest. No, to expect me to credit such things was to exploit a young dog's naivety far too far, I thought. But not long afterwards I heard tales from another quarter of another airborne dog. Had they all agreed to make a fool of me? But then I saw the dog-musicians, and from that time on I thought anything was possible; my intelligence was not limited by any prejudgments; I followed up the most absurd rumours and pursued them as far as I was able; in this absurd life what made least sense seemed to me to be more probable than what did make sense, and particularly fruitful for my research. That also applied to the aerial dogs. I learned all sorts of things about them, though to this day I have not succeeded in actually seeing one of them, but for a long

time now I have been firmly convinced of their existence, and they
have assumed an important place in my conception of the world. As
in most cases, in this one too it is not so much their skill that mainly
gives me cause for reflection. It is strange, it can't be denied, that
these dogs are capable of floating in the air—I am one with the pack
in my wonder at it. But as I sense it, what is much stranger is the
absence of meaning, the silent absence of meaning in these beings. In
general, they simply have neither grounds nor ground, they float in
the air, and that's all there is to it; life goes on its way; now and again
there is talk of art and artists, and that is all. But why, you good and
grounded pack, do they just hover in the air? What sort of sense is
there in their calling? Why is there no word of explanation to be had
from them? Why do they float up there, allowing their legs, the pride
of a proper dog, to shrivel away, separated from the nourishing earth,
why is it that they sow not and yet they reap, and are even, so it is said,
particularly well nourished at the pack's expense? I flatter myself that
my questions have brought a little movement into these things. There
is the beginning of some kind of cobbled-together grounds; there is a
beginning, but it won't get beyond a beginning. But at least it is something. And in the course of this, something is revealed that may not be
the truth—no one will ever get that far—but at least something of
the deep-rooted entanglements of the lie. For all the absurd phenomena of our life, and particularly the most absurd, allow grounds to be
established for them. Not completely, of course—that's the diabolical
thing about it—but enough protection against embarrassing questions. Take the aerial dogs once again for example: they are not arrogant, as you might think at first; rather they have a quite particular
need of their fellow dogs. If you try to put yourself in their place,
that's understandable. For of course they have to try to gain some
forgiveness for their way of life, or at least draw attention away from
it, cause it to be forgotten, if not openly—that would breach their
duty of silence—then in some other way. They do this, so I've been
told, by being almost unendurably chatty. They always have some tale
to tell, sometimes about their philosophical reflections, to which they
can devote themselves all the time because they have given up all
physical exertion, sometimes about the observations they make from
their exalted position. And although they are not greatly distinguished
for their intelligence—leading such an idle life, that goes without
saying—and their philosophy is as worthless as their observations,

and science can make hardly any use of it and isn't dependent on such wretched sources at all; in spite of this, if you ask what in the world these aerial dogs are for, you are always given the answer that they contribute a great deal to science. 'That is correct,' you reply, 'but their contributions are worthless and tiresome.' The rejoinder is a shrug of the shoulders, a change of subject, irritation, or laughter, and in a little while, if you ask again, you are told once more that they contribute to science, and in the end, if you are asked yourself soon afterwards and you're not really concentrating, your own answer will be the same. And perhaps it is good not to be too stubborn, and not acquiesce in acknowledging this justification of the aerial dogs' lives in their present numbers—that is impossible—but still to put up with it. They shouldn't expect more than that, that would be going too far, but they still expect it. They expect you to put up with more and more aerial dogs coming along. You have no precise idea where they come from. Are they multiplying by reproduction? Have they enough strength for that? They are not much more than a pretty pelt; what's the point of reproduction in their case? And if this improbability were possible, when is it supposed to happen? After all, you always see them alone, sufficient to themselves up in the air, and if sometimes they, so to speak, condescend to walk, it is only for a little while, a few affected steps and always strictly alone and deep in alleged thought, which they cannot tear themselves away from even if they tried—at least that's what they maintain. But if they don't reproduce, would it be thinkable that there are dogs who of their own free will give up a life with their feet on the ground, become aerial dogs of their own free will, and for the rewards of comfort and a certain skill choose this barren, cushioned life up there? It is not. Neither reproduction nor voluntary contact is thinkable. But all the same, the reality is that there are more and more new aerial dogs; that although the obstacles to our understanding seem insurmountable, a breed of dog once in existence, however strange, does not die out, at least not easily, at least not without something present in each breed that holds out successfully for a long time. Should I assume that what applies to this most esoteric, absurd, this strangest-looking of breeds, quite unfit for living, such as the aerial dogs are, does not also apply to my own breed? Even though I am not at all strange in appearance, the usual average, very frequently found at least in these parts, not outstanding for anything in particular, not to be scorned for anything in particular; in my youth and to some extent into my mature years, for as long as I wasn't neglecting myself and kept active, I was even quite a good-looking dog: my frontal view used to be particularly admired, the slender leg, the handsome pose of the head, but my grey-white-yellow coat, curling just at the ends, was also most agreeable—all that isn't strange; what is strange is only my nature. But this too, I should always remind myself, is firmly grounded in the general nature of all dogs. So if even the aerial dog is not alone, if here and there in the great world of dogs another one keeps on turning up and they can keep on getting another new generation even out of nothingness, then I too can be confident that I have not been left alone. However, these, dogs of my own kind, must have their own special destiny, and their existence will never be of visible help to me, if only because I will hardly ever come to know them. We are the ones who are oppressed by the silence, who want to break through it out of sheer hunger for air; true, the others seem quite comfortable with the silence, but they only seem so, just as the dog-musicians seemed to be making music calmly, but were in reality very agitated. But this appearance is powerful; you try to cut through it, but it makes a mockery of every onslaught. So how do dogs of my kind, my fellows, cope with it? How do they try to go on living in spite of it? Perhaps in various ways. For as long as I was young I attempted it with my questions. So perhaps I might stay close to the persistent questioners and that would be where I would find dogs of my own kind. For a while I also tried by overcoming my own nature, by overcoming myself, for indeed, more than anything I am troubled by the ones who ought to have the answers; I detest the ones who interrupt me with questions, which I mostly can't answer. Then again, who doesn't enjoy asking questions when he is young, so from out of the many questioners, how am I to discover the right ones? One question sounds like another, the important thing is its purpose, but that is hidden, often from the questioner as well. And after all, questioning is a general characteristic of dogs as a race, they all ask questions all at once, as if this were meant to blur any trace of the actual questioner. No, among the young ones, the questioners, I shall not find a dog of my own kind, nor shall I find them among the silent, the old ones. But what is the point of all these questions? I have come to grief over them; probably my companions are wiser than I, and employ very different, admirable, means to make this life bearable, means, as I can add from my own experience, that perhaps can help them at a pinch, have a reassuring, lulling, transforming effect, but in general are as powerless as my own, for however far I look ahead, I cannot see any success. But where, where are my fellows? That is my lament; that's just it. Where are they? Everywhere and nowhere. Perhaps my neighbour, three leaps away from me, is one of them, we often call to one another, and he comes over to me—I don't go to him. Is he my kind of dog? I don't know. True, I don't recognize anything of the sort in him, but it's possible. Possible, but even so, nothing is less likely. When he is away, by resorting to fantasy I can play at discovering plenty in him that is suspiciously congenial and familiar to me; but the moment he stands in front of me, all my imaginings are ridiculous. An old dog, smaller even than I am, and I am barely middle-sized, short-haired, with dragging feet and a weary droop to his head, and to add to that ill-health has caused him to drag his left hind leg behind him. I haven't for a long time had such close contact with anyone as with him; I'm glad that I can still put up with him tolerably well; when he leaves, I howl the friendliest things after him, not out of affection, it's true, but angry with myself, because whenever I watch him leaving I find him quite repulsive again as he creeps away with his dragging foot and his rump sagging far too low to the ground. Sometimes I feel as if I were mocking myself when I call him my fellow in my mind. In our conversations too he doesn't show any trace of fellowship; true, he is intelligent, and, considering the circumstances here, cultivated enough, and there's a lot I could learn from him, but am I looking for intelligence and cultivation? Our conversations are usually about local questions, and, made more clear-sighted by solitude, I am astonished at the sheer intellect it takes even for an ordinary dog, even in average, not-too-unfavourable circumstances, to eke out his life and protect himself from the worst of the usual dangers. True, science lays down the rules, but to understand them even at a distance and in the broadest outlines is not at all easy, and once you have understood them, that is when the really difficult part comes, applying them to the local circumstances; hardly anyone can help here; almost every hour there are new things to be done, and every fresh speck of earth makes its own particular demands. No one can say firmly of himself that he is permanently settled and now his life is running to some extent of its own accord, not even I can, though my needs grow fewer practically from one day to the next. All this never-ending effort—to what end? Only to bury yourself still deeper in silence and no longer, ever, be drawn out of it, not by anyone. They often praise the general advance of the race of dogs through the ages, and by that they probably mean the advance of science. Certainly, science advances, it is unstoppable; its advance is even speeding up, faster and faster. But what is so praiseworthy about that? It is as if you wanted to praise someone because with the increasing years he grows older, and consequently death approaches faster and faster. That is a natural process, and an ugly one too, and as I see it there is nothing about it to praise. All I see is decline, but by that I don't mean that earlier generations were better in nature; they were only younger, and that was their great advantage, their memory was not as overburdened as ours today; it was easier to persuade them to speak, even if no one managed to do so, but the possibility was greater, and it is of course this greater possibility that excites us so much when we hear those old, actually very simple, stories. Now and again we hear a word, a hint, and could almost leap up, if we didn't feel the burden of the centuries upon us. No—another thing I have against my own time—earlier generations were not better than more recent ones, indeed in a certain sense they were much worse, and weaker. In those days too, marvels did not walk freely about the streets to be snatched up at random, but the dogs were less—there's no other way I can put it—less dog-like than they are today; the organization of the pack was still loose; in those days the true word could still have had a say, could have determined the structure, altered it, changed it as anyone wished, turned it into its opposite. And that word was present, at least it was near, it hovered on the tip of your tongue, everybody could feel it. Today where has it gone? Today you could dig deep in your gut for it and you wouldn't find it. It may be our generation is lost, but it is more innocent than the older ones. I can understand the uncertainty of my contemporaries; indeed, it is not uncertainty at all, not any longer, it is that they have gradually forgotten the dream they dreamt a thousand nights ago and forgot a thousand times, so who will be angry with us just because of the thousandth time of forgetting? But I think I also understand our forefathers' uncertainty; we probably would not have acted differently. I would almost say we are fortunate that we were not the ones who had to burden ourselves with the guilt; rather, in a world others have already darkened we are able to hasten towards our death in almost guiltless silence. When our forefathers took the wrong way, they were scarcely thinking of taking an endlessly wrong way, they still had the crossroads literally in sight, it was easy to turn back any time they liked, and if they were uncertain about turning back, it was only because they wanted to enjoy a dog's life for a while longer. It wasn't a real dog's life yet, but it already seemed intoxicatingly good. How much better it was bound to be later, at the least only a little while later, and so they went on taking the wrong way. They didn't know what we can vaguely sense as we observe the course of history: that the soul changes more quickly than life does, and that when their dog's life was beginning to give them joy, they must already have had the soul of a pretty old dog, and were no longer as near to their starting-point as it appeared, or as their eyes, delighting in all the joys of being a dog, would have them believe. Who can talk of youth nowadays? They were the real young dogs, but unhappily their sole ambition was aimed at becoming old dogs, something that they couldn't fail to do, of course, as all subsequent generations demonstrate, and ours, the last, most of all.—Of course, I don't talk about all these things with my neighbour, but I can't help thinking about them when I sit facing him, this typical old dog, or when I bury my muzzle in his coat, which is already giving out the smell of skinned hide. There would be no sense in talking about these things, not with him, nor with anyone else. I know how the conversation would go. He would have a few objections to make now and again, in the end he would agree with me—agreeing is the best weapon—and the matter would be buried, so why bother to dig it up in the first place? Nevertheless, there is perhaps a deeper kind of agreement with my neighbour that goes beyond words. I have to go on asserting this, although I have no proof and may be under a naive illusion, simply because he is the only dog I have conversed with for a long time, so I have to hold fast to him. 'Are you perhaps my fellow after all? In your own way? Ashamed because everything has been a failure for you? You see, it's been like that for me too. When I'm alone I howl over it. Come on, it's better when there are two of us.' That is what I think sometimes, and I look straight at him. He doesn't lower his eyes then, but there's nothing to be got from him either, he looks at me blankly and wonders why I am silent and have interrupted our conversation. But perhaps this glance of his is his way of asking a question, and I disappoint him just as he disappoints me. In my youth, if other questions had not been more important to me in those days and I had been self-sufficient enough, I might have asked him out loud, might have received a dull agreement, less in fact than today, when he is silent. But aren't they all silent, just like him? What is there to prevent me from believing that they are all my fellows, that it wasn't just occasionally that I found a fellow inquirer, now lost and forgotten together with his meagre results, and no longer reachable across the darkness of the ages or in the jostle of the present; rather that I have always, for ages, had fellows, who all laboured in their own way, all without success in their own way, all of them silent, or cunningly prattling in their own way, as you do in this hopeless research. Then I would not have had to cut myself off at all, I would have been able to remain peacefully among the others, I would not have had to push my way out like a naughty child through the rows of grown-ups, who surely wanted to get out just as much as I did, and whose common sense was the only thing that put me off my stride, for it told them that no one gets out and that all efforts at pushing are stupid.

Such thoughts after all are clearly the effect of my neighbour on me; he confuses me; he makes me quite melancholy. He is cheerful enough on his own, at least I hear him when he is on his own patch bawling and singing—to my annoyance. It would be good to do without even this last associate, to give up pursuing vague daydreams of the sort that any association among dogs produces, however hardened against it you think you are, and to apply the little time left to me to my researches. The next time he comes, I shall crawl away and pretend to be asleep, and go on doing so until he stays away.

My research has also become disorganized; I've been getting slack, weary, I just go on plodding along mechanically where once I scampered with enthusiasm. I think back on the time when I began to investigate the question of 'Where does the earth get our nourishment from?' True, in those days I lived in the midst of my kindred, I would push my way where the pack was densest, I wanted to make them all witnesses to my work; their testimony was even more important to me than my work, for I was still expecting to make some kind of general impact. Of course, this gave me great encouragement, which is past and over for me now in my solitude. But in those days I was so strong that I did something that is quite unheard-of and against all our principles, which every eyewitness of the time remembers as something uncanny. In science, which otherwise aims at unlimited specialization, I discovered in one respect a remarkable simplification. Science teaches us that in the main the earth produces our nourishment, and then, once it has established this premise, it gives us the methods by which the various kinds of food can be obtained in the best way and in the greatest abundance. Now it is certainly correct that the earth produces our nourishment, there can be no doubt on that score, but it is not as simple as it is usually represented, to the exclusion of any further inquiry. Take the simplest events that happen every day: if we were completely inactive—and I have almost reached that stage already—and if after briefly watering the soil we were just to curl up and wait to see what would happen, then, assuming that there was any result at all, we would find our nourishment on the earth anyway. But even so, that is not the rule. Anyone who has kept even a slightly open mind towards science—and there are certainly not many of those, for the circles drawn by science grow larger and larger—will, even if he hasn't started from particular observations, easily perceive that the greater part of the nourishment we then find lying on the earth comes from above; indeed, depending on our individual agility and greed, we snap up most of it before it touches the earth. This is not to say anything against science, for of course the earth also produces this nourishment naturally; perhaps it is not an essential distinction whether it draws the one from itself or calls the other down from above, and the science that has established that cultivation of the soil is necessary in both cases, is not perhaps obliged to concern itself with these distinctions, for after all, as the saying goes: 'If you've the grub in your jaw, you've the answers for now.' Only it seems to me that science *is*, at least in part, and in a disguised form, concerned with these things, since it is familiar with two methods of obtaining nourishment, actually watering the soil and also the work of complementing and refining this in the form of spells, dance, and song. I can see a division here which corresponds, not completely, it is true, but all the same clearly enough, to my distinction. The cultivation of the soil acts in my opinion to obtain both kinds of nourishment and will always be indispensable; but spells, dance, and song have less to do with nourishing the soil in the narrow sense, but serve mainly to draw down the nourishment from above. In this conception I am supported by tradition. Our tribe seems to be putting science right on this point without knowing it, and without science's daring to defend itself. If, as science argues, those ceremonies are supposed only to serve the ground, perhaps so as to give it the strength to bring down the nourishment from above, logically they would have to take place entirely on the ground; everything would have to be whispered to the ground, sung before it, danced before it. And to my knowledge, science, it seems, demands no less. And now the remarkable thing: in all these ceremonies the tribe turns and points upwards. This does no harm to science; science does not forbid it and leaves the worker of the land free in this respect; in its theories it is thinking only of the ground, and if he carries out its theories on the ground, it is satisfied, but its train of thought in my opinion should really be more ambitious. And I, who have never been initiated further into science, cannot imagine at all how the learned can tolerate it when our tribe, fervent as it is, cries its magical spells upwards, wails its old traditional songs upwards into the air, and performs its vaulting dances as if it wanted to soar aloft, forgetting the ground for ever. Emphasis on these contradictions was my starting-point. Whenever, according to scientific theory, harvest-time drew near, I concentrated entirely on the soil; I scrabbled at it as I danced; I twisted my head just so as to see the soil as close as possible, later I made a little hollow for my muzzle and sang and declaimed so that only the soil could hear me, no one else, near me, or on top of me. The results for my research were scant; sometimes I didn't get any food, and was all set to rejoice at my discovery, but then the food came back again, as if at first wherever the food comes from was confused by my strange behaviour, but then recognized the advantage it brought and was happy to do without my howling and leaping; often my food came more abundantly than before, but then again it wouldn't come at all. With a thoroughness that until then had been unknown in young dogs, I made precise lists of all my experiments, thought now and again I was on the track of something that might take me further, but then it got lost once again in uncertainties. There is no disputing that my inadequate scientific grounding was getting in my way. Where was my guarantee, for example, that the non-appearance of food was brought about not by my experiment, but by unscientific watering of the soil? And if that was so, then all my conclusions were baseless. Under certain conditions, it might have been possible to create an almost totally precise experiment, namely, if I had succeeded in bringing down food from above, without any cultivation of the soil, wholly by the upwards-ceremony, and then in producing the non-appearance of food exclusively by means of the soil-ceremony. I even attempted something of the kind, but without any firm faith in it, and under imperfect experimental conditions, for it is my unshakeable opinion that a certain watering of the soil is always necessary, and even if the heretics who don't believe this were right, it still can't be proved, as watering the soil occurs from an urge, and within certain limits cannot help occurring. Another experiment, rather out-of-the-way, I admit, was more successful and caused something of a stir. Picking up on our usual way of catching at food from the air, I decided not to allow the food to fall, but also not to catch it. To this end, whenever food came, I would make a little leap into the air, but one that was calculated not to reach quite high enough; mostly it fell dully and unresponsively to the ground, and I would fling myself on it in rage, a rage not only of hunger, but also of disappointment. But even so, in isolated cases something different occurred, something really wonderful: the food did not fall, but followed me in the air; the food was chasing the hungry. It didn't go on for long, just for a short stretch, then it fell, or disappeared completely, or—the most frequent case— my greed brought the experiment to a premature end and I ate the stuff up. Anyway, I was happy then. There was a buzz going on around me; the others had grown restless and alert; I found my acquaintances more receptive to my questions; there was a light in their eyes that was seeking some help, though it might have been only the reflection of my own glances. I wanted nothing more. I was content. Until, of course, I learnt—and the others learnt with me—that this experiment had long ago already been described by the scientists, and had been more successful on a much grander scale than mine; it had not, it's true, been performed for a long time on account of difficulties with the self-control it required, and there was also no necessity to repeat it on account of its alleged insignificance to science. It proved only what was already known, that the soil did not only obtain its nourishment straight downwards, but also aslant, indeed, even in spirals. Well, there I stood, but I wasn't discouraged, I was too young for that, on the contrary, it spurred me on to what was perhaps the greatest achievement of my life. I did not believe the scientific devaluation of my experiment, but belief is no help here, only evidence, and that is what I wanted to produce, and with it bring this originally rather out-of-the-way experiment into the limelight and place it at the centre of inquiry. I wanted to prove that when I drew back from the nourishment, it was not the ground that drew it slanting down towards it, but it was I who was attracting it to fall behind me. However,

I wasn't able to develop this experiment; seeing the victuals before your eyes at the same time as conducting a scientific experiment—you can't keep that up for long. But I wanted to do something different, I wanted to abstain entirely from eating for as long as I could hold out, while of course avoiding any sight of food, any temptation. If I withdrew in this way, lying night and day with eyes closed, concerned with neither keeping nor catching food, and without any other measures, if, as I secretly hoped, but did not dare to assert, I concentrated only on the unavoidable non-rational soil-watering, and on my whispered songs and spells (I wanted to avoid dancing, so as not to weaken myself), the nourishment from above would descend of itself and without bothering to reach the ground would tap on my teeth to be let in—if this happened, then science would not, it's true, be refuted, for it has enough flexibility to accommodate exceptions and isolated cases—but what would the pack say, which happily does not have so much flexibility? For this would not be an exceptional case of the kind history has handed down to us, telling perhaps of someone who refuses out of bodily illness or melancholy to prepare his food, or hunt for it, or eat it, and then the pack unites in chanting their conjurations, and that diverts the nourishment from its usual path straight into the sick dog's mouth. By contrast, I enjoyed the best of health and strength, with such a splendid appetite that all day long it prevented me from thinking of anything else; you may believe me or not, but I was submitting to my fast of my own free will; I was capable of taking care of the descent of my nourishment myself, and I wanted to do so too, so I did not need any help from the pack, and even refused it most resolutely. I sought out a suitable spot in an out-of-the-way thicket where I wouldn't hear any conversations about eating, nor any lip-smacking or bone-crunching. I stuffed myself one more time until I was full, and lay down. If possible I wanted to spend the entire time with my eyes closed; as long as nothing to eat came by, it would be uninterrupted night for me, even if it lasted for days and weeks. I was supposed to sleep very little, though, or at best not at all, which made things more difficult, for of course I had not only to summon down the nourishment but also be on the alert that I wouldn't perhaps be asleep when it arrived; on the other hand, sleep was very welcome, for asleep, I would be able to go hungry for much longer than when awake. For these reasons I decided to parcel out my time carefully and sleep a great deal, but always for very short spells only. I managed this by always supporting my head when I was asleep on a weak branch which soon snapped and woke me up. I lay like this, sleeping or waking, dreaming or singing quietly to myself. At first, the time passed without event. Perhaps wherever the nourishment comes from had somehow not yet noticed that I was setting myself against the usual course of things, so everything remained quiet. I was slightly disturbed in my efforts by the fear that the dogs would notice my absence, quickly discover me, and take some sort of measures against me. A second fear was that, although according to science the soil here was infertile, simply watering it would yield the so-called chance-nourishment, and I would be tempted by the smell. But for the time being, nothing of the kind happened and I was able to go on hungering. Apart from these fears, at first I was calm in a way I had never noticed in myself before. Although I was actually working on undoing the science here, I felt almost comfortable, and filled with the proverbial calm of the scientist at work. In my daydreams I achieved the forgiveness of science; there was room in it for my researches also; it had the sound of consolation to my ears that however successful my researches might be—then especially—the life of the pack would by no means be lost to me; science was well-disposed towards me; science itself would take on the interpretation of my results, and this promise already meant fulfilment itself. Whereas until now I had deep down felt rejected, and had stormed my people's defences like a madman, now I should be received with great honour, the warmth of the dogs' massed bodies which I had longed for would flow around me; to high acclaim I should be carried swaying on my people's shoulders. Remarkable effect of the first stage of fasting. My achievement seemed to me to be so great that in my quiet thicket I began to weep for sheer emotion and self-pity—something incomprehensible, for if I was expecting my well-deserved reward, why was I weeping? Probably with contentment. I had never taken pleasure in my weeping. The only times I wept were when, rarely enough, I was content. On this occasion of course it soon passed. The beautiful images gradually faded as my hunger grew more serious. It was not long, all fantasy and all emotion speedily dismissed, before I was completely alone with hunger burning my entrails. 'This is hunger,' I said to myself countless times, as if I wanted to make myself believe that hunger and I were still twofold and I could shake it off like a tiresome lover, but in reality we were most painfully one, and when I explained to myself

'This is hunger,' it was actually the hunger speaking, mocking me as it spoke. A dreadful, dreadful time! I shudder when I think of it, not only on account of the suffering I lived through at the time, but above all because I didn't complete it, because I shall have to taste this suffering over again if I want to achieve anything, for to this day I still regard hungering as the ultimate, the most powerful method in my researches. The true path goes by way of hungering; the greatest result is only achieved with the greatest effort—if it *is* achievable—and the greatest strain for us dogs is to go hungry voluntarily. So when I think those times through—and brooding on them gives me profound pleasure—I am also thinking through the times still looming imminently over me. It seems as though you have to allow a lifetime to pass before you recover from such an experiment; all the years of my maturity come between me and that fasting, but I have still not recovered. When I begin fasting, very soon now, I shall perhaps have greater determination than before, due to my greater experience and deeper insight into the necessity of the experiment, but my powers now are even slighter than they were then, at the very least I shall begin to weaken at the mere expectation of the horror I have already met. Having a smaller appetite will not help me; it will only reduce the value of the experiment a little, and will probably force me to fast for longer than was necessary then. I think I am clear about these and other prior conditions; there have been plenty of preliminary experiments in the long interval; I have often enough nibbled at hungering, so to speak, but I was not yet strong enough for its extreme, and the natural assertiveness of youth is of course gone for ever. It vanished back in those days, in the midst of hungering. All kinds of thoughts tormented me. Our forefathers appeared to me as a threat. I think, though I do not dare say so in public, that they are to blame for everything; they are responsible for the dog's life we lead, so I could easily answer their threats with counter-threats. But I bow before their knowledge. It came from sources no longer known to us. That is why, however much I feel the urge to fight them, at the same time I would never actually overstep their laws; I only make sallies out through the gaps in the law—for which I have a particularly good nose. With regard to hungering, I rely on the famous conversation during which one of our sages uttered his intention to forbid it, whereupon a second advised against this with the question: 'Then who would ever hunger?' and the first allowed himself to be convinced, and withdrew the ban. But then the further question arose: 'Isn't hungering forbidden all the same, actually?' The vast majority of the commentators deny it. They regard the ban on hungering as lifted, supporting the view of the second sage, and therefore they are not frightened of any ill consequences that might arise even from an erroneous commentary. I had made sure of that before I began my hungering. But now, as hunger bent me double, and, already confused in mind, I constantly looked to my hind legs to save me, desperately licking them, chewing them, and sucking at them, right up to the rump, it seemed to me that the general interpretation of that conversation was absolutely wrong. I cursed the learned art of commentary. I cursed myself for having been led astray by it, indeed the commentary contains, as a child is bound to recognize—a hungry child, that is—more than one single ban on hungering. The first sage wanted to forbid hungering. What a sage wants is already done, so hungering was forbidden. The second sage not only agreed with him, but even regarded hungering as impossible, so onto the first ban he threw a second, a ban on the very nature of dogs itself. The first acknowledged this, and withdrew the express ban, i.e. after giving a full exposition, he commanded the dogs to use their intelligence and forbid hungering for themselves. A triple ban, then, instead of the usual one, and I had broken it. Now I could of course have obeyed belatedly right then and stopped hungering, but all through the pain there also went a temptation to go on hungering, and I followed it, as lustfully as I might another dog. I couldn't stop. Perhaps I was already too weak to stand up and seek out inhabited territories to save myself. I tossed to and fro on the dry leaves; I was no longer able to sleep; everywhere I heard noise; the world that in my life so far had been asleep seemed to have been wakened by my hungering; I imagined that I would never be able to eat again, for if I did, I would have to silence the world of noise that had been let loose, and I wouldn't be capable of it, though it's true, the loudest noise I heard came from my stomach. I often put my ear against it, and must have opened my eyes wide in horror, for I could hardly believe what I was hearing. And as it was becoming too dreadful, a frenzy began to take hold of my nature as well; I made senseless attempts to save myself; I began to smell food, delicious food I had not eaten for ages, childhood treats, more, I smelt the scent of my mother's breasts; I forgot my decision to try and resist any smell, or, more correctly, I didn't forget it; treating it rather as if it were a decision that fitted the situation, I dragged myself around with it in all directions, never more than a few steps, sniffing as if I were looking for food only to guard myself against it. I was not disappointed at finding nothing: it was only a few steps too far for me to reach; my legs had given under me too soon. At the same time, though, I knew that there was nothing there; that I was only making these slight movements from fear that I would finally collapse in some place which I would not leave again. My last hopes disappeared, my last temptations; I would perish here miserably; where was the point of my researches, childish efforts from a childishly happy time? Here and now it was serious; here and now scientific inquiry could have proved its worth, but where was it? Here and now there was nothing but a dog snapping helplessly into the void, watering the ground in sudden spasm after spasm without knowing it, but out of the jumble of all the conjurations in his memory no longer able to dig up a single one, not even the little verse spoken when a newborn was tucked under his mother. I felt as if I were separated from my brothers not by a short run, but infinitely far away from everyone, and as if I were really dying not from hunger, but because I had been abandoned. It was surely obvious that no one cared about me, no one beneath the earth, no one upon it, no one above, I was perishing from their indifference; their indifference said: 'he is dying', and that is how it would happen. And wasn't I of the same mind? Wasn't I saying the same thing? Hadn't I willed my abandoned state? All right, you dogs, but not so as to end like this, rather so as to reach out to the truth from this world of lies, where there is no one you can learn the truth from, not even myself, native citizen as I am of the world of lies. Perhaps the truth was no longer all that far away, only for me, who had failed and was dying, it was too far. But you don't die as quickly as a nervous dog thinks. I only fainted, and when I awoke and lifted my eyes, a strange dog was standing in front of me. I felt no hunger; I was very strong; there was a spring in my limbs, I thought—though I made no attempt to test this by standing up. Essentially, I saw nothing more than I usually might, a handsome but not all that remarkable dog was standing in front me; that's what I saw, nothing else, but even so I believed I was seeing more in him than I usually would. There was blood beneath me, which at first I thought was food, but straight away I spotted that it was blood I had spewed. I turned away from it towards the strange dog. He was gaunt, long in the leg, brown, flecked here and there with white spots, and with a fine, strong, inquiring gaze. 'What are you doing here?' he said, 'You must leave this place.' 'I can't go now,' I said, without any further explanation, for how was I to explain everything to him, and he too seemed to be in a hurry. 'Please, leave this place,' he said, restlessly lifting one foot after the other. 'Leave me,' I said. 'Go away and don't bother about me; the others aren't bothering about me either.' 'I beg you, for your own sake,' he said. 'Beg me for whatever reason you will,' I said, 'I can't walk even if I wanted to.' 'You're wrong,' he said with a smile. 'You can walk. It's because you appear to be weak that I am asking you to walk away now, slowly; if you delay, you'll have to run later.' 'That's my concern,' I said. 'It's mine too,' he said, sad at my obstinacy, and was obviously willing to let me stay for a while, and to use the opportunity to make friendly advances. At another time I would gladly have tolerated them from the handsome dog, but right then I couldn't understand it, I was seized by a horror of it. 'Get away,' I yelped, all the louder as it was the only way I could defend myself. 'Of course I'll leave you,' he said, drawing back slowly. 'You're a peculiar dog. Don't you find me pleasing?' 'You'll please me if you go away and leave me in peace,' I said, but I was no longer as sure of myself as I wanted to make him think. With my senses sharpened by hunger, I saw or heard something in him; it was just beginning; it grew; it came closer, and already I knew: even if now you can't imagine that you will nevertheless be able to get up, this dog certainly has the power to drive you away. And I looked at him, a dog who had only gently shaken his head at my rough answer, with growing desire. 'Who are you?' I asked. 'I am a hunter,' he said. 'And why don't you want to leave me here?' 'You are disturbing me,' he said. 'I can't hunt if you are here.' 'Try,' I said, 'perhaps you'll be able to hunt all the same.' 'No,' he said, 'I'm sorry, but you must go.' 'Leave your hunting for today!' I begged. 'No,' he said, 'I must hunt.' 'I must go; you must hunt,' I said, 'nothing but musts. Do you understand why we must?' 'No,' he said, 'but there's nothing about it to understand; these are natural, self-evident things.' 'Not so,' I said, 'you are sorry you must drive me away and nevertheless you do so.' 'That's how it is,' he said. 'That's how it is,' I repeated in annoyance, 'that's no answer. Which would you find easier, to give up hunting or to drive me away?' 'To give up hunting,' he answered without hesitation. 'Well then,' I said, 'that's a contradiction.' 'What sort of contradiction?' he said. 'My dear little dog, do

you really not understand that I must? Don't you understand what is
self-evident, natural?' I didn't answer any more, for I noticed—and
I was filled with new life as I did, the sort of life brought about by
terror—I noticed from unfathomable little signs, which perhaps no
one else would have been able to notice, that out of the depths of his
chest the dog was preparing to sing. 'You're going to sing,' I said.
'Yes,' he said gravely, 'I will sing, but not yet.' 'You're already beginning,' I said. 'No,' he said, 'not yet. But I am making ready.' 'You've
already begun,' I said. 'No,' he said, 'not yet. But make yourself
ready.' 'I can already hear it, even though you're denying it,' I said,
trembling. He was silent. And then I thought I could perceive something that no dog before me had ever experienced, at least there is
not the slightest trace of it in the tradition, and, filled with endless
shame and dread, I plunged my face in the pool of blood in front of
me. For what I thought I perceived was that the dog was already singing without yet knowing it, more than that indeed, that the melody,
separate from him, was floating through the air and above and
beyond him according to its own laws as if he didn't belong to it, and
it was making for me, only for me. Today, of course, I deny all percep-
tions of that sort, ascribing them to my oversensitivity at the time,
but even if I was mistaken, the error still has a certain grandeur; it is
the one reality, even if it was only illusory, that I salvaged from my
time of hungering and brought into this world. It shows at least how
far we can get when we are completely beside ourselves. And I was,
really, completely beside myself. In normal circumstances I would
have been gravely ill, incapable of moving, but I couldn't resist the
melody, which the dog soon appeared to take over for himself. It
swelled with increasing power; there were perhaps no limits to its
intensity, and at the time it almost burst my eardrums. But the worst
thing was that it seemed to be there only for me, this awe-inspiring
voice, which made the forest fall silent, only for me; who was I, that
I dared remain here, parading myself before it, befouled with my
blood. I got up shakily and looked down at myself. I was still thinking
'This isn't going to run, is it?' when I was already flying along, driven
by the melody, in the most marvellous leaps and bounds. I told my
friends nothing; I would probably have told them everything as soon
as I arrived back, but I was too weak at the time, and later it seemed to
be once again incommunicable. Hints I couldn't restrain myself from
making were lost without trace in our conversations. Physically, by

the way, I recovered in a few hours; mentally I still bear the marks to this day.

But I did extend my researches to the music of dogs. Certainly science was not inactive in this field either. The science of music is, if I am rightly informed, perhaps even more wide-ranging than the science of nourishment, and in any case has firmer foundations. This can be explained if we accept that it is possible to work in the latter field more dispassionately than in the former; in the one it is more a question of observation and systematization, while in the other it is above all a question of making inferences for practice. This has a connection with the greater respect accorded to the science of music than to the science of nourishment, though the first was never able to reach the tribe as profoundly as the second. I too was further away from the science of music before I heard the voice in the forest, further than from any other. Certainly my experience with the music-dogs had pointed in that direction, but I was too young then, and again, it is not easy to get your teeth into this science; it is regarded as particularly difficult, and in its superior way cuts itself off from the masses. In addition, although the music was the most immediately striking thing about those dogs, what seemed to me to be more important than the music was their unreachable reserve; perhaps there was nothing anywhere to resemble their terrible music; this I could discount, but from then on their essential nature came to meet me in every dog everywhere. But to dig deep into the essential nature of dogs, it seemed to me that investigation into nourishment was the most suitable, leading without going round about to the goal. Perhaps I was wrong in this. Even then one borderland between the two sciences attracted my suspicions. It was the theory of song as summoning our nourishment. In this case again I am held up because I never went seriously into music-ology, and in this respect I cannot, not by a long way, even count myself among the half-educated—and they are always held in particular contempt by science. This is something I have to bear in mind always. In front of a true scholar—and I have, sadly, proof of this—I would do badly in even the easiest examination in science. Of course that has its good reasons, quite apart from the circumstances I have already mentioned, first in my scientific incompetence, poor intelligence, bad memory, and above all in my inability to keep my scientific aim in sight all the time. I admit all that to myself quite frankly, even with a certain pleasure. For the deeper reason for my scientific incompetence seems to me to be an instinct, and truly not a bad instinct at that. If I wanted to boast and brag, I could say that it was this very instinct that destroyed my scientific abilities, for it would be at the least a very remarkable phenomenon that I, displaying as I do a tolerable common sense in the ordinary things of daily life, which are certainly not the simplest, and above all being able to understand, if not science, then certainly scientists very well, for that can be tested by my results, that I should have been from the start incapable of lifting a paw even onto science's first rung. It was this instinct that perhaps, simply for the sake of science, but a different science from the one practised nowadays, a science to end all sciences, made me value freedom above all else. Freedom! Certainly freedom as we have it nowadays is a pitiful growth. But in any case freedom, in any case a possession.

The Burrow

I HAVE fitted out the burrow and it seems to have turned out well.
From the outside only a great hollow is actually visible, but this leads
nowhere in reality, for after only a few steps you come up against solid
natural rock. I won't boast that I carried this stratagem out on purpose, rather it was the relic of my many failed attempts at building a
burrow, but in the end it seemed useful to leave this one hollow uncovered. It is true, some stratagems are so subtle that they become self-
defeating, I know that better than anyone, and it is certainly daring,
I agree, to use this hollow to draw attention at all to the possibility that
there is something here worth probing in the first place. Even so,
anyone who thinks I am a coward, and that I am only designing my
burrow out of something like cowardice, is making a mistake. A good
thousand paces from this hollow, hidden by a removable layer of moss,
is where the actual access to the burrow lies; it is made as secure as
anything in the world can ever be made secure, though certainly anyone can tread on the moss or push a foot through it, and then my burrow lies open to whoever wishes—though it will require certain not
very common abilities—to penetrate it and destroy it all for ever. I am
very aware of this, and my life, even now when it is in its prime, has
scarcely an entirely quiet moment; there in that place in the dark moss
I am mortal, and often in my dreams a lecherous snout is always snuf-
fling around it. I could, you might think, have covered this hole too,
the real entrance, with a thin top layer of tight-packed soil and further
down with looser earth, so that it would always give me very little
trouble in digging myself out again afresh over and over again. All the
same, that is not possible; simple prudence requires the possibility of
a quick way out for me; simple prudence, as so often, alas, requires
some risk to life; these are all pretty laborious calculations, and the
pleasure a keen mind takes in its own operation is sometimes the only
reason for going on calculating. I must have the possibility of a quick
way out, for despite all my watchfulness can't I still be attacked from a
quite unexpected quarter? I live in peace in the deepest depths of my
burrow, and meanwhile my enemy is tunnelling from somewhere
slowly and silently towards me; I don't mean he has a finer nose for
another's presence than I, perhaps he knows as little about me as I do
about him, but there are avid marauders who scrabble blindly through

the earth, and with the enormous extent of my burrow even they have a hope of stumbling upon one of my pathways somewhere, though of course I have the advantage of being in my own house and of being familiar with all the paths and their routes, so the marauder can easily become my prey—and one with a sweet taste. But I am growing old; there are many who are stronger than I am, and my enemies are numberless; it could happen that I might be escaping from one adversary and run into the jaws of another, oh, what is there that mightn't happen—anyway I have to be confident that somewhere there is an easily accessible, completely open exit where I no longer have to labour to get out, so that I do not, for instance, while I am digging away there desperately even though the soil is loose, suddenly—heaven preserve me!—feel the teeth of my pursuer in my flank. And it is not only external enemies from outside who threaten me, there are also some deep in the earth; so far I have never seen them, but legends tell of them, and I firmly believe in them. They are beings within the depths of the earth; not even legend can describe them, even those who become their victims have scarcely seen them; they come; you can hear their claws scratching just below you in the earth, which is their element, and already you are lost. It doesn't count now that you are in your own house, it is rather that you are in their house. Even my first way out will not save me from them, just as it probably will not ever save me at all, but destroy me. Still, it is a hope, and I cannot live without it.

As well as by this major pathway I am connected to the outside world by quite narrow paths which are seemingly without danger and allow me access to good, breathable air. They are made by field-mice, and I have been able to integrate them neatly into my burrow; they also enable me to catch a scent over a wide area and so give me protection; all kinds of such small creatures also come along them to me; these I eat up, so that I can live modestly on sufficient small game without leaving my burrow at all—which is of course very useful.

But the best thing about my burrow is its silence. Of course, this is deceptive. All of a sudden one day it can be interrupted, and then it's all over. But for the moment it is still there. For hours I can creep along my passageways, hearing nothing but the occasional rustling of some small creature, which I also promptly quieten between my teeth, or the trickling of earth, which tells me that some repair is necessary—otherwise, all is still. The forest air drifts in to me, it is both warm and cool, sometimes I stretch out and roll about in the passageway, full of well-being. It is good for one's approaching age to have such a burrow, to have found a shelter for oneself when autumn begins.

Every hundred metres or so I have widened the passageways into little round spaces, where I can curl up comfortably and rest. There I sleep the sweet sleep of peace, of desire satisfied, of purpose achieved, of house possessed. I don't know whether it is a habit persisting from old times or whether the dangers even of this house are strong enough to wake me, but invariably I start up from deep sleep and listen, listen into the silence reigning here night and day unchanging, smile, my mind composed again, and sink, my limbs relaxed, into a still deeper sleep. Poor wayfarer, unhoused, on the high road, in the forest, at best lying beneath a pile of leaves or among a pack of your kind, at the mercy of all the disasters of heaven and earth. I lie here in a clearing protected on all sides—there are more than fifty like it in my burrow—and the hours pass as I choose them, between dozing and unconscious sleep.

Not quite at the centre of my burrow, well judged for the event of extreme danger, not of pursuit exactly, but of siege, lies the main clearing. Whereas everything else is perhaps more the work of intelligence at full stretch than of physical toil, this citadel is the product of the hardest labour engaging every part of my body. There were some occasions when, desperate from physical exhaustion, I wanted to stop everything, I would fling myself on my back and curse the burrow, I would drag myself outside and leave the burrow lying there open. I was able to do that because I no longer wanted to go back to it, until after hours or days I would return in remorse, and might almost have lifted my voice in song at the sight of the burrow unharmed. Full of heartfelt joy, I would begin the work afresh. Work on the citadel became unnecessarily difficult. Unnecessarily because the burrow itself did not actually gain any advantage from the additional labour on it, for just at the place where the clearing was planned, the earth was very loose and sandy. The soil had to be practically hammered firm so as to shape the large, beautifully vaulted and rounded space. But for work of that kind I have only my forehead. So thousands and thousands of times, night and day, with my forehead I ran and butted the earth, I was happy if I pounded it till the blood flowed, for that was some proof that the wall was beginning to harden, and that is how, it must be conceded, I have surely earned my citadel.

This citadel is where I gather my provisions, everything I hunt inside the burrow that goes beyond my immediate needs, and everything I bring back from hunting outside I heap up here. The clearing is so big that provisions for half a year will not fill it. Consequently I can spread them out nicely, wander around them, play with them, enjoy their sheer quantity and the variety of their scents, and always have a precise overall view of what is there. I can always rearrange them, and according to the season I can make calculations in advance and plan my hunting. There are times when I am so well supplied that, out of indifference towards food in general, I don't touch the small creatures scurrying about at all, which I grant is perhaps improvident of me, though for different reasons. It comes with being busied so often in preparing the defences that I keep on changing or developing my ideas on how best to make use of the burrow for these purposes, though on a small scale, of course. It sometimes seems to me dangerous to be basing my defences wholly on the citadel, for after all the burrow's diversity also offers me more diverse possibilities; it seems more prudent then to distribute some of my supplies around, and lay up my stocks in a number of small clearings; I then assign roughly every third clearing to be a reserve store, or every fourth to be a main supply depot and every second to be an ancillary supply and suchlike. Or, in order to give a false lead, I will leave several paths completely out of use as depots for building up supplies. Or, quite arbitrarily, I will choose no more than a few clearings, relative to their distance from the main exit. It is true, every new plan of this kind requires hard work carrying supplies; I have to make the new calculations and then haul the loads to and fro. Of course I can do this undisturbed and without rushing, and it isn't so bad, holding these good things in your mouth, taking a rest wherever you might want, and nibbling at whatever you might fancy. It is worse when sometimes—usually when I start up from sleep—it seems to me that the current distribution is totally wrong and can lead to great dangers and has to be put right at once, on the instant, with no consideration for sleepiness or fatigue. Then I will hurry, then I will fly, then I have no time for calculations, for I am eager to carry out a completely new plan straight away; I grab arbitrarily at whatever my teeth come upon, I drag, I haul, I sigh, I groan, I stumble, and only some random change in the present state of affairs, which seem so terribly dangerous, will satisfy me. Until gradually, as I wake up fully, clear-headedness takes

over and I can hardly understand my hastiness, I breathe in deep the
peace of my house which I myself have disturbed, go back to my bed,
and tired once more, fall asleep immediately; then when I awake, as
irrefutable proof of my nocturnal labours, which now seem almost
like a dream, I find I have a rat or some such dangling from my jaws.
Then again there are times when gathering all my supplies in one
place once more seems the best thing to do. What use can the provisions in the small clearings be to me, how much can these hold anyway, and whatever you take there will block the track and one day it
might get in the way of my movements as I defend the place. Besides,
it is stupid, but true, that your self-esteem suffers if you can't see your
entire hoard all together so that you can tell at a glance what you possess. And in distributing all these stores around couldn't a great deal
be lost? I can't constantly be going galloping round all the twists and
turns of my passageways to see if everything is in good order. Of
course, the fundamental idea of distributing provisions around is the
right one, but only in fact if you have several clearings similar to my
citadel. Several clearings like it! Oh, indeed! Who is up to building
those? Besides, in the total design of my burrow it is no longer possible to find a place for them retrospectively. But I will concede that
this is a flaw in the burrow, just as there is always a flaw wherever you
have only one exemplar. And I admit too that all the time I was building it, I was obscurely aware—though distinctly enough, if I had
wanted—that the challenge of several citadels was growing within me;
I did not give in to it; I felt I was too weak for the enormous labour,
indeed I felt too weak to imagine that the labour would be necessary;
somehow I consoled myself with feelings no less obscure that efforts
which would otherwise be inadequate would for once in my case—as
an exception, as an act of grace, probably because Providence had a
particular care for my forehead, my pounding-hammer—be adequate.
Well, so I have only one citadel, but the obscure feelings that the one
I do have will be adequate this time have disappeared. Be that as it
may, I must be content with the one; for the small clearings cannot
possibly take its place, so now that this perception has developed in
me I begin to drag everything back to the citadel once more. For some
time now it has been a great comfort to me to have all the clearings
and passageways free, and see how the quantities of meat pile up in
the citadel, sending out their many intermingled scents as far as the
outermost passages. Each one of them delights me in its own way, and

I can distinguish them clearly even from a distance. All this usually brings especially peaceful times, and I move my sleeping places slowly, gradually, from the outer circles inwards; I immerse myself deeper and deeper in the scents until I can bear it no longer, and there comes a night when I storm into the citadel, rummage with all my might in my provisions, and stuff myself into total stupefaction with the finest I possess. Happy, but dangerous times! Anyone who knew how to exploit them could, without any danger to themselves, easily destroy me. Here too being without a second or third citadel also contributes to the damage; it is the vast, single, accumulated hoard that is my temptation. I try to protect myself from it in various ways—indeed distributing to the smaller clearings is in part another measure of this kind, but unfortunately, like other such measures, it leads through abstinence to even greater greed, which then capriciously alters my defence plans and gets the better of my intelligence.

After such occasions, to compose myself I usually re-plan the burrow, and after I have seen to the necessary repairs, I will often leave it, though always just for a short time. To live without it seems too hard a punishment, even to me, but I do see the necessity of getting out now and again. There is something almost like a ceremony about approaching the exit. In the times I spend at home, I keep away from it, I even avoid taking the passageway whose furthest ramifications lead towards it; also, it's not at all easy to wander around there, as I have designed a crazy little zigzag system of passages. That is the place where my burrow began; at the time I couldn't yet hope to be able to finish it as it stood in my design; I began half-playfully in this corner, and that is how my early delight in the work led to wildly building a labyrinth; at the time it seemed to me to be the crown of all buildings, but today I would judge it, probably more correctly, as on far too small a scale, amateur tinkering not really worthy of the total structure; theoretically it might perhaps be charming—here is the entry to my house, I used to say ironically to my invisible enemies, seeing them all suffocating in the entrance-labyrinth—but in reality it represents a folly with walls far too thin, which will hardly withstand a serious attack or an enemy fighting desperately for his life. So should I rebuild this part? I drag out reaching a decision, and it will probably stay the way it is. Apart from the great labour I would expect of myself, it would also be the most dangerous thing you could think of; at the time I began building I could work there relatively undisturbed; the risk was not much greater than at any other time, but today it would mean almost wilfully drawing the world's attention to the entire structure; today it is no longer possible. I am almost glad of it, for I still have a certain affection for this work of my early days. And if a major attack were to come, what ground plan for the entrance could save me? An entrance can deceive, divert, tease the attacker—and this one can do as much in an emergency, but a really serious attack is something I shall have to encounter immediately, with all the resources of the whole burrow and all the powers of body and soul—of course, that goes without saying. So let this entrance stay as it is. The burrow has so many weaknesses imposed on it by nature, so it might as well keep this one too, which was made by my hands, and fully acknowledged, though only in retrospect, to be a flaw. Nevertheless, that is not to say that I am not from time to time, or rather all the time, upset by this error. If, when I take my usual stroll, I avoid this part of the burrow, it is mainly because the sight of it displeases me, because I do not wish to look closely at a flaw in the building when that flaw has already been haunting my consciousness all too long. It is all very well for the flaw to persist incorrigibly up there at the entrance, but as long as it can be avoided I prefer to spare myself the sight of it. If I merely go in that direction, even though I am separated from it by passageways and clearings, I believe I have already fallen into a perilous situation; I sometimes feel as if my pelt were becoming thinner, as if I might be standing there with my flesh stripped naked, greeted at that moment by the howling of my enemies. Certainly, the very idea of an exit, where my house no longer shelters me, conjures up unwholesome feelings of this kind; nevertheless, it is this entrance structure too that especially torments me. Sometimes I dream that I have rebuilt it, altered it completely, rapidly, with a giant's strength, in one night, seen by no one, and now it is proof against all attack. The sleep in which that occurs is the sweetest sleep of all; tears of joy and relief still glisten on the bristles of my beard when I awake.

So I also have to cope physically with the grief the labyrinth causes me whenever I go outside, and I am both annoyed and touched if sometimes, just for a moment I take a wrong turning in my own construction, and the work seems still to be making an effort, wanting to prove, though my judgement has long ago been fixed, its justification for existing. But at that point I am beneath the covering of moss—which

I have sometimes allowed to grow and merge into the rest of the forest floor, for I do not stir out of the house for very long—and then all that is needed is a jerk of my head and I am in a strange land. For a long time I don't dare to make this little movement; if I didn't have to cope with the entrance labyrinth once more, I would certainly give up trying today, and drift back again. What? Your house is protected, self-contained. You live in peace, warm, well fed, lord, sole lord of a vast number of passageways and clearings, and all this you want to—not sacrifice exactly, I hope, but as it were abandon; certainly you are confident of winning it back, but you are still involving yourself in a gamble, one with all-too-high stakes. You say there are reasonable grounds for it? For something like that there can be no reasonable grounds. All the same I lift the trap-door cautiously and I am outside; I drop it cautiously and race as fast as I can away from the treacherous spot.

But I am not actually free; true, I am no longer squeezing my way through the passageways, but chasing through the open forest; I can feel my body fill with new energies for which there was, as it were, no room in the burrow, not even in the citadel even if it were ten times bigger. The food outside is better too; the hunt is harder, I admit, and success comes more rarely, but in every respect the result counts for more. I don't deny all this; I appreciate it and I enjoy it at least as well as everyone else, but probably far more, for I don't go hunting like a poacher out of thoughtlessness or desperation, but purposefully and steadily. Also, I am not destined for a life of freedom, to be at its mercy; on the contrary, I know that my time is measured, that I do not have to go hunting here for ever, but that, when I wish it, as it were, and am weary of life here, someone will call me to himself whose invitation I will not be able to resist. And so I can make the most of this time here, spending it without a care, or rather I could—and yet I cannot. The burrow preoccupies me too much. I ran away from the entrance fast; but I shall also return soon. I shall search out a good hiding-place for myself and keep watch night and day on the entrance to my house—this time from outside. You may call it foolish, but it gives me unutterable pleasure, more than that, it reassures me. I feel then as if I weren't standing and looking at my house, but at myself as I sleep, and as if I had the good fortune to be both deep asleep and at the same time able to observe myself keenly. I am, you might say, marked out to see the ghosts of the night not only in my vulnerable and sweet trustful sleep, but at the same time to encounter them in reality too, awake and energetic, with a strong and steady judgement. And I discover, remarkably, that things are not going as badly for me as I once thought, and as I shall probably think again, once I have descended into my house. In this respect—probably in others too, but particularly in this one—these expeditions outside are really indispensable. Certainly, however remote the site I chose for the entrance (the total plan imposed certain limitations anyway), a great deal of to-ing and fro-ing goes on up there nevertheless, if I sum up observations made over something like a week—though that may generally be the case in all habitable regions; even so it may be better to be exposed to a greater amount of such to-ing and fro-ing, which is carried along by its own impetus, than to be utterly alone at the mercy of the first intruder who comes prowling along. There are many enemies here, and even more to aid and abet them, but they also fight among themselves, and simply go careering past the burrow. In all this time I have never seen anyone actually probing at the entrance, fortunately for me—and for him too—for, frantic in my concern for the burrow, I would certainly have flung myself at his throat. It is true, though, some creatures also came along that I didn't dare to go near; I only had to sense their presence in the distance to be forced to flee; I can't actually say anything for certain about their reactions to the burrow, but it is probably sufficient to calm me down and for me to return before long, when I found none of them there any longer, and the entrance unharmed. There were good times when I almost told myself that the hostility of the world towards me had perhaps ceased or settled down, or that the strength of the burrow would relieve me from my previous deadly struggle. The burrow is perhaps a greater protection, I said to myself, than I have ever thought or, deep inside it, than I ever dared to think. It went so far that I sometimes had the childish wish never to return to the burrow at all, but settle down here near the entrance, spend my life observing the entrance, and find my happiness in constantly reminding myself of how soundly the burrow, if I were inside it, would keep me safe. Well, there is such a thing as a sudden awakening out of childish dreams. What kind of security was I observing here? Is it possible at all for me to judge the danger threatening me inside the burrow from the experiences I have had here outside? Are my enemies able to sense my presence properly at all when I am not in the burrow? They certainly have some sense of my presence, but only a partial one. And doesn't the persistence of a strong sense of a presence usually announce danger? So it is only half-experiments, quarter-experiments, that I have been trying out, apt to reassure me, and by lulling me into a sense of false security, putting me into very great danger. No, I was not observing my sleep, as I had thought; instead it is rather I who am asleep, while the destroyer watches. Perhaps he is among those who stroll casually past the entrance, always just making sure, just like me, that the door is still unharmed and ready for their attack, and they only walk past because they know the master of the house is not inside, or even because they know he is innocently lurking in the bushes nearby. And I leave my observation post, and have had enough of life outdoors and free; I feel as if I could learn nothing more here, not now and not later. And I dearly want to bid farewell to everything here, descend to my burrow and never come back, let things take their course and not hold them up with useless observation. But I have been spoiled by seeing everything that went on above the entrance for so long now that I find it very painful to carry out the business of descent, which can actually attract attention itself, not knowing what will happen behind my back and then behind the trapdoor, once it is closed. I try it out first on stormy nights by throwing down the spoils of my hunting; it seems to succeed, but whether it really does will only become apparent when I have gone down myself; it will become apparent, but no longer to me, or it will to me as well, but too late. So I give that up, and I don't go down. As an experiment I dig, sufficiently far away from the real entrance of course, a ditch no longer than I am myself and also closed over with a covering of moss; I crawl into the ditch, cover it over behind me, wait for carefully calculated stretches of time, longer and shorter, at various times of day, then I throw off the moss, emerge, and note my observations. They are extremely various, good and bad, but I do not find a general law or an infallible method for my descent. Consequently I am glad I have not yet descended by way of the real entrance and desperate that I shall soon have to do so. I am not far from deciding to go far away, resume my wretched old life once more, which had no security at all, but was a single teeming confusion of many dangers and consequently did not allow me to see, and fear, any particular danger as sharply as a comparison of my secure burrow with the rest of life constantly teaches me. Of course, such a decision would have been completely crazy, provoked simply by living in senseless freedom for far too long. The burrow is still mine. I have only to take one step and I am secure. And I tear myself free of all doubts and run in broad daylight straight towards the door, quite sure I shall raise it this time, but still I cannot do so. I run right over it and deliberately throw myself into a thorn-bush as a punishment, punishment for a guilt I do not know. For I admit, in the end I have to tell myself that I am right after all, and that it is really impossible to descend without openly abandoning the dearest things I have, everything round about, on the ground, in the trees, in the air, at least for a little while. And the danger is not imaginary, but very real. It does not have to be an actual enemy whose desire to follow me I have aroused; it can easily be any little innocent, any nasty little creature who pursues me out of curiosity and so, without knowing it, becomes the leader of the world against me; it does not even have to be her, perhaps it is someone—and that's just as bad as the other, in many respects it's the worst—perhaps it is someone of my own kind, an expert and good judge of a building, some brother of the forest, a peace-lover, but a vile rogue who wants a house to dwell in without building it. Still, if he did come now, if in his filthy greed he did discover the entrance, if he did start to work on it and lifted up the moss, if he did succeed, if he was agile enough to force his way in and had already disappeared so far inside that only his backside surfaced for just a moment, if all that were to happen so that I could leap on him at last in a mad rage, free of any doubts, bite him to bits, flay him to tatters, tear him apart and drink him dry, and straight away stuff his corpse down below with the rest of my hunting spoils, but above all—and that would be the main thing—so that I could be in my burrow at last, I would gladly admire even the labyrinth this time. But first I would close the moss covering above me and rest, I think, for the remainder of my life. But no one comes, and I am left to fend for myself. With my mind constantly absorbed with the difficulty of it all, I lose a great deal of my timidity; I no longer avoid the entrance, even outside; circling around it becomes my favourite activity; it is already almost as though I were the enemy spying out a suitable occasion to break in successfully. If only I had someone I could trust, and could station at my observation-post, then I could descend with confidence. I would contract with him as my confidant that he should observe the situation closely when I descend and for a long time afterwards, and knock on the covering of moss at any sign of danger, but not otherwise. That would make a completely clean sweep above me; nothing would remain, at most only the one I trust. For won't he want something in return for what he has done, won't he at least want to look round the burrow, but even this, to admit someone willingly into my burrow, I would find distressing. I built it for myself, not for visitors. I think I wouldn't let him in; even as his price for enabling me to enter my burrow I wouldn't let him in. But most certainly I couldn't let him in, because I would either have to let him come down by himself, which is beyond all imagining, or we would have to descend together, which would cancel out the very advantage he is supposed to give me by conducting observations when my back is turned. And what becomes of my trust? Can I trust him face to face in the same way as when I don't see him and when we are separated by the moss covering? It is relatively easy to trust someone if you are watching him at the same time or at least if you are in a position to watch him; perhaps it is even possible to trust someone from a distance, but from deep inside the burrow, that is, from a different world, to trust someone from outside is, I truly believe, impossible. But such doubts are not even necessary, it is sufficient simply to consider that during or after my descent all the countless contingencies of life can hinder the one I trust in fulfilling his duties, and what incalculable consequences the slightest hindrance to him can have for me. No, taken all in all, I don't have to complain at all about being alone and having no one I can trust. I certainly do not lose any advantage by it, and I am probably sparing myself some injury. But I can trust only myself and the burrow. I should have considered that earlier and anticipated the difficulty that is worrying me so much now. It would have been possible at least in part when I began building. I ought to have designed the first passage in such a way that it would have had two entrances, at an appropriate distance from each other, so that I would have descended through the one entrance, with all the unavoidable complications that involves, then have run quickly along the start of the passageway to the second entrance, lifted its moss covering slightly, which would have been put there for this purpose, and from there attempted to watch the situation for a few days and nights. This would have been the only right way. True, two entrances double the danger, but in this case my doubts would have to keep silent, especially as the one entrance, which was only planned as an observation post could be made quite narrow. At this point I am getting lost in

technical considerations, and beginning once again to dream my
dream of an utterly perfect burrow. This reassures me a little; my eyes
closed, it gives me delight to see distinct and not-so-distinct possibilities for building so that I can slip in and out unnoticed. Lying here
and thinking about it I have a high opinion of these possibilities, but
still only as technical achievements, not as real advantages, for where
is the point of all this unimpeded slipping in and out? It indicates an
unsettled mind, insecure self-esteem, impure desires, bad character-
traits, which become much worse in view of the burrow, for after all it
exists, and is able to fill one with its peace only if one opens up to it
completely. Well, right now, it is true, I am outside it, and I am looking for a possible way of returning, and for that the necessary technical arrangements would be very welcome. Still, maybe not all that
welcome. In the anxieties of the moment, aren't you underestimating
the burrow if you only regard it as a cave to creep into and hide in as
securely as possible? Certainly it is this secure cave as well—at least
it's supposed to be—and whenever I imagine being in the midst of
some danger, clenching my teeth and willing it with all my might, all
I want the burrow to be is simply and solely the hole meant to save my
life and for it to fulfil the explicit task I have given it as completely as
possible, and I am ready to absolve it of any other. But as things are,
in reality—in times of great distress this is something one cannot see,
and even in times devoid of danger one first has to learn to see—the
burrow may indeed offer a great deal of security, but not enough by
a long way, so will my anxieties about it ever completely cease?
These are different anxieties, prouder, richer in content, often long-
suppressed, but their crippling effect is perhaps the same as the worries brought by life outside it. If I had built the burrow only to secure
my life, I wouldn't feel cheated, but the relation between the tremendous labour and the actual security, at least insofar as I am in a position to feel it and insofar as I can profit from it, would not be in my
favour. It is very painful to admit that, but I must confess, it has to
happen, especially in view of the entrance there, which is now closing
itself against me, its builder and owner, indeed, clenches up tight. But
the burrow is not simply just a rescue-hole! When I stand in the citadel surrounded by my huge heaps of meat, my face turned towards
my ten passageways leading out from here, each particular one dug
deeper or banked up according to the total plan, straight or curving,
widening or narrowing, and all of them equally empty and still, ready,

each in its own way, to lead me further to my many clearings, and all
of these empty too and silent—then I am far from thinking about
security. Then I know deep down that this is my stronghold, which
I have won by gnawing and butting, scraping and stamping, from the
stubborn earth, my stronghold which in no way can belong to anyone
else, and which is so much mine that in this place I can in the end
calmly accept even the fatal wound from my enemy, for my blood will
seep away into my earth and will not be lost. And what else can be the
meaning of the pleasant hours I usually pass in my passageways, half
peacefully sleeping, half happily waking, passageways, calculated
exactly to fit my needs, for stretching out pleasurably, rolling about
childishly, lying dreamily around, falling blissfully asleep. And the
little clearings, each one familiar, each one, despite their complete
similarity, clearly distinguishable by the mere curve of its walls, they
embrace me more warmly, more peacefully, than any nest embraces a
bird. And everything, everything, empty and silent.

But if that is how it is, why am I hesitating, why am I more afraid
of an interloper than of the possibility that I might perhaps never see
my burrow again? Well, that, fortunately, is impossible. It would not
take any prior reflection for me to be clear about what the burrow
means to me; the burrow and I belong together so closely that I could
settle down here calmly, calmly for all my anxiety, and would not have
to make an effort to conquer my fears and against all my doubts, to
open the entrance; it would be quite enough for me to wait and do
nothing, for in the long run nothing can part us, and somehow in the
end I shall quite certainly go down to it. But of course, how much
time will pass until then, and how much can happen in that time, up
here as well as down there? And after all I am the only one who can
make it shorter, and do what is needed without delay.

And now, already unable to think for weariness, with head droop-
ing and legs unsure, half asleep, more groping than walking, I approach
the entrance; slowly I lift the moss, slowly I climb down. Distracted,
I leave the entrance uncovered unnecessarily long, then remind
myself of my omission, climb up again to put it right, but why should
I bother to climb right up? I only have to draw the moss covering
over; very well, so after that I'll just climb down again; and I finally
draw the moss covering close. It is only in this condition, solely in this
condition, that I am able to carry it out. So now I am lying underneath the moss on top of the spoils I brought in, surrounded by blood

and dripping flesh, and I could begin to sleep my longed-for sleep. Nothing disturbs me, nothing has followed me, up above the moss everything seems quiet, at least so far, and even if it weren't quiet, I don't think I could let taking observations hold me up. I have changed my place. I have come from the upper world down into my burrow, and I can feel the effect immediately. I have returned from a journey, numb and exhausted from the stresses and strains, but the reunion with my old dwelling, and with the work of fitting it out awaiting me, the need to take a quick look round all the spaces at least superficially, above all to press on as fast as I can to the citadel. All that transforms my fatigue, making me restless, eager. It is as if I had, during the second that I entered the burrow, slept deep and long. My first task is very laborious, and takes a lot out of me: it is to carry my hunting spoils through the narrow, loose-walled passages of the labyrinth. I push forwards with all my strength, and I manage it, but far too slowly; to do the job more quickly I haul part of the mass of flesh back and clamber over it, through it, so I have only a fraction of it ahead of me now and it is easier to move it forwards—though here in these narrow passages, which are not always easy to get through, even when I am unencumbered, I am so deep in this vast quantity of flesh that I could very well suffocate in my own supplies, indeed I can sometimes only survive their pressure by eating and drinking a way through. But my haulage efforts are successful, it won't take me too long to finish, the labyrinth has been conquered; taking a deep breath, I stand in a proper passageway, pushing the spoils down a connecting passage into a main route designed especially for the purpose, and leading steeply down towards the citadel. Now it is no longer hard labour; now the whole thing rolls and flows along almost of itself. In my citadel at last! At last I can sleep! Everything is unchanged, no disaster seems to have occurred; the slight damage here and there, as I see at first glance, can quickly be repaired. Only first, a long ramble down the passageways; that is not a burden, though, it is talking with friends, as I did in the old days—I'm still not that old, but my memory for many things is already quite clouded—or as I once did, or as I heard it used to be done. I begin now with the second passageway, deliberately slowly; now that I have seen the citadel I have endless time; inside the burrow I always have endless time, for everything I do there is good, and important, and fills my cup to the brim, as it were. I begin with the second passageway, break off my inspection halfway through, and move on to the third passageway, letting it lead me back to the citadel, so now I have to begin afresh on the second passageway anyway, and I turn the work into play, spin it out, laugh to myself and enjoy it and become quite bemused by the number of things to do, but I don't stop. For you, my passageways and clearings, and you above all, my citadel, I have come; I have counted my life as nothing after I was for so long stupid enough to tremble for it and delay returning to you. What do I care for danger now that I am with you! You belong to me, and I to you; we are bound together, what can befall us? Let the creatures throng up above if they want, and let their snouts be ready to push their way through the moss! For with its emptiness and silence the burrow welcomes even me, confirming what I say.

But now I am overcome by a certain sluggishness, and I curl up in a loose ball in one of my favourite clearings; I haven't inspected everything, not by a long way, but I do want to continue my inspection to the end; I don't want to go to sleep here, only I yield to the temptation of settling myself down as if I did; I want to see whether that will still succeed as well as it used to. It does, but I don't succeed in rousing myself: I stay here deep asleep. I have probably been sleeping for a very long time. I am woken out of the last traces of sleep only as they begin to fade; it must have been a very light sleep, for a scarcely audible piping rouses me. I understand it at once: in my absence the small creatures, too little noticed and too often spared by me, have tunnelled a fresh path somewhere; this path has joined up with an old one; the air is caught there, and that has produced the piping sound. What incessantly busy creatures they are, and how annoying their busy-ness! I shall have to listen closely at my passage walls and by making some exploratory excavations first establish where the disturbance is coming from; only then will I be in a position to dispose of the noise. Incidentally, I shall also be glad of the new trench as a new air-duct, as long as it accords somehow with the proportions of the burrow. But I shall take more notice of the small creatures than I have done up till now; not one of them shall be spared.

As I have had a great deal of practice in making inspections of this kind, it will probably not take long, and I can start straight away. True, there are other works waiting to be done, but this is the most urgent. It shall be quiet in my passageways. This noise, by the way, is a relatively innocuous one; I didn't hear it at all when I arrived, though it must certainly have already been present; I had to be fully at home again before I heard it; it can only be heard as it were by the ear of the real house-owner exercising his office. And it is not even there all the time, as other such sounds usually are; it has long intervals in between, which obviously derive from a build-up of the air-current. I start my investigation, but I do not succeed in finding the place where one ought to probe; I do embark on a few excavations, but only at random; of course, nothing comes of doing things in this way, and the hard work of digging and even harder work of filling-in and smoothing-off is for nothing. I am not getting any closer to the place where the noise came from; it can be heard at regular intervals, unchanged and thin, sometimes like piping, sometimes more like whistling. Now another possibility would be to leave it be for the time being; it is a great nuisance, it's true, but there can hardly be any doubt about what I have assumed to be the source of the noise, so it will not get any louder; on the contrary it might happen—though up till now I have never waited that long—that in the course of time, on account of further tunnelling by the little creatures, these noises will disappear of their own accord; besides, chance will often put one on the track of the disturbance, while a systematic search over a long time can come to nothing. That is how I reassure myself; I would much rather ramble further along the passageways and visit the clearings, many of which I haven't yet even seen again, in between gambolling around a bit in the citadel. But the noise will not leave me alone; I have to go on looking for it. Oh, the small creatures cost me so much time, so much time that could be better spent. In such matters it is usually the technical problem that attracts me; for example, depending on the sound, which my ear is adept at distinguishing in all its nuances, I conceive an idea of its cause, very precise, fit to be sketched, and then I have an urge to test whether the reality corresponds to this. With good reason, for as long as it cannot be established firmly, I cannot feel safe either, even if it were only a matter of knowing where a grain of sand falling down a wall is going to land. And in this respect even a noise of that kind is most certainly not an unimportant matter. But important or unimportant, however intently I search, I find nothing. Or rather, I find too much. It had to happen right in my favourite clearing, I think, head- ing off a long way away from it, halfway to the next clearing; actually, I think, the whole thing is a joke, as if I wanted to prove that it wasn't just my favourite clearing alone that had created this disturbance for me, but that there were disturbances elsewhere too, and with a smile I begin to listen. But I soon stop smiling, for truly, the same piping is here too. It is nothing, surely; sometimes I think that no one but me would hear it. I can hear it now, of course, more and more clearly, with an ear made keener by practice, although in reality it is exactly the same sound everywhere, as I can convince myself when I compare them. And it doesn't become any louder, I note as I listen, not right by the wall, but in the middle of the passageway. Then it is only with great strain, intense concentration indeed, that now and again I guess at rather than hear the breath of a sound at all. But it is this very sameness everywhere that upsets me most because it cannot be reconciled with my original hypothesis. If I had guessed the reason for the noise correctly, it should have reverberated with a louder sound coming from one definite place, the one I needed to discover, and then become fainter and fainter. But if my explanation was not the right one, what else could it be? There was still the possibility that there were two centres of noise which up till now I had only listened to while I was some distance away from both, and that when I came closer to one of them, its sounds certainly increased, but because the sounds from the other centre decreased, the overall result for the ear always remained approximately the same. I almost believed that if I listened very keenly I would recognize, though only very dimly, differences in the sounds which were in keeping with my new hypothesis. In any case, I had to extend my experimental range further than I had done so far. That is why I am taking the passageway downwards as far as the citadel and will start listening there. Strange, the same noise here too. Well, it is a noise produced by the scrabbling of some insignificant little animals who have made outrageous use of the time I was absent; in any case they are far from harbouring any ill intentions towards me; they are only busied with their own works, and as long as there is no obstacle in their way they keep to the direction they have once started on—I know all that, but all the same I find it incomprehensible, it agitates me and befuddles the sharpness of mind I need for my work, that they should have dared to approach the citadel. I don't want to make any distinctions as to the cause, but whether it was the depth of the citadel's site, imposing in any case, or its extent and the correspondingly strong draught that frightened off the burrowers, or simply news that this was the citadel which had got through to their dull wits, or the solemnity of the place—whatever the reason,

I had not noticed any signs of tunnelling in the citadel walls until now. True, animals would turn up, drawn in their masses by the powerful smells. Here was my best hunting. But they had dug their way through into my passageways from above and came running down them—anxiously, it's true, but strongly attracted. But now they were tunnelling into the walls as well. If only I had carried out at least the most important plans of my youth and young manhood, or rather, if I had had the strength to carry them out, for there was no lack of will. One of my favourite plans had been to separate the citadel from the earth around it, that is, to leave its walls with roughly the same thickness as my height, but as well as that to dig a space of the same thickness as the wall all the way round the citadel, except for small foundations which unfortunately could not be separated from the earth. I had always imagined this space—and I doubt if I was wrong—as the pleasantest dwelling-place there could be for me. Clinging to this curve, pulling myself up, sliding down, turning somersaults and then finding ground beneath my feet, and taking pleasure in playing like this literally upon the body of my citadel though not inside its actual space; able to leave the citadel, allow my eyes a respite from the sight of it, postpone the delight of seeing it again to a later hour, but still not have to do without it, but literally hold it tight in my claws, something impossible if you only have the one usual open entry to it; but above all able to keep watch on it, that is, be compensated for doing without the sight of it to such an extent that if you had to choose between the citadel and the hollow space around it, you would choose the hollow space for all the days of your life, only so as to roam up and down there and protect the citadel. Then there would be no noises in the walls, no insolent excavations right up to its open space; then peace would be guaranteed and I would be its guardian; I would not have to listen with reluctance to the small creatures digging, but with delight to something that now eludes me completely: the murmur of silence in the citadel. But all this beauty simply does not exist now, and I must set to work; I should almost be glad of it, for it concerns the citadel directly, and that lends me wings. However, it becomes more and more apparent that I do need all my energy for this work, which at first seemed quite light. At present I am listening in at the citadel walls, and wherever I place my ear, high or low, at the walls or down at the ground, everywhere, everywhere the same noise. And how much time, how much effort all this long listening to the noise demands, as it comes and goes! A small, self-deceptive consolation, if you like, is to be found in discovering that if you raise your ears from the ground here in the citadel, in contrast to the passages, on account of the vast extent of the open space, you hear nothing at all. Frequently it is only for rest, for reflection that I try out these experiments; I strain to listen, and I am happy to hear nothing. But in general, what has happened? Faced with this phenomenon, my earlier explanations fail utterly. But I am quickly forced to reject the other explanations that offer themselves too. You might think that what I hear is simply the small creatures themselves at work. But that would contradict all my experience; anyway, what I have never heard I can't all of a sudden begin to hear, even if it was always present. In the burrow my sensitivity towards disturbances has perhaps become greater with the years, but even so my hearing has by no means become sharper. It is simply the nature of the small creatures that you do not hear them; I would never have tolerated them otherwise; at the risk of starvation, I would have exterminated them. But perhaps—this thought too has sneaked in—it concerns an animal I am not familiar with. That might be possible; true, I have observed the wildlife down here long and closely enough, but the world is various, and there is no shortage of unpleasant surprises. But it would not be one single animal; it would have to be a large herd that had suddenly tumbled through into my territory, a large herd of little animals who outdo the small creatures as they can actually be heard, though not by very much because the noise made by their work is essentially quite slight. So it could be unknown animals, a herd migrating, just passing through, that are disturbing me, whose progress will soon come to an end anyway. So I could actually wait, and I wouldn't have to do any work that might in the end turn out to be superfluous. But if it is strange animals, why don't I get to see them? Now I have already dug a number of ditches to catch one, but found none. It occurs to me that it might be quite tiny animals, much tinier than the ones I am familiar with, and that only the noise they make is greater. So I examine the soil I have been digging, I throw up the clods so that they fall apart into the smallest of small crumbs, but the disturbers of the peace are not among them. Slowly I perceive that I shall achieve nothing with such random little excavations; all they do is let me root about in my burrow walls, scrabble here and there, with no time to fill in the holes; there are already piles of soil in many places, blocking my way, and my view, though this is only a minor nuisance. I can neither wander about now, nor look around nor rest; I have frequently fallen asleep for a while in some hole while I was working, with the claws of one paw clamped to the earth above me in my attempt, on the brink of sleep, to scrape down a lump of soil. So I shall change my method. I shall dig a really large trench in the direction of the noise, and, disregarding all theories, I shall not stop until I find its real cause. Then I will remove it if I am strong enough, but if not, I shall at least be certain. This certainty will bring me either peace of mind or despair, but whether it is the one or the other, it will be beyond all doubt, and justified. This decision does me good; all I have been doing until now seems overhasty to me, done in the agitation of my return. Not yet free from the cares of the world above, not yet fully received into the peace of the burrow, over-sensitive from having to live without it for so long, I had let myself be driven frantic, as I've conceded, by a very odd phenomenon. What is it after all? A faint piping, audible only at long intervals, a nothing which I won't say one could get used to—no, one couldn't get used to it—but without doing anything for the time being to counter it, one could, at least for a while, observe it, that is, listen closely every few hours and patiently note the results, but not, as I have been doing, trail my ear along the walls and tear up the earth almost whenever the sound became audible, not actually in order to find anything, but to do something that was correlative to the agitation within me. That will now change, I hope. And then again, I do not—as I angrily admit of myself even to myself, shutting my eyes—for the agitation is still trembling within me, exactly as it has been for hours now, and if good sense didn't restrain me I would probably want most to start digging anywhere, no matter whether there was something to be heard there or not, defiantly, mindlessly, just for the sake of digging, almost like the small creatures who dig either with no purpose to it, or just because they eat the soil. I am tempted by my new, rational plan, and then again I am not. There is nothing about it to object to, I at least don't know of any objection. As far as I understand it, the plan is bound to achieve its aim, but in spite of this, deep down I don't believe it; I believe it so little that I am not even afraid of the likely terror at what it might reveal, I don't even believe in a terrible revelation, indeed it seems to me that ever since the noise first appeared I had already thought about digging a trench systematically, and I hadn't begun on it until now only because I had no confidence in the undertaking.

Nevertheless, I shall certainly start digging, no other possibility remains to me, but I shan't begin straight away, I'll put the work off for a little while; if good sense is to come into its own again, it should be done thoroughly; I shan't rush into it. In any case I shall first make good the damage I have done to the burrow by rooting round so wildly; that will take time, but it is necessary. If the new trench is really to lead to its object, it is likely to be long, and if it is not to lead to its object, it will be endless; in any case this work will mean long absences from the burrow, none of them as bad as that episode in the world above. I can break off the work any time I like and go home for a visit, and even if I don't, the air from the citadel will waft over to me and envelop me as I work, but all the same it will still mean taking me from the burrow and delivering me up to an uncertain fate. That is why I want to leave the burrow in good order behind me; no one shall say that I, who do battle for its peace, was the one who disturbed it and did not repair it straight away. So I start scraping the earth back into the holes, work I know very well for I have done it countless times almost without being aware I was working, and in which, particularly as far as my skill in the final smoothing-off and finishing is concerned (this is certainly not mere self-glorification, it is the simple truth) I cannot be outdone. But this time I find it difficult; I am too distracted; again and again in the middle of working I press my ear to the wall and listen, and without caring let the soil I have only just lifted trickle back into the passage. I am scarcely able to carry out the final decoration, which requires greater attention. There are still unsightly bulges, cracks spoiling the effect, not to mention the entire sweep of the old wall, which cannot be restored when it is as patched-up as it is now. I try to console myself that the work is only provisional. When I return and peace is once again restored, I shall repair it once and for all, and everything shall be done on the wing. Indeed, in fairy-tales everything is done on the wing, and my consolation belongs to fairy-tales too. It would be better to do the work perfectly now, much more useful than constantly interrupting it to go wandering down the passageways and identifying new places where I can hear noises, which is, in truth, very easy, for all it requires is for you to stand in any old place and stay and listen. And I make still further useless discoveries. Sometimes it seems as if the noise has stopped, indeed, it pauses for long intervals, sometimes you miss these pipings, too often it is your own blood throbbing in your ears, then two intervals contract into one and for a little while you believe the piping is over for ever. You listen no longer; you leap up, your whole life turns upside down; it is almost like the opening up of the source from which there flows the silence of the burrow. You take care not to probe the discovery straight away; in search of someone you could once entrust it to without suspecting them, so you gallop to the citadel, remembering—because you have woken to new life with every fibre of your being—that you have eaten nothing for a long time, you grab something from provisions half-covered in soil and you are still gulping it down as you run back to the place of your incredible discovery; at first you just want to convince yourself of it once more, just in passing, just briefly while you are eating; you listen, but the briefest listening-in indicates at once that you have been shamefully mistaken; it is steadily piping away there, far in the distance. And you spit out what you are eating, wanting to stamp it into the ground, wanting to go back to work, not knowing which place to go to, some spot where it seems to be necessary, and there are plenty of them; you start doing something mechanically, as if it is only the foreman arriving and you have to go through the motions for his benefit. But you have been working hardly a few minutes like this before it may happen that you make a fresh discovery. The sound seems to have become louder, not much louder of course, it's always a matter of the finest distinctions, but a little louder, clearly recognizable to the ear. And this increasing sound seems to mean that it is coming nearer; and even more clearly than you can hear it getting louder you can literally see each step it takes as it comes nearer. You leap back from the wall; you try to review in one glance all the possibilities this discovery will bring in its train. You feel as if you had never actually fitted out the burrow as a defence against attack; that was what you intended, but contrary to all your experience of life the danger of attack and hence the preparations for defence seemed remote to you, not remote exactly (how could that be possible?), but far less important than preparations for a life of peace, which consequently had been given priority everywhere in the burrow. A great deal could have been done in that respect without disturbing the ground-plan; it had been neglected in a really incomprehensible way. In all these years I have been very fortunate; my good fortune has spoiled me, I was restless, but restlessness in good fortune leads to nothing. Actually, the first thing to do now would be to inspect the burrow thoroughly with an eye to its defence and to every imaginable

possibility relating to it, to undertake a plan for defence and a building-plan to match, and then to start on the work immediately, fresh as
a youngster. That would be the work needed immediately—for which,
by the by, it is of course far too late—but it would be the work needed,
certainly not digging some great investigatory trench, whose only
function in fact is to make me vulnerable, displacing all my energies
onto going in search of danger—in the idiotic fear that it wouldn't
come along soon enough by itself. All of a sudden I do not understand
my earlier plan; I cannot find the least sense in what once seemed so
sensible; once more I leave off work, and leave off listening too; I have
no wish to discover any further places with a greater volume of sound;
I have had enough of discoveries; I am leaving everything; I would be
content if I could only calm the conflict within me. Once again I let
my passageways lead me along; I reach some that lie further and further away, not seen yet since my return, and still completely untouched
by my scrabbling paws; their stillness is aroused at my arrival and
envelops me. I do not yield to it, I hurry on through it; I don't know
what I am looking for at all, perhaps just an occasion for delay. I wander so far out of my way that I reach the labyrinth; I am tempted to
listen in at the moss covering; things so far away, far away for the
moment, hold my interest. I climb up towards it and listen. Deep
silence; how beautiful it is here; no one troubles themselves about my
burrow down below; everyone goes about his business, which has no
connection with me, how have I arranged things to achieve this? Here,
by the covering of moss, is perhaps the only place in my burrow now
where I can listen for hours without hearing a thing. The complete
reverse of the situation in the burrow; what had once been the place
of danger has become a place of peace. The citadel, on the other hand,
has been carried away into the clamour of the world and its perils.
Even worse, there is in reality no peace up here either; nothing has
changed here, whether quiet or loud, danger still lurks above the
moss, as before—but I have become unresponsive to it: the piping in
my walls claims far too much of me. Has it claimed me? It is becoming louder, it is coming nearer, but here I am, winding my way up
through the labyrinth and lying down beneath the moss; it is almost
as if I am handing over the house to the piper. Have I something like
a new theory about the cause of the noise? Surely the noise comes
from the trickling of soil while the small creatures are digging? Isn't
that my definite view? Surely I don't seem to have departed from it?

And even if it doesn't come directly from the trickling, somehow it does so indirectly. And if it weren't connected to it at all, then there's probably nothing you can assume in advance, and you will have to wait until you have really found the cause, or until it simply shows itself. You can still play with hypotheses of course, even now. It could be said, for example, that somewhere far away there has been a break-in of water and what sounded to me like piping or whistling would actually be the sound of gushing. But apart from the fact that I have never experienced this kind of thing—the ground-water I found at the beginning I diverted immediately, and with this sandy soil it has not returned—apart from that, it is simply piping, and cannot be reinterpreted as gushing. But what good are all these exhortations to be calm; my imagination will not be still, and in fact I cannot get rid of the thought—there is no point in denying it to myself—that the piping comes from one animal, that is, not from several small ones, but from one single large one. There is a lot to be said against this: the noise is audible everywhere and always at the same strength, and steadily too, by day and by night. Certainly one was bound to incline at first towards assuming several small animals, but as I ought to have found them in the course of my excavations and instead found nothing, the only hypothesis left is the existence of one large beast, especially as the factors that seem to contradict this assumption are merely things that do not make the beast impossible, but rather make it dangerous beyond all imagining. That is the only reason why I have been resisting this assumption. I am giving up this self-deception. For a long time I played with the thought that the beast could be heard even at great distances because it works furiously; it digs through the soil at the speed of a walker at full stretch; the earth round about trembles where it is digging; even when it has finished, the after-tremors and the sound of the work itself combine in the great distance, and as I hear only the last of the sound as it dies away, I hear it sounding everywhere at the same strength. In addition, the beast is not heading for me; that is why the sound is constant; rather, there is a plan, though I can't make out its purpose; I am only assuming that the beast is encircling me—though this doesn't imply at all that I am maintaining it knows about me; probably it has already been digging some circles around my burrow since I have been observing it. Nevertheless the noise is becoming stronger now, which means the circles are closing in. The nature of the sound, the piping or whistling,

occupies my mind greatly. When I scratch and scrape at the earth
after my own fashion, it sounds quite different. The only explanation
I can give myself is that the beast's main tool is not its claws, which
might perhaps only be an additional aid, but its snout or muzzle,
which, quite apart from its evidently tremendous power, probably has
some kind of sharp edge. It probably pushes its snout into the earth
with a single great thrust, and tears up a huge clod; in this time I hear
nothing; this is the interval; but then it draws its breath once more for
a fresh thrust; this inhalation of air, which must make an earth-shat-
tering row, not only on account of the beast's strength but also on
account of its speed and eagerness to get on with its work, this great
noise I then hear as a soft piping. Nevertheless, what I still can't
understand is its ability to go on working without a stop; perhaps the
brief intervals also include the opportunity for a little break, but
apparently it has not yet gone as far as taking a proper rest; it goes on
burrowing day and night, always with the same fresh energy, with an
eye to its plan, carrying it out at top speed, and with all the skills
needed to realize it. But quite apart from its peculiar characteristics,
something is happening now that actually I should have feared, something against which I always should have been prepared for: someone
is advancing. How did it come about that everything was going on so
quietly and happily for so long? Who diverted the paths of my enemies
so as to give my possessions such a wide berth? Why was I protected
for so long, only to be exposed to such fear in this way? What were all
the minor dangers I spent so much time brooding over in comparison
with this one! Was I, as the burrow's owner, hoping to prevail over
everyone who might arrive? Simply as the owner of this great, vulnerable work I am of course defenceless against any serious attack; the
pleasure of owning it has spoiled me; the burrow's vulnerability has
made me vulnerable; any injuries to it give me as much pain as if they
were my own. This is just what I should have foreseen, and not
thought of defending only myself—and how carelessly and uselessly
I have done even that—but of defending the burrow. I should above
all have seen to enabling separate parts of the burrow, as many as
feasible, if they were attacked by anyone, to be cut off by falls of
earth, which would have to be achievable very quickly, from the parts
less threatened, that is, by such quantities of earth and to such effect
that the invader would have no idea at all that the actual burrow
lay just behind them. More, these falls of earth would have to be

suitable not only to hide the burrow but also to bury the invader. I did not take the smallest step towards anything of the kind, nothing happened in this respect; I have been as careless as a child; I have wasted my mature years in childish play; I was only playing with thoughts of danger, and fell short when it came to really thinking about the real dangers. And there were plenty of warnings. Anything approaching the present one didn't happen, it's true, but something similar did occur in the early days of the burrow. The main difference was simply that it was in the early days of the burrow. I was still working then as a little prentice on the first passageway; the labyrinth was only in its first rough draft; I had already opened up one small clearing, but it had gone completely wrong in its dimensions and in the treatment of the walls, in short, everything was at such an early stage that it could only be regarded as an experiment, as something that, if once your patience snapped, you could abandon immediately. Then it happened that once, during a working-break—I have always taken too many breaks—I was lying among my heaps of earth, when suddenly I heard a sound in the distance. Young as I was, I was more curious than anxious. I left my work and changed over to listening; at any rate I listened, and didn't run up to stretch out under the covering of moss so as not to have to listen. At least I did listen. I could make out quite well that it was some sort of burrowing, similar to mine, though it did sound rather fainter, but how much of that was to be put down to distance one couldn't tell. I was tense, but otherwise cool and calm. Perhaps I am in someone else's burrow, I thought, and now the owner is digging towards me. If my assumption turned out to be right, I would—for I have never looked for a fight nor felt the need to win—have moved away to build somewhere else. But after all, I was still young, and still without a burrow, I was still able to be cool and calm. And the way it all developed did not make me fundamentally any more agitated, only it was not easy to interpret it. If whoever was digging there was really endeavouring to reach me because he had heard me digging, and if he then changed course, as did in fact happen, then there was no way of being sure of whether he was doing this because by taking a break I had given him some point of orientation for his route, or whether it was because he had himself changed his mind. Or perhaps I had been completely deceiving myself and he never had been steering directly towards me. In any case, if the noise had for a while grown louder, as if it were coming closer, as a youngster

perhaps I would not at the time have been unhappy to see the tunneller suddenly emerge from the earth. But nothing of the sort happened, and after a certain point the sound of the tunnelling began to
tail off; it grew softer and softer, as if the tunneller were gradually
swerving away from his earlier course, and all of a sudden it broke off
completely, as if he had now decided to take the completely opposite
direction and was moving away from me, off into the distance. For a
long time I listened after him into the silence before beginning work
again. Now, this warning was clear enough, but I soon forgot it, and it
had scarcely any influence on my own building-plan. Between then
and now lie the years of my maturity, but it is not as if nothing at all
lay between them; I still take a long break in my work and listen at the
wall, and the tunneller has of late changed his mind; he has done an
about-turn; he has returned from his journey; he thinks he has left
me enough time in the interim to make my preparations for receiving
him. But on my side everything is less prepared than it was then; my
great structure stands there, defenceless, and I am no longer a little
prentice, but an old master-builder, and what powers I still have fail
me when it comes to a decision. But however old I am, it seems that
I would be glad to be even older, so old that I could no longer rise
from my bed of rest beneath the moss. Nevertheless, because in reality I cannot endure it up here, I do rise and, as if I had created for
myself up there not calm but new anxieties instead, I race down again
into the burrow. How were things when I left it last? Had the piping
become fainter? No, it had become stronger. I listen randomly at ten
different places and see my illusion clearly: the piping has remained
the same; nothing has altered. Up above no changes occur, one is
calm and elevated where time no longer exists, but down here every
moment makes the listener tremble. And once again I tread the long
way back to the citadel; everything round about seems to share my
agitation, seems to look at me, and look away again at once so as not
to upset me, but goes on nevertheless to make the effort to read from
my face the decisions that might save us. I shake my head: I still have
none. Also, I am not going to the citadel to carry out any plan. I pass
the place where I wanted to dig my investigatory trench; I examine it
once more; it would have been a good place; the trench would have
gone in the direction of most of the air-ducts, which would have
made the work much easier for me; perhaps I would not have had to
dig very far, would not have had to dig my way as far as the origin of

the noise, perhaps listening at the air-ducts would have been sufficient. But no reflections are strong enough to set me to working on
the trench. This trench is supposed to give me certainty? I am so far
gone that I have no desire at all for certainty. In the citadel I select a
fine collop of red meat, already skinned, and crawl with it into one of
the heaps of earth; it will be quiet there in any case—as far as quiet
still actually exists at all here. I nibble the meat delicately, think in
turn now about the strange animal, making its way in the distance and
then again about enjoying my provisions to the full, as long as the
possibility still remains to me. This last is probably the one plan I have
that can be carried out. Beyond that, I shall try to work out the beast's
plan. Has it gone wandering, or is or is it working in its own burrow?
If it has gone wandering, then it might be possible to come to some
understanding with it. If it really does break through to me, I shall
give it some of my provisions and it will go on its way. Go on its
way—I like that! In my pile of earth, of course, I can dream of everything, even of an understanding, although I know that there is no
such thing, and that the moment we see each other, indeed, the
moment we merely sense each other's presence nearby, we shall both
of us advance, equally blindly, neither of us sooner nor later than the
other, with a new and different hunger even if we have otherwise
eaten our fill, baring tooth and claw against each other. And as always,
we will be fully justified here too, for who, even if he had merely come
wandering by, would not change his plans, for his journey or for his
future, at the sight of my burrow? But perhaps the beast is digging in
its own burrow. If so, I cannot even dream of an understanding. Even
if it were such a peculiar animal that its burrow could bear to have
another in its neighbourhood, my burrow could not, at least not one
that could be heard. Well, the beast certainly seems very far away
now; if it would only withdraw a little further, the noise would probably disappear too and perhaps then all would be well again, as it was
in the old days; then it would be only a bad, but salutary experience,
it would push me into making a great variety of improvements; if
I have peace, and the danger is not immediately urgent, I am still
perfectly capable of all kinds of decent work. Perhaps, in view of the
enormous potentialities its great capacity for work seem to give it, the
beast will refrain from extending its burrow in the direction of mine,
and make up for it on another side. That too of course cannot be
achieved by negotiation, but only by the beast's own good sense or by

force on my part. In both cases the decisive thing will be whether the beast knows about me, and if so, what. The more I reflect on it, the more unlikely it seems to me that the beast has ever heard me at all; it is possible, though I can't imagine it, that it has some report of me from somewhere else, but probably it has not actually heard me. As long as I knew nothing about it, it can't have heard me at all, for I keep so quiet; there is nothing quieter than my reunion with my burrow; then, when I was digging on my experimental trench, it could well have heard me, even though my way of digging makes very little noise; but if it had heard me, I would have been bound to hear some sound of it too; after all, it would at least have had to interrupt its work frequently and listen, but everything remained unchanged, the*

SELECTED SHORTER PIECES

The Bridge

I WAS stiff and cold; I was a bridge; I lay across an abyss, the tips of my feet bedded in deep on this side, my hands on the far side; I had sunk my teeth fast in the crumbling clay. My coat-tails flapped at my sides. The icy trout stream roared in the depths. No tourists strayed to this inaccessible height; the bridge had not yet been drawn on the maps. So I lay and waited. I could not but wait; once a bridge is put up, it cannot stop being a bridge without falling down. Once towards evening—was it the first or was it the thousandth, I don't know—my thoughts were always muddled up and always going round and round; towards evening one summer, the stream was murmuring with a darker tone when I heard a man's footstep. Coming towards me, towards me. Stretch out, bridge, make yourself ready, you unrailed girder, support the man entrusted to you, adjust your balance imperceptibly to his uncertain footsteps, but if he begins to sway, make your presence known, and like a mountain god hurl him onto land. He came, tapped and tested me with the iron tip of his staff, then used it to lift my coat-tails and arrange them over me. He ran the tip through my bushy hair, and let it stay there a long time—as he gazed around into the distance I suppose. But then—just as in my dreams I was following him over hill and vale—he jumped onto me right in the middle of my body. I shook in violent pain, taken utterly unawares. Who was it? A child? An athlete? A daredevil? A suicide? A tempter? A destroyer? And I turned over—so as to see him. Bridge, turn over! I had not quite turned over before I was already plunging down; I was plunging down, and I was already being torn apart and pierced by the sharpened pebbles that had always gazed so peacefully at me from the raging water.

The Knock at the Courtyard Gate

IT was in the summer, a hot day. On the way home with my sister I passed by a courtyard gate. I don't know whether she knocked on it out of mischief, or absent-mindedness, or whether she just shook her fist at it and didn't knock at all. A hundred paces further on, where the highway turned left, the village began. It was unfamiliar to us, but at once people came out of the first house and beckoned—in a friendly way, but in warning, themselves terrified, and crouching low in their terror. They pointed towards the courtyard we had passed and reminded us of the blow on the gate. The owners are going to bring a complaint against us, and the investigation will begin right away. I was very calm, and calmed my sister down as well. She probably hadn't struck the blow at all, and if she had, there was nowhere on earth where a trial would be held on that account. And I tried to make the people around us understand this too; they listened to me, but withheld their judgement. Later they said that not only my sister, but I too, as her brother, would be charged. I nodded, giving a smile. We all looked back towards the courtyard, as if we were looking at a distant cloud of smoke, waiting for the flame. And really, we soon saw horsemen entering the wide open gate; dust rose, shrouding everything; only the tips of their tall lances were shining. And the troop had hardly disappeared into the courtyard before it seemed they had turned their horses round at once and were on their way towards us. I urged my sister to go: I'll clear up everything. She refused to leave me on my own; I said if she stayed, at least she should change her clothes so as to appear before the authorities wearing a better dress. Finally she complied, and set off on the long way home. Already the horsemen were upon us. Still on their mounts, they leaned down and asked after my sister. 'She's not here at the moment,' came the frightened reply, 'but she'll come later.' This reply was received almost indifferently; the main thing seemed to be that they had found me. There were chiefly two dignitaries, an energetic young man who was the judge, and his silent assistant, who was called Assmann. I was summoned into the parlour of the village inn. Slowly, shaking my head slightly and tugging at my braces, I bestirred myself under their keen gaze. I still rather thought that one word would be enough to release me, the city-dweller, from this horde of peasants—even with some signs of respect. But as soon as I had crossed the parlour threshold, the judge, who had started forward ready for me, said: 'I am sorry for this man.' But there was not a shadow of doubt that by this he did not mean my present state, but what would happen to me. The room looked more like a prison cell than a tavern parlour. Large stone flagstones, dark grey wall, an iron ring fixed into it somewhere, in the middle something that was half bench, half operating-table.

The Truth about Sancho Panza

SANCHO PANZA*—who, by the way, has never boasted of it—by providing a great quantity of chivalrous romances by evening and by night, managed so successfully in the course of the years to get his devil, whom he later named Don Quixote, off his back that the latter, all stability lost, went and performed the craziest deeds; these, however, having no definite target, which ought to have been Sancho Panza himself, did no harm to anyone. Sancho Panza, a free man, followed Don Quixote with equanimity and perhaps from a certain sense of responsibility on all his campaigns, deriving from them great and profitable entertainment till his end.

The Spinning-Top

A CERTAIN philosopher was always hanging around the places where children played. And if he saw a boy who had a spinning-top, he would be ready, lying in wait. The top would hardly begin spinning before the philosopher would pursue it so as to catch it. The children would raise an outcry and try to keep him away from their toy, but that didn't worry him. As long as he had caught the top while it was still spinning he was happy, though only for a moment. Then, he would throw it on the ground and be off. For it was his belief that insight into any small thing, including, for example, a top as it spun, was sufficient for insight into the universal. That is why he was not occupied with the great problems—that seemed uneconomical to him. For if the smallest small thing was really known, then everything was known. So that is why he was occupied only with the top as it spun. And whenever the top was about to be set spinning, he was filled with hope that this time it would succeed; and if the top did spin, his hope turned into certainty as he ran breathlessly after it, but then, holding the stupid lump of wood in his hand, he would feel sick, and the children's shouts, which till then he hadn't heard and which now fell suddenly on his ears, drove him away, reeling like a top beneath a clumsy whip.

Cat and Mouse

'OH,' said the mouse, 'the world grows narrower every day. At first it was so wide that I was afraid. I ran on, and I was happy that at last in the distance I could see walls to right and left, but these long walls hasten so quickly towards each other that I am already in the last room and there in the corner stands the trap I am running into.' 'You just have to change direction,' said the cat, and ate her up.

On Parables

MANY complain that again and again the words of the wise are only parables, but unusable in daily life, and daily life alone is all that we have. When the wise man says: 'Cross over to the other side,' he doesn't mean that we should cross over to the other side of the road, which we could do anyway if it was worth the trip; but he means some fabled other side, something we don't know, that can't be defined more precisely, not even by him, so can't be of any help at all to us here. All these parables actually mean is only that the incomprehensible is incomprehensible, and that we knew already. But the things we slave away at every day are something else.

At this, someone said: 'Why are you resisting? If you were to follow the parables, then you would become parables yourselves and consequently be free of your daily cares.'

Another said: 'I'll wager that this too is a parable.'

The first one said: 'You've won.'

The second one said: 'But unfortunately only in the parable.'

The first said: 'No, in reality; in the parable, you have lost.'

Give it up!

IT was very early in the morning; the streets clean and empty; I was walking to the railway station. As I compared the clock in a tower with my watch, I saw that it was already much later than I had thought. I had to hurry up, and my shock at this discovery made me uncertain of my direction. I did not know my way about this town very well.

Fortunately there was a policeman nearby. I ran up to him and breathlessly asked him the way. He smiled and said: 'From me? You want to find out the way from *me*?' 'Yes,' I said, 'as I can't find it myself.' 'Give it up, give it up,' he said, turning away with a wide swerve, as people do who want to be alone with their laughter.

APHORISMS

I

1. The true way passes over a rope which is not stretched high up, but just above the ground. It seems to be intended more for stumbling than for crossing.

2. All human flaws are impatience, cutting off systematic thought prematurely, seemingly fencing off the seeming issue at stake.

3. There are two cardinal human sins, from which all the others derive: impatience and apathy. On account of impatience they were driven from Paradise; on account of apathy they do not return. But perhaps there is only one cardinal sin: impatience. On account of impatience they were driven out; on account of impatience they do not return.

4. The shades of many of the departed are busy only with lapping up the river of the dead and its tides because they flow from us and still have the salt taste of our seas. The river recoils in disgust, flows backwards, and its current carries the dead back into life. They, for their part, are happy, sing hymns of thanksgiving, and gently stroke the horrified waters.

5. From a certain point on there is no return. This is the point to reach.

6. The decisive moment of human development is everlasting. That is why the intellectual revolutions that declare everything which has gone before to be null and void are right, for as yet nothing has happened.

7. One of the Evil One's most effective means of temptation is a challenge to do battle. It is like the battle with women, ending in bed.

8/9. A stinking bitch, mother of many pups, parts of her already rotting, who nevertheless meant everything to me when I was a child, a creature I cannot stop myself from thrashing, but shrink back from, step by step, even avoiding her breath, and who will, if I don't decide differently, drive me into a corner, already in sight, and with me and on top of me rot away completely, until the end—is it to my honour?—with the suppurating, worm-infested flesh of her tongue upon my hand.*

10. A. has a very high opinion of himself. He believes he is far advanced in virtue because he feels that, as an increasingly attractive target, he is exposed to an increasing number of temptations from directions previously unknown to him. But the true explanation is that a great devil has taken up residence within him, and the monstrous number of smaller ones turn up to serve the great one.

11/12. Disparity of views it is possible to have of, say, an apple: the view of the small boy, who has to crane his neck just to see the apple on the table-top, and the view of the master of the house, who takes the apple and freely offers it to his guest at table

13. One of the first signs of the beginnings of knowledge is the wish to die. This life seems unendurable, another life unattainable. One is no longer ashamed of wanting to die: one begs to be removed from the old, hated cell to a new one that one has yet to learn to hate. A remnant of faith also plays a part; during the removal the Lord will chance to come along the corridor, see the prisoners, and say: 'You are not to lock this one up again. He's coming to me.'

14. If you were crossing a plain, with the good will to get across, but all the same your steps took you backwards, it would be a matter for despair; but as you are clambering up a steep slope, as steep, say, as you yourself are viewed from below, it could also be that your steps backward are only caused by the nature of the ground, and you do not have to despair.

15. Like a path in autumn, it has hardly been swept clear before it is covered in dry leaves once more.

16. A cage went in search of a bird.

17. I have never been in this place before: breathing is different; next to the sun a star is shining, outdazzling it in radiance.

18. If it had been possible to erect the Tower of Babel without ascending it, that would have been allowed.

19. Do not let yourself believe the Evil One when he tells you that you could have secrets from him.

20. Leopards break into the temple and drink the sacrificial vessels dry; this is repeated over and over again; in the end it can be worked out in advance and becomes part of the ritual.

21. Tight as a hand holds a stone. But it holds it so tight only in order to cast it away that much further. But the way leads even that far.

22. You are the task set. No sign of a student far or near.

23. Your true adversary fills you with boundless courage.

24. The joy of understanding that the ground you stand on cannot be any bigger than [the space] your two feet can cover.

25. How can one take pleasure in the world except when one is taking refuge in her?

26. There are countless places to hide, only one refuge, but as many possibilities of refuge in their turn as there are hiding-places.

There is a goal, but no way; what we call way is hesitation.

27. The negative act is a task still imposed upon us; the positive is already given us.

28. Once you have taken evil to yourself, it no longer asks you to believe it.

29. The mental reservations with which you take evil to yourself are not your own, they belong to the Evil One.

The animal wrests the whip from its master and whips itself so as to become master itself, with no idea that this is only a fantasy, produced by a fresh knot in its master's lash.

30. The good is in a certain sense comfortless.

31. I am not aiming for self-mastery. Self-mastery is the desire to be effective in one fortuitous place within the infinite emanations of my spiritual existence. But if I have to draw such circles around myself then I would do better to stay still and merely gaze in astonishment at the tremendous complexity, and I will take home with me only the greater strength that *e contrario* the sight of it gives me.

32. Crows maintain that a single crow could destroy Heaven. There is no doubt about that, but it is not at all evidence against Heaven, for Heaven simply means: the impossibility of crows.

33. Martyrs do not underestimate the body, they have it raised upon the cross; in this they are at one with their adversaries.

34. His weariness is that of the gladiator after combat; his work was to whitewash a corner in a little office.

35. There is no having, only a being, only a being yearning for its last breath, for suffocation.

36. There was a time when I couldn't understand why I never got an answer to my question; today I cannot understand how I could believe I was able to ask. But of course I didn't believe at all, I only asked.

37. His answer to the assertion that perhaps he did have possessions, but no being, was only trembling and a thudding heart.

38. There was one who was astonished at how easily he walked the way of eternity; actually, he was racing along it downhill.

39. One cannot pay the Evil One in instalments—and is always trying to do so.

It might be conceivable that Alexander the Great, despite the successes of his youth in war, despite the splendid army he had built up, despite the powers he felt within him to change the world, might have stopped short at the Hellespont and never have crossed it, not from fear, not from indecision, not from weakness of will, but from earthly weight.

39a. The way is infinite; there is nothing to subtract, nothing to add, yet everyone still measures it by his own childish yardstick. 'Assuredly you also have this yard of the way still to walk; it will not be forgotten you.'

40. Only our concept of time makes us call the Last Judgement by that name; actually it is a drumhead court-martial.

41. It is a consolation that the imbalance of the world seems only to be numerical.

42. Sinking a head full of revulsion and hate onto one's chest.

43. The hounds are still playing in the yard, but their quarry will not escape them, however fast it is now speeding through the forest.

44. Ridiculous, the way you have put on your best harness for this world.

45. The more horses you hitch up, the faster it goes—I mean, not tearing the block out of the foundations, which is impossible, but tearing the reins and so travelling empty and joyful.

46. In German the word 'sein' means both 'being' and 'belonging to him'.

47. They were given the choice of becoming kings or the messengers of kings. As children do, they all wanted to be messengers. That is why there are nothing but messengers. They race through the world and, as there are no kings, shout their proclamations, now meaningless, to one another. They would gladly put an end to their miserable lives, but they dare not because of their oath of loyalty.

48. To believe in progress is not to believe that any progress has already happened. That would not be a belief.

49. A. is a virtuoso, and Heaven is his witness.

50. Man cannot live without an enduring trust in something inde-structible in himself, though both the indestructible as well as the trust may remain for ever hidden from him.* Remaining hidden has one possible expression in the belief in a personal god.

51. The mediation of the serpent* was needed: evil can seduce man, but not become man.

52. In the duel between yourself and the world, act as second to the world.

53. One should cheat no one, not even the world of its victory.

54. There is nothing else apart from a world of the spirit; what we call the world of the senses is the evil in the spiritual world, and what we call evil is only the requirement of a moment in our eternal growth.*

By the strongest light one can dissolve the world. Seen with weak eyesight she becomes firm; with weaker, she acquires fists, seen with even weaker sight she becomes bashful and shatters the one who dares to gaze on her.

55. Everything is a cheat: trying for the least degree of deception, remaining stuck in the usual ones, trying for the highest degree. In the first instance one is cheating the good by wanting to make it easy for oneself to acquire it, and cheating evil by setting it far too unfa-vourable terms of battle. In the second instance one is cheating the good by not aspiring towards it, and so not even in earthly things. In the third instance one is cheating the good by removing oneself as far away as possible from it, and cheating evil by hoping that raising it to its highest pitch will make it powerless. To judge from this, the second instance is to be preferred, for one always cheats the good, but in this case not, at least so it appears, evil.

56. There are questions we couldn't pass over, if we hadn't been freed of them by our nature.

57. To express anything outside the world of the senses, language can only be used by way of hints and intimations, but never in any way even approaching metaphorically, for, as it corresponds to the world of the senses, it deals only with possession and its associations.

58. One lies least only when one lies least, not when one has least opportunity for lying.

59. A tread on a stairway that has not been worn down by footsteps is in its own eyes only a piece of dreary wooden carpentry.

60. Anyone who renounces the world is bound to love humankind, for he is renouncing their world too. That is how he begins to have some inkling of humankind's true nature, which cannot but be loved, assuming that one is its equal.

61. Anyone within the world who loves his neighbour is doing no more and no less wrong than anyone who loves himself. There would remain only the question whether the first is possible.

62. The fact that there is nothing else but the world of the spirit robs us of hope and gives us certainty.

63. Our art is one of being blinded by truth; the light cast on the distorted face as it shrinks away is true, nothing else.

64. The expulsion from Paradise is in its main part eternal: so the expulsion from Paradise is indeed final, and life in the world inescapable, but the eternity of the process nevertheless makes it possible not only that we could remain in Paradise for ever, but that in fact we are there for ever, whether we know it here or not.

66. He is a free and safely tethered citizen of the earth, for he is tied by a chain which is long enough to give him free run of all earthly spaces, but only long enough for nothing to drag him across the borders of earth. But at the same time he is also a free and safely tethered

citizen of Heaven, for he is also tied by a heavenly chain with similar dimensions. If he wants to reach earth, he is choked by the heavenly collar, if he wants to reach Heaven, by the earthly. And in spite of this, all possibilities are open to him, and this he can feel, indeed, he refuses to ascribe it all to an error when he was first shackled.

67. He chases after facts like a beginner learning to skate, and what is more, one who is practising on forbidden ground.

68. What is more joyful than a belief in a domestic god!

69. In theory there is one possibility of perfect happiness: to believe in the indestructible in oneself and not to strive towards it.

70/71. The indestructible is one; it is every individual human being, and at the same time it is common to everyone, hence the uniquely inseparable union of all humanity.*

72. In the same person there are insights which though utterly divergent, nevertheless still have the same object, so that the only inference that has to be drawn is that there are divergent subjects in the same person.

73. He devours the scraps that fall from his own table; that is how for a while he is more full up than everyone else, though he forgets how to eat from the table above; but that is how the scraps stop falling too.

74. If what is supposed to have been destroyed in Paradise was destructible, then it was not crucial; but if it was indestructible, then we are living in a false belief.

75. Test yourself against mankind. It makes the doubter doubt, the believer believe.

76. This feeling: 'I shan't drop anchor here,' and immediately feeling the surging, heaving tide around one.

In reverse. Watchfully, anxiously, hopefully, the answer creeps round the question, in despair searches her unapproachable face, follows her on the most meaningless paths, that is, the paths that lead as far away from the answer as possible.

77. Having to do with people is a temptation to self-scrutiny.

78. The spirit will only become free when it stops being used as a support.

79. Sensuous love is a deception to divert us from heavenly love; it could not do this by itself, but as it unconsciously has the element of heavenly love within it, it can.

80. Truth is indivisible, so it cannot know itself; whoever wants to know it cannot but be Lie itself.

81. Nobody can desire what deep down ultimately harms him. If nevertheless it has this appearance in certain individuals—and perhaps this is always the case—then the explanation is that somebody within the person desires something that is certainly useful to the latter, but severely harms a second somebody, who is drawn in partly to judge the case. If the person had sided with the second right at the start and not only when the judgement was made, the first somebody would have been eliminated, and with him the desire.

82. Why do we complain about the Fall? It is not on that account that we were driven out of Paradise, but on account of the Tree of Life, so that we would not eat of it.

83. We are not sinful merely because we have eaten of the Tree of Knowledge, but also because we have not yet eaten of the Tree of Life. It is our condition that is sinful, independently of guilt.

84. We were created to live in Paradise; Paradise was destined to serve us. Our destiny has been changed; it is not stated whether this has also happened with the destiny of Paradise.

85. Evil is an emanation of human consciousness at certain points of transition. It is not actually the world of the senses that is illusion, but its evil aspect, which, it is true, in our eyes forms the world of the senses.

86. Since the Fall we have in essentials been equal in our capacity to know good and evil; nevertheless this is the very issue where we look for our own particular points of advantage. However, it is only beyond this knowledge that the true distinctions begin. The appearance of the contrary is produced as follows: no one can be satisfied with this knowledge by itself, but has to endeavour to act in accordance with it. However, we have not also been given the strength to do this, so he has to destroy himself, even at the risk of not receiving the necessary strength even by these means, but there is nothing else left to him except this last resort. (That is also the meaning of the threat of death when it is forbidden to eat of the Tree of Knowledge; perhaps it is also the meaning of natural death.) Now, he fears this attempt; he would rather undo his knowledge of good and evil (the term 'the Fall' derives from this fear), but what has happened cannot be undone, only clouded over. It is to this end that rationalizations arise. The whole world is full of them, indeed perhaps the entire visible world is nothing else than the rationalization of humankind, desiring for the space of a moment to be at peace. An attempt to falsify the fact of knowledge, to turn knowledge only into the goal.

87. A faith like a guillotine, so heavy, so light.

88. Death is before us, rather like a picture of Alexander's battle* on the schoolroom wall. It depends on our actions in this life whether we darken or even wipe out the picture.

90. Two possibilities: to make oneself infinitely small, or to be so. The first is perfection, implying inactivity, the second beginning, implying action.

91. Towards avoiding a verbal error: what is to be destroyed by an action must have previously been held quite firmly; what crumbles away, crumbles away, but cannot be destroyed.

92. The earliest idol-worship was certainly fear of things, but related to that, fear of the necessity of things, and related to that, fear of the responsibility for the things. This responsibility seemed so vast that mankind did not dare burden even one single non-human with it, for mankind's responsibility would not be relieved sufficiently by the

mediation of merely one being; an encounter with merely one being would still be far too tainted by responsibility, and that is why they gave each thing responsibility for itself, and more than that, they also gave these things a commensurate responsibility for humankind.

93. For the last time psychology!*

94. Two tasks set at the beginning of life: limiting your circle more and more, and constantly scrutinizing whether you haven't gone into hiding somewhere outside your circle.

95. Evil is sometimes in the hand like a tool: recognized or unrecognized, it yields without contradiction to being laid aside, if one has the will.

96. The pleasures of this life are not its own fear, but *our* fear of rising to a higher life; the torments of this life are not its own, but our self-torment on account of that fear.

97. Only here suffering is suffering. Not so as to suggest that those who are suffering here will be lifted up to another place on account of this suffering, but in such a way that what is called suffering in this world will, in another world, and liberated from its opposite, be bliss.

98. The idea of the infinite breadth and abundance of the cosmos is the result of the combination, driven to its utmost, of laborious creation and free self-contemplation.

99. How much more depressing than the most implacable conviction of our present sinful condition is even the weakest conviction that our temporality will be justified in eternity. Only the strength to bear this second conviction, which in its purity fully embraces the first, is the measure of faith.

There are many who assume that as well as the original great deceit there is in every case a small particular deceit set up especially for them, so that if a drama of love is being performed on the stage, the actress will also have, besides the false smile meant for her lover, another special smile behind his back intended for the quite specific spectator in the furthermost gallery. That is going too far.

100. There can be such a thing as knowledge of the diabolical, but not a belief in it, for there cannot be more of the diabolical than does exist.

101. Sin always comes openly and can be grasped immediately with the senses. It strikes at their roots and is not to be torn up.

102. All the suffering around us we too must suffer. We all have not only a body but a development, and that leads us through every pain, in one form or another. Just as a child develops through all the stages of life until old age and death (and deep down, each stage seems unattainable to the one before it, whether in fear or longing), so we develop likewise (no less deeply bound to humanity than to ourselves) through all the suffering of this world. There is no place for justice in this connection, nor for fear of suffering either, nor for interpreting suffering as merited.

103. You can withdraw from the suffering of the world. You are free to do so and it is in keeping with your nature. But perhaps this very withdrawal is the one suffering you could avoid.

104. Mankind has free will, of three kinds:
First, he was free when he willed this life; now, however, he cannot undo what he has willed, for he is no longer the person who willed it then, unless he could do so to the extent that he carries out what he willed then by living.
Secondly, he is free in being able to choose his life's path and the way he walks it.
Thirdly, he is free as the one he will once again be, who has the will to make his way through life under all circumstances, and in this manner come to himself; that is a way, it's true, which can be chosen, but in any case it is so labyrinthine that it would leave not a spot of this life untouched.
Those are the three kinds of free will, but because they are simultaneous, they are also one kind, and it is so fundamentally one kind that it has no place for a will, neither free nor unfree.

105. The means this world uses to seduce us, as well as the sign guaranteeing that this world is only a crossing-place, are the same. Rightly so, for this is the only way this world is able to seduce us, and it corresponds to the truth. But the bad thing is that after a successful seduction we forget the guarantee, and so in fact the good has led us into evil, the woman's glance has tempted us into her bed.

106. Humility gives everyone, even the lonely and despairing, the strongest relationship to his fellow man, and that immediately, though only if the humility is total and lasting. It is able to do this because it is the true language of prayer, both worship and the firmest commitment. The relation to one's fellow man is the relation of prayer, the relation to oneself is the relation of striving; it is from prayer that the strength to strive is drawn.

Is it possible then for you to know anything else but deception? Once the deception is destroyed, you will not be permitted to look at it else you will be turned into a pillar of salt.*

107. Everyone is very kind to A., rather in the way one tries to protect a billiard table even against good players, until the great player comes, examines the table keenly, refuses to put up with any hasty mistake, but then, when he begins to play himself, goes at it with utter recklessness.

108. 'But then he went back to his work as if nothing had happened.' That is a remark we are familiar with from an immense, vague number of old stories, although perhaps it does not occur in any of them.

109. 'One cannot say that we lack faith. On the other hand the simple fact of our life is utterly inexhaustible in its religious value.'
    'This, you say, is a religious value? But one cannot not-live.'
    'It is in this very "cannot not" that the crazy power of faith is hidden; it finds its form in this negation.'

It is not necessary for you to leave the house. Stay at your table and listen. Do not even listen, only wait. Do not even wait. Stay completely still and alone. The world will offer itself to you for unmasking; it can't help it; it will writhe before you in ecstasy.

II

6.I.20.
Everything he does seems extraordinarily new to him. If it didn't have this fresh vitality, it would, he knows, to judge from its intrinsic value, inevitably have come from the old slough of hell. But this freshness is deceptive, makes him forget it, or take it lightly, or admittedly see through it, but painlessly. After all, it is today, without doubt, this very day, when progress sets out to progress further

9.I.20
Superstition and principle as means of making life possible: by way of the heaven of vice the hell of virtue is won. Superstition is simply*

A segment has been cut out of the back of his head. With the sun, the whole world can see inside. It makes him nervous; it distracts him from his work; and it annoys him that he is the one excluded from the spectacle

The presentiment of ultimate release is not refuted if the next day one's captivity still remains unchanged or is even harsher, nor yet if it is expressly declared that it is meant to have no end. All this may form the necessary prior condition of ultimate release.

There is no occasion when he is adequately prepared, but he cannot even reproach himself with this, for where in this life, which so painfully requires us to be ready at any moment, might there be time to prepare oneself; and even if there were time, is it possible to prepare oneself before knowing the test, that is, is it possible to come through a natural test, not artificially constructed, at all? That is why he has long since been utterly ground down; it is remarkable, but also consoling, that he was prepared for that least of all.

He has found the Archimedean point,* but has used it against himself. Evidently it was only on this condition that he was allowed to find it.

13 [January 1920]
Everything he does seems to him to be extraordinarily new, but also,

in keeping with such an impossible wealth of new things, extraordinarily amateurish, scarcely tolerable even, incapable of becoming part of history, breaking the chain of the generations, interrupting for the first time the music of the world down to its deepest depths, though up till now it had always been faintly sensed, down to its deepest depths. Sometimes in his arrogance he is more afraid for the world than for himself.

A prison he could have come to terms with. To end as a prisoner, that would be a goal for a life. But it was a cage with bars. Indifferently, imperiously, as if at home there, the roar of the world flowed in and out through the bars. The prisoner was actually free; he could take part in everything; nothing outside escaped him; he could even have left the cage, after all, the bars were yards apart; he wasn't even imprisoned.

He has the feeling that by being alive he is blocking his own path. In turn he takes this block to be proof that he is alive.

14 [January 1920]
Himself he knows; the others he believes. This contradiction saws everything he has to bits.

He is neither bold, nor careless. But he is not timid either. He would not shy away from a life of freedom. Life has not turned out like that for him, but that does not worry him either, just as he does not worry about himself. However, there is a Somebody, utterly unknown to him, who is deeply, persistently worried about him, only about him. Sometimes at a quiet moment these worries of Somebody's concerning him, particularly their persistence, cause him an agonizing headache.

He lives with wits scattered. His elements, a free-living gang, fly about the world. And it is only because his room belongs to the world that he can sometimes see them in the distance. How is he to take responsibility for them? And can it still be called responsibility?

Everything, even the most ordinary things like being served in a restaurant, he has to take for himself by force with the help of the police. This makes life very uncomfortable.

17.1 [1920]

The bone in his forehead obstructs his way (he rams his forehead bloody against his own forehead).

He feels a captive on this earth. The sadness, weakness, diseases, delusions that prisoners suffer break out in him, no consolation can console him because it is all mere consolation, delicate, head-aching consolation in face of the crude fact of his captivity. But if you ask him what he really wants he is unable to answer, for he has—it is one of his strongest pieces of evidence—no idea of what freedom looks like.

Many deny their misery by referring to the sun. He denies the sun by referring to his misery.

He has two opponents; the first puts him under pressure from behind, from his origins; the second blocks his way forward. He does battle with both. Actually, the first is supporting him against the second because he wants to press forward; likewise the second is supporting him against the first, because he is driving him back. But this is only in theory, for it is not only the two opponents who are present, but he himself as well, and who really knows what his intentions are?

He has many judges. They are like an army of birds sitting in a tree. Their voices are confused; questions of rank and jurisdiction cannot be disentangled, and they are constantly changing places. Individuals, however, can be picked out and recognized

There are three kinds:*

He is tormented by the surging movement of all life, of others and his own, self-tormenting, sluggish, faltering, because it carries with it the never-ending compulsion of thinking. Sometimes this torment seems to him to precede the events. When he hears that his friend is to have a child, he recognizes that in his thoughts he has already suffered on account of it.

He can see two things: the first is calm reflection, judgement, scrutiny, outpouring, filled with life, and impossible without a certain ease. Their number and possibilities are endless; even a woodlouse needs a fairly wide crack for shelter, but no space at all is needed for these activities; even where there is not the smallest crack, they are able to interpenetrate one another and live on in their thousands upon thousands. That is the first thing. But the second is the moment when one is summoned to account for oneself, when one is unable to utter a sound, and is thrown back on the reflections, etc., but now faced with a hopeless future, one cannot paddle in them any longer, one becomes heavy, and sinks down, cursing.

2.II.20

He recalls a picture representing a summer Sunday on the Thames. The entire breadth of the river was filled far and wide with boats waiting for a lock to open. In all the boats there were high-spirited young people in bright, light clothes, lying almost right back, surrendering freely to the warm air and cool water. As they were all sharing it, their friendliness was not confined to the one boat; jokes and laughter were being passed on from one boat to the next.

He imagined that in a meadow on the bank—the banks were barely hinted at in the picture, where everything was dominated by the assembly of boats—he himself was standing. He was observing the party, which wasn't really a party, but could surely be called one. Of course he wanted very much to take part in it, he was practically reaching out to it, but he was obliged to tell himself frankly that he was excluded; it was impossible for him to fit in there; it would have demanded so much preparation that not only this day, this Sunday on the river, but many years too, and he himself, would have passed by; and even if time had stood still here, it would have had no other outcome; his entire lineage, upbringing, and physical development ought to have been conducted differently.

So that is how far he was from these trippers, but equally, how close, which was harder to understand. After all, they were human beings like him, nothing human could be entirely alien to them, so if one investigated them fully, one could not but discover that the feeling that overwhelmed him and excluded him from the river-trip was also alive in them—though it's true, it was far from overwhelming them, but ghost-like only lurked in dark corners somewhere

15.II.20

This is what it was about: once, many years ago, I was sitting on the slopes of the Laurenziberg,* sadly enough, to be sure. [I was looking closely at what I wished for my life. It emerged that the most important or the most attractive, was the wish that I might develop a view of life (and—this was necessarily bound up with it—was able by my writing to convince other people of it) in which life would keep its natural grave falling and rising but at the same time be acknowledged no less clearly as a nothing, as a dream, as a floating. A beautiful wish, perhaps—if I had wished it properly. Rather like wishing to hammer a table together tidily, meticulously, with a craftsman's skill, and at the same time do nothing. But not so that they could say: 'Hammering is nothing to him,' but rather 'Hammering is real hammering to him, and at the same time it is nothing too,' which would of course make the hammering become even bolder, even more resolute, even more real, and, if you like, more crazy. But he couldn't wish in that way at all, for his wish wasn't a wish, it was only a defence, a decent domestication of nothing, a breath of cheerfulness he wanted to give to nothing, which, though he had scarcely taken his first conscious steps into it at the time, he already felt to be his element.] He was bidding a kind of farewell then to the illusory world of youth, which, by the way, had never deceived him directly, but only allowed him to be deceived by what all the authorities around him had told him. That is how the 'wish' inevitably came about.

His only evidence is himself; all his opponents defeat him immediately, but not by refuting him—he is irrefutable—but by being their own evidence.

The basis of human unions is that the strong self of one appears to have refuted other individuals, in themselves essentially irrefutable; for these individuals that is a sweet consolation, but it lacks truth, and so will never last.

Once he was part of a group monument. Around some raised centre there stood, in well-thought-out array, symbolic figures representing the military estate, the arts, the sciences, the crafts. He was one of this number. Now, the group has long ago been dispersed, or at least he has left it, making his way through life alone. He no longer even has his old profession, indeed he has even forgotten what he represented then. It is probably this very forgetting that produces a certain sadness,

insecurity, restlessness, a certain longing for past times which clouds
the present. And yet this longing is an important element of vital
energy, or perhaps vitality itself.

He does not live for the sake of his personal life, he does not think for
the sake of his personal thinking. He feels as if he were living and
thinking under the pressure of a family for which, even though it has
itself more than abundant energy for living and thinking, he nevertheless signifies, according to some law unknown to him, some formal
necessity. For the sake of this unknown family and these unknown
laws he cannot be discharged.

Original sin, the ancient wrong committed by man, consists of the
accusation man makes and never ceases to make, that a wrong was
done to him, that the original sin was committed against him.

18.II.20
Two children were hanging around in front of Casinelli's shop window,* one a boy about six years old, the other a seven-year-old girl,
dressed expensively, talking about God and sin. I lingered, standing
behind them. The girl, Catholic perhaps, thought that only telling
lies to God was an actual sin. Stubborn, as children can be, the boy, a
Protestant perhaps, asked what telling lies to people, or stealing, were.
'A very great sin too,' said the girl, 'but not the greatest. Only sins
against God are the greatest; for sins against people we have confes-
sion. When I confess, the angel comes straight away and stands
behind me, only you don't see him.' And, getting tired of being half-
serious, for fun she spun round and looked behind her. 'You see,
nobody is behind me.' The boy turned round just as fast, 'Look,' he
said, not caring that I was bound to hear him, and not giving any
thought to it either, 'the devil is standing behind me.' 'I can see him
too,' said the girl, 'but I don't mean him.'

He does not want consolation, but not because he doesn't want
it—who wouldn't want it—but because seeking after consolation
means dedicating one's life to this work, on the edge of his existence,
always living almost outside it, scarcely knowing any longer for whom
one is seeking consolation, and so not even being capable of finding a
consolation that works (consolation that works, not one that is true
consolation, for that does not exist)

He guards himself from being fixed by his fellow humans. (A human being, even if he is infallible, sees in the other only that part for which the strength of his sight, and the nature of his sight, is adequate. But like everyone, only to an extreme, he is obsessed with restricting himself to the limits set by the strength of his fellow man's sight.) If Crusoe had never left the highest, or, more correctly, the most visible point of the island, out of defiance, or humility, or fear, or ignorance, or longing, he would quickly have come to grief, but when he began to explore his whole island and to enjoy it without considering the ships and the weakness of their telescopes, he kept himself alive and in the end—though to common sense it did not in logic necessarily follow—he was actually found.

19.II. [1920]
'You are making a virtue of your necessity.'

'In the first place, everyone does so, and in the second it is exactly what I am not doing. I let my necessity stay necessity; I'm not draining the swamp, I live in its fever-laden miasma.'

'And that is just what you are making into a virtue.'

'Like everyone, as I said. Besides, I am only doing so on your account; so that you stay kind to me, I do my soul harm.'

My prison cell—my stronghold.

Everything is permitted him—except forgetting himself, and with that everything is forbidden him again, down to the one thing that is at the moment necessary for the whole.

A narrow mind is a social requirement. All virtues are individual, all vices social; what are regarded as social virtues, such as love, unselfishness, impartiality, self-sacrifice, are only 'astonishingly' diluted social vices.

The difference between the 'Yes and No' he says to his contemporaries and the one that he actually should say, might correspond to the difference between death and life; that too he can only grasp as a faint awareness.

The reason the judgement of posterity on an individual is more right than that of his contemporaries lies in the dead man himself.

He reveals himself in his true nature only after his death, only when he is alone. Being dead is for the individual what Saturday evening is for chimney-sweeps: they wash their bodies clean of soot. Then it becomes visible whether his contemporaries have harmed him more than he has harmed his contemporaries. In the latter case, he was a great man.

The power to say no, this most natural expression of the continuously changing, renewing, dying, reviving, human fighting-organism, is something we always have, but not the courage; all the same while to live is to say no, it follows that to say no is to say yes.

With his dying thoughts he does not die. Dying is only a phenomenon within the inner world (which will continue to exist, even if it too were only a thought), a natural phenomenon like any other, neither joyful nor sad.

'He is prevented from rising by a certain heaviness, a feeling of being secured against any event, a dim sense of a resting-place made for him and belonging only to him; but he is prevented from lying there by a restlessness that drives him from his bed, he is prevented by his conscience, by his endlessly beating heart, by the fear of death and the desire to prove it false, all this prevents him from lying back, and he rises up again. This up and down, and a few accidental, fleeting, obscure observations made along these ways, are his life.'

'Your description is bleak, but only with regard to the analysis, where it reveals a fundamental flaw. It is indeed the case that man rises, falls back, rises again, and so on, but it is also at the same time, and with greater truth, not the case at all. He is one person, hence his flying includes resting, his resting includes flying, and both are again united in each individual, and the union of the union in each and so on, up to, well, up to real life, and anyway this description too is just as false, and perhaps even more deceptive than yours. From this region there is simply no way to life, though there must have been a way from life to here. That is how lost we are.'

The stream you swim against rages so wildly that in some absence of mind you despair sometimes at the desolate stillness you are paddling in, so infinitely far have you been driven back in one moment of failure.

29 [February 1920]

He is thirsty and separated from the spring only by a thicket. But he is divided: one half of him has a view of the whole, can see that he is standing here and the spring is nearby; but a second half notices nothing; at best he is dimly aware that the first half can see everything. But because he notices nothing, he is unable to drink.

EXPLANATORY NOTES

THE AEROPLANES AT BRESCIA

4 *Gabriele d'Annunzio*: (1863–1938), Italian poet and novelist, perhaps best known for the novel *Il trionfo della morte* ('The Triumph of Death', 1894). He had already, in 1908, flown with the aviator Wilbur Wright, and would become a fighter pilot in the First World War. One of his most famous feats was the 'flight over Vienna', in which he led nine planes on a 700-mile round trip to drop propaganda leaflets on Vienna in August 1918.

5 *Otto*: Max Brod's younger brother Otto (1888–*c.*1944 in Auschwitz), also a novelist.

Cobianchi: Mario Cobianchi (1885–1944), Italian aviator, later famous for his flight over the Leaning Tower of Pisa on 22 January 1911.

Cagno: Alessandro Cagno (1883–1971), Italian racing driver and aviator, who in 1910 founded Italy's first flying school at Pordenone near Milan.

Calderara: Mario Calderara (1879–1944), Italian aviator, who in 1909 became the first Italian to obtain a pilot's licence.

6 *Rougier*: Henri Rougier (1876–1956), French racing driver and aviator. At Brescia he won the prize for altitude, narrowly beating Curtiss, and at the Grand Prix air display at Berlin in September 1909 he won the prizes for distance and altitude. On the day when Kafka saw him, Rougier reached a height of 117 metres.

Curtiss: Glenn H. Curtiss (1878–1930), American aviator. A motorcycle racer and engine designer, he was called 'the fastest man in the world' for reaching a speed of 136.36 miles per hour in 1907 on a motorcycle he had designed himself. In August 1909 he took part in the world's first air meet, the Grande Semaine d'Aviation at Rheims, where he won the speed contest by flying 10 kilometres in just under 16 minutes and beating Blériot by six seconds. He received the second French pilot's licence ever awarded (Blériot got the first).

Moncher: Guido Moncher (1873–1945), aviator from what is now the Italian region Trentino–Alto Adige; until 1919 it belonged to Austria as South Tyrol, and had a large Italian-speaking population which wanted it transferred to Italy.

Anzani: Alessandro Anzani (1877–1936), Italian aviator. Having been world motorcycle racing champion in 1906, he experimented with the design of aeroplane engines and developed the lightweight three-cylinder engine cooled by air instead of water which made possible Blériot's Channel crossing on 25 July 1909.

Blériot: Louis Blériot (1872–1936), famous for having recently made the first Channel crossing by air on 25 July 1909. At Brescia, as described here, he won the Grand Prix for flying 50 kilometres in 49 minutes and 24 seconds.

7 *Leblanc*: Alfred Leblanc (1869–1921), French aviator, assistant to Blériot.

11 *Wright*: Orville Wright (1871–1948), who with his brother Wilbur (1867–1912) had made the first experimental flights with manned gliders at Kitty Hawk, North Carolina, from 1900 onwards, and the first flight in a petrol-powered flier on 17 December 1903. Orville took part in the Grand Prix air show at Berlin in September 1909. This sentence was probably added immediately before publication in order to bring the article up to date.

Latham: Hubert Latham (1883–1912), Anglo-French aviator. He tried to cross the Channel by air on 19 July 1909, but engine-failure obliged him to establish a different record by landing his aircraft on the sea for the first time. At the Grand Prix air display at Berlin in September 1909 he won the prize for speed.

A COUNTRY DOCTOR: LITTLE TALES

12 *Bucephalus*: the war-horse ridden by Alexander the Great is named 'Bucephalus' in the life of Alexander written by Plutarch (*c.* AD 46–120), and is said to have been vicious and intractable until Alexander tamed him—a marked contrast to his sedate modern life as a lawyer. Alexander was the son of Philip, king of Macedonia.

gates of India: various medieval legends, known to Kafka through his reading of Jewish folk-tales retold by M. J. bin Gorion and others, may be recollected here. Some told how Alexander's military expedition to India brought him to the gates of Paradise, though he was unable to enter. Another medieval tradition asserted that the giants Gog and Magog, or the lost tribes of Israel, were confined in Central Asia behind Alexander's Gate. In Ezekiel 38: 15 it is prophesied that 'Gog' will emerge from the north with a mighty army and attack the people of Israel; this may have suggested the northern nations of 'At the Building of the Great Wall of China', the nomads of 'An Ancient Manuscript', and the Tartar-like doorkeeper of 'Before the Law'. See Andrew Runni Alexander, *Alexander's Gate, Gog and Magog, and the Inclosed Nations* (Cambridge, Mass.: Mediaeval Academy of America, 1932), and Malcolm Pasley, 'Kafka's Semi-private Games', *Oxford German Studies*, 6 (1971–2), 112–31 (pp. 120–1).

14 *pair of horses*: the doctor's two horses suggest a mock-heroic allusion to pairs of horses in Homer, and even more to Goethe's quasi-Homeric narrative poem *Hermann und Dorothea* (1797), canto 5, lines 132–50, where Hermann harnesses his 'brave stallions' to his cart. Kafka read the poem on 19 February 1917.

16 *by higher authority*: Kafka here uses an incongruous piece of bureaucratic jargon.

the bed: an ironic parallel to the climax of the story 'Legend of St Julian the Hospitalier' (1877) by Gustave Flaubert, one of Kafka's favourite authors. In this ironic retelling of a medieval legend, the saint's supreme test is to get into bed with a leper and clasp the leper to warm him. The leper turns into Jesus and carries the saint up to heaven. By contrast, Kafka's story ends without any further supernatural intervention.

19 *Imperial Palace*: Kafka's fascination with China extended to translations of Chinese poetry: early in their acquaintance he quoted to Felice Bauer a poem by 'Yan-Tsen-Tsai' (1716–97) expressing his own conflict between love and literature (letter of 24 November 1912, *Briefe 1900–1912*, ed. Hans-Gerd Koch (Frankfurt a.M.: Fischer, 1999), 259). He also read travelogues about modern China by Julius Dittmar, which described the subjection of the Chinese to the European powers: hence perhaps the allusion to the helplessness of the Emperor. See Rolf J. Goebel, *Constructing China: Kafka's Orientalist Discourse* (Columbia, SC: Camden House, 1997).

jackdaws: Kafka knew that his own surname meant 'jackdaw' (Czech *kavka*); references to jackdaws, crows, or ravens in his works are a kind of enigmatic signature.

20 *the law*: suggests the Jewish Law, while the 'doorkeeper' appears in Jewish legends as guardian of the various forecourts leading to heaven. Kafka himself described this story as a 'legend' (diary, 13 December 1914). On its affinities with Jewish legends, see Iris Bruce, *Kafka and Cultural Zionism* (Madison, Wisc.: University of Wisconsin Press, 2007), 99–103. 'Man from the country', *'am ha'aretz*, literally 'countryman', also implies someone ignorant of the Jewish law; the Yiddish equivalent, *amorets*, means 'ignoramus'. Kafka's diaries confirm that he knew this expression (see 26 November 1911).

21 *Tartar's beard*: the doorkeeper's threatening appearance, and his Central Asian provenance, link him with the nomads of 'An Ancient Manuscript'.

24 *purity*: an allusion to the Jewish requirement of *shehitah* or ritual slaughter in which an animal was killed with one stroke of a sharp knife across the throat and allowed to bleed to death. The early twentieth century saw a lively debate about whether this practice was cruel or not.

25 *top engineers*: the ten engineers appear to represent the ten contemporary writers who contributed to the anthology *Der neue Roman* ('The New Novel'), which Kafka received probably in February 1917. Malcolm Pasley has identified them as follows: (1) Kafka's friend Max Brod (1884–1968); (2) the left-wing poet Rudolf Leonhard (1889–1953), represented in the anthology by an essay on Heinrich Mann; (3) the French novelist Anatole France (1844–1924); (4) the Danish critic Georg Brandes (1842–1927), represented by an essay on France and hence described here as giving the third engineer explanations that have not been asked for; (5) Heinrich Mann (1871–1950); (6) the Yiddish playwright Ossip Dymow or Osip Dymov (1878–1959; real name Yosef Perlman); (7) the horror writer

Gustav Meyrink (1868–1932); (8) the Expressionist playwright and prose writer Carl Sternheim (1878–1942); (9) Maxim Gorky (1868–1936, real name A. M. Peshkov); (10) Hugo von Hofmannsthal (1874–1929). These identifications are further explained in Pasley's article 'Franz Kafka: "Ein Besuch ins Bergwerk"', *German Life and Letters*, 18 (1964–5), 40–6.

30 *eleven sons*: following Kafka's lead, Malcolm Pasley identifies the 'sons' with the following stories: (1) 'A Dream', criticized as 'too simple'; (2) 'Before the Law', where the 'fencing pose' may allude to the dispute between K. and the Chaplain in *The Trial* about the interpretation of the parable; (3) 'A Message from the Emperor', alluding to the lyrical tone of the story; (4) 'The Next Village', criticized as 'lightweight'; (5) 'An Ancient Manuscript', perhaps alluding to the naivety of the shopkeepers; (6) 'Jackals and Arabs', where the son hangs his head as the jackals do; (7) 'In the Gallery', where the young man's attitude combines 'disturbance as well as respect for tradition'; (8) 'The Rider on the Coal-Scuttle', originally intended for inclusion in *A Country Doctor*, but then excised and hence perhaps 'far away'; (9) 'A Country Doctor', seeming to criticize its dream-like qualities; (10) 'The New Advocate', referring to 'cross-questioning'; (11) 'A Brother's Murder', which ends in 'destroying the family'. Pasley justifies these attributions more fully in 'Drei literarische Mystifikationen Kafkas', in Jürgen Born *et al.*, *Kafka-Symposion* (Berlin: Wagenbach, 1965), 21–37 (pp. 21–6).

35 *bear fruit*: an incongruous but unmistakable quotation from Goethe's poem 'Prometheus' (1774): 'because not all my dreams blossomed to maturity' (Goethe, *Selected Verse*, tr. David Luke (Harmondsworth: Penguin, 1964), 19).

38 *Achilles*: according to Greek legend, the hero Achilles was dipped by his mother Thetis in the river Styx to make him invulnerable, but as she held him by the heel, that was the one place where he could be wounded.

39 *Hagenbeck*: Carl Hagenbeck (1844–1913), who founded the zoo in Hamburg in 1907; Kafka had probably read his autobiography *Von Tieren und Menschen* (1909) and knew about the method of 'gentle training', relying on psychology rather than force, which was applied particularly to apes.

Peter: this may allude to a well-known performing chimpanzee named Consul Peter who displayed his feats in Prague in 1904; wearing a jacket, he would eat his dinner, pour wine from a bottle into his glass and drink it, and then light a cigarette and lean back in his chair to digest his meal in comfort. Newspaper reports about him are quoted by Hartmut Binder, *Kafka: Der Schaffensprozeß* (Frankfurt a.M.: Suhrkamp, 1983), 198–9.

news-hounds: this corresponds to a pun in the original: Kafka has 'Windhunde', literally meaning 'greyhounds', but also suggesting 'Windbeutel' or 'wind-bags'.

A HUNGER ARTIST: FOUR STORIES

64 *to understand it*: perhaps an echo of a semi-proverbial line from Goethe, *Faust I*, line 534: 'If you don't feel it, you will never capture it.'

BLUMFELD, AN ELDERLY BACHELOR

82 *game*: cf. how in *The Castle* K., a morose character like Blumfeld, is told that his two playful assistants (as tiresome as the balls and as useless as Blumfeld's trainees) were sent to him 'to cheer him up' (*The Castle*, tr. Anthea Bell, Oxford World's Classics (Oxford: Oxford University Press, 2009), 204).

100 *regardless*: Kafka's manuscript comes to an abrupt end here.

AT THE BUILDING OF THE GREAT WALL OF CHINA

104 *Tower of Babel*: see Genesis 11: 1–9, where the descendants of Noah build a tower which is intended to reach to heaven, and are punished for their pride by being made to speak different and mutually unintelligible languages.

110 *ancient times*: in this passage Kafka adopts and exaggerates the standard Western topos of China as an immobile and stagnant civilization: see Goebel, *Constructing China*, 76.

THE HUNTSMAN GRACCHUS

This text consists of a number of fragments, which are reproduced here without attempting to weld them into a coherent narrative. Divisions between the fragments are indicated by asterisks. This and the following fragments, down to 'Then there happened', are from Kafka, *Nachgelassene Schriften und Fragmente I*, ed. Malcolm Pasley (Frankfurt a.M.: Fischer, 1993), 305–13.

113 *sabre-swinging hero*: as the events are located in Riva on Lake Garda, Hartmut Binder identifies this as the statue of St John of Nepomuk which stood at the harbour of Riva until 1916 (illustrated in Binder, *Mit Kafka in den Süden: Eine historische Bilderreise in die Schweiz und zu den oberitalienischen Seen* (Prague: Vitalis, 2007), 26, 101–3). The saint holds a candle, not a sword: Kafka seems to have changed the statue rather as in *The Man who Disappeared* he gives the Statue of Liberty a sword instead of a torch.

114 *Gracchus*: the name of an ancient Roman family whose most famous members tried to reform the corn laws in the second century BC and were murdered by their aristocratic antagonists; it also suggests 'jackdaw' (Latin *graculus*) and hence Kafka's surname (Czech *kavka*, 'jackdaw').

Salvatore: Italian for 'Saviour'. Combined with the recurrent motif of the dove, this introduces an allusion to Christ and his power to restore the dead to life; but it is an ironic allusion, for the Mayor cannot restore

Gracchus to life and in any case Gracchus does not wish to be restored but rather to die properly.

115 *earthly waters*: Lake Garda is connected with the sea via the rivers Po and Mincio (Hartmut Binder, *Kafka Kommentar zu sämtlichen Erzählungen* (Munich: Winkler, 1975), 200).

on the move: after this Kafka has stroked out the following passage:

'The huntsman has turned into a butterfly. Don't laugh.'

'I'm not laughing,' the Mayor protested.

'Very perceptive of you,' said the huntsman. 'I'm always on the move.'

The butterfly is an ancient symbol of the immortal soul.

Julia: perhaps a reminiscence of Shakespeare's *Romeo and Juliet* (*Romeo und Julia* in German), which is set in Verona, some forty miles from Riva. Juliet, wearing her wedding-dress (cf. p. 117: 'I slipped into my shroud like a girl into my wedding-dress'), is cast into a death-like sleep; Romeo, thinking she really is dead, commits suicide; Juliet, on awaking and finding Romeo dead, does the same. See Frank Möbus, *Sünden-Fälle: Die Geschlechtlichkeit in Erzählungen Franz Kafkas* (Göttingen: Wallstein, 1994), 23–6.

116 *No one will read . . . help me*: this fragment seems to fuse the identities of the Huntsman Gracchus and of Kafka the writer.

bushman: a native of what was then a German colony, South-West Africa (now Namibia), who seems to be reversing colonial power-relations by pointing his spear at a European. See John Zilcosky, *Kafka's Travels: Exoticism, Colonialism, and the Traffic of Writing* (Basingstoke and New York: Palgrave Macmillan, 2003), 180.

117 *6 April 17*: this fragment occurs in Kafka's diary: *Tagebücher*, ed. Hans-Gerd Koch, Michael Müller, and Malcolm Pasley (Frankfurt a.M.: Fischer, 1990), 810–11.

Is it really true: this fragment in dialogue form comes from a later notebook: Kafka, *Nachgelassene Schriften und Fragmente I*, 378–84.

INVESTIGATIONS OF A DOG

133 *aerial dogs*: the original, 'Lufthunde', seems to be a pun on 'Luftmenschen', people who live by their wits. There may be a more specific implication that Western Jewish writers are too detached from the solid ground where the narrator-dog and most of his fellows live: the journalist Anton Kuh, whom Kafka knew personally, described many contemporary Jewish writers as 'Luftgaukler', aerial jugglers (quoted in Binder, *Kafka Kommentar*, 280).

THE BURROW

182 *unchanged, the*: Kafka's manuscript breaks off in mid-sentence.

SELECTED SHORTER PIECES

In Kafka's notebooks these texts are untitled. We have used the titles added by Max Brod, as they have become well known, except that we have given the title 'Cat and Mouse' to the text that Brod called 'Little Fable'.

185 *Sancho Panza*: the down-to-earth companion of the deluded knight in Miguel de Cervantes' *Don Quixote* (1605, 1615).

APHORISMS

Kafka originally wrote the aphorisms in part I, and others—along with records of day-to-day life, notes on his reading, and short narratives—in a series of octavo notebooks when staying with his sister in Zürau in the winter of 1917–18. He then, probably in late February 1918, wrote a selection of them on separate sheets of paper, numbered them (not quite accurately: there is no '65' or '89'), added a few without numbers, and placed them in a folder. He separated some from the next by horizontal lines. Max Brod published this sequence in 1931 under the title 'Reflections on Sin, Suffering, Hope, and the True Way'. Those in part II are taken from Kafka's diary for 1920, and were printed by Brod under the title 'He'.

189 *upon my hand*: in Kafka's original notebook this paragraph has the heading 'A Life'.

193 *hidden from him*: cf. the following passage from Schopenhauer: 'All philosophers have made the mistake of placing that which is metaphysical, indestructible, and eternal in man in the *intellect*. It lies exclusively in the *will*, which is entirely different from the intellect, and alone is original. . . . the intellect is a secondary phenomenon, and is conditioned by the brain, and therefore begins and ends with this. The will alone is that which conditions, the kernel of the whole phenomenon; consequently it is free from the forms of the phenomenon, one of which is time and hence it is also indestructible. Accordingly, on death consciousness is certainly lost, but not what produced and maintained consciousness; life is extinguished, but with it not the principle of life which manifested itself in it. Therefore a sure and certain feeling says to everyone that there is in him something positively imperishable and indestructible.'—Arthur Schopenhauer, *The World as Will and Representation*, tr. E. F. J. Payne, 2 vols. (Clinton, Mass.: Falcon's Wing Press, 1958), ii. 495–6.

the serpent: see Genesis 3.

eternal growth: Schopenhauer argues that palingenesis or rebirth is a widespread and highly plausible theory, but he does not see it as in any way progressive; Kafka may have known at second hand about the Jewish mystical doctrine of *Tikkun* or metempsychosis, in which successive lives are the setting for a striving towards perfection.

195 *all humanity*: again cf. Schopenhauer: 'In the phenomenon, and by means of its forms time and space, as *principium individuationis*, it is thus evident

that the human individual perishes, whereas the human race remains and continues to live. But in the being-in-itself of things which is free from these forms, the whole difference between the individual and the race is also abolished, and the two are immediately one. The entire will-to-live is in the individual, as it is in the race, and thus the continuance of the species is merely the image of the individual's indestructibility.' *The World as Will and Representation*, ii. 496.

197 *Alexander's battle*: Kafka may have in mind Albrecht Altdorfer's painting *The Battle of Alexander at Issus* (1529), on display in Munich, which he had visited in November 1916.

198 *psychology!*: probably not psychoanalysis, but the psychology of Franz Brentano (1838–1917), with which Kafka was familiar. In *Psychology from an Empirical Standpoint* (1874) Brentano advocated introspection as a means of psychological knowledge. Kafka's note is therefore a warning against excessive self-examination.

200 *pillar of salt*: in Genesis 19: 26, Lot's wife, fleeing with her husband from the cities of Sodom and Gomorrah which the Lord is destroying, disobeys the divine command by looking back, and is turned into a pillar of salt.

201 *is simply*: Kafka's sentence breaks off here.

Archimedean point: the Greek mathematician Archimedes (287–212 BC) is supposed to have illustrated the power of the lever by saying: 'Give me a firm spot on which to stand, and I will move the earth.'

203 *three kinds*: Kafka did not complete this sentence.

205 *Laurenziberg*: a hill, called Petřín in Czech, on the left bank of the Vltava (Moldau) in Prague; it is covered with parks and was a favourite place for Kafka to take walks.

206 *Casinelli's shop window*: a lending-library in Prague.

MORE ABOUT | **OXFORD WORLD'S CLASSICS**

The Oxford World's Classics Website

www.worldsclassics.co.uk

- Browse the full range of Oxford World's Classics online

- Sign up for our monthly e-alert to receive information on new titles

- Read extracts from the Introductions

- Listen to our editors and translators talk about the world's greatest literature with our Oxford World's Classics audio guides

- Join the conversation, follow us on Twitter at OWC_Oxford

- Teachers and lecturers can order inspection copies quickly and simply via our website

www.worldsclassics.co.uk

American Literature

British and Irish Literature

Children's Literature

Classics and Ancient Literature

Colonial Literature

Eastern Literature

European Literature

Gothic Literature

History

Medieval Literature

Oxford English Drama

Poetry

Philosophy

Politics

Religion

The Oxford Shakespeare

A complete list of Oxford World's Classics, including Authors in Context, Oxford English Drama, and the Oxford Shakespeare, is available in the UK from the Marketing Services Department, Oxford University Press, Great Clarendon Street, Oxford OX2 6DP, or visit the website at www.oup.com/uk/worldsclassics.

In the USA, visit www.oup.com/us/owc for a complete title list.

Oxford World's Classics are available from all good bookshops. In case of difficulty, customers in the UK should contact Oxford University Press Bookshop, 116 High Street, Oxford OX1 4BR.